Praise for Lauri

"Hilarious." —*Seattle Post-Intelligencer,* on *The Idiot*
the Flaming Tantrum of Death

"[Laurie Notaro] writes with a flair that leaves you knowing she would be a gal you could commiserate with over a bucket of longneck beers. If you need to laugh over the little annoyances of life, this is a book for you. If you need to cry over a few of them, *Flaming Tantrum* can fit that bill, too."

—*St. Louis Post-Dispatch,* on *The Idiot Girl and the Flaming Tantrum of Death*

"A double-handful of chuckle-worthy vignettes . . . Notaro blends sardonic, often self-deprecating comedy with disarming sincerity."

—*Publishers Weekly,* on *The Idiot Girl and the Flaming Tantrum of Death*

"[Notaro's] quirky humor, which she's previously showcased in her cult-classic essays on girly dorkdom, runs rampant."

—*BUST,* on *There's a (Slight) Chance I Might Be Going to Hell*

"Notaro is everywoman. She is every woman who has ever made a bad judgment, overindulged (you pick the vice), been on a fad diet, been misunderstood at work, been at odds with her mother or been frustrated with her grandmother's obsession with Lifetime TV, while somehow being a little too familiar with the conflicted, star-crossed personages of those movies."

—*San Antonio Express-News,* on *I Love Everybody*

"[Notaro] may be the funniest writer in this solar system."

—*The Miami Herald,* on *Autobiography of a Fat Bride*

Also by Laurie Notaro

The Idiot Girl and the Flaming Tantrum of Death

There's a (Slight) Chance I Might Be Going to Hell

An Idiot Girl's Christmas

We Thought You Would Be Prettier

I Love Everybody (and Other Atrocious Lies)

Autobiography of a Fat Bride

The Idiot Girls' Action-Adventure Club

Spooky Little Girl

a novel

Laurie Notaro

Villard Trade Paperbacks · New York

Spooky Little Girl is a work of fiction. Names, characters, places, and incidents are the products of the author's imagination or are used fictitiously. Any resemblance to actual events, locales, or persons, living or dead, is entirely coincidental.

A Villard Books Trade Paperback Original

Published in the United States by Villard Books, an imprint of The Random House Publishing Group, a division of Random House, Inc., New York.

Library of Congress Cataloging-in-Publication Data

Notaro, Laurie.
Spooky little girl: a novel / Laurie Notaro.
p. cm.
ISBN 978-0-345-51097-6 (pbk.)
1. Future life—Fiction. I. Title.
PS3614.O785S66 2010
813'.6—dc22 2010001858

Printed in the United States of America

www.villard.com

2 4 6 8 9 7 5 3 1

To my Nana, who I hope is eating Italian cookies, having coffee, and playing cards with her friends and my Pop Pop (and maybe even Frank Sinatra) wherever she is now. We miss you.

Contents

Spooky
Little
Girl

chapter one You Win

The very moment when the cab pulled up to the curb, Lucy Fisher knew that she was seeing something exceptional.

Directly in front of her fifties-ranch-style red-brick house, a woman dressed in flowing white was wrestling with nothing short of a cloud in Lucy's yard. For a ridiculous moment, Lucy's mind determined that it was a dilapidated angel desperately trying to climb back aboard her ride, almost like a surfer that had toppled off a board.

But a second later, Lucy realized it was simply a homeless lady, complete with stolen grocery cart, trying to shove a shimmering white mass into a huge dirty plastic bag, like processed meat into a sausage casing. Lucy sat there, nearly smiling at the curiosity that she was witnessing as the cloud flapped against the woman's head, briefly slapping her face as if she was about to be bound with the wrappings of a shiny Gabor sister mummy.

It took less than a fraction of the next second for Lucy to suddenly—and clearly—realize that the white mass was no cloud at all.

"HEY!" she shouted, furiously popping the door open and flying out of the backseat as if a superpower had been activated. "HEY! What are you doing! Put that back! That's my dress! *That is MY wedding dress*!"

"That'll be twenty-two seventy, lady!" the driver called after Lucy as she bounded across the street toward her house and the homeless woman.

But Lucy failed to hear him. When she came within an arm's length of the woman, she grabbed two handfuls of satin and lace and tugged the dress out of the woman's grasp as hard as she could.

"Give me that!" Lucy snarled, tugging, pulling. "What are you doing with my dress? Give me my dress!"

"This is my dress now!" the woman, who was twice Lucy's size, hissed back, and she jerked the dress back with all of her might. "You can't change your mind! You can't leave all of this out for the taking and then just change your mind when someone else decides they want it!"

"Twenty-three fifty," the cabdriver called again, this time louder.

"Give me my damn dress," Lucy shouted as she tugged harder. "I just had my last fitting for it. *Give it to me!*"

"It's mine!" the woman yelled back. "I found it just laying here. Finders keepers!"

"It is accruing twenty-nine percent interest on my Visa, and that makes it mine!" Lucy gathered all of her strength, gritted her teeth, locked eyes with her opponent, and then pulled as hard as she could, producing a shriek from the woman that was loud, high-pitched, and shrill, like she was coming apart.

How did she do that? Lucy thought. *How did she do that without opening her mouth?*

And then Lucy understood. The satin and lace, once taut between the women, was now slack, although neither had let go. Lucy looked down at the tear, which had screamed as it was being ripped, now frayed, open, and destroyed. The two women looked at the mess in their hands, neither one saying a word.

"Okay, then," the homeless woman finally said as she dropped her end onto the ground. "You win."

"Twenty-five even, and the meter is still running," the cabdriver called impatiently.

Lucy looked up from the white mess in her hands, through the collection of light brown curls that had fallen into her face, and finally saw what the cabdriver saw. What the homeless woman saw. What every car passing on the street in front of her house had seen.

Her life. Spread out all over the lawn, littered in the gutter, spilling out of the bed of her truck that was parked in the driveway. Her brand-new thirty-six-inch television sitting in her front yard like a postmodern flamingo; her laptop bag, with the corner of her computer peeking out of it, flung onto the ground like a stepping stone. Her grandmother's antique rocking chair tipped up against the mailbox as if someone had recently been dumped out of it. Her clothes, her photo albums, her everything, was spread out over the front lawn, on exhibition, for anyone to come and poke at, pick through, gawk at.

A comforter. A lamp. A saucepan.

"If it works, I'll take that TV," the cabdriver said, chuckling. "Or even if it don't work, I'll still take it. Meter's still running, lady."

Lucy turned around and marched back toward the cab. "Pop the trunk," she demanded of the driver. She reached into the back-seat, grabbed her purse, and then yanked her suitcase from the trunk.

"Here," Lucy said as she tossed a twenty and a five at the driver, and looked at him with sharpened eyes. "Go rent to own your own flat screen."

And then, because she wasn't sure what else she should do, she rolled her suitcase to the sidewalk in front of her house, with her tattered wedding dress shoved underneath her arm, stood there for a moment, and wondered what the hell was going on.

An hour and forty-five minutes earlier, Lucy's plane had touched down on the runway in Phoenix after returning from what was supposed to have been a fantastic weeklong vacation in Hawaii. She had left Martin, her fiancé, and her job as a dental hygienist to travel to the tropical paradise with her best friend and co-worker, Jilly, and their friend, the office receptionist, Marianne. Instead, the trip defied their expectations as soon as they arrived. Their luxurious boutique accommodations were nothing more than a roadside motel with a museum-quality collection of insects; the discount-brand sunscreen Lucy had purchased was cheap for a reason; and it was suspected that either the pig or some shellfish the girls gobbled at the luau could have rightly benefited from a little more time in the cooker. Lucy spent the majority of her seven days in Hawaii fighting off ants and mosquitoes in a shabby motel; watching her skin burn, bubble, and peel like a paper label off a jar; and trying to master a lopsided, dirty toilet with missing floor bolts.

None of that, however, could hold a candle to the trip's high point, which began when she was simply having some drinks in the motel bar with Marianne, who was on a mad prowl for a vacation fling. The receptionist was less than versed at the art of flirting and might have been more successful in making a match had she invested in a hairbrush and attended to the area of her upper lip, which didn't look so much like a lip as it did a pelt. While that sort of fur growth is great on a kitten, Lucy thought, it just didn't reap the same snuggle rewards on a woman who often had Cheetos dust clinging to hers. Lucy never had too many problems attracting men; she only had trouble attracting men who weren't already married, weren't unemployed at the moment, or weren't just going into or just coming out of rehab. Her warm, strong eyes were clearly her best feature and made her look openly approachable, followed by a definitive straight nose and genetically predisposed perfectly aligned teeth. She looked friendly and fun, and was just unpolished enough to look like she knew how to relax and have a good time.

And that's just what Lucy was trying to do, that last night at the hotel bar. She just wanted to relax and have fun, but as the night mercilessly dragged on, she began feeling tired and weary.

After too many rounds of drinks, Marianne finally zeroed in on a target and tried desperately to capture the attention of a man sitting on the opposite side of the motel bar, despite the fact that he was wearing a T-shirt that stated DEFINE GIRLFRIEND.

Lucy breathed a sigh of relief when the guy finally sent Marianne a drink and then asked if they wanted to join a poker game upstairs. Lucy reluctantly agreed after much persistence and arm-tugging from Marianne, under the condition that Lucy was going to stay for five minutes only. She had had her fair share of slushy umbrella drinks and wanted nothing more than to go to bed like Jilly had hours earlier, but she also knew she couldn't let Marianne go alone. The moment they stepped foot into his room, it was Marianne who shot back down the hall toward the elevator without any warning, shrieking that she'd left her key card at the bar and that she'd be right back.

Suddenly, a beer was in Lucy's hand, and she sipped it. Not only was it warm and bitter, but it tasted downright odd. Skanky guy, skunky beer. She sat in a side chair, waiting for Marianne's return, and when the guy leaned back on the bed and smiled at her, Lucy's stomach flipped. She stood up to say she was going to wait for her friend in the hall, and the nausea of the undercooked shellfish hit her again. Luckily she was able to make it several steps and shut the bathroom door behind her before getting sick. After splashing cold water on her face, Lucy finally stumbled out of the bathroom ten minutes later to find that Marianne had still not returned, the television was off, and the guy was smiling at her.

"You know, if you brush your teeth," he said as he sat up, "we could still have a good time."

Lucy wanted to vomit all over again. Her pulse pounded in her temples. She looked at him, picked up her purse that was sitting at the foot of the bed, and then opened the door to find Marianne coming down the hallway with her key card in her hand.

"Hey," Lucy said to the guy before she shut the door, "Define 'asshole.'"

By the time the plane touched ground in Phoenix, Lucy didn't want anything more than to simply go home. She couldn't wait to fall onto her own creaky couch, pet her dog, Tulip, and crack open whatever cold drink she could find in the fridge. She was excited to see Martin, and hoped that they could spend that night watching old movies on TV, their favorite way to spend any night.

Waiting for the trio of girls to emerge from behind the security gate was Warren, Jilly's broad, tall, bearded, and jolly husband, who had agreed to give Marianne a lift home, too. Lucy looked around for Martin but didn't see him anywhere.

"I'm sure he's just running behind," Lucy said, and smiled, although she couldn't help feeling a bit disappointed that he wasn't there to meet her. He'd probably had a late truck come in at Safeway, where he was the manager of the produce department and had to unload it. *That's Martin. Got busy, lost track of time, forgot to call. Probably doesn't know he's late,* she thought. *I wonder if he even remembers that I was coming come today. If I didn't know better, I'd swear that man was having an affair with a head of cabbage.*

Warren came forward with a huge grin and gave Jilly a kiss on her freckled cheek and a quick squeeze before he picked up her bag.

Lucy flipped open her phone and speed dialed Martin's number.

"Just what I thought," she said, and laughed a little when it went straight to voice mail. "I'm sure that there are five hundred heads of lettuce demanding his attention."

Jilly nodded and smiled. "Nah. I bet he's down at baggage claim, waiting with a big bouquet of flowers," she reassured Lucy. "You just wait and see. Martin, forget anything? You're insane, or your blood alcohol level still hasn't recouped yet."

But when they descended the escalator to baggage claim, there was no bouquet of flowers waiting for her, no Martin. She tried his cell again. Straight to voice mail.

"What should we do?" Jilly asked Lucy after she saw her hang up again. "Warren brought the truck . . . so there's only room for three of us. . . . I could have him drop us off and then come back."

"I can be back here in forty minutes," Warren confirmed.

"No, that's silly, that's silly," Lucy said, shaking her head. "I'll try him again, and if I don't get ahold of him, I'll take a cab. How much could it possibly be, ten, fifteen bucks?"

"Are you sure?" Jilly asked, tucking a strand of her straight strawberry blond hair behind her ear. "Warren doesn't mind."

"I'll take a cab." Lucy laughed. "I'm a big girl. I should have called him this morning to remind him. He just forgot. I'll see you at work tomorrow. I swear I'm fine."

"All right," Jilly agreed, hesitantly. "Are you sure?"

"Absolutely. I'll see you guys tomorrow," Lucy said firmly.

"See you tomorrow, Lucy," Marianne called as she waved. The three of them started for the parking lot.

The cab had circled the Safeway parking lot two times when the driver asked Lucy if she wanted to go around again. Martin's beat-up red Ford Ranger truck was nowhere in sight. Lucy had figured that the cab could just drop her off at the store, Martin could run her home, and they'd save a couple of bucks, but it wasn't working out exactly as she had hoped.

"No," she said, shaking her head. "Maybe I should run inside and see if he's on lunch or something."

"Your dime," the driver said. "Meter's running."

Lucy could see her fare was already almost twenty dollars, and she didn't have much more than that in her purse. If she ran around Safeway for several minutes, she wouldn't have enough to pay her fare if Martin wasn't around, let alone a tip.

"Just take me home," she said, sighing.

After Lucy had rather unsuccessfully won the tug of war over her wedding dress and the cab had driven away, she found herself standing in front of her house, shaking her head, trying to make sense of things. She fished her house keys out of her purse and started up the driveway, dragging her suitcase behind her, the ruined dress under her arm. As she passed the bed of her truck, she saw heaps of her clothes, shoes, purses, everything from her closet. On the lawn was her television, computer, books, photo albums, a blanket her grandmother had crocheted. Everything she owned, everything that was hers. Lucy's head spun like she had downed a six-pack and gone on a Tilt-a-Whirl ride. Her mind searched for any reason that could clarify the scenario. Had they been robbed and everything out here was not worthy of stealing? Or worse, had some part of the house caught fire and this was what had been saved? Did Martin have some sort of yard sale, after which he had neglected to bring anything back inside the house? Were they being evicted, was the house being foreclosed on, had he stopped making payments and not told her? What was going on, what had happened? Where the hell was Martin?

As she neared the front door, she dialed Martin's cell again, praying for him to answer. The phone rang, rang, rang, and then, again, went to voice mail.

"CALL ME BACK," Lucy demanded into the phone. "What happened? Everything's out on the lawn. *Would you please call me back?* Are you all right? What is going on?"

She tried to insert the key into the lock, but it wouldn't fit.

The key, *her* key, refused to slide into the lock. She tried it again, this time with more force. It wouldn't fit. She took a step back and took a deep breath. "This can't be happening," she said aloud, then took the key again and with all of her might, with her teeth grinding, tried to shove it into the keyhole, but to no avail. Had they been evicted and the locks changed? But when she looked in the living room window, everything appeared normal. There was Martin's La-Z-Boy recliner, their nasty burlap couch, the coffee table. All was as it should have been.

This was unbelievable. She let go of the suitcase, took a step back from the door again, closed her eyes, and tried to calm down.

But Lucy knew she wasn't very good at calming down.

She raised her hand and threw her useless key ring against the front door as she screamed.

Suddenly, she heard barking. There, inside the house, standing at the window, was Tulip, Lucy's old, graying golden retriever mix.

"Hi, sugar," Lucy said, immediately feeling her blood pressure drop as she put her hand up to the window. "How are you, sweetheart? Are you being a good girl? Are you? Did you miss me? I missed you. I really did. Do you know why the TV is next to the mailbox and why my panties are scattered all over the bed of my truck? Do you? Do you know what's going on? I wish you could tell me."

Tulip licked her side of the glass where Lucy had put her hand, then sat, panting patiently. She barked again, moving her head almost in a nod, her eyes on Lucy the whole time. She had been Lucy's best friend for years, since the day Lucy had found her at the pound as a puppy. Flea-bitten, shivering, and scared, Tulip had come home with Lucy, and from that day on, they had slept in the same bed, watched the same television shows, and celebrated life's accomplishments together. Tulip was always there to cheer Lucy up, to comfort her when she needed it, and to be the one constant thing that Lucy always knew she could depend upon. Tulip made Lucy feel grounded and safe and always loved. Tulip was everything a dog should be to its person: a valued member of the family, a dear friend, a skilled secret keeper. And when Lucy met Martin three years ago, Tulip came along with the package, as did her basket of balls and hair-covered bed when Lucy eventually moved into his house. Now, standing on the other side of the glass, Tulip wagged her tail and pawed at the window, barking slightly in a very definitive way, as in, "Don't just stand there, come in!"

From inside her purse, Lucy heard the ring of her phone. She grabbed it.

"Martin?" she asked into the receiver, without so much as looking at who was calling.

"No," Lucy heard on the other end of the phone, followed by a quick little laugh. "It's Jilly. I got a call from—Wait, you mean Martin is still MIA? That boyfriend of yours is a workaholic."

"Well, I'm at the place that apparently used to be my home," Lucy replied, as the severity of the situation started to sink in. "Jilly, everything I own is tossed out on the street and I have no idea why. I don't know what's going on. All of my clothes are in the bed of my truck, the furniture I inherited from my grandmother is in the yard, and I just fought a homeless woman for my wedding dress, which is now ripped to shreds. The locks to the house have been changed. I can't get in! Martin won't answer his phone, he won't call me back, and I can't even get inside to get Tulip. He wasn't at Safeway. I drove around the parking lot twice. I don't know what to do. I have no idea what to do. I think he has thrown me out."

"Just stay there," Jilly advised. "Warren and I will be there in ten minutes."

Lucy put the phone back into her purse and shook her head, then looked at her dog on the other side of the glass. Tulip didn't take her cocoa-colored eyes off Lucy for one second.

Tulip panted. Lucy tried to smile for her, to make sure Tulip knew everything was going to be all right. She walked into the yard, grabbed the closest box—full of several pairs of her favorite cowboy boots, including a treasured vintage pair from the forties—and tossed it into the bed of the truck. Another box, brimming with purses and shoes, was the next to go. A stack of books from dental school. A pile of white and pastel-colored uniforms for work.

A box of wedding invitations that Lucy had just gotten back from the discount printer and had decided to put off addressing until after she returned from Hawaii, even though the wedding date was only eight weeks away.

She had thought she would have plenty of time.

chapter two The Sinister Potential of Chicken Skin

It wasn't going to be a big wedding, anyway, Lucy had rationalized when she'd found herself daydreaming about her vacation instead of getting a pen and sitting down at the kitchen table. It didn't really even matter when she addressed the invitations. Just a few friends in the backyard with the reception catered by the barbecue place down the street, Martin's favorite. Martin didn't like big things, didn't like to make a fuss. He was a direct path kind of guy. If he was at point A and he needed to be at point B, he'd go from A to B, and that would be it. No turns, no sidetracking, no pausing, no stops, just travel the most direct route. Their vacations or weekend trips were always like that. No plans for a detour to see fossilized dinosaur bones embedded in the side of a mountain, because he'd say it all looked like rock, couldn't tell which was which, anyway; no point in stopping to take a picture of a dozen vintage Cadillacs, half buried nose first in the ground at an angle corresponding to that of the Great Pyramid, if you could already see them from the highway; and why would a grown woman want to stop and have lunch at Flintstones Bedrock City on the way back from the Grand Canyon when that cartoon wasn't even on the air anymore?

Thus, when Lucy finally got her sliver of an inheritance check from the sale of the family farm after the death of her grandmother a year earlier, she knew exactly what she was going to do with it. With nonchalant disregard to her upcoming nuptials, she spent almost the last dime of her inheritance on the Hawaii trip, justifying the cost by categorizing the trip as her bachelorette party and something of a last hurrah. Martin had already informed her that any extended honeymoon was out of the question; work was too busy, as it was spring and this was his season to make his department shine. Maybe they could take a weekend and camp in Sedona, but nothing longer than that. When Lucy suggested going to Jerome, a former mining town turned artsy enclave, Martin gave her a long look.

"We'd have to stay in a hotel up there," he reminded her. "Why pay for a hotel if you have a tent?"

So when Lucy got her inheritance, she already had her mind made up. She didn't want to take any sort of vacation she would have to drive to, which were all the vacations she had taken with Martin. She wasn't going to camp in a tent, or sleep in a roadside motel with worn carpet and stiff polyester bedspreads and thin beige plastic buckets for ice. She had done all of that for him, and to be honest, she never had any longings about sleeping on the ground in a tent for a week without bathing, like a Joad. Wherever she went on her vacation, she was going to fly. She was going to go as far as she could imagine. She immediately decided on the most un-Martin place she could think of: Hawaii. It was that simple. *Hawaii.* She imagined herself laughing on the beach and sipping frivolous drinks under exotic trees with fringe. She wanted to stay at a fancy hotel, eat steak and shrimp and roasted boar, and wake up early to walk along the beach, even if she didn't have a point A or point B already in mind.

So she called Jilly and proposed that they go. Warren was game. He was up for the girls having a good time for themselves, and then Marianne mentioned that she'd always dreamed of going to Hawaii. Splitting the hotel room three ways sounded great. Lucy pitched it to Martin as sort of a "last hurrah" girls' weekend before she and he tied the knot; Marianne found a great deal on a beachfront "resort." Lucy bought her ticket. And while it turned out that it wasn't the most glamorous vacation on earth and she had spent the most memorable moments of it puking in some sleazeball's bathroom, getting away from home had given her time to think, time to laugh, and time to realize that maybe it wasn't such a sin that she hadn't quite gotten around to addressing those invitations just yet.

Martin was a good man. He had good bones, a good heart, a kind voice. He was a quiet man with a gentle character. Typically on-the-dot dependable. So nice anyone could always count on him to help them move. And if there was anything Martin was, it was satisfied. Satisfied with his job managing the produce department at Safeway, waking up at three in the morning to make sure cabbage was in, unloaded, and stacked in the display cold case with just the right spacing. Satisfied with his thirteen-year-old red dented truck with a frozen driver's side window and a seat belt so tired of being wound that it could only give enough length to be fastened if he tugged hard at it twice and let it go gently a third time. Satisfied with the spring popping up on the left side of the brown plaid couch every time he'd get up, satisfied with waiting for a movie to go to rental before he would see it, satisfied with basic cable. Satisfied with not complaining once when he would come down with a cold. And, by all accounts, he had been satisfied with Lucy.

Martin had lived his life the way that good men do. Lucy knew that the moment she met him, and she also knew that as far as men went, she had never done any better. She felt safe with him, and taken care of. She knew she would never have to worry about anything as long as Martin was around. He wasn't a yahoo with an on-again, off-again job, a gaggle of kids stringing behind him, or a probation officer he had to visit once a week. He didn't start drinking beer at noon on a Wednesday, and there was not one crazy ex-girlfriend who would crank call him at midnight or drive by the house. He was a guy who washed cucumbers, smiled at every customer, and answered whatever question anyone might have about a radish. His nails were always clean, and his flattop was always neatly trimmed at a precise length. He wasn't unnecessarily tall; he simply rose to an average height. And he had a full, friendly face, ruddy cheeks, and light blue eyes that twinkled when he smiled, which was frequently. Looking at Martin, no one would ever say he was ruggedly handsome or of model pedigree, but he could have easily been an archetype for the nice, friendly guy.

Although he was kind to Lucy—he would always offer the popcorn bowl to her first on the Friday nights when he rented movies on his way home—he wasn't fanatical about her. It sometimes seemed to her that Martin had figured one day that the time had come to find himself a companion, and instead of going to the pound, he'd looked around the produce department and had seen an average-height lady with pretty brown eyes, in her late twenties and dressed in white scrubs with her regular everyday curly light brown hair pulled back into a ponytail with a plain rubber band, about to take down a display of Granny Smith apples by pulling at the ones on the bottom. And so he'd smiled.

Martin smiled often. He was a big smiler. But after some time, Lucy began to notice that he rarely grinned, never beamed, and hardly laughed the way she loved to laugh. He chuckled, might snicker at a silly joke, but Martin never seemed to let go with a hearty guffaw or even so much as a chortle.

Sometimes in a moment of furious impatience, Lucy would look at Martin and wonder when he was going to *start.* When he might surprise her and go faster than thirty-five miles per hour. He never did. He coasted. A smooth, even coast, no bumps, no jolts, no sudden turns. It seemed as if there was a spark inside Martin that was never going to thrive into anything bigger; a spark that could just never go off, catch fire, and blaze madly. When he proposed to her, he simply came home from work, put his car keys on the hall table, held a ring out in the palm of his hand, and asked, "What do you think about that?"

Lucy thought maybe it was her, maybe she was the one who was keeping that spark from roaring into a fire, but she wasn't sure what else she could do to fuel it, and besides, she already knew that Martin had never set a fire inside of her, either. She loved his sensibility, his kindness, his stability, but as far as electrical current went, the bathroom lightbulb burned brighter. Certainly, they weren't on fire, but they were warm enough. And there was Martin and Lucy, small sparks going off on either end of the couch, with a popcorn bowl between them. And Tulip snoring on her dog bed at their feet.

Remarkably, they had really only been in one argument, very early in their relationship, for the whole three years they had been a couple. It was a ridiculous explosion about fried chicken; Martin had brought home original style, and Lucy liked the skinless extra crispy kind. She hated the flop and rubbery texture of chicken skin. She could barely stand to touch it, let alone pull a sheet of it off her dinner. In an instant, Lucy became angry, and when Martin simply shrugged, said he was sorry, and that he would make it a point to get skinless extra crispy next time, she became furious. As Martin looked at her blankly, Lucy fought the chicken skin fight alone, stoking her own fire that Martin refused to fan, building it into an inferno that led to her storming out of the house and hitting the Round About, the bar where she knew Jilly and Warren would be enjoying happy hour as it evolved into double-vision hour.

She spent that night laughing and talking to people she hadn't seen in a while, old drinking buddies that had wondered where she'd vanished to. When she made it back to Jilly and Warren's booth after another trip to the bar, Warren was laughing with an oily-looking guy Lucy had never met, and Jilly was rolling her eyes in disgust. "Pay no attention to him," Jilly whispered. "We call him Icky Ricky. I'm just nice to him because I have to be, but you don't."

"And who is this fine young filly?" the newcomer said as he turned his mustached face toward Lucy, shooting a wave of cigarette and beer breath at her. "I'd like to buy you a drink, miss!"

"I'd like to buy you a toothbrush," Lucy replied.

Lucy did her fair share of ignoring Icky Ricky and danced, laughed, joked with old friends, forgetting about her fight with Martin. The next morning, before Lucy even opened her eyes, she smelled something terrible, the scent of stale beer, Taco Bell, neglected trash, and dirty socks. She knew right away that waking up with "eau de single guy's apartment" was not a positive sign by any means. She breathed a tremendous sign of relief when she swung her legs around the side of the futon she was on and saw her jeans still intact on her lower body. Even her boots were still on, but that was about all she knew.

Beside her she saw the back of a head with shaggy brown hair that was clearly not Martin's neat flattop. The shaggy head rolled over, and in its place was a nasty, oily little mustache.

Oh, my God! a little voice in her head gasped. *Icky Ricky!*

"Where's my stuff?" Lucy demanded, kicking blankets and sheets patterned with a rainbow on them that were crumpled on the floor, not daring to pick them up with her hands to look under them.

"And a good morning to you, too, little lady," he said, seeming offended. "All your stuff's in the living room—on the couch, maybe, I dunno where you put it. Are you usually this nasty in the morning?"

"Only on the mornings that I wreck my life," she replied. Lucy found her purse and jacket by the front door on a chair and immediately rifled through her purse to find her keys. She heard shuffling from the bedroom.

"Hey, how 'bout we go grab something to eat?" Icky Ricky said as he emerged from the bedroom, his hair homelessly askew.

Lucy gave him a disgusted look. "No. I'm going home," she replied, finally finding her keys at the very bottom.

"Okay, then," Icky Ricky said, looking puzzled. "We could do a drive-through at McDonald's, get a little breakfast burr-eeto?"

"Are you kidding me?" Lucy said as she turned and faced him. "Don't read anything into anything, all right? Nothing happened here. Nothing. I don't know what I'm doing here, but I am leaving and going home."

"Good luck with that, unless you know how to fly!" he said with a laugh that came close to a snort as he reached across his chest and scratched his armpit. "Your car ain't here. You car's still at the Round About. You got sorta liquored up, miss, so much you couldn't drive. You could barely walk all by yourself, so I put you in my car and started to take you home, but you passed out cold before I even hit the corner. I don't know where you live, so I brought you back here and put you to bed. Like a gentleman. That's what I am. A *gentleman*."

Lucy felt a churning ball of sickness develop in her stomach. It suddenly hit her. She didn't remember anything past saying goodbye to Jilly and Warren when the jukebox began playing one of her favorite songs. What had she done? A fight over *chicken skin*. And now here she was, waking up on a dirty rainbow, standing in the middle of Icky Ricky's stinky apartment, about to ask him for a ride back to the bar.

"Let me find my keys," he said, more than a little discouraged. "Come on, not even just a quick run-through for a burrito? How about if just I get one?"

When Lucy pulled into the driveway, Martin was at the kitchen table with a cup of coffee. He looked up to see her as she opened the door and walked into the house.

"I saw your car at the Round About this morning," Martin said plainly. "You spend the night at Jilly's?"

Lucy shook her head.

Martin paused for a moment and just looked at her.

"I made a mistake, Martin, but I swear to you nothing happened," she began. "I woke up someplace I didn't plan on waking up, but nothing happened. I drank too much, and then I drank more and someone tried to take me home but didn't know where I lived, so . . ."

"This person, Lucy," he said quietly. "This person was a man?"

Lucy nodded. "I swear to you nothing happened, Martin. I promise. I would not lie to you. I made a mistake, I acted foolishly. But not one thing happened."

Martin looked away and then looked back at her.

"All right," he said slowly. "I'm going to choose to trust you, Lucy. But if this happens again, I'll know I've been made a fool of, and I won't ask any questions. I'll just call it a day. Do you understand?"

"Completely," Lucy replied immediately. "Absolutely."

That was three years ago. It had been the biggest event in their relationship, and when it was over, it was almost forgotten. Since then, they had developed a full Lucy and Martin history: holidays, vacations, birthdays, favorite television shows, inside jokes, photo albums, their own side of the bed, who got which drawer in the dresser.

No matter how mundane, or regular or sparkless, they had built a life.

A Lucy and Martin life.

And she could never look at chicken again, alive, dead, fried, or roasted, without feeling her head spin.

By the time Jilly and Warren pulled up in their truck, Lucy had managed to squeeze just about everything into the bed of her truck, except for her grandmother's rocking chair and the television. After helping Jilly and Warren load those up in their truck, she walked back to the front door to a waiting Tulip, who she could barely see anymore. It was getting dark and there were no lights on in the house.

"I love you, my good girl," Lucy said as she put her hand up to the glass, to which the dog reciprocated with raising her big, clunky paw. "I will come back for you, okay? Okay? I will see you soon, sweetheart. I promise."

Tulip looked at Lucy steadily and blinked. Then she emitted a tiny, almost inaudible little whimper.

Lucy's eyes burned.

"No, no, no, I'm coming back," Lucy said softly. "No crying, okay? Be a big girl."

With that, Tulip dropped her paw and tilted her head slightly.

"That's my girl," Lucy said. "We will get this figured out. We will find out what's going on. I will see you soon, I promise."

Jilly and Warren were waiting for her. She had to go. She was saying her last goodbye to Tulip when she saw something move back in the shadows, in the kitchen past the living room. Something moved. She saw it. It was slight, but it was there.

"Martin," Lucy said, and squinted her eyes to get a better look, but it was getting dark and all she could really see was a jumble of unidentifiable shadows.

"Martin!" she called this time. "Martin! Please talk to me. Tell me what's going on! Is that you? Is that you in there? *Is that you? Why are you doing this? Goddamn it! Why are you doing this? Talk to me!*"

There was no answer. She stood as still as she could, staring, watching the stillness in the kitchen, a kitchen she thought she'd be drinking a cold Pepsi in by now. Then she saw movement again, just as slight, and instantly felt foolish. The oscillating fan in the kitchen, she realized. It moved the blinds on the sliding glass door when it turned.

Lucy walked backward to her truck, waving to Tulip continuously, until she reached the driveway and could no longer see her.

"Lucy," Warren called out from the driver's side of his truck. "There's one last box on the lawn. You can toss it in the back here."

Lucy shook her head. "Those are my wedding invitations." She shrugged as she opened the door of her truck. "I don't think I'll be needing them."

From the corner of her eye, Lucy saw something white flutter out of the cab and onto the concrete of the driveway below. It was an envelope. She picked it up. She saw right away that it was Martin's quick scrawl that had written her name on the front.

Inside, the letter said simply:

> *You know I will take good care of Tulip until you can come and get her. My day off is Thursday. You can pick her up then.*
>
> *Martin*

chapter three I Will Totally Date a Midget

Lucy had just pulled in behind Warren's truck in the driveway of her best friend's house when Jilly walked over to her.

"Do you know what happened?" Jilly said, her hands in the front pockets of her jeans. "Why would Martin do something like this?"

Lucy shook her head. "I have no idea, I really don't," she said honestly. "He won't answer his phone. This note he left me says absolutely nothing. Nothing happened. We didn't have a fight, we didn't have words. Jilly, it's just impossible. How can everything be fine one minute and then completely upside down the next?"

"Lucy, well, maybe everything wasn't fine," Jilly said reluctantly. "Did you ever get any feeling that Martin was . . . I don't know, that maybe he was messing around?"

"Three hours ago I would have said no," Lucy replied, her voice rising. "But now that I'm homeless, I suppose anything is possible. I would never expect Martin to do this, so I guess, sure. He could have been messing around with a cashier or the girl in the bakery who makes birthday cakes. Sure, why not? It makes about as much sense as anything else. Because he didn't just throw me out—he blasted me out like a rocket! I don't know what I'm going to do."

"Well, you know you can stay here until this all gets figured out," Jilly reassured her. "But in the meantime, I have to tell you something, and I know you've had to deal with big stuff today, and if this could wait, believe me, I wouldn't be telling you now. Nola called. There was a problem with the deposit from the office for the day before we left for Hawaii."

Nola, the office manager of the dental practice the girls worked at, was easily excited and had a tendency to inflate anything that wasn't noted on her schedule into a drama worthy of a prime-time cable network hour. Her position in Dr. Meadows's office consumed her whole life, and considering that Nola's time was a little free after she clocked out, her entire life force was focused on the office. Lucy and Jilly often mused that Nola's home life was so hollow that she kept a baby monitor on her nightstand with the twin monitor placed strategically in an open desk drawer at the office, or tucked behind a silk plant, so she could listen to the office sleep at night. Rumor had it that Nola had once had a beau, who had broken her heart years earlier, leaving Nola no other choice but to throw herself into the workings and minute details of a dental office.

Every important duty was Nola's responsibility by design; she needed it that way. But there was one exception. Every night at the office, Marianne would total out the day's tally, and whatever was paid in cash and checks that day would get put into a sealed envelope and handed over to the designated deposit person, who would go to the bank on their way home. This method was devised after Nola saw the same man at the same ATM two nights in a row. She became convinced that he was casing her deposit habits and was hatching a plan to kidnap her and sell her into the sex trade in an

Eastern Bloc country, like she'd seen in a segment on human trafficking on *48 Hours Mystery*. The following morning she called an urgent staff meeting and demanded that everyone in the office take turns making the deposit and visiting different bank branches all over town, and she had indeed made a schedule. It was now everyone's duty to make the deposit when it was their turn.

"So there's a problem with the deposit," Lucy replied to Jilly snottily. "What was the problem? Did Stranger Danger pop up at one of Nola's spots and she's now wearing a black negligee and marabou slippers somewhere in Estonia?"

Jilly shook her head and grinned. "No. The deposit wasn't made. The bank never got it. She's been tracking it all week to see if it was credited, but it never was. And . . . it wasn't Nola's deposit," Jilly replied. "It was the one from your night."

"My night?" Lucy said, her hands flying up to her mouth in horror. "It was my night? I forgot to make it? *Oh, no!* Shit. I was so excited about the trip that I ran home and just started packing. I must still have it. It's here somewhere. I think I had my black bag that day."

Lucy climbed up into the bed of the truck and found the box of purses and shoes, then handed it down to Jilly.

"Here's the black bag," Jilly announced after digging for a few seconds. She opened the purse, and there was the deposit.

Lucy looked at Jilly, and they both broke out in laughter that immediately sliced the heavy tension that had caused Lucy to break out in a nervous sweat.

"Whew!" Lucy said with a massive rush of relief. "I can't believe I forgot it. I guess I was in a bigger rush than I thought."

"This is such good news," Jilly said, smiling and shaking her head. "Such good news. I thought Nola was going to have your head. All right. Let's get your stuff into the garage and then we can get you settled in. You've had a long day."

"I don't think I've ever had a longer one," Lucy said in agreement, and started to unload.

As soon as Lucy walked through the door of the office the next morning, Nola bolted into the foyer, her squat figure moving quickly toward Lucy. She had the body of a stout fifth-grade boy—petite in stature but solid in the middle, with several curves on her, though not one of them was desirable. Despite her lack of feminine shapeliness, Nola's face was soft, her peachy cheeks always a little bit flushed, and her eyes were a deep aqua green. Her chin was delicate and well proportioned to her heart-shaped face, and her black hair, thick and enviably shiny, was always closely cropped in a style women usually waited until retirement age to acquire. She was in her early thirties and would have been considered almost pretty if it wasn't for the bulb of a peasant nose that was stuck in the middle of so many enviable features. The nose rendered her not to an unattractive level but to simply plain and unremarkable. She knew this, and had determined a long time ago that what she could not attain with the benefits of beauty, she would take by force and will. With all her might pushing forward like a train, Nola speed walked in through the foyer, her right arm pumping furiously like an oil drill, her left arm pointed at Lucy sternly.

"Dr. Meadows and I need to see you immediately," she said as harshly as her dimpled face looked, resembling the closest thing to an angry donut Lucy had ever seen.

"I know. Jilly told me about the missing deposit," Lucy replied, trying to ease the situation, pulling the deposit from her purse. "I have it right here. I'm really sorry."

Nola looked at Lucy and smirked. "I said Dr. Meadows and I need to see you," she repeated.

"Okay." Lucy nodded, eager to settle the situation. It was all very easily explainable, she knew; it was a mistake, a silly, stupid accident, but she was sure Dr. Meadows would understand. It was the first deposit Lucy had ever forgotten about or had made late. She had never been in trouble at the office before, all of her job performance reviews had been positive, and she had faith that the dentist would see this for exactly what it was: a touch of irresponsibility and distraction, but nothing more than that. She had worked for this man for almost two years. Jilly had gotten her the job when the previous hygienist had suddenly quit and they'd needed someone in a hurry. It was a good office, a solid practice, and she knew she was lucky to have the job.

Nola escorted her back to Dr. Meadows's office, where he was already sitting behind his large mahogany desk.

"Dr. Meadows, I'm very sorry this happened, but I can explain—" Lucy started, and then stopped when the dentist raised his hand.

"Do you have the deposit, Lucy?" he asked plainly.

Lucy nodded and handed it to him. Nola looked over her shoulder and watched her carefully.

He took a letter opener, sliced across the virgin seal of the envelope, and pulled out the contents of various checks and cash. The dentist went through it slowly, and then stopped when he got to a particular check.

"Well, it all seems to be here," he said, without looking up.

"Of course it's all there," Lucy said with a laugh in response to the absurdity of what she was hearing. "The envelope was sealed. I never opened it. Why would I open it?"

"There was a check in the deposit that was of a sizeable amount," the dentist said, without a trace of the robust and usually jovial and friendly man Lucy knew. "When the amount didn't show up in the account, well, let's just say that questions arose."

"Questions?" Lucy found herself saying. "What questions? You can clearly see I never opened that envelope."

"Well, Lucy," he continued, looking at Nola and then back to Lucy. "When twenty thousand dollars fails to be accounted for, it becomes a serious situation."

Lucy's mouth dropped open. "Twenty thousand dollars?" she said, not even believing the amount herself, and then she turned to Nola. "You gave me an envelope with twenty thousand dollars in it and didn't bother to *tell me*?"

"For precisely the reason we're talking to you now, that's something we didn't care to broadcast," Dr. Meadows said without any further explanation.

Lucy paused for a moment, until it fully hit her. "You think I tried to *steal* that money?" she asked angrily. "How could I steal a check that wasn't made out to me, a check in an envelope that you can clearly see has never been opened?"

"There are ways. They can be washed. It's really very simple. I've seen it done," Nola said very matter-of-factly, then quickly added, "On TV. It was on *Primetime Live.*"

"I only have basic cable," Lucy shot back. "I don't get the criminal mastermind channel."

"And then there's also an issue of pharmaceuticals that went missing before you girls left on vacation," Dr. Meadows interrupted. "Several bottles of sedatives are not where they should be."

Lucy could not believe what she was hearing. She shook her head in exasperation. "I don't know anything about that," she said simply, looking Dr. Meadows in the eye. She would never have done something to jeopardize her job, let alone anything as outlandish as washing checks and stealing meds. She had celebrated holidays and birthdays with the people in this office, including Dr. Meadows. He knew her better than that.

"So I'm going to ask you to submit to a drug test, Lucy," the dentist said. "I'm asking everybody. I'm not singling you out because of the deposit. Drug use—and theft—will not be tolerated in this office. That's something I can't risk."

"I have absolutely no problem with that," Lucy offered. "I'll take any drug test. I have nothing to hide."

From nowhere, Nola produced a plastic cup with LUCY stretched across the middle of it in marker. Lucy took the cup and headed to the bathroom, where Nola posted herself right outside the door.

Lucy would have found the entire episode laughable, except that five minutes later, her employer came into the break room, where Lucy was waiting. He looked at her for a moment before saying anything.

"You tested positive for cocaine," he said simply. "I have to say I didn't expect that."

"That is impossible," Lucy asserted. "It is absolutely impossible. That test is wrong. It's *wrong*. This is insane. It's a mistake. Do another test. There's no way that's right. No one's done cocaine since 1987, except for Fleetwood Mac cover bands!"

Instead of arguing, Dr. Meadows went to the supply cabinet and pulled out another test. Lucy stood there in amazement, wondering how she had never noticed bulk urinalysis drug tests in Costco. This time, Lucy stood next to Dr. Meadows as he opened a new pouch and lowered what looked like a multipronged dipstick into the urine sample. After the five minutes of laborious dead silence between Dr. Meadows and herself, Lucy saw the results on the test strip herself. A red line appeared after COC.

"I'm sorry, Lucy. I'm going to have to let you go," the dentist said. "It looks like you've made some poor decisions. You've become a liability to this office, and we can't run a practice that way."

"This whole thing is a joke, right? Are you filming this for some crazy show that Nola watches? If you are, I will totally date a midget," Lucy said firmly.

"Nola will give you your last paycheck," he said. "I'm sorry it turned out this way, Lucy. Best of luck to you."

And with that, he turned and walked away, as Lucy stood in the break room, her head swirling almost as quickly as it had when she'd thrown up on vacation in that guy's toilet. Jilly appeared at the doorway.

"What happened?" she asked. "Are you okay?"

Lucy shook her head. "My test came up positive for coke," she said with a little laugh and a shrug.

Jilly looked puzzled. "What? When did you do *coke*?" she asked.

"Oh, I dunno," Lucy responded. "When was the last time I got my hair frosted? Long before you could buy a twelve-pack of drug tests at the mall and have your boss mix it up in the break room next to the coffeemaker. I don't know what happened, Jilly. I haven't done coke since my boobs were able to hold up a tube top on their own. I don't even *like* coke. I hate the way it's bitterness clings to the back of your throat. All I know is that the test is wrong. And they don't believe me."

"Lucy, you've got to say something," Jilly insisted.

"Oh, I did," Lucy said, laughing again in futility. "So we did the test twice, and the second time I watched with my own eyes as Dr. Meadows stuck a gloved hand into my pee and twirled the stick around like it was a very dirty martini. I'd rather take an unemployment check than watch that again. And that's not all. They think I was trying to steal the deposit. Apparently, there was twenty thousand bucks in there that Nola neglected to mention. And you'd better be prepared to submit a sample yourself. Dr. Meadows said they're drug testing everyone because some sedatives are missing from the cabinet. You know how I thought yesterday was the crappiest day ever? Nope. It somehow got topped."

"What are you going to do?" Jilly asked, putting a soft hand on Lucy's arm.

"Good question," she replied. "I'm already a coked-out embezzler, so maybe I'll hit either a street corner and wait for my pimp or a karaoke bar that plays a lot of Stevie Nicks songs. Big deal. So they fired me. Fired me from a job where I spend my days scraping plaque buildup and rotten food from the mouths of people who don't know how to brush their teeth. Do you know I spent roughly sixty percent of my workday watching people spit? I could go to China if I wanted to see that all day long."

"Try calling Martin again," her friend pleaded.

Lucy took a deep breath. "I have," she admitted, exasperated. "I've been trying to call him since last night, and I tried again this morning. He's disconnected his cellphone and the house phone. What did I do? I don't know what the hell I did. Maybe I'll find out what this is all about when I get Tulip on his day off, on Thursday. I'm still in shock. I can't believe any of this is happening."

"Maybe you should go down to the store and try to talk to him," Jilly suggested.

"Confront Martin?" Lucy laughed. "At work? No way. Only if I never want to straighten this out. I've never known him to do anything remotely like this, but I do know that when Martin is ready to talk, he'll talk. All I can do is hope he will call me back, but if he's this upset, it's got to be on his own terms. Maybe he just needs time to calm down from whatever freaked him out, but my hope is not high. He threw me out without so much as one word of explanation. Truthfully, that's not something I want to lock into for a lifetime, you know? Cold feet is one thing, but this?"

"Yeah, you're right. You can stay at our place as long as you need to," Jilly reassured her.

"Thanks," Lucy said with a nod before Jilly gave her a hug, but Lucy already knew that although it was a selfless offer, it wasn't an option. How long could she sleep on Jilly's couch with no job and no references to get another one? How long could she bunk in the living room of a generous friend when she had hardly any money saved to get her own apartment? Easily, she would need to work for a month or two before she'd have enough money for a month's rent and security deposit. No one was going to rent to her if she was unemployed. And despite Jilly's love for Tulip, how could Lucy ask that her friends take in her dog, too? Lucy had one, and only one, option, so after she got everything she had from her cubby in the break room and her last measly check from Nola, she sat in the cab of her truck in the parking lot of the doctor's office and dialed her cellphone.

Flagstaff wasn't that far away, Lucy told herself. Two hours, two and a half, tops. She could haul all of her stuff up in one day, and easily make the drive down to get Tulip on Thursday. It was simple. Staying at her sister's was really the only thing she could do. The only true way family can throw you out is with an appearance by the sheriff holding a warrant.

And Alice was the only family Lucy had left besides an odd cousin here or there. They had been raised by their grandmother Naunie, a fiery no-nonsense woman with an inch of patience that burned up quicker than an oil-soaked candlewick. When they were barely toddlers, Lucy and Alice were collected and taken to the family farm by Naunie after both their parents had been killed in a car accident. Lucy and Alice grew up there with the help of an uncle until he was pulled into a combine the way a vacuum cleaner sucks up a penny. After that, it had just been the three of them, making do and creating a family of their own, depending only on each other. It was times like this that Lucy knew she could count on her sister.

"It'll only be for a little while," Lucy told Alice. "Won't take me long to get my stuff together and figure something out. Plus, I haven't seen you for a while. It'll be good to catch up."

"Actually, I could use the help around here. Things are a little tight," Alice replied. "I haven't gotten a child support check in months, and I just put almost everything I had into getting a new transmission for a car I shoulda junked years ago. I would love to have you, Lucy."

"And Tulip, too?" Lucy almost hesitated to ask.

"No question. Jared would love to have a pal to run around with in the backyard. A nine-year-old boy has more energy than he ought to," her sister added. "It would be wonderful if your nephew got to know you better. The divorce was hard for him. My ex-husband has a new family now, so apparently, it was easy for him to forget about his old one. It will be a good distraction to have you and Tulip here."

So with help from Warren, Lucy once again loaded up the back of the truck with everything she could squeeze in, and left the remainder piled in the corner of Jilly's garage, promising to come and claim it when she had all of this trouble sorted out. Before she left, Jilly made sure Lucy set herself up with a free email account since her old one was through the cable company back at Martin's house. This way they could keep in touch, even if it was a while before Lucy got really settled.

"If your phone ever gets shut off, at least you can pop into one of those Internet cafés and check your email for a dollar," Jilly said as Lucy put her keys in the ignition and turned the engine over. "Don't let me lose you, Lucy."

Lucy looked at her friend quizzically and laughed. "How you gonna lose me, Jilly?" She smirked. "You've got a bunch of my stuff sitting where your car should be. I always come back for what's mine!"

"All right, then," Jilly said as she smacked the window frame with her hand and smiled. "You go on and go. You've always been nothin' but trouble."

Lucy laughed, and then backed out of the driveway and headed for I-17 in her truck, the bed covered with tarps and ropes to hold everything down. Whatever Lucy owned that wasn't in the bed of the truck or stashed in Jilly's garage was in her pocket. She was the only one who had failed the drug test in the office, and when Nola had handed her check over, she'd done so with the side note that Lucy's benefits were paid up until the end of the month, including life and health insurance, but once the month was over, the benefits ended. Nola had also said that if Lucy had any plans to file for unemployment, she should know that Nola would see to it directly that Dr. Meadows would appeal it on the grounds of financial fraud. So Lucy had cashed her last paycheck—less than a couple hundred dollars—and with what she had left in the bank, the grand total rolled to $430, folded in a lump, in the front right pocket of her jeans.

On the drive up north, she tried not to remember what had crumbled over the last couple of days. Every time her mind snuck over and picked at that spot, she changed the station on the radio and tried to find a song she knew the words to. She laughed at the cliché when Gloria Gaynor wailed through the static that she would survive, and Lucy gave in and wailed along with her. *I'm not going to focus on any of it,* she told herself firmly. *I'm going to take what I've got and move on to something else, something new, something different. This is a whole new chance for me. A brand-new chapter in my life. I get to start over with not one single string.*

Lucy switched the radio station again. She sang along, mumbling at first, then clearer, more legible, and louder, and then as loud as she could.

Outside the truck on the interstate, the tall, spired cacti were flashing by less and less, slowly overcome by the dusty green brush that signaled that she was leaving the desert.

Lucy looked over and saw the brush form one continuous sage-colored blurry line. For the first time in what seemed like forever, she was glad.

It had been a while since Lucy had been up to Alice's, but when she pulled into the dirt circular driveway, the house looked shabbier than she remembered it, almost as if tweakers had spent the night and sucked some life out of it. A dry brown pot of withered petunias sat next to the door of the light blue, weathered, low-slung wood-paneled house. The posts of the spilt rail fence leaned in various, unintentional directions. Pine needles from the towering trees blanketed the ground everywhere, enough that it looked like they hadn't been raked up in years. Lucy knew it had been hard for Alice since she and her husband had split the year before, so if Lucy's living at the house would help her sister out, it made everything seem a little brighter. She decided that this would be good, for her to get out of Phoenix for a while, clear her head. She could water flowers or fix a fence. She wished she had been able to bring Tulip with her, but in two days, she'd be able to drive back to Phoenix to pick her up and really start everything all over again.

The front door opened, and Alice, tall and thin, her wispy hair back in a ponytail, stepped outside. With a wide smile, she came toward Lucy, walking down the driveway, barefoot, with her arms open wide. The joy on her face charged Lucy, and when they finally embraced in an earnest hug, Alice emitted a glad, true deep-throated laugh.

"I am so happy you're here," she said as she held Lucy close to her.

"Me, too," Lucy agreed with a full smile.

"I'm so sorry about Martin," Alice said with a squeeze, and then she pulled back to look at her sister. "You haven't heard from him at all?"

Lucy shook her head as she pulled back. "He wouldn't call me back, and now his number's been disconnected," she said with a shrug. "There's not much I can do, you know? Maybe he'll talk to me when I go pick Tulip up. He'll have to say *something.*"

Alice held Lucy at arm's length. "And what about work? Is there any way to sort that out?"

Lucy shook her head again. "I was the only one who came up dirty, and I still can't tell you why," she answered. "But I've decided to look at this as an opportunity to start over again. New job, new life, new everything. Who knows what tomorrow will bring, right?"

Later that night, Lucy opened the oven door and pulled out a beautifully browned pan of meat loaf made from Naunie's beloved recipe, while Alice gave the mashed potatoes one last whirl with the hand mixer. Jared put the plates on the kitchen table, and lined the forks and knives along the sides of them, and Lucy ruffled his hair as she reached over and placed the meat loaf on a trivet square in the middle. He smiled as he sat down at the dinner table. His Aunt Lucy had bought him a present, a little iPod he could keep in his pocket and listen to while taking the bus to and from school. Lucy knew she didn't have the money to be buying things like that, but it hadn't been that expensive, and when he'd showed it to his mother at the store display when they had all been out that afternoon, his face had lit up. It seemed to Lucy that he hadn't had much to smile about for a while, and that she should have been there for him long before this. The player made him happy, which, in turn, made Lucy happy. Besides, she was heading to the unemployment office first thing tomorrow, ready to battle any claim against her that Dr. Meadows might make, so week after next, there would be money coming in whether or not she had found a job yet.

"Naunie's meat loaf!" Alice said excitedly as she placed the potatoes next to the meat loaf. "It smells so good. I can't wait to eat it. I miss all of her home cooking, and tomorrow I get to have a meat loaf sandwich for lunch right after I have my yearly review at work, in which, crossing fingers, I will get a nice big raise."

Lucy dropped a huge spoonful of mashed potatoes onto Jared's plate. "Of course you're going to get a raise. You've been working at the school district since you guys moved up here. This here is lucky meat loaf, you know! You can't eat Naunie's meat loaf and not be lucky!"

"All right, then. In that case, you're going to have good luck at the unemployment office," Alice said, raising her can of Diet Coke.

"To a raise and to early retirement," Lucy joked as she raised her soda can and Jared raised his glass of milk. "Cheers!"

"And to Naunie's meat loaf," Alice interjected. "Cheers!"

"What do you remember about Naunie?" Lucy asked her nephew after the toast.

"Well," Jared began after he took a forkful of fluffy, creamy potatoes. "I remember one summer when we were visiting the farm on vacation and she made me go out and run the hose over that big pig named Willy, who I think really liked being washed, because he snorted and then he smiled at me. The next night she said, 'Isn't Willy a good pig?' and I said yes, that he was very nice. And she said, 'No, not nice! *Tasty!*' and took another bite of her pork chop."

Lucy nodded. "Well, you know, she had a habit of doing that," she said simply, as Alice slid a slice of the meat loaf onto Jared's plate.

"You learned not to get attached to anything on the farm, even smiling pigs. Do you remember anything else about her?"

"She seemed pretty cranky most of the time," Jared said honestly. "But she did make good Willy chops."

"You know, your Naunie was something else," Lucy offered. "Not only could she dress and fry up a pig, but there wasn't anything she couldn't do—and if she didn't know how to do something when she started, she'd figure it out until she was finished. She never left anything undone. She had an iron will, that cranky old lady."

"We were able to get the car fixed with the money when we sold her farm," his mother reminded him. "And we bought you a new bike. I remember you being pretty happy about that."

Her son nodded. "I do like my bike," he said with a smile.

"It's a good thing you still have that money from the farm," Alice said to Lucy. "That will be a nice cushion for you until you find something."

Lucy stopped. She didn't know what to say. She now felt terrible about blowing the money on a vacation when Alice was struggling with simply paying for necessities. How could she possibly say that she had taken her share of the farm that her grandmother had broken her back to keep going and had blown it on a lousy trip to Hawaii? Lucy was quickly ashamed at what she had done with her portion, the pinnacle of the vacation spent hurling into a stranger's toilet after drinking some hot, bitter beer, a bitterness that had hung in the back of her throat just like—

Lucy gasped and nearly dropped her fork.

Holy shit, she thought. *Holy shit*.

He laced my beer. That asshole roofied my beer with coke while I was waiting for Marianne.

Holy shit.

"Lucy!" Alice yelled as she ran into the house, the door slamming loudly behind her. "Lucy! I need your truck! My car won't start! Where are your keys?"

Lucy shot awake on the sleeper couch when she heard Alice yelling. Light filled the living room in dusty yellow streams that stretched across the room.

"What?" Lucy mumbled groggily.

"I need your keys!" Alice demanded, poking her head through the doorway that connected the living room and kitchen. "My review! My review is in twenty-five minutes, Lucy! I can't be late. God, I can't be late. *Where are your keys?*"

Lucy struggled to remember where she'd put them. Had she placed them on the kitchen counter? Were they in her purse?

"I d-dunno," she stammered groggily. "Kitchen counter, purse. One of those."

She heard Alice searching the counter, then the collision of metal keys against one another as she scooped them up.

"Got 'em," she said right before her head popped back into the doorway. "Is it all right? Can I take the truck? I can't wait for the bus, I won't make it."

"Sure," Lucy said, her eyes still adjusting to the light. "I don't have to get Tulip until Thursday. How far is the unemployment office? Can I take a bus or a cab?"

"I have the bus schedule on the refrigerator door," Alice said quickly. "Look for the courthouse on the map. The office is right across the street from it. I'll see you tonight?"

"Yeah, I'll see you tonight," she replied, still half-asleep and trying to fully open her eyes.

"Good luck!" she called after Alice, a millimeter of a second before she heard the door slam again.

With her finger firmly pressed on the map on top of the spot for the courthouse, Lucy searched out the window, trying to figure out where she was. She didn't know the town very well, but she remembered certain landmarks from her trips up before. She had just passed Alice's favorite diner, and she was sure she was readily approaching the bar where she had had one of her last affairs with Jack Daniel's. The bus emitted a loud gasp as it pulled to a stop, the doors creaking open.

"Next stop, courthouse," the driver announced over the intercom, to Lucy's relief, particularly since Lucy had explained to the driver when she'd gotten on the bus that she had no idea where she was going. The bus driver, a ruddy, plump woman in her sixties, had patted her hand and told her not to worry; she would make sure Lucy knew when the courthouse stop was. A minute or two later, Lucy saw a large, brick clock tower with a spire on top that she knew had to be the landmark. Sure enough, the bus pulled directly in front of it and stopped, and the doors flapped open with several mechanical groans.

"Courthouse," the driver announced, then turned and pointed to Lucy. "This is you, sugar," she said with smile, and Lucy picked up her things, slipping in line with the other riders filing their way out. She waved at the driver before she disembarked with a little "Thank you!" and the bus driver waved back and smiled.

On the street, it had bloomed into the perfect spring day. The sky was a clear, bright blue, the kind of blue Michelangelo used when painting the heavens in the Sistine Chapel. The sun shone a perfect, soothing white, just enough to tint the day with a bounce. A slight breeze fluttered by, blowing several strands of hair into Lucy's face.

She smiled and tucked the hair behind her ear, noting how glorious the sun felt on her skin. It was a good day. Map still in hand, she scanned the buildings around her as she walked down the block, looking for anything that resembled the unemployment office. When she came up empty, she looked across the street, and there she saw it, sitting exactly parallel to the courthouse, with DEPARTMENT OF ECONOMIC SECURITY in gray and gold lettering across the window.

As Lucy waited to cross the street, a car pulled up next to her, all windows rolled down for its passengers to enjoy the gorgeous day. The melody coming from the car was familiar, but Lucy couldn't name it until the song surged into the chorus, and that was when she smiled and shook her head as Gloria Gaynor once again declared that she was going to survive.

Lucy turned to check the time on the clock tower: It was 12:34, lunchtime. At first she cursed herself for getting there just in time for the lunchtime rush, but then she laughed at herself when she realized that there was no lunch hour rush when you were unemployed. Lunchtime lasted all day. She heard the walk signal sound and moved forward, but then another gust of wind blew a chunk of hair over her eyes just as she stepped from the curb into the street. When she finally got the hair tucked behind her ear again, she heard a loud torrent of a roar rushing at her with a force that was fast and consuming. Lucy looked up and saw the horrified face of the bus driver who had been kind enough to let Lucy know when her stop was. In a slice of a second so thin there was no measurement for it, that roar pulled her forward, sucked her backward, and then, without hesitation, swallowed her.

chapter four Don't You Ever Wonder What Happened to Sugar Pie?

Lucy woke up to the sound of a man snoring beside her, but before she found out who was making the rumble, she realized that all she saw was white.

A warm, glowing white the color of cream, soft and easy to fall into.

And then Lucy realized that her eyes were still closed.

With a knee-jerk reaction, her lids flew open and she sat up, looking around. To her left and to her right were single beds, lined up in row after row after row, for almost as far as she could see. There must have been a hundred of them. In each bed, a person slept, with the exception of a few people here and there, who, like Lucy, were quietly looking around and trying to answer the simplest of questions: where were they?

A long, deep snore erupted again. Lucy turned to peer at her neighbor, a middle-aged man with a double chin and a stout nose that clearly had taken most of a lifetime to develop to its current enormity. Lucy watched him, settled deep in an enviable sleep, as he inhaled through his cavernous nose and then exhaled through his mouth, his lips rippling with every escaping breath. She'd become somewhat hypnotized by the rhythm of his snoring, when suddenly an image of the horrified bus driver's face crashed into her consciousness like a bolt of lightning.

Lucy gasped, stunned and confused. Her head took a moment to restart, and then, one by one, she began gathering the pieces together. The bus. She'd been on the bus. Something must have happened with the bus. She remembered the wind had been blowing, gentle at first, and then it had become stronger. She remembered the glare of the noon sun and her hair blanketing her eyes, blinding her as she stepped off the curb, then the bus driver's face, her eyes wide and terrified, towering high above Lucy behind a sheet of curved glass. It was a blur, nothing more than a bite of a moment. That was it, then nothing. Nothing until she had woken up to a snoring neighbor. She was still puzzled, knowing that something had happened. Maybe she'd fallen. She must have fallen and hit her head, and had been taken here, a hospital of some sort, although truth be told, it looked more like an orphanage. Lucy didn't see any sort of medical equipment beside any of the beds, and looking up and down the aisles, she didn't see a trace of a nurse or a doctor. She briefly checked herself over—wiggled her toes, made sure she had all ten fingers, bent her knees, felt for any missing pieces of skull or for a head bandage she might have missed. Everything was fine. She was fine. She was whole. Nothing missing, all parts accounted for. She felt extremely rested and relaxed. She felt great. In fact, she felt fantastic.

Oh, shit, she realized as she slapped the blankets on the bed. *Oh, my God. No wonder.* County. She was in a county hospital. No wonder there wasn't anyone around or a nurse to be had. *Damn it,* Lucy swore to herself. *How the hell did I wind up in county? Where's my purse?* she thought, whipping her head around to scan the table beside her. She saw her cowboy boots lined up neatly by the side of the bed, but nothing else. *I've got to find my purse,* she thought adamantly. *My insurance card is in my purse. Besides, I'm fine. I am perfectly okay; there is no need for me to stay in a hospital anyway, county or otherwise. I probably had a tiny concussion, but I am fine now.*

Her purse. Where was her purse? Lucy realized that it must have gotten lost during all of the commotion. Clearly someone had called 911 and an ambulance had brought her here. Who knew where her stuff had ended up? Another wave of dread washed over Lucy. If they didn't know who she was, then they hadn't known who to call to inform of Lucy's whereabouts, or even how she was. Alice had to be worried sick. It was clearly already morning, and the last thing Lucy remembered was looking at the clock on the courthouse at 12:34 the day before.

Lucy searched the side table for a phone. The table was empty save for what looked like an old intercom speaker the size of a small alarm clock. On it was a red button, which Lucy instinctively pushed.

"Nurse!" she called into it, trying not to sound too frantic. "Nurse! Anybody! I need to make a phone call. Can anyone help me?"

Lucy released the red button and waited for a response. After several seconds, she heard a staticky crackle, and then a tinny woman's voice replied, "Please report to the front desk."

What? Lucy thought, taken aback. *The front desk?* Where was the front desk? Which way was *front*? All Lucy could see were rows and rows of beds. There didn't seem to be any end to them. Then, as if on cue, Lucy looked down at the foot of the bed, on which was perched a tiny little metal sign that read in small, chipping red letters, FRONT DESK, with an arrow pointing to Lucy's left.

Anxious to get Alice on the phone to let her sister know that she was all right, Lucy pulled back the covers, to discover that she was fully clothed in what she had been wearing when she'd butted heads with the bus the day before—her jeans, a white broadcloth shirt, and a brown corduroy jacket.

Wow, I guess that's county for you. Look at that. So cheap they can't even let you suffer in a hospital gown. How generous. You have to be sick in your own clothes. Not that she'd rather be wearing a hospital gown, but still. Something a little more comfortable would have been appreciated. Then again, she didn't exactly remember being uncomfortable, either. In fact, she thought she might have had one of the best night's sleep she had ever had. She didn't recall tossing or turning, waking up, being thirsty, needing to fluff pillows, or even pulling up covers. None of the snorers—and judging by the symphony erupting all around her bed, there were plenty of them—had disturbed her sleep in any way, and Lucy was a light sleeper, evidenced by how many times a night she had to wake Martin to have him turn over when he snored. *Hooray for concussions,* Lucy thought. *They make you sleep like the dead. If there was a concussion in a pill,* she thought, and smiled, *they could run Ambien right out of business.*

Lucy swung her legs over the side of the bed and pulled her battered black square-toed cowboy boots on. She tried to be quiet, but knocked her engagement ring on the rails of the bed while pulling on her right boot, sending a metallic echo ringing throughout the hall. As the exaggerated echo bounced off wall after wall after wall, Lucy winced and stood still, waiting for the shouting and grumbles that she was making too much noise.

But nobody said a word. Nobody even moved or stirred. It was quiet as the battery of slight, wispy breaths and alternate snores rose and fell, building and collapsing as the rest of the ward continued to slumber.

When she finally reached the front desk after trudging past what seemed like an eternity of beds full of sleeping patients, the pleasant woman seated behind the desk looked up at Lucy, smiled, and said, "Please proceed to this room."

She handed Lucy a slip of paper with "SD1118" printed on it, and then pointed to her left. "The SD wing is that way."

"I just want to check out, or release myself," Lucy tried to explain to the woman, but the woman simply smiled in return.

"That way," she repeated pleasantly again.

"Can I make a phone call?" Lucy asked. "My sister has no idea where I am."

"SD1118 is where you're supposed to be," the attendant concluded. "You'll find everything you need in there."

Lucy knew she was getting nowhere with the woman, so she smiled in return, nodded, and started off in the direction the woman had instructed. Lucy was bound and determined to find a phone somewhere. All down the hallway were doorways with heavy-looking old wooden shellacked and paneled doors, each marked with brass letters and numerals, as in SD1098, SD1099, SD 1100. Every door was closed, creating a long, windowless tunnel of glossy, dark wood that glimmered from the fluorescent lights above. There was no hint as to what might be inside—a classroom, a lounge, or an office that might have a phone. Lucy trudged on until she arrived at door SD1118, paused for a moment in front of it, and then turned the ornate brass doorknob and stepped inside.

Two rows of university-type plastic desks—chairs with writing surfaces attached—sliced through the center of the classroom. The desks faced a lectern that rested on a small, raised stage littered with what looked like theater props, including a stack of books, dishes, some odd pieces of old furniture, and several old steamer trunks. The seats were filled with a wide assortment of people—there was a rail-thin gentleman in a very clingy and shiny blue cycling outfit, complete with helmet, resembling a human lollipop; a large, thick middle-aged man in camouflage coveralls and a matching vest; a blond middle-aged attractive woman in a body-hugging pink ski suit; a man with graying temples in casual vacation wear; a young guy, maybe just out of his teens, with shaggy hair, who just stared at the ground; and a woman who looked to be about Lucy's age, in an entire wet suit complete with flippers, a diving mask resting on the desk.

Lucy was baffled by the assortment of people, each of whom whipped their heads up and stared at her as she entered the room. *Either I'm in the psych ward portion of the hospital or I'm at a casting call for a church or an antidepressant commercial,* she thought.

"Is this SD1118?" Lucy hesitantly asked, in response to which the camo guy, flipper girl, and bike guy nodded their heads.

"Are you here to check out?" Lucy ventured again.

"I'm fine, and I just want to fill out whatever paperwork and go home," the flipper girl said adamantly. "The staff around here is not helpful, and they just told me to come to this room."

Lucy nodded in response. "Me, too," she said, and felt compelled to take the open desk next to the girl.

"How long have you been waiting?" Lucy asked.

"Not long, a couple of minutes," flipper girl said, shaking her head. "But I just want to get back to my vacation and call my boyfriend. We have things scheduled and planned today, you know? I can't be sitting around here all day waiting to find out if I can leave. I *would* just leave if I knew the way out. I haven't seen one exit sign! That's a fire code violation, you know. I'm going to report them."

"Yeah," Lucy replied. "Is it morning, do you know? I can't figure out how long I've been here."

"Me, too. I have no idea," flipper girl said. "I just woke up in a room full of other people. I didn't know there were such weird hospitals in the Bahamas. They don't even have nurses here!"

Lucy tried to smile but was a bit puzzled, until she realized that the flipper girl was not as well as she might have imagined and was clearly still suffering from some concussion side effects or perhaps a psychotic break. It was a weird hospital, all right, and woefully understaffed, but what else would she expect from a county hospital in Flagstaff, Arizona?

Lucy suddenly stopped. Scuba diving in Flagstaff, Arizona?

"You were scuba diving around here?" she asked her newfound friend. "Where did you go?"

Lucy immediately regretted her actions, because the last thing she had patience for was engaging in conversation of any sort with a person disoriented with reality.

The girl got a wide smile on her face. "Well, when my boyfriend told me we were going on vacation to the Bahamas, I couldn't believe it, I was so excited!" she gleefully related. "So we made a deal; he said he would go and take the Anna Nicole Smith Farewell Tour with me in the Bahamas if I would go shark feeding with him. He said it would be fun, and it was something he had always wanted to do since he saw an article about it in *Maxim*. I said okay, and Anna Nicole was an idol of mine, so I couldn't say no. Have you done it?"

Lucy shook her head.

"Oh, you have to do it while you're here!" flipper girl exclaimed. "At first it is terrifying. I mean, they take you out way into the ocean, far, far from land and put you in the water, hand you a chunk of bloody fish, and then the sharks are suddenly coming at you! I know it sounds crazy, but it was thrilling. The sharks just rip that fish right out of your hands and then the shark-feeding people give you another one. So I was holding that, and the biggest shark came at me with its mouth wide open, and it was swimming so fast! It got closer and closer, and suddenly it was right there. I mean right there, inches from me! It was like a video game, but real. And I guess that's when my oxygen cut out. The hose probably bent in all of the excitement. I passed out. And then I woke up here. I hope I didn't ruin it for anybody else on the trip. Don't you ever wonder what happened to Sugar Pie? I'm Bethanny, by the way."

"I'm Lucy," she said, extending her hand, which Bethanny took.

"What happened to you? Why are you here?"

"You know, it was the dumbest thing," Lucy started with a small laugh. "I stepped in front of a bus. I know. Sounds crazy, but my hair blew into my face, and all of a sudden there I was. The last thing I remember was the look of absolute horror on the bus driver's face. She must have had great reflexes, though, because me versus a bus . . . Well . . . I, um, yeah. I guess I—I don't know. I guess I hit my head? But I feel fine. I feel great. I'd just like to call my sister. Do you happen to have a phone I could use?"

Bethanny shook her head. "All of my stuff was on the boat. I hope my boyfriend has it," she replied.

"Does anyone have a phone I can use?" Lucy asked, turning around to face the other people in the room.

The bike guy shook his helmet head; the fellow in the Hawaiian Tommy Bahama shirt shrugged listlessly. The housewife in the pink ski suit pursed her two raft-like lips together and mouthed "No" while looking dramatically despondent. The shaggy-haired kid didn't even bother to respond at all.

"I have a phone," the guy in camouflage offered as he reached into the pocket of his vest and pulled it out. "But it's dead. I guess I need a charge."

The door to SD1118 opened one more time, and in stepped a little wrinkled old lady with fiery red hair. She was wearing a long black robe and dirty blue house slippers. In her arms was a stack of binders and folders that she held close to her chest.

"Hello," she announced loudly and cheerily in a scratchy voice as she sauntered over to the lectern and slapped the pile of folders down on top of it. "My name is Ruby Spicer, and I am here to guide you through your Transition."

No one in the group said a word. They simply sat and stared at Ruby Spicer, not really knowing what to do.

"We have a lot of work to do to get you where you need to be. Anyone know where they are? Do we have any detectives in the house?" the old woman asked with a crooked smile, her voice crackling almost like static on occasion, her red lipsticked mouth stretching over a full set of nicotine-stained teeth.

The bike helmet—along with Bethanny and the velvet housewife—shook his head. The others, like Lucy, were busy trying to put together the pieces of a puzzle they hadn't seen and couldn't even begin to imagine.

"You don't need to *guide* me," Bethanny protested. "I just want to sign my release forms and go back to the hotel."

"What's the last thing you remember before you woke up, dear?" Ruby asked, pointing to Bethanny. "What is the last thing you remember seeing?"

"A shark?" Bethanny snipped, throwing up her hands.

"And you?" Ruby asked, pointing to the guy in camouflage.

"My son. He was coming up in front of me, through the brush. He was aiming at something behind me. I bet it was a five-pointer. I bet he bagged it!"

"And Sir Ten Speed?" Ruby prodded. "What do you remember?"

"Well, I remember I was heading for a sizeable hill with a steep grade on my recumbent bike, so I opened my Hammer Gel concentrated carb meal and was squeezing it into my mouth when I saw a Hummer come around the bend."

"And you in the tropical print?" Ruby asked.

Tommy Bahama sighed impatiently. "I was on a plane, eating the snack mix," he fired off sharply. "And I remember coughing. That's it. That's the last thing I remember. I don't know what that has to do with this little game."

"Anyone see a common thread? Young man?" the old woman said to the shaggy-haired guy, whose face was obscured by his precisely cut mane as he stared relentlessly at the floor.

He shrugged, his head still hanging down.

"Young man, I'm talking to you," the old woman repeated.

"I dunno. I was wasted, old lady," he said, relenting, still without looking up.

Ruby sighed and rolled her eyes.

"Miss, what do you recall?" she asked the velvet housewife.

"I was on a ski lift, and it was so cold! Suddenly it felt like I had two ice blocks in my bra!" she admitted.

"And you?" she continued, moving on and meeting Lucy's eyes.

Lucy looked back. And as she looked at the old woman, she slowly began to shake her head.

"No," she said quietly.

"What do you remember?" the old woman asked again.

"No way," Lucy said forcefully. "I don't— *No*. On Sunday, my fiancé dumped me by throwing all my stuff out on the street, on Monday I was fired for having a dirty drug test because a skanky guy my stupid friend was trying to hook up with roofied me on my vacation, the office manager where I used to work thinks I was trying to steal twenty thousand dollars, and *now* you're trying to tell me that *that bus*—"

Lucy stopped and shook her head and crossed her arms in defiance. "No," she said again pointedly. "No way. Absolutely not."

"Trying to tell you what?" Bethanny said in a panic. "Trying to tell you *what*?"

Lucy continued to shake her head.

"I'm just going to break it to you as gently as the situation allows, dears," Ruby said with a kind smile. "You're dead. You're all dead. Welcome to Sudden Death—or as I like to call it, Surprise Demise—room 1118."

chapter five Why Am I Wearing Underwear?

"Now, I realize what I just said may seem like a terribly turbulent way to start our acquaintance," Ruby informed the speechless and stunned group before her. "But after guiding countless sections of the freshly expired through their Transitions, I've found that being up-front, first and foremost, is not only the most effective method, but the most helpful. You're dead. You've all died very unexpectedly, and my job is to assist you with your initial Transition. This is Intro to Sudden Death, a primer for this particular stage in the death process."

"Do you mean denial, bargaining, and acceptance?" the bicyclist wondered.

"If I died, where are my already dead family members?" Tommy Bahama asked. "I thought they were all supposed to show up to welcome me!"

"I want to speak to your manager!" the housewife cried in a panic. "I demand to see Jesus! *And his mother.*"

"I don't understand where we are," Bethanny said, still confused by the fact that her vacation had ended so abruptly. "Am I not going on the Auna Nicole Farewell Tour?"

"Listen," Ruby interjected, trying to calm things. "We have a lot of ground to cover, so let's clear up some confusion. You are in the Transition Center. That's where you woke up this morning, in the dormitory. That's where you'll be staying until our section is complete. I'll be handing out room assignments before you leave."

"Oh, that's ridiculous," the snow bunny housewife objected. "So you're saying I'm dead *and* I'm staying in a dorm, like in college? I gained fifteen pounds in that dorm. And I'll tell you right now, if there's some nosy-body RA sniffing around, I'm not discussing my eating habits with *anyone*. I demand an upgrade. I'll pay for it. I have plenty of frequent flier miles."

"There are no upgrades, I'm afraid," Ruby informed her. "This is all we've got. Everyone gets the same thing. There's no sliding scale."

What the hell is a Sudden Death Transition Center, Lucy thought as she sat back and watched the reactions of the others around her, almost as if it was a television show and she was just tuning in. Could she really be dead? she wondered, then immediately wanted to smack herself for being so foolish. It was a dream. The whole thing was bizarre enough to be a dream, and once she realized that she was trapped in the reality-show portion of her subconscious, she decided that she really should simply sit back, enjoy the show, and wait until she woke up. It was like free entertainment. After all, there were worse dreams to be stuck in. She could have been making out with Carrot Top or being chased through a mall by a bear with a goat head, all while trying to figure out a way to stop in at the food court to get a Beef 'n Cheddar at Arby's without getting mauled. Truly, this was a great dream. The detail was amazing; the premise was fascinating. She was already looking forward to recounting the whole bizarre episode to Alice in the morning over their first cups of coffee.

"If I'm dead," queried the hunter, as if he could catch the old woman in a trap, "why am I wearing underwear?"

"This is bullshit, lady," Tommy Bahama bellowed suddenly, his face about to rupture with anger. "What kind of joke are you playing on us?"

"This is no joke, Mr. Russell," Ruby replied, her smile quickly dropping into a stern no-nonsense look. "You choked on a peanut from your in-flight snack because you never really did learn to chew properly due to the fact that you lack the virtue of patience and you can be a real pain in the ass. You were in a hurry to board the plane, you were pushy when you ordered your drink, and you made a face when the flight attendant handed you merely one snack bag. You tore it open, poured the contents into your mouth, and barely masticated one time before a peanut rolled into the back of your throat and lodged itself there. After coughing several times and making several useless simian-like motions to capture someone's attention, you choked to death and then collapsed onto your fold-down tray, breaking it. You are a Sudden Death, Mr. Russell, and simply put, you were not expected. You all met a surprise tragic ending. This wasn't in the cards for any of you, but *here you are*."

"What are you all pissed about?" the shaggy-haired youngster finally said in a tense voice. "I'm the youngest one here! Look at everything I missed out on. I just turned twenty-one! I haven't even begun to live yet! The rest of you already lived; you're old. I was young. You were all going to die soon anyway. But you all have nothing to complain about. I didn't even get a chance!"

"Well, Mr. Morse, I would say your chances were never really all that good, being that you drank yourself into a stupor, lost consciousness, and *then* lost control of your bladder while snuggled under your grandma's old electric blanket, and fried yourself like a chimichanga."

The youngster's jaw went slack, and after a moment he stared straight back down at the floor again.

The bicyclist raised his hand. "I was hit by a Hummer, is that correct?" he asked. "Is that what you're saying? A gas-sucking, environmentally disastrous vanity car ran me over?"

"Well, not exactly," Ruby offered. "He was a little too close to you, and as he passed, the side mirror whacked your head from behind and rendered it into a projectile, you could say. It then bounced several times, due to the foam core of the helmet, and then finally rolled behind a bush, resting next to a Big Mac wrapper and a Styrofoam cup."

"I was decapitated and then wound up as litter," the bicyclist concluded. "That is a ridiculous way to die. I somehow thought my ending would be more . . . significant. Earnest, if you will."

"Don't we all hope that, Mr. Marks?" Ruby said, trying to be comforting. "We all carry the hope that our death will not be in vain, or that it will assume some higher translation, maybe even taking on metaphoric stature. In life, we all want our deaths to be magnificent and relevant. And in your case . . . I'm sorry, no."

"I still don't understand why I'm here," the ski bunny said. "I think a mistake has been made. I don't see how I'm supposedly dead. If I'm dead, how did I die? Avalanche? I fell off the ski lift? Did I hit a tree on my last run?"

Ruby nodded, then ran her finger down the top sheet of a stack of papers before her. "Mrs. Wootig, Mrs. Wootig . . . Ahhhh, I see. It seems your assets froze, then exploded. Apparently if you had gone for a respectable C cup or even merely a single letter with your augmentation, you wouldn't be here right now. It would have just been a case of frostbite. They went like grenades, it says here. Oh, that's terrible. *Terrible*. And as long as we're on the subject, Mr. Granger, in the camouflage, if there was any doubt in your mind, your son did bag a 250-pound buck, but it was you. Did you see that coming when you bought him his first BB gun for his eleventh birthday? Really? Not even a bit, not a hint? Curious. All right, then. So . . . We have fish food, bed wetter, flying head, buck shot, peanut sucker, boobsicles and that brings us to Lucy, who we all know got flattened like a shoe insert by a city bus. According to my list, I think we're all here."

I *have* to remember that, Lucy stressed to herself. She could see Alice shooting coffee out of her nose over boobsicles. She hoped she could remember it all—waking up and thinking she was in a county hospital, trying to find her classroom, looking for a phone, thinking Bethanny was a mental patient, finding out she was a Surprise Demise, who lost a head, who got shot, or eaten by a shark, all of it. This dream had to be lasting for hours, she realized. This was the longest dream she'd ever had. This was incredible entertainment!

"Can I sleep now that I'm dead?" Lucy offered up sarcastically with a hearty laugh. She figured, hell, if this was her dream, she ought to get a couple of one-liners in. "Has it been half an hour yet? Does the devil know I'm here? Whoa, I feel drunk—that must be some powerful embalming solution! Can I have my next one on the rocks?"

"This is crazy! I don't think you're funny, Lucy!" Bethanny objected. "I am not dead. I'm talking; you can see me. Send me back! I want to go back!"

"Bethanny, dear," Ruby said as she slightly raised her right hand, "the only part of you that hasn't been completely digested yet in the GI tract of a sea monster is your right leg, and it's stuck on a coral reef at the bottom of the ocean. Angelfish have already nibbled on it. An eel is flirting with it. No one simply wants to be a leg, do they? Do they? Just one nibbled-on leg?"

Bethanny returned Ruby's soft look with an embittered pout that rendered her face a light shade of port wine.

"I can't believe I'm not an angel!" she finally erupted as she stomped

a flipper to the floor with a loud, rubbery snap. "*Why* am I not an angel? I bet Anna Nicole is an angel! This isn't fair! I want to be sitting on a cloud, spying on people! I want to wear flowy robes and have a good singing voice! I want to hit Mariah Carey high notes!"

Ruby waited a moment before she said anything.

"True, you didn't make it to a higher level, but that could be due to a variety of things—maybe you didn't have enough time in the game to really complete all of the tasks you needed to before your leg drifted to the bottom of the ocean, or a three-ton city bus rendered you one-dimensional, or your head rolled into a pile of garbage," she attempted to explain to her charges. "Maybe you were thinking about making a contribution to the humane society but bought yourself a frilly, fancy push-up bra instead. With insufficient insulation, I might add. Maybe you didn't say you were sorry enough times when you knew you were wrong. Maybe you told a homeless vet to get a job instead of giving him a dollar to get some soup. Maybe you voted for George Bush one too many times. Maybe you put guns into the hands of children, who knows? I don't know. I do know the reasons for every one of you are different, but this is your chance to make it up, to sort of fix things."

"Am I really in Hell because I wanted to have a beer with George Bush?" Bethanny asked sadly.

"Oh, Bethanny," Ruby said sympathetically. "Please don't be sad. This is not Hell. Hell is in a different part of the building altogether. This is your chance to shine, so to speak. Because if there ever was an afterlife, this is it. Your same life, but after you're dead. You're all going back.

"My dears, you're in ghost school."

My subconscious is amazing, Lucy thought after being told this latest information. *Now I'm a ghost? Classic. I've never been a ghost in my dreams before. I've been chased, suddenly pregnant, lost, late for a plane, trying repeatedly to dial a phone, taking a test I never studied for, watching a tornado coming toward my house, flying over mountains, but I've never been a* ghost in ghost school *before. That is a first. It's just like a little ghost classroom, too,* Lucy noted as she looked around. *Here I am, sitting at a desk with a bunch of people around me that I don't particularly like, with a crazy old woman at the front of the classroom who's our teacher. And now I have to find someone to have lunch with.*

But suddenly, Lucy got a feeling that something wasn't quite right. A flush of alarm engulfed her and she immediately froze. Something was off. Something didn't fit. If she was having a dream about school, she realized, there was always a constant. Always. Whether she was taking a test, trying out for cheerleading, being called on to make a presentation she hadn't prepared for, there was always one common thread.

Always.

Lucy hesitated before she looked down, but when she did and saw her jeans and her corduroy jacket and saw that they were indeed on her, she realized quickly that she could not be dreaming.

She was not naked.

And if she was in a classroom and was not naked, there was no way this could be a dream, and if this wasn't a dream, that meant that she was, very much so, dead.

And not only dead, but a spook.

"Oh, my God, I'm dead," Lucy suddenly gasped, and then emitted a stunned laugh. "So I didn't make it. I didn't make the cut. I didn't make advanced choir in junior high because I had mono, I didn't make it into college because I slept through my alarm and was too hungover to take the SATs, and now I even DIED and I haven't made the cut to the afterlife. I'm just a ghost. I don't even get to be *all the way* dead. I was always picked last, and this is just like being an alternate. I always knew the white light was bullshit!"

"Now, now, now, there are some benefits to being at this level, you know," Ruby quickly interjected, trying to calm Lucy. "You need to see this more positively. There is a white light, but it's not one you want to go into, and I'll explain that in more detail when we reach that section in your training.

"You are all dead, and rest assured you are *all the way* dead, Lucy. There's no such thing as a dead alternate. You died. That means that aside from being born, you have completed the hardest thing in life. It's something you never have to do again. What is the thing everyone is afraid of the most? *Death.* And guess what? You did it! It's over for you! You never have to worry about dying again. All right, so maybe you didn't get an A plus in life, maybe you're a C lifer and so you ended up here, but hey, it's a huge relief, right?"

No one could help but nod in agreement, including Lucy, who bobbed along with the crowd, desperately trying to keep her head from spinning off. She alternated every five seconds between being completely numb and wanting nothing more than to get up and run screaming out of the classroom, but she had no idea where she was or where she should go, and if Hell was indeed in a different part of the building, she was clearly better off staying put. She tried to calm herself down by reminding herself that getting hysterical wasn't going to help matters any, plus the fact that none of the other newly dead were becoming unglued, so maybe there was no reason to panic. But as Lucy looked at each of them, she saw that they also had mixed flashes of disbelief and confusion on their faces. She found comfort in their apparent discomfort.

"You're dead. Congratulations!" Ruby continued. "That means, as of today, you're all retired. No more work. You never have to go to work again. Rat race is over. You crossed the finish line. You never have to fill out another tax form, pay another bill, worry about getting audited. *You're dead.* You'll never get another cold, you'll never wind up in the hospital, you'll never break a bone. You'll never have gas or pass a kidney stone. You never have to bathe again, shave again, or floss again. You'll never have to go to a job you hate. You never have to wait in line. You never have to diet."

Mr. Granger, the hunter who'd taken a rifle blast to his abdomen, raised his hand.

"I was planning on losing a couple of pounds before my son killed me," he explained. "Can I work on that here? Do you guys have a gym, or even a treadmill? I think I'd do well on a Bowflex. But I think I'll stay out of the sauna!"

The dead students chortled.

Ruby winced. "That's a tough one," she began. "But it brings us to a good point. Although you all have the image of your earthly form, physically things have changed for you. You are no longer flesh and bone in the traditional sense. Frankly, all that stuff does is eventually fail you and get in the way. Your form now is more adaptable, it's portable and flexible. The energy of what made you alive is what you are now. That is what has survived. It's what exists."

"You mean our *spirit*?" Bethanny asked.

"Certainly, you can call it that," the teacher confirmed. "Everything in the earthly form is energy, propelled by energy, composed of energy. It's all energy, but in different forms, in different versions. Even your earthly bodies were composed of energy, but the strongest force of energy is what you are now. You are now the most powerful part of what you were. What I'm here to do is teach you how to work with your new form. I can see you here—we can all see each other—but back on the earthly level, our energy is transparent, unless you *want* it to be otherwise. But modifying your energy takes practice and skill, as well as a couple of tricks. That is what we will be focusing on in your course work here. After which you'll go on to your individual assignments. But I'm afraid losing weight isn't an option. You have no weight to lose. The way you are at the moment of your death is the way you are for, well, forever."

Bethanny's face boiled back to red again. "I have to wear a wet suit for all of eternity?" she screeched. "I can't walk around in these flippers! This is just asking too much. I'm in rubber here. I'm basically dressed in a *tire*! Had I known that this was going to be my eternal fashion projection, I would have worn my curvy jeans and strappy sandals to feed that stupid shark. I don't see how this is fair. You need to start warning people before they get devoured."

Ruby smiled. "Like I said, you were a surprise to us, dear, even though you were dressed like a walrus with press-on nails. I don't think you'll find anyone in here who believes a shark was not going to find you appetizing. You were like a floating pig in a blanket. But this brings us to one of the most exciting parts of Transition," she said excitedly as she pulled out something that resembled a magazine from the bottom of her stack of folders and binders. "I agree that wearing a wet suit would not only be cumbersome for your assignment in the afterlife, but a little ineffective as well."

Ruby stepped down off the stage and walked over to Bethanny as she flipped through the pages. "Here we go," she said, and she laid it into the girl's eagerly awaiting rubber arms. "Pages thirty through sixty are considered the women's section, although we do have some crossover for our alternative lifestyle specters, in the 'Ladies but Gents' section. Now, don't be hasty. Make sure you've looked at everything before you make your decision. This is for your entire assignment, remember. There are no returns once you've made your choice."

Bethanny gasped, and a smile spread across her face as she went from page to page. Lucy couldn't help but put her mania aside for a moment and steal a peek at what Bethanny was flipping through. It looked like a catalog, filled with images of clothing and costuming for just about any era, style, or role.

"Oooooh," Bethanny cooed as she pointed to a pretty woman in flowing robes, looking almost like a Greek goddess. "'The Ethereal White Lady.' Oh, I like that one a lot. It looks very comfortable and could be rather formfitting, too, if need be."

"Very popular." Ruby nodded at the selection. "We do a lot of White Ladies. It's probably the closest to Angel Wear you'll find of all the choices. And just think of how lovely that's going to look underwater. I mean, I think we're talking legendary."

Lucy couldn't peel her eyes away. There were grand Civil War–era ball gowns, several different Victorian dresses boasting bustles of black silk and long ebony veils of netting, several pages of wedding gowns for every century and decade, offerings made of basic fabrics for Viking maidens, a whole section for royal court wear from Elizabeth I to Victoria, waitress and nurse uniforms, what seemed like a whole section of the costuming from *Oliver Twist,* and even the most basic selection of simply a loincloth and a string of lumpy beads..

"Is this a catalog of morgue wear?" Lucy asked unbelievingly. "This whole thing is for ghost fashion?"

"Not everyone dies in the most appropriate outfit, Lucy," Ruby reminded her. Then she slyly shot her eyes over to Mrs. Wootig, whose lips barely rested above the collar of her puffy ski jacket. "In fact, some would look completely ridiculous attempting to spirit in what they were wearing during expiration. Appearance is ninety percent of this job, and if you don't look the part, you're wasting everyone's time. Don't dress as the ghost you are; dress for the ghost *you want to be.*"

"I like this one, too," Bethanny said, tapping another image with her finger. "'The Titanic.' The beading on it is fantastic, and it looks like there's a Wonderbra built right in. This is a knockoff of Kate Winslet's dress, isn't it?"

Ruby shrugged and gave a mischievous smile.

"Aha! I thought so. I could haunt in this. I could *really* haunt in this!" Bethanny said excitedly. "Does Celtic flute background music come with this dress? Please say yes."

"May I—" Mr. Marks, the bicyclist, said quietly. "May I see that when you're done?"

"Do we have to pick an outfit from the dead catalog?" Lucy asked as she raised her hand. "I'd really rather not spend my time as an apparition looking like I'm trick-or-treating."

"Certainly not," Ruby reassured Lucy. "It would be ridiculous to have an assignment, for example, in a Las Vegas casino and have an operative dressed like Scarlett O'Hara. It's not realistic, and no one would believe it. The locale, purpose, and attire all need to go hand in hand. Otherwise, you should just throw a sheet over your head and rattle some chains. You can stay exactly as you are, Lucy—after all, you are haunting as yourself. None of you are going to be character ghosts. If you feel comfortable in what you are wearing, so be it. It's completely up to you."

"Maybe I should come back as a mermaid," Bethanny murmured to herself.

"You keep mentioning these 'assignments,'" Lucy said. "When are we going to find out what they are? And when do we go? And how long do they last? And what happens after that?"

"In due time, dear," Ruby informed her. "You've already had a lot to process so far. Today's only the first day of the rest of your death. There is plenty of time to walk through everything. However, time isn't the same measurement here as it is in earthly terms, and you need to understand that. A day *here* isn't necessarily a day *there*. That's important to keep in mind, because beginning tomorrow, you're all going to take your own field trips. You'll all be going back to observe your funerals, memorial services, wakes, whatever it is that your families and friends have arranged. Hopefully, this will bring you some necessary closure, which is essential if you're going to move on to the next level. You don't need to worry about being spotted; you'll be able to observe everything unnoticed, but you don't have the required skills or training to make yourself known. If you've ever wished you were invisible, this is your dream come true. After your trips, you'll all come back here and I can answer any questions you may have."

Lucy suddenly felt a wave of relief wash over her, and her uneasiness settled somewhat. She was going back. She would see everyone. Familiar faces, familiar ground. There had to be a way to figure out how to get back there for real, right?

"We'll meet here first thing in the morning, and then I'll escort each of you to your destinations. Then I'll return to bring you back. And tonight, if anyone is interested, we have several activities scheduled, as there always are. There's bingo, karaoke, Rollerblading, dance lessons, and there are several theaters in the Transition Center. I know one of them is playing *Topper* this week, which, although it's cute, is not what I would call *accurate*. I hate to be a stickler for those sorts of things, but ghosts are not born. They are *made*! Cary Grant made it look so easy! And between you and me, he is even more charming in spirit. The other theaters are playing all the new releases in case you didn't get to see something you wanted to prior to meeting your hideous and mostly gruesome deaths. There is also a video game arcade if you are so interested, Mr. Morse. Luckily for you, it does not serve alcohol, but as an ethereal being, you no longer have body functions anyway. See? That's another plus to no longer having a pulse! No need for pit stops! There are coffee shops and a couple of restaurants, but to be honest, they're just for show. Is anybody hungry?"

Everyone shook their heads, just noticing for the first time that they weren't hungry or thirsty, and no one even had the inclination to want anything of sustenance.

"Another plus! One more thing you don't have to bother with! However, we understand that it may be hard to break the rituals and habits of eating, so the cafés and bistros are there just to make you feel more comfortable and at home. You'll even be able to taste the food, but it's really nothing more than an illusion of sorts. Finally, I'm going to hand out your room assignments along with a Transition manual that provides most of the basic information you'll need."

Ruby stepped down off the platform and handed each of her pupils a silver binder thick with pages.

"Read Section One before we meet again as a group, the day after your funerals," she said as she passed the last one to the hunter. "And we'll be ready to move on to our first exercises. I'm going to let you all go a little early so you can explore your new surroundings—there's a map included in the manual that makes it very easy to find your way around the Transition campus."

Bethanny leaned over and peeked at Lucy's room number, which was written on a sheet of paper on top of her manual.

"You're in 895!" she squealed. "Look! I'm in 897! Thank goodness we'll be close! I'll find it on the map!"

While Bethanny scoured the hallways and landmarks of the Transition Center diagram, Lucy halfheartedly flipped through the pages of the binder without really looking at them. Would it be possible to escape from this place and get her life back? Slip back in, right where she left off? If so, she had some choice words for a couple of people, namely Martin and Dr. Meadows. She had more than a piece of her mind to hand to both of them. Wouldn't it be amazing to suddenly appear at her own funeral while they were mourning and weeping, march right up to each asshole, and tell them exactly what she thought of them? A broad, full smile spread across Lucy's face, and she chuckled aloud at the thought. *Oh, I get to see Martin tomorrow, all sobby and guilty. Baby. He* should *feel guilty,* she reassured herself. *Throwing all my shit out on the lawn. Who does that? Who does that and then refuses to even provide a reason? I bet Nola will be there, too. Maybe I can pinch her. I would loooooove to pinch Nola, right on the soft, fleshy back part of her arm where it's the most tender and leaves a nice, smug bruise. Had I known that that day at the office would be the last time I saw Nola, I would have told her to get a life and some other choice things, something witty and wicked.*

But then she would see Alice, too, and her nasty pinching thoughts immediately melted away. *I didn't spend enough time with her,* she thought. *She was a wonderful sister.* Alice was definitely the better of the two sisters, she knew, but she had always known that. Alice, just a year older than Lucy, was always cleaning up Lucy's messes when they were kids, covering for Lucy when she would stay out late as a teenager and drive Naunie nuts, and then, later, when they became grown-ups and Lucy spent too much time with a beer in her hand and never had enough money to pay rent, while at the same time Alice was getting ready to settle down and start her own family.

Jilly and Warren would be at the funeral, she was sure, and probably Marianne, too. Maybe she would even get to see some people from high school. People from high school always find a way to show up at funerals; word spreads like wildfire. *I wonder who's gotten fat, who's gone bald, and who has squeezed out a litter of kids already.* Maybe even some patients would show up, but only, Lucy hoped, the ones who flossed regularly and didn't have plaque caked around their teeth like mud on boots. *This will be great. It will be just like "This Is Your Life, Lucy Fisher" without having to talk to anyone I want to avoid.* And, actually, most of all, she wanted to see Tulip. Sweet Tulip, she thought. Lucy was sure that upon hearing the news, Martin would have brought the dog up to Alice's. Jared and Tulip would become best friends instantly, she had a feeling. It would be great for all of them to have each other, especially now.

I wonder what I'll be wearing, she went on to ponder. *I wonder what Alice picked out. I had better not be in some sort of prom dress or*—Lucy wilted with horror—*that wedding dress.* Thank God it was stuffed in a box in the back of Jilly's garage where Alice couldn't find it, unless Jilly offered to dig it up. *I have to admit, I am a little excited at seeing myself. I can't wait to see what my makeup and hair look like. It's done by a professional, so it better look good. Better than good, I had better look* great. *This is my last public appearance. I* have got *to make an impression!*

I hope they play decent music—but honestly, if they play "Wind Beneath My Wings" I don't know if I'll be ecstatic or furious. Such a toss-up there. I hope they play some Allman Brothers. Oh, my God! Oh, my God! Oh, my God! she thought, getting instantly excited. *The EULOGY I forgot about the EULOGY! Oh! This is so fantastic! I wonder who it will be. Who will write the Lucy eulogy? This is just delightful! Maybe it won't be just one person. Maybe they'll take* turns. *I've been to funerals like that, where almost every person there got up and said how giving and selfless and beautiful and wonderful the dead person was and how the world is a bleaker, sadder, less lovely place now. Oh, I really hope that's on the agenda,* Lucy thought. *I could sure use a little pick-me-up right now. Nothing like a eulogy to kick-start your self-esteem.*

Oh, Lucy said to herself, *I think I am really looking forward to tomorrow. I am very excited about my funeral.*

Lucy heard a resounding *thud* as Bethanny slapped her binder shut and turned toward her neighbor.

"Our rooms are right by a bowling alley and a nail salon," she quipped cheerfully. "This is going to be *just* like going on a cruise, but with no stops."

And with that, the two freshly dead girls got up and went in search of their new homes.

chapter six Shake and Bake

The moment after Lucy's eyes snapped open, she met the morning with a rushed sense of anticipation. At first, she was puzzled by the excitement, but it only took a small pause for her to remember, and she was invigorated.

It was the day of her funeral.

She pushed off the motel-issue blankets and jumped out of bed. She ran to the mirror tacked on the wall above the dresser and peeked at herself; Ruby was right. No need for a shower. Her hair wasn't a nest of tumbled curls and stray strands the way it usually was in the morning, giving her a homeless "I hear voices" look. In fact, her coiffure looked exactly the way it had last night before she'd gone to bed. Her teeth didn't beg to be brushed, and her mouth lacked that mucky feeling that normally drove her nuts when she woke up. As soon as she changed out of the plain pair of soft white pajamas she'd found in the dresser, into her regular clothes and she was ready to go, which was good, because her assigned dorm room didn't come equipped with a shower, bathroom, or even a sink. It was just a simple room, Super 8 motel style, with a twin bed, a small desk, a dresser, and a couple of light fixtures. Nearly monastery-like in its simplicity, the room wasn't decorated for Lucy to fall in love with it; it was there to provide some necessities and a place to get some peace and quiet.

Next door, Lucy could hear Bethanny in number 897 rustling about, opening and closing drawers, and then a *rap-tap-tap* on the wall.

"Lucy!" she called in a muffled voice. "Are you ready?"

"Almost," Lucy called back. "I just need to get my boots on."

Lucy had just pulled her left boot on and had smoothed her jeans down over the shaft when Bethanny knocked on the door and then let herself in. Lucy stopped, looked at Bethanny.

"Aren't you getting dressed?" she asked her neighbor, who was standing in the doorway in her pair of white pajamas and white slippers.

"I'm not spending one more day in that wet suit," Bethanny declared. "Do you know that if I was alive, I would have been chafed all over! This is the only other thing I have, and it's far more comfortable."

"Have you decided on anything from the catalog?" Lucy asked, stepping into the hallway and closing the door to number 895 behind her.

Bethanny shook her head. "I am torn between the White Lady and the ballerina from *Swan Lake,*" she said, clearly flustered. "And then there's a great Cleopatra outfit that I am drooling over, but it looks kind of hard to sit down in, unless there's some sort of Lycra involved. What do you think? Do you think they'd make a stretch Cleopatra dress? You're so lucky that you died in your own clothes."

"I'm just so happy I didn't perish in heels," Lucy commented as they walked to SD1118. "I can't imagine. I'm so glad I died with my boots on."

Bethanny gasped, as if suddenly struck by even more tragedy. "Oh, no! If I go with *Swan Lake,* I'll have to go around on tiptoe, and I'll just end up cramping," she said sadly. "And if I go with Cleopatra, the outfit comes with sandals made out of grass, which is just ridiculous. I don't know why a nice pair of ballet flats or espadrilles wouldn't work. But *Swan Lake* has the crown, and I really wanted the crown. Maybe I should just do Dead Bride. I don't know. I'm so confused."

"Bethanny, can I ask you something?" Lucy ventured.

"Sure," the girl in pajamas replied.

Lucy hesitated for a moment. She wasn't quite sure how to say it.

"Do you believe we're really dead?" Lucy finally said. "I mean, this is all so unbelievable. One minute, we're living, and the next minute, we're getting ready to crash our funerals. Doesn't that seem weird to you?"

Bethanny looked at Lucy, then shook her head of shoulder-length blond curls, now freed and bouncy since she had ditched her wet suit. She looked much younger than Lucy had first thought, her skin a glowing peachy-pink, her teeth perfect and white, and not a single wrinkle gathered around her eyes. Lucy guessed that the poor thing couldn't be more than in her very early twenties. She was little, barely rose above Lucy's shoulder, and had tiny, crushable little bones. That shark was a bastard, Lucy thought. That was in no way a fair fight.

"I don't know," Bethanny said honestly. "How else would it feel to be dead *but* weird. I've never been dead before. I guess I wouldn't expect it to be any other way but kinda freaky."

Lucy nodded in affirmation. "Yeah," she agreed. "It's an experience like no other. I'll say that much. Are you looking forward to your funeral?"

"Not really," Bethanny said with a wince. "I mean, we've only been dead for a day. What kind of party can you organize in that amount of time? I'm afraid it will be kind of lame."

"You know, I don't think we've been dead for just a day," Lucy replied. "Remember Ruby said that time is different here than it is there? Who knows how long we were 'asleep' in the big dorm? I have a feeling we might have been there for a while, kind of like in a dead sleep. There were only a couple of other people who were awake. The rest were still snoring away."

"Yeah, I wondered about that, too." The little blond girl nodded. "So maybe there was time to plan a big party after all? I hope they got a DJ! Are you looking forward to yours?"

"Like you can't imagine. I hope they bury me on a hill, under a tree. Someplace green with grass. Phoenix has some cemeteries that are nothing but dirt and headstones. No, thank you. I'd really like something by a lake. I'd like a view; that would be great. Wouldn't a view be great?"

Bethanny looked at Lucy a bit puzzled. "But you're not there," she said as she looked up. "You're here. You'd never get to see the view except for today."

Lucy took it in for a moment and then laughed. "You're absolutely right," she said just as they approached the door of SD1118. "What do I care about a view I will never see? Unless I'm haunting my grave . . ."

"Hello, ladies," Ruby said jovially, clapping her gnarled hands together as both girls walked into the classroom. "Who's ready for a funeral, huh? I wanna see you girls get excited! You typically only get one of these, you know, unless you're Abe Lincoln or you get exhumed during a trial."

The old woman's smile was contagious, and both Lucy and Bethanny caught it.

"I'm ready," Bethanny squeaked.

Ruby put one arm around Bethanny and the other hand on her shoulder and squeezed affectionately. "You know, there are some things I need to fill you in on about your trip," the old woman said. "So I'm going to take Lucy first, and then you and I will talk about it, okay? And maybe we'll find you something to wear around here besides pajamas."

Bethanny grinned from ear to ear. "It's really going to be special, isn't it?" she squealed, barely able to contain herself. "They got a DJ, huh? Oh, I am so excited to go dancing! I am going to have the best funeral *ever,* I just know it! It's going to be a great party! And really, I don't mind the pajamas, they're very comfortable. I would love some shoes, though. If you have anything with a kitten heel and a peep toe, that would be my first choice!"

"We'll see what we can do. But in the meantime, you can go over the catalog again. I'll only be a minute," the old woman said with a smile, and then turned to Lucy. "Are you ready, dear? I just delivered Mr. Russell to his service. Boy, what a chunky family he had, all lined up at the buffet, forks poised like spears. There was so much food there I thought a pharaoh had died! I'm surprised more of them haven't choked to death on foodstuffs, to be honest."

Lucy followed Ruby out of SD1118 and into the hallway.

"Are you looking forward to this, Lucy?" the instructor asked.

Lucy couldn't help but nod and smile. "I am," she admitted. "I'm also very excited to see how we're going to get there. Are we going to tele-transport? Fall to earth? Sail on a ghost ship? Repel? Wormhole? Please say it's a wormhole. I've really got all my hopes kind of pinned on that one."

Ruby stopped dead in her tracks and burst out laughing. "Funny. That's as good as the 'seven people you meet in heaven,' " she whispered as she leaned toward Lucy.

She then stepped forward and pushed a small, circular, and

slightly protruding button in the wall, after which two metal and rickety doors slowly slid apart in opposite directions.

"Really? Where did you get an idea like that? No, we're not taking a—what did you call it?—a wormhole?" Ruby said as she stepped forward and entered the compartment behind the doors. "We're taking the *elevator*."

"An elevator?" Lucy questioned with a laugh as she followed the old woman in. "All the way . . . down there?"

"Why do you assume we're going down?" Ruby chuckled, pressing another button that sent the noisy doors sliding jerkily shut. "We may be going up. But yes, we're taking the elevator all the way there. Listen, from what I hear, it's a tremendous improvement over taking the stairway. It wasn't so long ago that we'd have to walk the whole way. If you had died a hundred or so years ago, we'd be hoofing it."

"A stairway? You've got to be kidding me. Was it hard to climb?"

"How would I know? I wasn't even born then," Ruby responded. "But I know it would sure take a lot longer."

Lucy was surprised. From the woman's black cloak and her wrinkled, puckered face, Lucy had just assumed that Ruby was as old as the ages, and had been a figure at ghost school since the beginning of time. It never occurred to her that Ruby's alive time may have just paralleled her own.

"Wait—how old are you?" Lucy ventured.

"What, you think I'm a vampire? As old as the pyramids, maybe? Did I know Queen Victoria, Genghis Khan, Lizzie Borden? Did I ever date a Viking? Was I here when the universe was created? *Was* the universe created? Hell if I know. I did the twist at my prom. I watched the Beatles on the Ed Sullivan show. I've been here for a while, but not as long as you think. I got here a couple of years ago—maybe. It's hard to keep track. The space-time continuum isn't the same as what you're used to, you know."

Lucy was shocked. "Really? But your robe— I just thought, I don't know, druid, Puritan, Spanish inquisitor, Salem witch trials?"

"This thing?" Ruby said as she looked down at her dark woollen robe, complete with hood. "No! I saw *The French Lieutenant's Woman* on TV. I made one for myself because it rained eight months out of the year where I lived, and I could go shopping in it and not get wet. It looked so practical. Plus, I liked my privacy. No one could see me. Coulda been Meryl Streep under here. It was nobody's business what I bought. Look, this thing is just a blanket with arms. It's a Snuggie. I was a fashion pioneer, you know."

"So—you were wearing that when you passed? How did you die?"

"Well, my arms were free, you know," Ruby started, then hesitated, waving her arms all around. "So I would wear this sometimes at night, reclining in my chair, and I like my cocktails. Who doesn't, right?"

"Sure," Lucy agreed.

"Well, you spill once, you spill twice, you spill a couple of times, and this thing has to be dry-cleaned and it's quite absorbent. It's a pain," the old woman said simply, then shrugged. "I lit a cigarette, and I don't know. Maybe a lit ash fell, and that, with maybe too much vodka soaked into the fabric, well, I went up like a Roman candle."

"You're kidding," Lucy replied.

"Nope. Why would I kid?" Ruby replied. "Why would I kid about spontaneously combusting?"

"Wow," Lucy said, amazed. "I've never met anyone who spontaneously combusted before! Did it, um, hurt?"

"Come on," Ruby chided. "You got squashed by a bus. Did *that* hurt?"

Lucy laughed. She liked Ruby. She seemed like someone Lucy

would have enjoyed spending time with when they'd still been breathing. She couldn't help but feel a little sad that they had never gotten the chance.

"Why aren't you a ghost?" Lucy suddenly asked her.

"But I *am* a ghost," the cloaked one answered. "In fact, I am an excellent ghost. You happen to be looking at one of the best. I caught on to haunting as if I was born to do it. I was so good at the trade that the higher-ups asked me to stay on and help teach the incoming dead. Surprise Demisers are the slowest to learn. Our pupils didn't expect to be where they are quite so fast. It's a lot to process. The old, the sick, they've had time to prepare, or even just think about it, absorb it a little. But in SD, there are a whole lot of factors at hand besides learning how to flicker the lights or turn the water faucet on. Today, Lucy, you're tearing off the Band-Aid. This is a very vital step for you, closing the door of your old world behind you and moving forward into a new and frankly, I think a much more exciting existence."

"I'm excited to see my sister and my friends," she admitted. "And I'm hoping someone brought my dog."

"Ah, I miss my dogs more than anything," Ruby said, closing her eyes hard for a second. "But I know they're being well taken care of. My nephew has them."

A teeny bell rang, and the rickety doors began to open slowly. Beyond the doors, Lucy saw a very nicely decorated hall, as if she was in the foyer of a very stately manor house—or funeral home.

"We're here," Ruby let her know, and they stepped out onto a gleaming white marble floor. Lucy looked at Ruby, unsure of what she should do next. "You're through those double doors over there."

Ruby raised a cloaked arm and pointed toward a set of carved ornate doors to Lucy's left. Two lovely and towering flower arrangements flanked the sides of the doorway, each resting on an elegant and matching Chippendale side table.

Beautiful flowers, Lucy thought. *That's a good start. I wanted some like those for my wedding.*

One of the doors was already ajar, and Lucy heard the hint of organ music drifting out into the foyer.

"I guess I should go?" she asked Ruby uncertainly, and then she heard the *clop-clop-clop* of dress shoes coming from behind them. Lucy turned and saw a tall middle-aged man dressed in a somber dark suit walking briskly from the hall behind them.

"I have to fart!" Ruby loudly announced to the man.

"Ruby!" Lucy scolded, sharply turning around to face the old lady, shocked at what she had just done.

But the man's stride did not break, his pace didn't slow, he simply kept walking past the two of them and toward the set of ornate doors flanked by the twin flower arrangements.

"Look!" Ruby yelled even louder, and pointed at the man. "He looks like he hasn't seen a ghost!"

Once he reached the doors, he stopped, quietly opened the one that was ajar, and slipped inside.

"He didn't hear you," Lucy said, surprised, and then, she was surprised again because she should have known better.

"You can move among them," Ruby informed her. "You can sit where you like. You can even sit *on* them, although I wouldn't really recommend that. Some of them really smell close up. You can say what you wish, you can run into them, yell in their ear, do a striptease, or actually try to fart. They can't hear you. Your skill level is below basic. No one will see you, feel you, or know you're there. You're simply invisible. And you won't be seeing these people for a while, Lucy, so take it all in."

Lucy nodded, listening to Ruby's every word.

"Any questions?" Ruby asked.

"I have four million questions for you," Lucy laughed. "But for right now, I just go in there and watch?"

"Do whatever you feel like doing. You might want to hang back for a little while and see what feels natural," Ruby advised. "Wander around. Listen. Make the most of it. Understand what's happening here."

Lucy nodded.

"And, Lucy," Ruby said, gently touching Lucy's arm, "it might not be the way you envision it. It might be completely different than what you think it's going to be like. Not only the service but your reaction. They might play lousy music. There may be some folks you don't care for that show up. Funerals are always full of surprises. Know that whatever happens, it's okay. And when you're ready to go, call me. Just out loud, call me. I'll be there to bring you back."

Lucy nodded again.

"Good luck," Ruby said, patting Lucy on the arm before turning and walking down the short hallway. She pushed the button on the wall and stepped back into the elevator. Lucy heard the doors close with a metallic clank.

She stood there for a moment, looking at the set of double doors, telling herself to take a step. But she couldn't. Her legs wouldn't move, and her eyes focused only on the set of doors that separated her from the people she loved most in the world. And, then again, possibly some she didn't.

Suddenly, a fire of panic flew up her spine and she resisted the impulse to run to the elevator and push the button, but when she turned around, the elevator was gone, replaced with the same paneling that matched the rest of the wall.

She wanted nothing more than to yell out "Ruby!" and get whisked back to the Transition Center again, but she knew that would be foolish.

This is ridiculous, she thought. *What am I afraid of? I know everyone in there. They can't even see me. I can do whatever I like. What am I afraid of?*

And as Lucy stood there, barely more than a yard away from the doors to her funeral, she began to understand. This was the last time she'd see most of these people for a long time, the last time she could pretend to be alive in an earthly place, even if it was at her funeral. But she had to go in. There wasn't a choice of fight or flight. She had to go in and see for herself—see her family, her friends, and, ultimately, even herself. That, of course, was going to be the most bizarre moment of all. She imagined her body would sort of look like the doll a nurse had brought to her sixth-grade class to teach mouth-to-mouth resuscitation on, but with a curly brown wig plopped on its head and lipstick in a shade Lucy would hopefully prefer. Behind those doors was the unknown, she told herself, and then she quickly realized she'd already crossed into the greatest unknown, the one every single person in that room was terrified of. *I've done it. I've done it and it was a piece of cake. Well, so far.* There was nothing, not one thing, left in Lucy's world to be afraid of. Summoning up all of her bravery, Lucy took the necessary steps forward to get to the door, lifted her arm up, opened her palm, and reached for the door handle, which slipped straight through her hand. She tried it once more, and again her hand moved straight through it, although she could feel the solid handle pass through, cold and hard. It didn't hurt; she simply felt its presence, as if her hand was moving through the object like a cloud.

Hmm, she thought, wondering how she was going to get into the room.

Well, she finally concluded, *if my hand can go through that handle, then maybe I can go through this.* She took a few steps backward, focused all of her concentration on the door, and marched right into it, feeling the door pass through her, almost like walking through a large, determined ocean wave.

Quite pleased with herself, Lucy now found she was inside the viewing room, which was small, quiet, and had about ten rows of folding chairs. She saw the backs of the heads of three people—Alice in the middle, Jared next to her, and an unknown female head on Alice's other side. The middle-aged man in the dress shoes, obviously the funeral director, stood off to one side with his hands folded, and another man, also dressed in black, sat in the very last seat of the first row. The music was slow and organ-y—almost like Muzak but far more somber and slow, and although she recognized the melody of the song, it wasn't in the right context. She couldn't place it.

"Deee, da-deee, da-deee," Lucy hummed to herself.

I wonder what time this thing is going to start. I must be here awfully early. She heard a sniffle. It was Alice. The funeral director plucked a tissue out of the box on the table next to him and went toward her, offering it to her. Alice gently took it, and then quietly blew her nose.

Quickly, Lucy walked toward the front of the room. She wanted to put her arms around her sister and tell her it was all right. She was fine. She was in a—well, not a *better* place, but sort of an okay place. There were free movies, free bowling, and she didn't have to pay rent. And she would never have another bad hair day! That was something to celebrate, right?

"Alice," Lucy called as she picked up her speed, walking past the rows of chairs. "Alice! I'm here. It's Lucy. I'm right here."

Alice sniffled again just as Lucy turned the corner of the first row, just as the funeral director suddenly leaned forward to provide Alice with another Kleenex. Lucy walked right into him, and at the moment of their collision, he hiccuped.

"Excuse me," he said quietly as Alice lifted the Kleenex from his hand.

Lucy knelt in front of her sister, the sensation of running into the funeral director still hanging on her. It was quite unlike the door handle, which had been cold and solid; this had been more like running into a wall of warm Silly Putty.

"Alice, it's me," she whispered. "I'm here. It's okay. I'm all right. I'm fine. Everything is going to be okay."

No response. She put her hand on Alice's knee, all warm and Silly Putty-ish, and patted it gently. Alice looked up, almost right at Lucy. She took a deep breath, still staring in Lucy's direction.

"Whew," Alice exhaled. "It's okay. I'm all right. I'm fine. Everything is going to be okay."

Lucy sat up. *She heard me. She heard me. Well, she didn't hear me, but she must have heard me.*

"I'm sorry, Mom," Jared said. He was dressed in a nice navy-blue jacket a little too small for him, and he put his arm around Alice's shoulders. "I loved Aunt Lucy, too."

Alice nodded, and blew her nose again.

"I love Jared right back," Lucy said.

"She loved you right back, sweetie," Alice said. She cradled her son's face in her hand and then gave him a quick kiss on the forehead. "We can start now, Mr. Harris. We're ready."

"Are you sure?" the funeral director asked, looking a little taken aback.

Lucy also couldn't believe what she was hearing. Starting already? But no one was there. Not one of her friends, no co-workers, no sobbing friends from high school, not even one single patient whose plaque she had scraped off their nasty old teeth. What the hell did Alice mean she was ready to start? No one had come yet! Where were Jilly and Warren, and Marianne? *Where was Martin?*

And then suddenly, Lucy realized something else was missing—something vital.

Like Lucy.

"I'm not even here yet, Alice!" Lucy said, shooting up to her feet. "You can't start the funeral without the corpse! A funeral without a body is—is—just *a meeting*! You have to wait for me to show up! *You have to wait for the body!*"

"Did—" Mr. Harris began delicately. "Did you want to wait a little bit longer for guests, Ms. Fisher?"

Alice shook her head, a tissue pressed hard against her nose.

"No," she said. Then she looked up. "It's just us here—me, Jared, and my neighbor Susan, who was so kind to drive us. And Reverend—I'm sorry, Reverend, I've forgotten your name . . ."

"Reverend Gary, of the Jesus, Mary, and Joseph Assembly," he said, and nodded primly.

"And Reverend Gary of Jesus, Mary, and Joseph," Alice replied. "So thank you for asking, Mr. Harris, but we can begin."

Lucy's head spun. She grasped for a chair, and collapsed into the one next to Susan. "This can't be happening, this can't be happening, this can't be happening," she muttered over and over.

Da, deee-da, deee-da . . . The melody above her floated from the speaker.

Lucy shook her head unbelievingly, shook it, shook it, shook it. *I can't believe it.*

Suddenly she jumped up out of the chair—shot out like a rocket, really—and began jumping up and down in a furious, frantic, angry motion.

"I got hit by a bus!" she screamed at the top of her lungs. "I got hit by a friggin' bus and no one has come to my funeral? What is the point of getting hit by a bus if no one shows up to the service? You have got to be shitting me. You *have got* to be shitting me! And

I just realized the song you're playing at my stupid no-show funeral is 'I Will Always Love You.' Why don't you just kill me again, huh? Kill me again. Send another bus over, and I'll run right out and jump in front of it, okay? Would that be okay? Think we can muster up a couple of people that way?"

And then without any warning at all, she quickly geared up and kicked the chair she had just been sitting in with all of her might, and though she felt her leg shoot right through it, to her surprise, it moved just a little.

Just a *little.*

Mr. Harris walked back over to the wall and pressed a button on something that looked like a thermostat. The volume of the music slowly lowered, moment by moment until there was not a trace of it left in the room. It had disappeared, just like Lucy.

The light also softened, and Reverend Gary ambled up to the front of the room and stood behind a lectern next to a table that sported a massive spray of silk flowers, a plain and shiny vase, and a picture of Lucy taken at Alice's wedding, wearing an enormous floppy pink hat. She'd been Alice's maid of honor, and unfortunately for Lucy, her sister had just gotten cable while planning her wedding, had seen *The Godfather* one too many times, and had been tragically influenced by the joyous scene of Connie Corleone's nuptials. Convinced she could re-create the magic, Alice had planned each detail of the marvelous event accordingly, including the bridesmaid's hats, although Lucy had protested that she looked much more like Squeaky Fromme trying to shoot President Ford than she did a nubile Italian maiden in a classic film. Despite Naunie's impossible promises of getting Frank Sinatra to drop by and perform, the wedding went on, Godfather-style, with gallons of wine and trays of Stouffer's lasagna. Sadly for Alice, it was not Sonny

Corleone who ended up in the bathroom with another pink floppy hat wearer, but her brand-new husband.

Lucy despised that photo, but told herself she shouldn't worry about it, since there was no one there to see it. She sat back down in the chair, folded her arms in a pout, and waited for her undoubtedly shitty eulogy.

"I did not know Lucy Fisher," Reverend Gary began, extending his left arm toward the flowers. "But we are here today to celebrate her life and honor her passing."

Great. Let's celebrate, Lucy thought irritably. *Pop some champagne. I bet the cork will knock out an eye.*

"In the awesome finality that is death, we remember Lucy Fisher," he continued, again stretching out his left arm toward the table, flowers, and photograph. "With kindness and love, not only as a beloved sister, but also as a cherished aunt."

Well, that was nice, Lucy thought, softening a little, but still not uncrossing her arms.

"Although she met her end in a way that was unique, unsettling, and that left the courthouse intersection closed for two days, Lucy Fisher," Reverend Gary went on, "will be with us always."

Reverend Gary's left arm again traveled to his left, and this time it hung there for several seconds.

That's a nice thought, Gary, Lucy wanted to shout, *especially since I'm not even* here *now.*

Gary's arm remained outstretched.

Oh, no, Lucy thought.

Or am I?

Lucy suddenly sat up straighter. She looked at the table. Saw flowers, a vase, a photograph. Saw flowers, a jardinière, a photograph. Saw flowers, an urn, a photograph.

Jesus, Mary, and Joseph, she said to herself. *She shake and baked me. Alice shake and baked me.*

I'm in *that thing. Holy shit, I'm in* that thing.

She canned me like preserves.

All I am is dust in the wind.

How is Martin—once she finds him—supposed to cry over my gorgeously made-up dead body if I look indistinguishable from the stuff that shot out of Mount Saint Helens?

I look like the killer of Pompeii.

Oh, my God, Lucy thought, *I would throw up if I still had a working stomach.*

Instead, Lucy jumped up, ran toward the back of the room—picking up speed as she raced—and without much thought, ran right through the heavy, ornate set of double doors, not feeling much of anything.

Outside in the massive hallway, Lucy paced up and down, up and down, trying to take it all in. Just like that, Lucy's life was gone. She was just gone. Poof. Vanished. Not to be eulogized, not to be mourned. Not to be missed.

"Hey," she heard someone call, and she turned around to see a portly man in bright yellow golfing attire staring at her from the opposite side of the hallway, next to a set of doors identical to those on her side of the hallway.

"Me?" she mouthed as she pointed to herself.

"Yes!" he said, and chuckled. "Yes, you!"

"You can see me?" she said aloud.

"Of course I can!" He laughed, then moved his hand straight through the Chippendale table that flanked the set of doors. "I saw you stampede right through that door like a buffalo!"

"Oh." She nodded, understanding his ghostly identification gesture. "I just had to get out of there."

"A bit overwhelming, huh?" He chortled. "I know how you feel. This thing has been going on for almost an eternity, people taking turns talking, telling stories. There was a string quartet, a slide show presentation. There were even some people that couldn't make it who sent in videos. After this, they're going over to the club to unveil a statue of me taking a swing. Can you believe it? Got a girl in there now singing 'Wind Beneath My Wings.' I had to take a break. I was getting a little choked up myself, you know? How much can one guy take at his funeral? Standing room only. What a way to send a guy off."

Lucy tried to nod, and smiled faintly.

"How's yours going?" he asked, nodding in the direction of Lucy's doors.

"Good, good. I got 'I Will Always Love You,'" was all she could manage to say.

"All right, then," the yellow golf man said, tipping his little yellow golf hat. "I'm heading back in. Don't wanna miss too much. I'm taking a running start this time; you've inspired me!"

And just like that, the man began running, his belly flopping, and in a flash like a chunky bumblebee, he vanished through the doors.

If Lucy had had any doubts about truly being dead, they were gone, and if she'd still had any visions of slipping back into her life, she knew now they were ridiculous.

Never, in her entire life or death, had Lucy felt more alone.

There was only one thing left to do.

"ROOOO-BEEEEE!" she bellowed.

chapter seven Boomerang

"Lucy, what happened to you?" Bethanny said after she pushed the door to SD1118 open and saw her friend slouching in her seat inside. "I knocked on your door a couple of times last night, but you didn't answer. If you went bowling without me . . ."

Lucy shook her head. "No, I didn't go bowling," she assured the perky blonde, who was now dressed in a tank top with a number pinned to it, stretchy shorts, and athletic shoes. "Nice outfit. Better than pajamas. I'm sorry. I just needed to decompress a little, have some alone time."

"Ruby brought it over. There was a marathon in record heat yesterday, and more people survived than they thought," Bethanny explained. "These are extra ghost clothes, I guess. Did you see someone you didn't want to see at your funeral?"

Lucy couldn't help but laugh. "No. I was very happy to see who I saw," she said simply, not wanting to talk about it. "How was your trip?"

Suddenly, Mr. Russell, still in his Tommy Bahama wear, opened the door and stepped inside, followed by Mr. Marks, the bicyclist, and Mr. Granger, the hunter.

"Well, I couldn't believe it." Mr. Granger chuckled. "I have never worn a suit in my life! I guess I should just be happy they didn't have me stuffed and mounted!"

"Chuck, that's hilarious!" Mr. Marks commented. "I can just see you standing in someone's living room, upright and ready to pounce, just like a grizzly!"

"I'm telling you, Elliot," Chuck replied, "it's no less funny than having your head stapled back on and the seam hidden with a turtleneck!"

All three men laughed heartily.

Mrs. Wootig entered the room, still surrounded by her puffy jacket, tailed slightly behind by Mr. Morse, the guy who had electrocuted himself by wetting his bed during a drunken blackout. To Lucy's surprise, he was grinning ear to ear, and the hair was almost swept entirely off his face.

Lucy wasn't the only one who noticed. When Ruby swept into the class a moment later, she stopped in front of him, cocked her head, and grinned.

"Why, Mr. Morse, not so glum today, I see?" she mentioned.

He held up his hand, his fingers stretched far apart. "*Five* girls that I wasn't related to cried at my funeral," he bragged. "*Five of them*. And two of them—well, one really—is super hot. The other one would be hot, too, if she got that one tooth fixed. The other three were okay, but I was just amazed they came. I didn't even think they knew I was alive! Being dead is so cool. I love being dead. And you can call me Danny. That's a great name! Danny of the Dead!"

"Well, I think that's wonderful, Danny," Ruby said, moving on to her lectern and plopping her stack of binders and folders right on top of it, just as she had on the first day of class. "Who else would like to share their experience from yesterday?"

Mrs. Wootig's arm shot up.

"My service was at the finest church in San Diego," she gushed. "You have to pass a board vote to get in. Sixty-seven cars in my procession. It was the fifth-highest attended funeral in the history of the church. I came in behind the president of the Junior League. Of course, there was an invitation list. Every seat was taken, although I was a bit disappointed there was no red carpet. It was a wonderful day, except that I heard one of the girls in my tennis class whisper to another that she heard I'd died in a liposuction accident! Can you believe such a preposterous thing? It's absolutely ridiculous. She obviously never got a very good look at my ass. I completely survived my liposuction!"

"Well, there is no doubt you'll be buried in the shallowest grave of them all, Mrs. Wootig," Ruby said, and grinned.

"Oh, you bet I will," Mrs. Wootig heartily agreed. "I'm sure my husband paid extra for that."

"Mrs. Wootig, now that we're getting to know one another a little better, what would you like for us to call you?" Ruby asked.

Mrs. Wootig looked like she was stumped. She furrowed her brow as much as her Botox would allow, and thought very, very carefully. For ten seconds. Thirty seconds. A full minute.

She finally looked up when genius struck, and she smiled at Ruby. "I would like to be called," she began, "Countess."

Ruby looked away for a moment and then reattached her gaze to the woman.

"But I'm afraid you're not a countess," Ruby explained. "You're the mother of two sons of young adult age, one of whom locks himself in his room for substantial periods of time, listening to German death metal music and badly drawing flaming skeletons with enormous breasts, and the older one was just thrown out of college for running a gambling ring on campus. Your husband bilks people out of their savings by claiming to remove mold from their houses, but is really just using a big vacuum, and that's just one of his business scams. I don't know many counts who pretend to clean up mold with a Hoover, I'm sorry to say."

Mrs. Wootig sighed heavily and rolled her eyes. "Fine," she conceded. "Mrs. Wootig, then."

"Mr. Russell, how was your day?" Ruby prodded, attempting to move on.

"Well, I got to see a lot of old friends that I had lost touch with, and that sure was nice," he replied, and somehow, Lucy thought, the Hawaiian print didn't look quite so garish on him today. "There was a huge buffet at the reception, and everyone was just stuffed. It looked great. And listen to this, I have great news: The company I was going to see that day felt so bad about me dying on my business trip that we got the account! How's that, huh? Isn't that impressive? Yep. 'Good ole Kirk.' That's what everybody said. 'Bringin' them in even after he's croaked! He'll do anything to land 'em!' At the office, I heard there's talk of naming the cafeteria after me!"

"Congratulations, Mr. Russell," Ruby replied, and offered a petite round of applause, which everyone else eventually joined in on.

"Call me Kirk," he said, his chunky face beaming. "Kirk Russell. No, Goldie Hawn is not my girlfriend! Don't I wish? Ha, ha, ha!"

Bethanny's hand went up next.

"I didn't get a funeral because, well, pretty much every part of me is still missing, but I did get a DJ!" she interjected cheerfully. "I was so excited! They had a memorial service at my favorite club, and my boyfriend had an open bar, so everyone had a great time. Two people even had sex in the bathroom! That tells you right there it was a great party!"

Another small round of applause went out for Bethanny and her cocktail service.

"My family is doing well," Chuck added. "They all met at our favorite hunting lodge, shot a moose, and had a big barbecue. I hope this doesn't sound like I'm bragging, but it was the best funeral I've ever been to. My brother even brought a keg!"

The rest of the class nodded and murmured their congratulations.

"I'd like to share my experience," Mr. Marks, with the shiny spandex ass, offered as he exuberantly raised his smallish girl hand. "As a result of my untimely execution by the side mirror of a planet-destroying Hummer, my cycling club staged a protest, it got on the news, and as a result, a bike lane just may be created from the point where my body rode off on the bike and finally fell over, to the point where they found my head. All they need to do is raise the funds for construction materials! My decapitation may not be irrelevant after all!"

Lucy looked at the beaming Mr. Marks, realizing that she was inexplicably irritated by the sheen of his toothpick Jazzercise legs in shorts eleven sizes too small, the fact that his ass was the size of a four-year-old's, and that he was still wearing his helmet. She couldn't help but sigh.

"Lucy?" Ruby asked quietly, leaving it open-ended.

Lucy said nothing for a moment, just sat and shook her head.

"People staged a protest for you, Mr. Marks," she finally said. "How could you possibly think you were irrelevant? Kirk is getting a cafeteria named in his honor, the countess's funeral had a guest list, Chuck's Clan of the Cave Bear over there slaughtered and gorged on a sacrificial moose, Danny discovered he had weepy groupies, and Bethanny's friends celebrated her by getting laid in a bathroom like they were at Studio 54 and had just snorted an eight ball with Bianca Jagger. I hope you all consider yourselves very lucky, because at my funeral, guess what? Nobody showed. Not my friends, co-workers, or my very recent ex-fiancé. No one except my sister, my nephew, and cameo appearances by some strangers. Other than that, nobody came. No one could be bothered to come. You worried about being irrelevant, Mr. Marks, but I can tell you how it feels to have it confirmed."

"Oh, Lucy," Bethanny cried, throwing her bony pixie arms around her ghost friend's neck. "I'm so sorry. I bet there's a very good explanation for why your friends didn't come. Maybe there was another funeral they had to go to that day. I bet there's a good reason!"

"Maybe they got the days mixed up," Mr. Marks said kindly. "That happened to my neighbor. The dates were printed wrong in the newspaper."

"Maybe someone's car broke down and they were all coming together," Chuck offered.

"Who cares if no one came," the countess remarked. "How did you look?"

"Another great surprise," Lucy replied. "I would have to say I probably looked overdone. Or like an ashtray at a casino at the end of the night. I was roasted and packaged in a 'parts is parts' pot. All facets of me are now all mixed together, public and private. I'm a canister of human crumbs. I live in a jar like *I Dream of Jeannie*. Being cremated never even crossed my mind when I was alive. I had this vision of looking fantastic in my casket. Roses around my head, maybe holding some flowers, looking peaceful and lovely. I have to admit that I wanted very badly to leave an impression, you know?"

Ruby clucked her tongue and stepped down from the podium.

"That is a masterpiece of understatement," she interrupted. "There certainly was an impression, Lucy. It was an impression from a three-ton city bus that left a tire track across your face. We all know you did not win that fight, so the truth is that your sister probably had no choice. And, not to be tacky, but there is always the issue of funding, dear. An ashes to ashes send-off is a little more economical than finding you a pretty mausoleum or a marble headstone. And besides, how much should it really matter to you? You should know more than ever that it's simply a symbol for the living. I know you are very upset about the attendance, but forget about who wasn't there. People don't get mad at you because you die, and decide to stop speaking to you."

"But I had such high hopes and was so looking forward to it," Lucy cried. "I mean, I'm only going to get one funeral, and I'm rather disappointed at how this one turned out."

Ruby reiterated what she had told Lucy the day before when she'd walked out of the elevator doors at the funeral home to find her student upset.

"This experience is different for everyone," the old woman said to the class. "Some people are elated, and some wind up distraught. I'm sorry this was the way it turned out for you, Lucy, but the important thing is to focus on the people who were there and not the people who were missing. I've had students who didn't get a service at all, didn't have one person they knew present when the time came, and no one said a word about them. It was just a body and a guy with a shovel. I've even heard of people who wound up in the trash, a little cardboard box with a bag of ashes inside. No vase, no *I Dream of Jeannie,* and no sister to take them home with her."

Lucy knew it was true, the same way she knew it was true that by being dead, she might have been able to exact some revenge on both Nola and Martin for destroying her life as she knew it, and she'd just wanted to enjoy that. If there had been any way to make the bus feel guilty, she would have been happy to see that, too. But that, in itself, was no reason to be upset about a funeral that didn't quite live up to her expectations. Lucy saw that her anger was foolish, senseless, and a waste of her last moments with her sister, and she suddenly wished she had the chance to go back and attend her funeral all over again. She should have spent more time with Alice and Jared. Who knew when she was going to see either of them again.

"This exercise should have demonstrated to all of you that although you still do exist in this form, the way that you were has come to a conclusion and the door is now closed," Ruby explained. "That was the point of yesterday. It's a necessary understanding if we're going to proceed with the next section of your Transition. If we're all at that point, we can move forward. Now, did everyone get a chance to read through Section One of your binder?"

"I did," Bethanny said immediately.

The men in the group all nodded affirmatively, Mrs. Wootig simply looked straight ahead as if she had heard nothing, and Lucy avoided Ruby's eyes altogether.

"Lucy, what did you find most interesting about Chapter One, 'Your New Spectral Self'?" Ruby asked.

"Oooooo," Bethanny whimpered, shaking her hand in a frenetic motion. *"Can I answer? Can I answer? Can I answer?"*

Ruby did not turn her gaze away from Lucy, and patiently waited for a reply.

To tell the truth, the last thing Lucy had wanted to do the night before was snuggle up in her motel bed with a nice binder full of stupid homework. She had had the worst day of her death, and by her calendar, it had only been her second one. The more she'd thought about it, the more angry she'd become. It was just another hoop to jump through to reach some unknown destination. It was bullshit, she'd decided, and she'd felt set up that she'd even had to go back to her funeral at all. What purpose had it served, aside from humiliating her, as if her last days of life hadn't been enough of that? She didn't see the point of knowing that no one had bothered to show up to pay their respects, mainly because no one had had any respects to pay. That was obvious. "Thanks, Jilly," she had said out loud. "Thanks, Warren. Thanks, Marianne, Nola, Dr. Meadows, and thank you most of all, Martin. Nice to see all of you." *What a shining example of fairness he turned out to be. I'm glad I didn't wind up with him,* Lucy had told herself. *I am so glad that I didn't end up in that house stuck with him and all the pieces of his boring Martin life. No matter why he threw me out, I don't care,* she'd continued. *He did me a favor.*

The more Lucy had thought about it, the more angry she'd become, pissed off, furious, forgotten, and stuck in a strange place and with people she had known a day. What other hoops was she going to have to jump through in this idiotic place? How many tricks would she have to perform? She'd never wanted any of this. She'd never had a choice. This just suddenly was. Well, she'd told herself, she did indeed have a choice. She had a choice whether or not to follow any more rules, and the answer was no. She was not going to read whatever ridiculous chapter in her binder, to hell with it. She wasn't going to read it. Instead, she'd begun to cry, and as she'd sobbed on her drab little bed, she'd thankfully drifted off.

Ruby was still looking at Lucy, waiting for an answer. Lucy took a deep breath.

"I didn't read it," she admitted. "After I came back from my funeral, I just didn't feel up to it. So I went to sleep."

Ruby's expression didn't change, and she didn't take her eyes off of Lucy.

"Everyone needs to be engaged in their education here," the old woman said sternly. "If you don't work hard in this class and reach your utmost potential to be successful in your assignment, you will be roaming the earth for who knows how long. Everything you learn in this class will be put into practice once you return back to Earth and begin your assignments. Your success or failure there will determine if you move on to the infinite level. This is true whether you are completing unfinished business or your mission is to help the living in some way. If you don't complete your assignment, if you don't meet your objective, you will never move on and will remain exactly where you are for eternity. I am here to tell you that none of you want that. You need to move on to the next and ultimate level; it's what you lived your whole lives for. The strength of the skills you develop here is of utmost importance. Any of you want to hang around for centuries, running around as hysterical harpies like Anne Boleyn or Bloody Mary, showing your bloody head to tourists or terrifying little girls at slumber parties because you simply couldn't bring yourself to pay attention in class and learn how to spook effectively?"

Everyone in the class, including Lucy, shook their heads.

"I didn't think so," Ruby said, nodding in affirmation. "So let's get started."

Lucy learned, as she followed the lesson in Chapter One along with the rest of her classmates, that the spectral self she currently embodied was still only a temporary form used while embarking on her still-unknown assignment.

According to her handbook and Ruby, after her assignment was complete and she had reached her objective, a promised land of sorts awaited Lucy and her fellow Surprise Demised. Referred to in the manual as "The State," their final destination was, at best, cryptically described as "a glorious retirement beyond the most elaborate imagination," lending the inkling that it was a place well worth the wait.

Before that destination was reached, however, it was clear to Lucy that there was a long road ahead of her, according to the manual from which Ruby read out loud. There was the duration of her spectral training, and then her assignment, which the book informed her would "last a length of time depending on your deployment of skills and the dedication infused into the mission."

"What if I fail?" Bethanny suddenly cried out loud. "What if I fail my mission? Will I go to Hell? Have people failed and gone to Hell?"

"You won't fail," Ruby assured all of them. "I make good ghosts. Plus, the devil is on sabbatical right now, anyway. He's got a gig on AM radio, and I heard he got tangled up with triplets known as OxyContin, Lorcet, and Vicodin. He's not coming back for a while. There is no failing. You're stuck down there until you finish, like Anne and Mary."

To be blunt, Lucy didn't get it. She was left confused and puzzled after covering this information, and wondered what sort of mission she could possibly be sent on. Maybe American ghosts went to the offices of the KGB to eavesdrop on secret meetings and plans, and Russian ghosts dropped plutonium tablets into the teacups of English spies, and English ghosts were dispersed all through the countryside to castles and manors to keep tourism thriving, as Ruby had said. But surely there were infinite numbers of the dead, as new ones were arriving every day and old ones, like every executed member of royalty from the Middle Ages on, were still hanging around. One thing was for sure—if Lucy had to put on a little ghost white shirt and black tie and ride a little ghost bike trying to convince people that seagulls were magic, she'd rather do her time on AM radio next to Beelzebub.

Lucy couldn't imagine an existence as a hapless ghost stuck in the rut of incompetence; it sounded repetitive, dull, and boring, particularly after centuries. She hoped with all of her might that she would receive a nice assignment, perhaps in a fancy New York hotel where she could be witness to juicy trysts, high-stake deals, celebrities on vacation, and who knows what else, spending her days wreaking havoc with the hot and cold shower knobs and her nights ripping comforters off sleeping supermodels.

Without even thinking, Lucy raised her hand.

"Is it possible to put in a request for where you would like to serve on a mission?" she asked Ruby, who immediately chuckled and smiled.

"Heavens, no," her instructor replied. "Remember, I told you that you were going back to your own life."

"Yes, but I thought that meant I'm going back as me, as Lucy Fisher and not, like, Liza Minnelli. So as long as I'm me, can I pick where I go?" she continued. "I mean, as long as I'm just shaking beds and moaning here and there, what's the difference where I do it?"

Ruby looked utterly insulted. "First of all," she began a little harshly, "paranormality is not just rattling chains and moaning in the middle of the night, you know. It is an *art form*. And we'll see how much of a master you are once we start your training. Who knows? You may only be able to manifest yourself to the level of a shadow person, and let me tell you, once a shadow, always a shadow. That's the bottom rung for ghosts, my friends. What kind of hereafter is that, skulking around in hallways and never being able to fully project? Is there anything sadder than a forlorn mist that looks like a petrified fart?"

Kirk and Chuck both emitted hearty laughs.

"I don't want to be a shadow person," Bethanny said, and pouted. "I think I've finally settled on an outfit, and I really want people to see it."

"Don't worry, Bethanny," Ruby said, trying to console her. "You just need to pay attention and focus. And, Lucy, when I say back to your old life, I mean you are really going back to some facet of your previous existence. I don't know what it will be, but there's a role for you to play in setting something right that is undone."

"I don't like the sound of that," Lucy admitted. "Can you give me an example of a mission? I'm trying to wrap my head around this thing, and I'm having kind of a hard time."

"Me, too," Bethanny admitted, and the rest of the class followed suit with various murmurs and nods.

"I think you are missing the whole point of why you are all here," Ruby continued. "You're here because you did not reach your full potential in life when you had the chance. You missed opportunities, maybe left things unsaid, or didn't come through on promises you made. Everyone who gets to The State had reached those objectives in life; they were successful in making a difference. They had left a good mark on the world when their time was up. It wouldn't be fair or just to let those who didn't leave a good mark slide on in without doing the necessary work. This is your second chance. Do you understand what that means?"

Lucy, in fact, did understand. She understood immediately, and it shocked her. She nodded her head slightly at Ruby.

"Atonement," she said quietly. "I sucked as a person. I was a disappointment, a failure, a flake. This is judgment day, right?"

There was a pause in the room, a pause that was filled with every person in it understanding the scope of what it was that had delivered them to SD1118.

"Hey," Ruby finally said, breaking the heavy silence. "Everybody. Listen. I didn't make it to The State, either. You can each think of your time as a specter however you wish, but for me, I just prefer to consider it as doing extra credit."

All of the Surprise Demisers, even Bethanny, looked horribly solemn.

"Even I don't know what or where you'll be going. That's not up to me. You're here to do in death what you didn't do in life," Ruby said, and shrugged. "And you're stuck down here until you get it right."

chapter eight What a Lovely Ghost

Lucy's hand hovered tentatively over the lightbulb, which glowed brilliantly bright, white, and, quite clearly, very hot.

"Go on," Ruby urged as she looked on with the rest of the class. *"Grab it."*

Lucy's hand didn't move. It remained still and steady as Lucy's eyes were transfixed on the burning, shining bulb.

"Grab it!" Ruby insisted again, this time nearly spitting with impatience.

Under Ruby's careful tutelage, Lucy and the rest of her Surprise Demise class had worked their way through the first chapter of the ghost school binder while trying to fathom the work before them. Today they were taking theory and putting it into motion. The culling of energy—the cornerstone of every ghostly skill—was the first exercise all the students needed to master, combining the forces of focus, concentration, and pure will. It was Lucy who Ruby had called onto the stage first to test her skill.

The objective of today's lesson was to transfer the power of the lightbulb into themselves, or, in other words, to suck the power up like a spectral vacuum. "Think of your hand as a magnet," Ruby instructed, "a strong magnet pulling up a thread of paper clips."

As soon as Lucy leveled her hand over the shining bulb that was screwed into a lamp sitting on a table at the front of the class, she could feel it immediately, but it was not the sensation simply of heat that she felt. It contained much more than that. In fact, it was everything but that. The palm of her hand tingled at first, but that lasted only a few seconds, and then she began to feel the power draw, almost like her hand really did have the pull of a magnet. It seemed to her as if she was filling up like a balloon, bit by bit, slowly, increasing her strength and reserve, almost like getting warm with the heat of a campfire.

"Can you feel that?" Ruby asked, and Lucy nodded quickly. "All right, then, grab it!"

Lucy still hesitated. She had foolishly burned her hands on lightbulbs before, and this one burned brighter than any one she had ever seen. She was perfectly fine with her hand skimming the surface of it.

"Lucy," Ruby said firmly. "Are you afraid it's going to hurt you?"

"Hurt me?" Lucy nearly laughed. "If I put my hand on that thing, I know for a fact I'll hear the sound of a steak hitting the grill at Sizzler."

"Lucy, you're a sweet girl, but," Ruby said as she raised her cloaked arm and swung it toward Lucy, slapping her hard and fast across the face with a crack that rang as sharply as a boxing bell, at the precise moment when Lucy looked up at her.

Lucy gasped, as did everyone else in the room. Then Lucy took several steps backward, her mouth hanging open. She tried to say something, but the stun of being hit left her speechless.

It was Elliot, safely tucked inside his bike helmet, who ventured the first reaction.

"Pardon me, but I don't see why that was absolutely necessary," he said quietly, lest Ruby turn and charge after him. "I'm sure with a little coaxing, you could have forced Lucy to burn all the flesh off her hand had you been kinder and more pragmatic."

Ruby did indeed spin toward the poor bicyclist, her finger pointed directly at his shiny little body.

"See?" she proclaimed. "See? That's the point! That's the point I'm trying to make. Lucy, I just slapped you very hard, and I'm sorry, but did I hurt you? Are you in pain?"

Lucy stopped for a moment and assessed the degree of the sting, then burst out into a full chuckle. "No," she said, shaking her slapped head. "I actually don't feel a thing. It didn't hurt. I guess you just scared me."

"No pain," Ruby said, throwing up her hands. "No active nerve endings, no pain. Get it? Now, will you please grab the damn bulb? You can't swim if you don't jump off the pier, and you can't materialize if you don't have enough energy."

Lucy laughed and nodded, then stepped forward, opened her palm, and wrapped her hand completely around the illuminated ball.

The rush was instant. Whatever pull Lucy had felt simply by holding her hand over the source was compounded a hundred, maybe a thousand, times. She felt nearly electric herself, as if she had been swallowed by an incredible light and now had become part of it. She even felt as if she glowed. It felt like the first time she'd taken a drag off a cigarette, that charge that becomes all encompassing and hits you like a wave.

Then, as quickly as she had felt that intensity, it began to dissipate, the force of it diminishing, becoming weaker. Ruby looked at her and smiled.

"What Lucy felt was the absorption of an initial force of energy, which is almost overwhelming, but after a few seconds, it begins to ease and trickle off," the teacher explained. "Lucy, what you need to do now is draw up as much energy as you possibly can. Concentrate on the power. Pull it up."

Lucy centered her mind on the bulb, imagining that she was pulling the light from the bulb right up into her palm, then her hand, and then her arm. She felt the charge become stronger, and the more intensely she focused, the greater it became.

"Wow," Bethanny said from her chair. "Lucy, there's a light all around you!"

Lucy looked at Ruby and smiled.

"That is how you harness energy," Ruby explained. "Now, we can see the light around Lucy, which is a shine, but on a mortal plane, the effects would be different. In the physical realm, Lucy would be forming a mist right about now, which is the first phase of materializing. In order to project a true image, she's going to need a bigger energy source, especially with those ecologically friendly bulbs everybody has that have about a watt apiece in them. Worthless, I'm telling you. I don't know who calls that progress. You could eat one and not get a decent shine."

Elliot, still fearful of having the old woman lunge at him, simply cleared his throat and looked the other way.

Wanting to be a good example, Lucy collected all of her concentration and aimed it directly at the light that shone through her fingertips. She felt herself begin to almost buzz, as if she was plugged directly into an electrical outlet.

"She's getting brighter," Bethanny whispered.

Lucy bore her eyes into the lightbulb, drawing the energy out, out, out. She could feel it becoming the strongest yet, when suddenly, she heard a loud *POP!* and saw her hand go dark as she instinctively drew it quickly back. The bulb had exploded, sending minuscule shards of glass all over the stage.

"Did I do that?" Lucy asked, taken completely aback.

Ruby nodded. "I believe you did," she confirmed. "I guess I'm just glad I didn't use a spotlight for our first lesson. As a ghost, though, you really don't want to be blowing lightbulbs out all over the place. If you're haunting lazy people who never change lightbulbs, you've lost a great power source. Besides, you want to haunt, not menace. Being a menace will bring you more trouble than it's worth."

"We can only get energy from lightbulbs?" Chuck asked dismally. "I guess I'm going to spend a lot of time massaging lamps, considering my size."

"No, no, no," Ruby corrected him. "Size does not matter. You'll use as much energy as someone Bethanny's size. Remember, you no longer exist in the physical sense, you have no weight. You're energy; you're light. You exist in the sense that those things do."

"This is getting too heavy for me, man," Danny quipped, shaking his head. "I'm totally into the ghost thing, but I'm not getting this whole 'how I exist' thing. I can see everybody. I can touch everybody. And I really want to grab that lightbulb."

"The lightbulb is not your only source of energy, quite the contrary," Ruby went on. "It's just the simplest and most common form. You can draw energy from almost anything—an appliance, radiator, anything with a battery, an electric substation, a dog's shock collar, even the atmosphere, especially if the weather is right and a thunderstorm is ionizing the air. Why do you think people associate dark and stormy nights with the spooky things and ghosts?"

"Ahhhhhh," the students said in chorus.

"You can even take energy from the living," their teacher explained. "You don't need much; they won't notice it. Look at what Lucy was able to do with just forty watts."

"I refuse to touch strange living people," the countess declared. "They might be wearing Walmart clothes."

"It does seem a little vampirish," Lucy added.

"Not at all. You're drawing so little that they truly won't even notice, and the chubby ones have extra, anyway," Ruby said plainly. "And honestly, if you can draw some energy from a menopausal woman, you'd be doing her a favor. Mrs. Wootig, you don't have to touch them. Once you've sharpened your skills a bit, you'll easily be able to siphon the energy with some focused concentration. You probably won't have to touch any poor people. Ever hear of a cold spot? That's exactly what that is. That's simply one of us gathering enough resources to interact in that physical world."

"We can actually bring the temperature of a room down?" Kirk asked with a chuckle. "I thought only my ex-wife could do that. On second thought, she was dead on many levels. . . ."

"Ha, ha," Chuck guffawed along. "I love a good dead joke."

"Oh, my God! Oh, my God!" Bethanny suddenly shrieked as she jumped completely out of her seat. "I almost forgot to tell you guys! They found my leg! They found my leg!"

A round of hearty applause filled the room, along with some congratulatory hugs.

"That's wonderful news, Bethanny," Ruby commented, and walked over to give the little girl a squeeze.

Bethanny took a deep breath and beamed gloriously. "A little kid found it while he was looking for shells. It washed right up onto the beach, and at first, the lifeguard thought it was a giant shrimp! But it was my leg, as if to say, 'Here I am! Here's Bethanny's leg! Look at me!' "

"I'm so happy they found a part of you," Elliot added.

"You know what this means?" Bethanny squealed to everyone, then waited for an answer that never came.

"A *funeral*!" she answered herself. "I finally get a real funeral!"

"That is such good news," Lucy said with a wide smile, and patted her friend on the back.

"And on that wonderful note, let's get back to our lesson," the instructor called, and walked back over to the small stage. She came back rolling a large full-length mirror on casters from the rear portion of the platform and guided it to the front. "Lucy, you're losing some of your shine, so let's see if we can charge you back up a bit. Once you gather your energy, it is essential to use it within a reasonable period of time. It will slip away quickly, so make the most of your time when you have it. That's why there's so much activity in kitchens—cabinet doors opening and closing, dishes rattling, faucets being turned on and off—because that is the hallmark of a ghost who simply cannot hold his shine and acts out like a monkey. In time, you'll learn how to sustain it, so you can make your presence known in any location."

Lucy walked back to the stage, where Ruby positioned her directly in front of the mirror—a mirror that did not reflect Lucy's image. In fact, it didn't reflect anything.

She laughed. "Is this a carnival mirror, one of the trick ones?" she asked as Ruby took the lamp off the table and replaced it with a toaster oven.

"Not exactly," Ruby answered. "I need everyone to gather around Lucy for this portion of the lesson. This mirror will reflect the way you appear on the physical plane. Right now you don't even appear, there's nothing there."

Lucy's classmates got up from their seats and mingled behind her. Not one of them was visible in the mirror.

"We're invisible," Kirk said as all of them studied the empty frame. "Just like we were at our funerals. But we can see each other . . . because ghosts can see each other since we're on a different plane?"

"I saw another ghost at my funeral," Lucy added. "His was across the hall from mine. He saw me run through a pair of doors."

"Exactly," Ruby confirmed. "We can see each other, but few on the other level can, unless you want them to. Another spectral spirit would be able to see that shine around her. One spirit will always be able to see another spirit, even if they're not charged. They will look whole and full to you, just like they did when they were alive. You can tell a ghost from a living person by the shining around them. It's like a little golden energy field buzzing around them like an outline—you will carry that with you, no matter what. Lucy, I want you to focus on the toaster oven, and draw from it."

Lucy stood up straight in front of the mirror, even though she couldn't see herself. She looked at the toaster oven and focused steadily on it, reaching out her left hand to touch the top of it. Again, she felt the surge of energy from the small kitchen appliance rush into her arms and over her shoulders.

"Focus," Ruby coached. "Good, good, keep going. Your shine is getting strong. You're building up a nice reserve. Keep it going, keep it going . . ."

The countess was the first to gasp; in the mirror, a mist formed. It was a loose shape, but still, it was a shape. Lucy saw it, too, and centered her concentration even further. The shape became denser, although still transparent, and became more defined.

"You're doing fantastic, Lucy," Ruby encouraged her student. "Just a little bit more. Concentrate."

Excitement built from her classmates—they couldn't believe what they were seeing. Lucy's cloudy reflection was becoming more definitive; the shape of her shoulders appeared, the color of her brown, curly shoulder-length hair, the contour of her face.

"Is that an eye?" Elliot whispered. "I think I see an eye!"

"Whoa," Danny added. "I know I see a nostril. Houston, we have a nostril."

And, with Lucy's hand planted firmly on the top of the toaster oven and the light around her getting brighter and deeper, Lucy's face slowly began to form in the mirror, an eye, an eye, a nose, a mouth.

It was a faint image, as if it had been lightly screened on a thin piece of silk, or a magical piece of linen, but it was there.

"Look," Bethanny breathed, "it's Lucy!"

Lucy smiled broadly, and, as if on cue, her translucent reflection smiled right back.

"Congratulations, my dear." Ruby beamed. "You're a lovely, lovely ghost."

chapter nine PTDS

As the students in SD1118 conquered chapter after chapter in their silver binders, the promise of their ghostliness had begun to take shape. Ruby led them along a path of spirit discovery, each one of them revealing new facets of themselves. Halfway through the binder, everyone was finding their niche and discovering exactly what sort of spook they aspired to be. While all the students were comfortable with the basics—materializing and fading; collecting energy from the living, which resulted in delightful goose bumps in the warm-blooded; tapping on shoulders; and learning how to quickly and nimbly move just out of eyesight—some of the student spirits were obviously more gifted at one paranormal activity than another.

Who would have thought that Chuck, a man who'd had a gun rack bolted inside the cab of his Ford truck, would be an unrivaled master at spectral whispering and would send a shiver up another ghost's spine simply by calling their name? No one would have expected that Elliot, a slight man who could have easily shopped in the JCPenney girls' department for his wardrobe when alive, possessed such a highly developed talent for generating loud, booming footsteps that mimicked a pirate's heavy boot. And then there was Danny, the once lonely and bitter musician, who finally realized his calling was door slamming and blowing out candles; he was honing his talent to enact both challenges *simultaneously*.

It was almost as if death had opened a brand-new door and introduced the Surprise Demisers to new talents, abilities, and even possible genius. Kirk Russell, for example, surprised everyone with his ability to delicately hover behind someone and blow a slight, gentle stream of air onto an exposed neck or ear, a maneuver that was guaranteed to produce not only a shriek, but a frantic, panicked race to escape a house. The countess even brought her game to the arena with a playful yet nearly sinister cackle that could bounce for centuries off castle walls. And with Bethanny's flowing, curly blond hair and her facial features nearly in miniature, she was of course mistaken for a haloed angel, much to her ethereal delight. To bring her point home, the perky towhead practiced for hours and hours in her spare time and came close to perfecting a definite flowing levitation, although she never left the ground without her familiar complaint that if she just had a fan to make her hair billow, she could get the effect absolutely perfect.

Lucy, however, was not really very good at anything.

Sure, she had had her moment in the spotlight the first day she'd materialized with the rest of her class looking on in admiration, but to be blunt, it was as if she had peaked at the moment when she'd seen the tiny caverns of her nostrils, and all the air had rushed out of her spectral balloon. It was at that moment that Lucy realized she did not want to be there. She didn't want to be a ghost, she didn't want to be dead, and she certainly didn't want to go out on a haunting mission. The rest of the class charged on with their studies, and Lucy watched as they tackled each section with enthusiasm and clapped along when Elliot was able to make his first floorboard creak and Danny was able to turn a battery-operated train on with a touch of his finger and some good old ordinary phantom-y determination.

It wasn't that Lucy didn't want to be a good, effective ghost; she did, but she simply found that her heart really wasn't in it. She was tired. After getting thrown out of her house, losing her job, getting killed by a bus, and not having one single friend attend her funeral, Lucy couldn't help but feel a tiny bit bitter, especially about the funeral thing. It's easy to feel a lot better about almost anything as long as friends are behind you, but when they simply fail to show up, it's just another knock in the teeth. Everyone else in the class, as far as Lucy knew, just died one day and wound up here, while Lucy's life had been falling apart, chunk by chunk, until destiny decided enough was enough and blew a blinding visor of hair into her face, almost as if to end the misery. She was more than a little fed up with changes and just wanted to stay in one place for a while and adjust. To anything. Instead, she found herself in a ghost classroom being pelted with one lesson after the next—how to turn lights on and off, how to drop forks and knives from the silverware drawer onto the floor, what to do when the living sit on you or walk right through you, how to make small objects teeter and slide off a table, or how to misplace keys or tilt a photo or painting just the slightest bit off center.

Lucy, frankly, was sick of it. They had all been told that as soon as their training was complete, they'd be off to another new place for their assignment, another adjustment she'd be expected to make. All Lucy really wanted to do was stand up and scream, "I have post-traumatic death syndrome!" in hopes that everyone would take pity on her and simply leave her alone. Instead, she delivered a half-assed attempt at almost everything, and it didn't go unnoticed.

"It's almost as if you don't care how to switch television channels in the middle of a show the living are watching," Bethanny said sorrowfully one night when the girls were picking up a few games at the Soul Bowl. "The only one who is worse than you is the countess, and that's because she'll watch anything as long as it's in English. You really need to try, Lucy. How are you going to get to the next level if you don't succeed in your assignment?"

Lucy took a deep breath and shook her head. "Maybe I just need to hang out for a while." She exhaled as she shrugged. "Maybe I'm not ready to go on my assignment just yet, you know? It's not like it's that hard to change the channel anyway. You just punch the button on the remote control when they aren't paying attention. Big deal."

"You're going to fail, Lucy, if you don't watch it," her once sweeter-than-pie friend warned sharply, her confidence freshly fueled by her levitation flair. "Then you'll be stuck down there forever. I just want to do my job and move on so that I can relax for all eternity. Do you think they'll have tanning beds in The State? I think they should, if it's eternal and everything."

Bethanny wasn't the only one who was keyed in to Lucy's lackluster attitude. In the middle of the lesson of moving small pieces of furniture, Ruby halted her demonstration when she noticed Lucy doodling in her binder, and promptly asked her to step outside of SD1118.

"You seem a little disconnected, Lucy," the instructor said after her student closed the door behind her. "You've seemed that way for the past several sections. This is important stuff, and it's essential that you pay attention. Is anything wrong?"

Lucy wasn't thrilled about being confronted about her academic failure, even though she truly liked Ruby and thought she was a wonderful teacher. Her anger got the better of her, and now that it had been tapped, there was no stopping it.

"Of course there's something wrong," Lucy replied. "*I'm dead.* Cut down before I was even thirty. I didn't get a chance to start anything. I didn't get a chance to finish anything. All of sudden, my turn at life is over, and now I'm sitting in a classroom trying to bump around a chair even though I'm invisible? Is this it? What was the purpose of my life?"

Ruby stood looking at her student for a while, while Lucy also stood quietly and averted her gaze.

"I am very sorry, Lucy," she finally said. "I agree that you didn't get a fair shake at your time being alive, but we are powerless about that. I'm here to help you get to The State, and I promise you, it will be worth all of the effort you can muster. If we can get you there, you'll have endless days of elation and solace; everything you have been through will have been worth it. You'll see. Think about the happiest, most comforting moment of your whole life and imagine that stretched out before you with no end. But you won't get there without one hundred percent of your effort."

Lucy scoffed and almost rolled her eyes, but held herself back.

"Who cares about moving furniture?" she rebuffed. "I don't. I can already make it move. I don't feel like being a ghost. I didn't pick this. I'm sorry, Ruby, but this is all just stupid to me. I feel like I am wasting my time."

"To the contrary, dear," Ruby replied. "Time is all you have, and there's quite a bit of it. I don't want to hear centuries from now that you're still trapped down there, roaming dusty rooms and scaring the crap out of people because you didn't bother to learn the right way and ended up going rogue. There's no happy ending for those spooks whose only skill is to terrify. They never get the job done.

And please tell me what you mean when you say you've already moved furniture. It's quite difficult and is an advanced technique, so if you can indeed do it without training, I'd like to see it."

"I moved a chair, just like how you showed us in class, but I was much angrier. It was at my funeral. I kicked it, and I saw it move. It didn't move a lot—it didn't tip over or anything—but it definitely moved."

"Do you think you can do it again?" Ruby asked.

Lucy shrugged. "I can give it a shot," she replied, in response to which Ruby opened the door to SD1118, stepped aside, and let Lucy enter.

Lucy's opponent stood defenseless on the stage, in a designated part that was charged to simulate the atmosphere of a much more solid plane, as in that of the living.

Ruby had released the rest of the students on a short break, not only to prevent Lucy from being embarrassed should her claims not be realized, but also to not put any undue pressure on her and hamper her potential.

"Do you want me to charge up first?" Lucy asked, and pointed to the vast array of appliances, lamps, and outlets that the students used to get enough energy to do the exercises.

"No, no," Ruby said, shaking her head. "It wouldn't help anyway. For something like this, we would have to move way beyond a toaster oven or a television set. You'd need to really plug into a fuse panel, tap into a streetlight, or, if you were lucky, catch the stream from a nearby substation. Just go ahead and do whatever you did when you made the chair move before."

Lucy positioned herself in front of the chair, took a moment, and then kicked it as hard as she could. Her foot sliced through the plastic folding chair like a baseball through a vat of Jell-O, and Lucy knew it. She felt her leg move through the object without so much as a jiggle.

"Hmmmm," Ruby commented. "Maybe that chair is too much for you."

"It's not," Lucy insisted, shaking her head. "The chair I kicked was much heavier than this one. I mean, it was a chair in a funeral home, you know? It was wooden, not this cheap plastic folding chair stuff. I want to try it again."

"Sure," Ruby said, and shrugged.

This time, Lucy raised her leg, positioned it square in the center of the chair, and kicked it with all her might. Again, the chair might as well have been made out of water, as Lucy's leg sailed through it, without budging the chair an iota.

"Nah," Ruby said, shaking her head and waving her hands. "Stop. I didn't think you could do it. Don't worry. It's pretty hard, and you shouldn't be embarrassed. I don't think you were lying. Exaggerating a little, but I know you thought you were telling the truth."

"But I *was* telling you the truth," Lucy protested.

Ruby unabashedly laughed a deep, throaty chortle. "Okay, kid, sure, whatever. You say you moved a chair. But you've kicked it twice now and nothing's happened. What am I supposed to believe? Did you move a chair, didn't you move a chair, who knows? If you say you can move that chair and expect me to believe you, then you'd better prove it, and so far, you haven't. But you know what I think? I think you're too busy feeling sorry for yourself to take charge of your own eternity. Guess what, Lucy? We're *all* dead. We *all* died. It wasn't fair to *any* of us. And you know what else? If you were as selfish in life as you are in death, it's no wonder there were rows and rows of empty chairs at your funeral, and that clears up the mystery of how you ended up here in the first place, now, doesn't it?"

Lucy didn't know what to say. She felt all of her anger collect in a tight little ball that quickly rose from her stomach, spread across her shoulders, and then exploded in her temple in a fiery, acidic blast that made her head throb.

Still looking straight at Ruby, in less than a second she reared up and blasted the chair, delivering all of the rage, fury, and exasperation that had been building up inside her since she had arrived.

And in response, the chair not only moved, but tipped backward and then fell forward the tiniest bit in a slight but undeniable rock. Lucy couldn't believe it. She stared at the chair as if what she'd done had been a Herculean feat, as if she had just lifted a car off of a baby.

From below the stage came a sharp, shrill one-note shriek that mirrored what Lucy felt, and she turned to see a lithe black blur of a figure hopping up and down, clapping and screaming in complete delight.

"You did it! Oh, Lucy! You did it! That was marvelous, how wonderful! Spectacular!" Ruby cried with glee, and she walked quickly toward the stage. "You moved the chair! You really moved the chair!"

"I told you I could do it," Lucy replied, ecstatic that she had actually done it, but still quite upset at her instructor's comments. "You doubted me."

"I *pushed* you, Lucy," Ruby explained. "On the first two tries, you had nothing fueling you, so I decided to press your most obvious buttons. Was that fair? No. But I needed something to help me light the fire, and it worked. Don't forget I was there right after the funeral. I saw the state you were in. I needed you to tap into the same source that gave you the power to move that chair then. You've completed an incredibly difficult task, Lucy. I only know of one other student who has been able to do what you just did without extensive training. That's how rare it is. And it should also key you in to just what kind of talent you may have within you, if you just *try*."

Lucy nodded, relieved to know that Ruby's inflammatory comments had been pointed for a reason. She also recognized that most of what Ruby had said had hit a nerve, even though she hated to admit it. Ruby was right. Lucy did feel sorry for herself, and she knew that if any kind of future awaited her on the other side of the ghost horizon, she was the only one who could pull it off. No one else was going to do it for her. Kicking the chair had felt good, it had felt liberating, and it had been a much needed release.

Lucy smiled, and Ruby returned a warm, earnest smile.

Lucy then kicked the chair as if it were her own ass, and they both giggled when it tipped completely over.

chapter ten From Here to Eternity

Before any of the students had realized it, the last day of school had arrived.

To reward them for being such attentive students and working so hard, Ruby had decided to take it a little easy on the Surprise Demisers' final day together. As soon as the students all rolled in, she took them to one of the theaters to see *Ghost*. Ruby regarded it as one of the best comedies ever made, and cackled particularly loudly when Patrick Swayze's character projected himself completely onto Whoopi Goldberg's and Demi Moore's characters in some darkened alley. Then he lit up the alley with his accompanying orb of light and bent down and actually kissed the Demi Moore character.

"Look at that!" the old woman howled, pointing at the screen. "A full apparition with exceptional definition, in color, and not a power source in sight! You can't take that much power from the living unless they're hooked up to a life-support machine! And he's a ghost kisser, too! I guess I forgot to teach that section, ghost love. I don't know who the spirit consultant was on this movie, but they were obviously still breathing!"

After the movie, they returned to the classroom, where Ruby paced before them while everyone settled in.

"Let's say I was haunting my Aunt Nancy, who has lost her wedding ring and is heartbroken about it," she tossed out. "I've found it under the microwave. How am I going to let her know, and what power sources can I use to complete the task?"

The classroom wasn't silent for very long before several hands popped up.

"Elliot," Ruby chose. "What am I going to do?"

"Well," he started, "I would use the power from the microwave itself, and somehow move the microwave to reveal the ring."

Ruby pursed her lips together in a pondering look and nodded. "I can see the power source as the microwave," she replied. "But some microwaves are pretty heavy, especially the old ones. My Aunt Nancy never buys anything new, and that microwave weighs more than her bed. What do I do now? Be creative!"

Danny was the next one to shoot up his hand. "I'd keep knocking on the microwave until she got the hint."

"Aunt Nancy is older than me," Ruby replied. "Deaf as a post."

"Unplug it?" Kirk Russell offered. "This way, she thinks it's broken, has someone move it to see what's the matter with it, and there's the ring!"

"Points for creativity!" Ruby yelled, giving Kirk a little round of applause. "But . . . unless you have a really strong charge, unplugging something might be very difficult, especially if you have to move the microwave to do it. Any thoughts?"

As the students pondered the puzzle, the room became more and more hushed for long seconds, then, finally, for a full minute.

"I have an idea," Lucy suddenly said, breaking the quiet.

"Shoot," Ruby responded.

"I take a paper towel, toilet paper, tissue, something light that I can handle easily without the use of a lot of power, and poke it through the vents on the back of the microwave. Then, when it overheats, Aunt Nancy thinks it's broken, and like Kirk said, she has someone move it, and voilà, her ring."

"I think that's a perfect solution as long as you don't let the paper towel catch on fire," Ruby said. "If you turned my Aunt Nancy into an SD-er, there'd be hell to pay, and not just the one down the hall. Great job, Lucy!"

The class rewarded her with a nice round of "Good job, good job," "Nice work," and "Way to go!"

"So I have a friend that I'm haunting, and her boyfriend just broke up with her. How can I cheer her up without flipping her out?" Ruby queried.

"This one is mine," Bethanny said, and she didn't even wait to raise her hand. Instead she simply stood up.

"First," she began without any cue from Ruby, "I'd check to see if any of her favorite movies were on that night, and then change the channel at the appropriate time to make sure she knew they were on. Then I would spray her nicest perfume to make her feel pretty. Then I would knock down all of the pictures of him she had up. And I'd hide anything of his so she wouldn't be reminded of his beastly self."

"If she had any Aretha Franklin on her iPod, I would certainly cue 'Chain of Fools' and push play when it was most needed, like every morning when she woke up," the countess chimed in.

"If the phone rang and it was his number that popped up on the screen, I'd disconnect," Chuck said emphatically.

Ruby beamed from ear to ear.

"Great work, everyone, very creative, nicely inventive. I like that," she complimented the class. "You've all been paying a lot of attention. Now, remember, what's the first rule of ghosting?"

"The best kind of ghost," recited the class in unison, "is the kind you never know is there."

"Beautiful," the old woman gushed. "And the second rule?"

"There are no such things as coincidences," the class chimed, once more in chorus. "Only ghosts on duty."

"Now here's rule number three of ghosting," Ruby said with a wry smile. "What do you do when ghost hunters come?"

The question was met with silence for several reasons, with different scenarios rushing through each of the students' heads.

"You know this one. You know it. It's right in front of your faces," Ruby teased.

"If anyone thinks they're going to hunt me," Chuck asserted boldly, "the tables will turn. The prey shall hunt the hunter! I am the haunting hunter! When I was alive, I used to get knife catalogs!"

"If we're going to be hunted, I want a ghost gun *right now,*" Bethanny cried in a panic. "Or at least some kind of spirit pepper spray. I need something to defend myself! I'm the smallest ghost here! Do you see how small I am?"

"I refuse to touch a gun," Elliot pronounced defiantly. "I will counter the attack with reason, sensibility, and a touch of goodwill."

"I demand a bodyguard," the countess said simply. "Or a ghost guard. Or an apparition guard or a guard for whatever the hell it is I am now. You're not sending me into some sort of jungle where I'm going to be pursued like invisible big game."

"Calm down, calm down, please," Ruby said, raising both hands. "No one needs a gun or a bodyguard, all right? I'm sure all of you are going to be perfectly fine. But when ghosts violate rule number one and tip the living off to their presence, it's not typically a big deal. In fact, sometimes it can work to your advantage. But when ghosts go rogue and start acting on their own behalf and do not follow the recommended conduct guidelines, there can be trouble."

Ghost hunters, Ruby went on to explain, were not really hunters but more like enthusiasts. They were living beings that were fascinated by ghosts. They weren't sure if ghosts really did exist or if spirits were figments of the imagination, but these enthusiasts were interested enough to investigate ghosts in their spare time and buy equipment for it. Usually, they were just a bunch of people who didn't mean any harm, who just wanted to gather evidence that ghosts and the paranormal did in fact exist. They did this by taking pictures and using voice recorders, thermal imaging cameras, and energy sensors. Sometimes, Ruby went on, they would try to provoke a spirit into creating an action or effect. These ghost buffs might shout insulting things or ask stupid questions.

"I have even heard of one ghost hunter asking a spirit he was trying to coax, 'Do you realize that you're dead?' " Ruby laughed, as did the members of the class. "I'm sure the spirit wanted to respond, 'Well, I don't eat, I move through walls, no one can see me, and I haven't gone potty in sixty years. You're kidding me, I'm dead?' "

The class all nodded, and laughed even harder.

"Keep a cool head," their teacher advised, "and don't fall into the trap." The best thing to do when the ghost hunters show up is right in front of your face, she said again.

Play dead, she concluded.

"What would be the big deal?" Kirk asked. "So what if they knew we were there? They can't do anything to hurt us. We're already deceased."

"True, true," Ruby agreed. "Typically, those people don't want to hurt you. They want to interact with you, which can be flattering and make you feel special. But the minute you make a move, make a sound, speak, knock on a wall, or are detected by thermal imagery, the gig is up, my friends. Because after the ghost hunters come, the psychics and mediums are oftentimes bound to follow, and they are the dangerous ones."

"I think all of that is hooey," Chuck declared. "I can't believe you're telling me those people are for real."

"Most of them aren't," Ruby said, trying to be reassuring. "But every now and then, you'll get a real one. They're few and far between, but they are out there, and through some mix-up, they're very much in touch with both worlds, ours and theirs. They are sensitive to the living and the non. You'll find many animals have this ability as well. They have an awareness that goes beyond the physical, and they can sense and know what's around them. People typically lose that the moment they are born."

"That doesn't sound so bad," Lucy added. "It might be nice to be able to talk to someone through a psychic telephone, so to speak. Maybe I could send a message to my sister, or they could even help us complete our assignment."

"Mmm, mmm, mmm, I know the lure is irresistible," Ruby cautioned. "But when the psychics—and I mean a real one, which, as I said, is rare—show up, it is time to hightail it out of there just in case. Don't even bother playing dead. If they're real, they will find you. And they will want to help you over to the other side."

"But we're already on the other side," Danny said with a grin. "We've already broken on through."

"Exactly," Ruby agreed. "That's the point. We're already on the other side. We've just come back to do some extra credit so we can move on to The State. But they don't know that, and in the effort to 'help' us—like the living can even remotely help the dead, can you imagine?—they will try to draw you into the light so you can 'pass' over and find peace."

"So the light is bad?" Lucy questioned.

Ruby shook her head. "No, the light isn't bad," she said quietly. "The light is *horrific.* It is not a light. It's an energy tunnel that has been in place since the beginning of time. It is misunderstood as a passageway to the other side, but it is not. It's real purpose is to filter out the bad and leave the good, but it can only do so much. If you get sucked into that tunnel, the density of it will render a spirit into a non-energy particle, like a speck of dust."

The students were speechless, and Ruby continued in such a serious tone that they knew what she was saying was the truth.

"The rings around Saturn?" the teacher began. "Filled with the foolish who thought there was an easy way out. You must fight the pull. Go into the light, and you'll spend an eternity orbiting around a dead planet as space debris. Throwing plates at the living, stacking chairs in a pyramid, and having three priests throwing holy water at you is no way to meet your objective. *Amityville Horror*? Amityville Idiots. I believe they're now located in the yellow band of Saturn's second ring. I mean, really. Whose idea was the marching band and a flying pig with red eyes? Your objective is to help, not to terrify. That's the surest way of getting yourself petrified. And it's for eternity. There's no going back."

"That's so sad," Bethanny murmured.

"It's not sad, dear," Ruby corrected her. "It's the most ghastly existence you could ever imagine. I don't want that for any of you. I wouldn't want that for my worst enemy, and believe me, I have a couple."

"I don't understand," Lucy interjected. "The living often have near-death experiences where they claim to see the light, and they go into it, feeling peaceful. How can the light be so bad, then?"

Ruby adamantly shook her head. "Those people aren't seeing the light," she informed them. "Do you remember your first morning here? Do you remember waking up in the bed in the big reception dorm? Before you opened your eyes, what did you see?"

Lucy remembered. It had been calming, comfortable, peaceful. She had felt so rested. It had been soft and welcoming.

"White," she recalled. "I saw white."

"You were no longer physical," Ruby added. "There was no reason to see darkness. Close your eyes now. What do you see?"

Lucy saw the same white, the white of a brilliant, soft sun, the white of everything good and nothing bad. They all closed their eyes; they all saw white.

"That's what those people see, and if they make it to The State, they very well may see family and friends who have also made it up to that level," Ruby explained. "But if they lose the battle and are transferred back to a physical plane, the white vanishes, as does everything that goes along with it. Psychics cannot reach where we are. They can only reach us if we are *where they are.* They have no idea that the light they think of as good is actually the worst thing possible for any spirit. If a psychic is trying to pull you into the light, resist as much as you possibly can, use whatever power you possess to escape. Do whatever you can to avoid it. Nothing is out of bounds at that point. Even scaring them is acceptable."

"Like writing 'Boo!' on a steamed-up mirror the way Patrick Swayze did in *Ghost*?" Bethanny asked.

"If you can fog it up, sister, then you should write all over it," Ruby confirmed. "It's one thing for them to think you're there. It's quite another for you to deliver proof and watch them jump through their skin. Just remember to plug yourself in first so that you have enough energy to physically operate in the world of the living."

"I'm looking forward to being a ghost," Danny remarked. "I can do whatever I want, whenever I want to. I can ride a bus for free, I can go to the movies for free, see a band for free, and I never, ever have to take a shower. I can't wait."

Lucy silently agreed. She couldn't wait to get to her destination so she could finally settle in someplace for a while. She hoped that she would be assigned to Alice, because if anyone needed help, it was her sister, and that was help Lucy was more than happy to give. Sure, she'd direct Alice to find rings, car keys, spare change that has sunk below the cushions. She could even get all charged up and maybe clean the house for her sister while she was at work; Alice was so harried, she'd never even notice. Maybe she could guide Jared with homework, or perhaps fend off a bully. Lucy was excited now about the assignment. She had to be going to Alice's; where else could she possibly be assigned? That was someplace she wouldn't mind hanging out for a while, and, in a way, that had sort of been the plan all along.

"Don't get too comfortable, young man," Ruby warned. "As much as you think you'll like mixing it up back on your home turf, you'll have a more glorious existence in The State. You might like being back on the living plane for now, but your goal needs to be making it to your forever level."

"Have you ever been there?" Danny asked.

"Do you know what it's like?" Elliot questioned.

"Do they have cosmetic procedures there?" the countess wondered aloud. "They have to have wonderful doctors."

Ruby shook her head and shrugged. "I'll be truthful," she replied. "I was there for a very short time. But I will tell you that it was the most beautiful place I had ever been. It was lovely and tranquil and calm. It was everything I had hoped an eternity would be. However, it is different for everyone, because everyone is different. No two spirits experience it the same way, so I can't really tell you what it will be like for you. But I can tell you that you will be glad you are there. It's everything you could ever want or need."

"I don't understand why you didn't stay, then," Bethanny piped up. "Why come back and teach?"

Ruby laughed a light, choppy little laugh. "Oh, dear," she responded. "Because I did not make it to The State. It was simply shown to me as an incentive to come and teach for a little bit before I moved on. I came here, where I was needed more, instead of going back to the living plane to haunt. And with that little story, I have a surprise for some of you."

The instructor went back behind her lectern, and then reemerged with several boxes that she presented to Bethanny, Elliot, and the countess.

Bethanny looked as delighted as a child opening the biggest box on Christmas morning. She beamed when she held up her flowing silken White Lady gown, draping it across her so the rest of the class could get an idea of exactly how ethereal she planned on being.

Elliot blushed when he opened his box, and smiled widely. The first thing he pulled out of the box was a leather sandal with what looked like ropes hanging from each side, then what appeared to be a ladies' white tennis outfit, and then a knee-length linen cape with a little braided belt that did, indeed, match his shoes.

"Wow," Chuck said, hesitating. "Are you . . . John Belushi in *Animal House*?"

"No." Elliot giggled gleefully. "I'm Socrates! I'm a thinking ghost!"

The countess had not opened her box, but left it closed on her lap, her arms holding on to it, almost like straps.

"Mrs. Wootig, aren't you going to show the class?" Ruby asked her.

"No," she replied quickly. "I'd rather try it on in my room."

"I can guarantee you that it will fit," Ruby added. "It was custom-made for you."

"Come on," cajoled Kirk, who was sitting next to her. "Let us see it."

The countess shook her head adamantly.

"Fair is fair," Elliot squealed, pretending to whip her with his little tiny belt. "I showed you mine!"

"I don't think so," she countered immediately, holding the box tighter.

"Come on," Kirk laughed. "Let us see. I'll bet you picked something out from the Princess Diana line."

The countess said nothing but firmly shook her head and kept shaking it until Kirk quickly and nimbly snatched the box from her lap and ran several seats away with it, where he popped off the top and began digging. From her seat, Lucy couldn't see anything but flashes of bright pink and what looked like feathers.

A Muppet? she thought. The countess was going to haunt as a Muppet? Where was she assigned to, Sesame Street?

"Kirk, give that back," the countess demanded, standing up, her arms running straight down her sides, curled up at the end in little rocklike fists.

"Oh, come on, Vicki, I'm just talking a peek!" he said, laughing.

Vicki? Lucy thought as she sat up. *Vicki? The countess is a Vicki? Who said Vicki? When did she say Vicki?*

Kirk continued to chuckle as Vicki Wootig stood motionless, watching, becoming more and more scarlet by the moment until she resembled a red potato. She tried to grab her outfit away from Kirk's grasp as he lifted the pink birded mess up for all to see and it unfolded as a transparent, silken lady robe with a flock of marabou feathers that Lucy and Bethanny both recognized as the issue for a Gold Rush Brothel Madam.

Lucy was forced to avert her eyes while the rest of the class sucked in a collective gasp.

"KIRK!" Vicki said harshly, and stomped her foot. He then

gasped and bunched it back up, and together, Kirk and Vicki fumbled to shove it back into the box.

"Somehow, I don't think Vicki was counting on being alone in her room when she tried that on later," Lucy whispered to her petite blond friend.

"Talk about *ghost love*." Bethanny shuddered. "Can ghosts barf?"

"I wish they could, dear," Ruby replied.

In a huff, Vicki plucked the box from Kirk's grasp and looked around the room as if she was nonplussed.

"What?" she demanded of all of them as she frantically shrugged. "*What?* So what if they exploded and killed me. I paid for them, and I'll be damned if I'm not going to get any use out of them!"

Vicki then stomped back to her seat, where she sat down in an exasperated huff.

"They were brand goddamned new," she growled.

The class sat quietly in the rich moment while Countess Vicki avoided everyone's eyes.

"All right, then," Ruby finally said, sealing the moment with a clap. "Tomorrow's your big day. I'm very proud of all of you, and I know you're going to be effective, wonderful ghosts. I'm sorry I didn't get to meet any of you until we were all dead, but I hope to see you all in The State very soon, or at least when my teaching assignment has concluded. Deal?"

"Deal!" her students enthusiastically agreed, except for Vicki, who was still looking everywhere anyone wasn't.

"Tomorrow, you'll find out your assignments," Ruby concluded with a smile. "I hope each one of them is a place you want to be."

chapter eleven That's a Lot of Kissing for a Sister

Lucy's cheek itched.

Still half-asleep, she reached up to scratch it, and felt something odd under her head. It was rough, nubby, and irritating. It felt almost like burlap, and Lucy quite quickly realized that it wasn't her pillow her head was resting on, and it wasn't her bed in room number 895 she was lying in.

Her eyes flew open, and the first thing she saw was blurry lines of white and orange slicing through a dull brownish background, the lines of whatever her face was smooshed into. Lucy then recoiled, because whatever it was, it stank. Concentrated notes of mustiness, age, dust, pet, and general unpleasantness lingered around her head like a stink fog. She instantly sat up to escape the stench, and realized she had been lying on an fraying burlap couch that was every bit as old as she was.

It was a couch that people had obviously spent countless hours on, reading books, flipping through channels, and watching rented movies with a bowl of popcorn nestled in between them. It was the kind of couch that a dog would have no problems lumbering up onto to take a nice afternoon nap, and the kind of couch where if something spilled on it, it wasn't even close to a tragedy, and it was maybe not even worth cleaning it up. The kind of couch that was miserable to sleep on, as the middle sagged and the spring on the left side shot up with a loud announcement every time an occupant rose from the cushion, which was battered and becoming threadbare in the middle.

Lucy hated this couch. Lucy loathed the couch. It was uncomfortable, smelly, and old, and she had come to the conclusion that having no couch at all was better than having this couch.

She knew because it was her couch that she woke up on, plopped right in the middle of Martin's dark paneled living room.

In complete disbelief, Lucy laughed disgustedly and shook her head. *Well, this is a nasty trick,* she thought. *Par for the course. You have got to be kidding me.* She had almost fully convinced herself that she'd be assigned to Alice and she had gotten her hopes up. She should have known that death was going to be a little bit more unaccommodating than that, a little more sneaky than placing Lucy in the spot where she could really do the most good. And to just plop her on the couch was almost snotty. She'd thought at least she'd have a chance to say goodbye to her classmates, particularly Bethanny, and to say thank you to Ruby. But nope. They'd just thrown her ghost ass out on the sofa and left her. Somebody obviously thought they knew better. When Ruby had mentioned that they would find out what their assignments were in the morning, Lucy had hardly thought it would be because she would simply wake up in it.

I just can't believe it, Lucy thought, and snickered sarcastically, feeling astoundingly betrayed. *What the hell am I doing here? I'm supposed to be doing* good *here? For Martin?* Martin, the most reliable, sensible, plainspoken man on the face of the earth? Martin, who'd never needed a helping hand from anyone the entire time she had known him? Martin, Mr. Point A to Point B? Martin, who had kicked her out of their house without one single word of explanation? You mean the man who hadn't bothered to even show his face at her funeral?

"This is just a nightmare," Lucy spat angrily at no one. She was gritting her teeth together when she heard a spastic snore erupt from the other end of the couch. Looking toward the sound, she couldn't help but instantly smile when she heard another snort and saw Tulip, who lay curled up and snoozing at her feet.

"Tulip," Lucy whispered. "Tulip!"

The sleeping dog twitched a little, and Lucy hoped that Ruby was right—that some animals could sense, see, and hear spirits. She reached over and tickled the bottom of Tulip's hind paw, and the dog automatically flinched and pulled it back. Lucy smiled again, knowing Tulip had felt her. Lucy scratched the dog's belly lightly, just enough to touch the dog's fur without pressing too hard and falling through. Within several moments, Tulip's eyes began to flutter and she opened them slowly, glancing over at the owner of the wonderful hand that was delivering such a delightful belly rub. She raised her head slightly, simply peering over, and then in one sudden, momentous movement, she was leaping toward Lucy with tail wagging and excited, happy pants.

"Oh, my sweet girl," Lucy said as she scratched both sides of Tulip's face, trying to be careful. With a sudden jerk, the dog passed right through her arm and then pounced through Lucy's torso.

"You goofball!" Lucy laughed, gloriously happy to see her best friend again. "I have missed you so much! So much! Have you been a good girl? Huh? Huh? You're always a good girl, my little sweetheart. How I have missed you!"

By Tulip's exuberant response of licks meant for Lucy's face that passed into thin air, and her continued prancing, Lucy knew that Tulip had missed her, too. It seemed like a thousand years had passed since she had said goodbye to her friend through the plate glass window of the living room as the sun was setting and it was getting dark.

"I'm sorry I didn't come to get you," Lucy apologized. The smile in the dog's eyes made Lucy want to melt. "But I told you I'd come back, and see? I did!"

Lucy swore that Tulip was smiling. The dog tried to lick her face again, and got even more excited when Lucy laughed.

"Tulip! What's going on in there?" Lucy heard someone call from the kitchen. "Come on, girl. You need to go outside?"

It was Martin. Lucy had hoped he wouldn't be awake yet so she would have just a little bit of time to get a handle on being back in this house before she had to see him. It was still somewhat dark. Only slivers of sunlight had begun to break through the windows.

With the promise of a venture outside, Tulip leapt off the couch and headed for the hallway, then stopped and looked behind her, just to make sure Lucy was coming, too.

"I'm coming, I'm coming," Lucy reassured her as she got up from the couch, half expecting to hear the spring pop back up, and a little surprised when she didn't. She suddenly realized she smelled coffee; it had been such a long time since she had even thought about coffee, let alone smelled it. Used to be every morning she wouldn't even be able to speak until she'd had at least half a cup, infused with two teaspoons of sugar and a huge gulp of vanilla Coffee-mate. Now the smell of coffee was familiar but distant, almost like a waft of cigarette smoke to someone who had kicked the habit.

Lucy padded into the hallway after her dog until Tulip was a step away from the entryway of the kitchen and stopped. Again, Tulip turned around to make sure Lucy was behind her, and when she saw Lucy still in the hallway, she gave a tiny whine.

"All right, all right," Martin said, and Lucy heard the scrape of his chair scooting back along the linoleum floor. "Hang on, Miss Tulip. I'm comin'."

And then, suddenly, there was Martin as he passed right before Lucy to let Tulip out the back door, his closely cropped flattop still neatly buzzed, his ruddy cheeks still rosy and vibrant. He was wearing the robe Lucy had bought him for Christmas the year before, a blue and cream plaid flannel with navy piping. Lucy had always thought it looked nice on him, and she saw that it still did. It made him look warm and dependable, like the Martin she thought she had known.

Coffee cup in hand, Martin shuffled to the back door and opened it for Tulip, who kept hesitating and looking back. She would start to go through the door, then pull back, looking to see if Lucy was coming, too.

"Go on," Lucy whispered, waving her fingertips forward in an effort to let the dog know she was okay.

"Go on, Tulip," Martin said, half laughing. "In or out? What are you looking at? Did you forget a bone back there?"

Martin turned and headed down the hall, and within three steps, he was there, right next to Lucy, who had pressed herself up against the wall.

"I don't see anything," he concluded as he searched the floor with his eyes, then flipped on the hall light. Lucy winced, convinced he could see her. "Nope. There's nothing here, Tuly."

He turned the light off, headed back to the kitchen, and gently scooted the dog outside with his hand on her fanny. "Just go potty and you can come right back in," he coaxed. Tulip obliged, and with one final look back, she went out the back door, which Martin then closed.

Still in the hall, Lucy leaned against the wall as she watched him refill his coffee from a coffeemaker she had bought on sale at Penney's right after they had moved in together. It made terrible coffee, and the handle had broken off from the lip of the glass pot within a week of her buying it. By then, she had lost the receipt, couldn't return it, and was stuck with it. Which was fine. Martin didn't mind. He'd just click it back into place and watch it spring off midway as he was pouring, which would leave a little coffee spill every time.

Martin shuffled over to the kitchen table and sat back down in the aluminum chair, made to look like a vintage fifties diner set with curved corners and red plastic upholstery that boasted glitter in it if you looked hard enough. Lucy moved to the opposite wall of the hallway so she could see him.

He looked fine, she noticed. He looked regular. He still looked just like Martin. Nothing had changed about him, not one thing. Everything about Lucy had changed, including her "alive" status, but Martin, he was a constant. He did not look like a man who had thrown his wife-to-be out of the house without explanation, and he certainly did not look like a man who had thrown his wife-to-be out of the house without explanation and had then heard that she'd been shoved by the hand of destiny into a smack down with a stupid city bus.

Not at all.

Maybe it was in his eyes, Lucy thought. Maybe that's where his regrets lived. That's where they had to be. She decided she needed to see his face close-up, and when she did, it would all make sense to her. She would suddenly understand why Martin had made the decision that he had and that had led to Lucy becoming a Casper, and if it even mattered to him at all.

Lucy stepped from the hallway into the kitchen, stood in front of the stove for a moment, and then saw her move. She slipped into the diner chair next to Martin at the table, where he was reading the morning newspaper.

She cupped her hands underneath her chin and waited for him to notice her, notice anything, to even feel the slightest bit of something. But he didn't. He went on reading the paper, his eyes focused on the print, not even remotely aware that dead Lucy was mere inches from him and wanting to communicate from beyond the grave, or urn, or mayonnaise jar, or whatever.

"Martin," she said aloud.

Nothing. No response. He kept reading, uninterrupted, then turned the page.

"MARTIN," she said louder, but again, there was no answer, not a hint of indication that he'd heard anything.

She raised her hand up and flicked the corner of his paper, which did bend and tremble, but nothing more, and with a response flick of the paper, he straightened it back out again. Then Lucy took a deep breath and blew, blew straight at him, straight at his face, determined to get him to look at her.

She could see by a slight startle that he had felt it, and he shuddered slightly. He put the paper down, got up from his chair, and walked over to the back door, which he found completely closed. He glanced back over to the kitchen table with a somewhat puzzled look on his face, and a moment later heard Tulip scratching the other side of the door.

"MARTIN!" Lucy yelled as loudly as she could this time, and as Tulip trotted into the house, he looked back toward the living room and replied, "YES?"

He'd heard her. He'd actually heard her. And had answered her.

Lucy giggled with delight. Maybe this wasn't going to be that bad of a gig after all. This could actually turn out to be a lot of fun, haunting the crap out of Martin, especially now that she knew he would reply to phantom voices. *Poor Martin,* Lucy thought, still giggling, *he's been living alone for too long.*

He paused for a moment, listened intently, then asked, "YES?" again, this time louder.

"What?" another voice called out from another part of the house. "Did you say something?"

Another voice. A female voice. A voice Lucy swore she knew. Perhaps it was Martin's mother or sister who might be visiting, helping him through this difficult time. Of course he couldn't be alone, Lucy realized. That would be really hard after what had happened. Hopefully. After she'd gone, after she'd died. Lucy was sure Martin had to feel terrible about it. Who wouldn't? It made sense to her that he would have someone come and stay with him until time got around to healing things, and Lucy found herself almost feeling bad for him. She was feeling a bit sorry she had doubted his ability to mourn. No one would want to do that alone. *Look at him,* she said to herself. *He's wearing the robe I bought him. It must be symbolic. He's holding on to the pieces of me that he has left.*

Tulip padded over and sat next to Lucy, and she gently patted the dog's head.

"Did you say something?" Lucy heard again, this time much clearer and louder, and then suddenly another figure was in the kitchen, the figure of a woman in a white, fluffy robe and wearing matching fluffy slippers. Lucy saw only the back of her.

In the dimly lit kitchen, she saw the figure reach over and put her arms around Martin's neck, and then kiss him on the cheek.

"Why are you wearing that old thing?" the woman said, picking up the collar of the blue plaid robe. "I thought you got rid of this."

"Nah, nah," Martin replied, shaking his head. "It's a good robe, nice and not too warm. Comes in handy, especially on a morning like this when it's starting to get warm. I felt a chill this morning, gave me goose bumps. I thought I had left the door open, but I guess it's just the cold weather coming in."

Warm weather? Lucy was puzzled. Spring right around the corner? When Lucy had walked out in front of the bus, it had already been spring. It had been a beautiful, brilliant day. How much time had gone by, she wondered. Just how long had she been dead?

"Oh, just toss it," the woman said, kissing Martin again. "I'll buy you a new one. And then it will be from me, and not *her.*"

That's a lot of kissing for a sister, Lucy thought. *That's a lot of kissing even for a mother. Kind of gross for either one, to tell the truth. And what's this "her" business? Let him remember me the way he wants to remember me, for crying out loud. No need to get pushy. And let the man go,* she wanted to shout. *You're hanging off him like an orangutan! Sister, mother, whomever. He's a man, not a jungle gym.*

And, as if on command, the woman dropped her arms and grabbed an empty coffee mug from the cabinet. She poured herself a cup from Lucy's broken coffeemaker, spilled a little onto the countertop, and began walking toward the table. Lucy quickly scrambled up out of the seat and wedged herself next to the refrigerator to get out of the way.

And as the woman neared the kitchen table and the light hanging over it, Lucy saw that she was not Martin's sister.

It was not Martin's mother.

About to sit down in Lucy's seat next to Lucy's dog and drink coffee from what was probably Lucy's mug, was Nola.

chapter twelve The Big Reveal

Nola liked stupid TV.

For two days, Lucy had been anchored on the itchy sofa with the office manager who had gotten her fired and was now living in Lucy's house. They sat watching mind-numbing television shows full of people getting makeovers, getting face-lifts, or having their homes redone or renovated as a result of social mockery, having a crush on a guy at work who didn't notice, or having a medical malady that was so serious that only a grand piano and some framed posters could fix it. Nola especially liked the episodes in which women got dental work or were awarded some sort of facial implant for their suffering. Episodes in which, upon the big reveal, the accountant, who'd never noticed the victim before, now suddenly did, thus guaranteeing courtship, marriage, and a litter of offspring with unfortunate bone structure. What Nola couldn't watch on live television she recorded, and was able to bring up with the push of a couple of buttons on the remote. Mr. Basic Cable, it seemed, had upgraded his viewing possibilities to the status of infinite.

It's not that Lucy was surprised that Nola was a champion of causes such as buckteeth or chipped teeth, weak chins, and scoliosis, but what was amazing was just how much of the schlock she could watch while still craving more.

When it came to the plight of the orally malformed or spinally challenged, Nola was insatiable, especially if they were getting their makeup professionally done or were on the receiving end of a new house with angel wallpaper and a hot tub.

And Lucy, unfortunately, sat there right alongside her. It wasn't that Lucy wanted to watch these shows or be within a thousand-mile radius of Nola, but she really didn't have a choice. The 1950s ranch house was small, and the available options of where Lucy could spend her off-duty ghost time were rather limited. She could hang out in the living room, where Nola was much of the time; in the kitchen, where Nola was when she wasn't in the living room; in the bathroom, where Lucy could very well be trapped should Nola barge in and then do something unholy; in Martin's "hobby room," which was packed with camping and fishing equipment; or in her old bedroom, which was no option at all. Much to Lucy's dismay, she'd arrived on a Saturday, and after Martin had scooted off to work, it had been Nola's humanitarian duty to tune in to every corporate-sponsored tale of woe, tragedy, and overbites that had been televised that week, and Lucy, frankly, had had no choice but to join in.

She had quickly realized that the days of spooks and specters were long, drawn-out affairs, full of watching people conduct their intricately boring lives and not having any control over her own time. If she wanted to flip through a magazine on the table, she'd have to wait until the living left the house, much like if she wanted to watch TV on her own, or play with the dog. There was only so much spooking one ghost could do in a day's time; while it might be fun to flicker the lights or turn on the alarm clock at 3 A.M., self-control was key. Too much tinkering might have disastrous results, and Lucy knew she had to pace herself. It was no wonder that some ghosts went mad and started carrying their heads like purses simply to scare the living for the sake of a cheap thrill; thrills and excitement or the mere task of even being occupied were all too hard to come by when you observed but didn't exist. She could go for a walk around the neighborhood, but that was about it; in the suburban sprawl that was this town, anything remotely interesting, like a movie theater, was miles away, and Lucy had no idea what the bus schedule was, let alone her newfound bus-related terror. She was, in a sense, stuck in limbo. She actually found herself yearning for the days back at ghost school, where at least she could interact with others. But being dead in a real-life environment was some excruciatingly boring stuff, with a whole lot of nothing to do. Plus, it was fairly safe to say that in her two days' time back at the house, Lucy still had not figured out why she'd been placed there or what her objective was supposed to be.

However, Lucy had already arrived at the conclusion that once she unleashed her wrath, it would all come raining down on Nola, Nola, Nola. She did her best to distance herself from what was right before her eyes—Nola living in *her* house with *her* boyfriend and *her* dog. *Nola living her life*. The thought of it made Lucy nauseous, furious, vengeful. Lucy had to stop herself from thinking the obvious questions and trying to figure out the answers, because it was all too much. She knew she couldn't take it. But every thirty seconds or so, Lucy glanced over at Nola, sniffling on the couch because a little boy with no bones got a bunk bed in his new bedroom, and she wanted to kick Nola like she had kicked the chair at her funeral. Nola was deserving of it, so deserving. But Lucy did something else instead. As the little boy was being carried into his new bedroom painted with racing stripes and bold, empowering colors, as soon as he crossed the threshold, Lucy simply reached over and pushed the power button on the remote.

While a cloud of blackness swallowed the TV screen, Nola shrieked as if a surgeon had just rammed a six-inch needle under her kneecap. Nola fumbled for the remote, tried to recapture the precious moment of highest emotional exploitation that she had desperately been waiting for.

How did this even happen? Lucy said to herself as she shook her head. She couldn't help but wonder. *How did this pairing even come about, how does it even make sense? Seriously. This is what Martin replaced me with? Nola? And no one stopped it?*

Over the last couple of days, she had observed them as a couple, had tried to figure it out, had watched their interactions, and she still didn't have a clue. Martin was still Martin, simple, self-sufficient, matter-of-fact. Nola was fawning, overachieving, annoying in her inconsequential details.

"Oh! Oh! Oh! Don't eat yet, Martin! I put the fork in the wrong spot. Let me fix that!"

Or:

"There's too much salt in these instant potatoes, Martin. Too much salt! I have to watch my sodium. I'm never buying this brand again."

Or:

"I am covered in Tulip fur. I've just given up on wearing any dark colors at all. And that's terrible, because purple is my color. People have always said that."

Or:

"Oh, you're already watching something? I'm sure it will be better than the show I've been waiting to watch all week about the girl who lost both eyeteeth in a softball accident and is getting a makeover and a new wardrobe so she can learn how to camouflage her thick hips. But I'm sure your show will be good, too. I guess."

Lucy could barely stand it. It was all she could do to not plug herself into the fridge and then try to tip it over on the office manager in the middle of dinner.

But she couldn't do that, because that was not her mission, and if she didn't complete her mystery objective, she'd be stuck in this house with Nola and Martin until she could eventually see through them, too.

Then Lucy had a terrible thought. What if this was not a new pairing? What if this had not spontaneously happened post-Lucy? What if Nola was the reason why Lucy had found her stuff on the sidewalk? What if this was the reason Lucy had lost her job, because it had all been set up from the beginning? If Lucy could have felt ill, she would have, but instead, she waited until Nola left the room for another snack, and when she was officially out of sight, Lucy kicked her Pepsi can over, completely soaking her treasured arsenal of ladies' magazines with the rushing sticky sweet soda.

If Nola had possessed a finer ear, she would have heard Lucy laughing heartily when she saw her nemesis's face after she walked back into the living room and discovered the mess, and then she would have heard the laughter abruptly stop when Nola scowled, turned, and huffed, "Oh, Tulip! Bad dog! Bad dog! You are not worth the trouble, and *you are trouble*!"

Lucy reached down to where Tulip sat loyally at her feet, and scratched the good dog's head.

"Don't listen to her. You're a good girl, Tulip," Lucy reassured her, but Tulip didn't look so sure.

"Bad dog!" Nola snipped again, pointing her nasty finger at Tulip. Then she returned to mopping up the runny mess with the napkin she'd pulled from the collar of her shirt, where she'd already had it tucked in from snacking.

Lucy sneered at her. *What you have coming,* she thought as she shook her head. *Oh, what you have coming, dear Nola.*

Thankfully, Nola returned to work on Monday, and Lucy had the run of the house. She was free to do what she pleased, and the sense of freedom was a tremendous relief. No longer being trapped by Nola's presence was delightful, and Lucy was not bothered by Martin's days off, just like when she'd been alive. That was because Martin rarely took any time off, and when he did, you could count on him to have his tackle box in the cab of his truck by 6 A.M., next to a steaming mug of coffee as he pulled out of the driveway.

Lucy had the days to herself and her dog, but she still felt rather limited. She knew it was wise to stay in the house rather than venture out with Tulip, even though there was nothing more that she wanted to do than take her for a walk. Once, she was staring out the window and saw a dog come trotting along, no leash, no harness, just as free as a bird. A couple of paces behind was its owner, bringing up the rear and smiling. From that distance, it had been difficult for Lucy to see if the person was outlined with a shine, and Lucy had wondered if the person was real, flesh and blood, alive, or if the owner was like her, weightless and earthbound. Instead, Lucy and Tulip played ball in the living room, hide-and-seek, and Lucy gave Tulip little doggie massages, which Tulip greatly enjoyed and which caused her floppy tongue to loll out of her mouth. When Nola and Martin arrived home at the end of the day, Lucy simply stayed as far away from them as she could, which she knew was not helping her mission any. The whole scenario simply disgusted her, and she thought the best way to deal with it—for now—was to simply remove herself from what little interaction they had with each other.

At night, Lucy made peace with the couch or roamed restlessly through the house. She had been back for less than a week, and already the days and nights were beginning to blur into one another as if she was a hostage. Although she liked the idea of "falling asleep" at nighttime, it was simply a ritual she felt comfortable with more than anything she got a benefit from. She never felt tired or sleepy, never felt the aches and pains of the day creep up on her at night the way she had before city-bus impact. Curling up on the sofa or in her little ghost school Super 8 bed was nothing more than a link to her former life, something that had been the only constant between life and death, aside from the clothes she'd entered the big sleep in.

Now quite dead, Lucy realized that there were far more hours in the day when there was nothing to do, nowhere to be, and no one to talk to. Martin had been quite thorough in picking through their belongings and culling her stuff, it had become apparent. There was nothing left of Lucy in the house—not a picture on the wall, not one of her books, none of her music, nothing. He had even replaced the calendar she had bought at the beginning of the year and tacked up in the kitchen. She had singled out important dates, such as their birthdays; Lucy's Hawaiian vacation; her return date, including the flight number and time; the date of their wedding, writing little notes for each date. Even that, apparently, was too much of Lucy for Martin to tolerate. The calendar was gone, replaced by a free one from AAA. He really had eradicated her from everything, Lucy noted as she scoured the bookshelves, magazine rack, and even the pantry.

"Hmmmm," Lucy said out loud to Tulip as she peeked at the shelves of food on one of her first days alone in what used to be her house. "Tons of Little Debbies, but not an Oreo in sight. But look, here are some cookies for you!"

After pulling some energy from the fridge, she grabbed the box, noticing they were the generic store brand and not Tulip's favorite kind of liver snaps, which Lucy had always made sure to have on hand for her. She held out the store-brand biscuit to Tulip, who simply sniffed it and then turned her head.

"I'm sorry," she said as she ruffled the dog's head with her hand. "*My* snacks are gone, too."

Lucy heard a clanking noise and then a loud thud in the living room, and she recognized that familiar racket of the mail being delivered through the slot in the front door. Lucy motioned Tulip to follow her as she made her way to the living room to commence with Lucy's newfound best part of the day—going through the magazines, ads, and bills of the daily delivery of mail. It wasn't snooping, she decided. The dead can't snoop. And besides, even if it was snooping, who was she going to tell? In just several days' time, Lucy had discovered some fascinating things about her hosts: that they were planning a tropical cruise, based on the pamphlets and advertisements that were delivered; that Nola had a three-year subscription to *Homemakers* magazine; and that she had allowed her membership to Totally Ladies! gym to lapse. It was amazing, Lucy thought, the things you can gather just from a tumble of mail that you can't even open.

And then she saw something she hadn't expected.

It was a letter, addressed to her. Lucy Fisher. It wasn't anything dire, just a letter from a wildlife organization asking for a donation and offering some free return address labels as a gift. As Lucy stared at the name on the envelope, she realized that she was feeling something she hadn't experienced for a while. She felt sort of alive. She felt alive at the thought that someone out there believed her to be alive. Alive enough to write them a check, anyway. That letter, there on the floor, was hers. It was addressed to her. And she wanted it. She had basically no possessions, only what she'd been wearing when she'd died. She had not one other single thing. Not that she needed anything; she didn't, which was a definite checkmark in the "pro" column of not having a pulse, but she wanted this. A letter and some labels that were for Lucy Fisher. She needed this something that said, that proved, she had been here. That she had lived. There wasn't even a body left to prove that.

Lucy searched for the remote and turned on the TV. She waited a minute or two until it was fully on, had stopped flickering, and had a full, complete screen. Then she took ahold of both corners on top and pulled, pulled, pulled, pulled up so much power that the screen began to flicker with weakness. After Lucy felt charged enough, she grabbed her letter and opened it, poring over all of the little rectangular stickers with her name on them, each embellished with picture of a wolf, polar bear, or baby seal in one corner. She sort of liked the stickers and was a little sorry that she didn't need them for anything, but they still made her feel lively. Lucy scanned the room for a good place to hide the letter. She was limited by what she could do physically, so she couldn't be terribly elaborate by taping it behind a china cabinet or shoving it under a heavy mattress. But upon another look, she thought she had found something equally as effective in the hiding department: under the cushion of the stinky burlap couch. With one flip, the battered cushion was up and the letter was safe, nestled in secrecy and surrounded by stench.

Lucy was quite pleased with herself, and had plopped down on the exact cushion to cement the deal when she heard the doorbell ring. She panicked. She could feel that she still had quite a bit of charge left, and was terrified that someone would see her bouncing all over the dilapidated couch in all of her visible glory. Quickly, she scurried off the couch and scrambled behind it, hoping that whoever was at the front door hadn't been doing a little pre-doorbell spying through the window.

The doorbell rang again, and this time, Tulip got up and went to the door, then rang out her own small but determined bark.

"Oh, just go away," Lucy whispered at the unwanted intruder, who was now effectively bothering her.

But Lucy's wishes were of no consequence to the visitor, who then decided that since ringing the doorbell was not effective, banging on the front door just might be. This, however, dully irritated Tulip, whose small bark generated to much louder on the second round.

"Oh, come on!" a voice called out sternly. "I know you are in there! Open this damn door! Open it now!"

Lucy panicked. They must have seen her. She hoped it wasn't a neighbor, or relative, or someone that had mistaken her for Nola. The mere thought made Lucy shiver. She shrank down even farther behind the couch, trying to mold herself into a neat little invisible ball.

"All right, that's it!" the voice outside warned. "I'm coming in!"

Oh, no, Lucy thought. *Shit. This is someone with a key, and there is no place I can go where they won't see me. I'm at almost a full charge and I don't know how to drain! How do I drain? How do I become, at the very least, transparent or wisps of smoke?*

"Lucy!" the voice called, shocking her and sucking in all of her attention. "We're coming in!"

And right through the front door marched Ruby Spicer, complete with her heavy, dark monkish robe, and by the looks of things, she had brought some friends.

chapter thirteen Three's a Ghostly Crowd

"Lucy?" Ruby called out after she had marched right through the front door and into the living room, a collection of figures behind her on the other side of the door. "LUCY! I don't have time to play games, you know!"

"Ruby?" Lucy called excitedly as she rolled out from behind the couch and scrambled to her feet. "Wow! I am so happy to see you! Did you come to get me? I knew there had been a mistake! Am I going to Alice's now?"

Ruby laughed a little and shook her head. "I have a bigger surprise than that," she said, and then motioned behind her. *"Come on in!"*

Lucy watched in amazement as three figures took several steps, passing right through the front door, and stood alongside Ruby. On her right was a tall, lanky man of indeterminate age who slumped slightly at the shoulders; next to him was a dour-looking woman wearing a black Victorian dress complete with bustle, her hair pulled tightly back into a bun; and on the other side of Ruby was a smaller figure, clad in what Lucy could clearly recognize as the same Ethereal White Lady gown that Bethanny had chosen. She was a tiny, wrinkled old lady with short, cropped white hair. She had deep creases around her eyes, which looked kind but also twinkled with just a touch of fire. These were eyes that Lucy knew, and that Lucy loved.

"Naunie!" Lucy gasped as she rushed to the old woman, scooping all of her white lady finery up into her arms. Naunie responded with a firm, taut hug that signaled just how long-awaited the reunion was.

"Lucy," her grandmother whispered in her ear. "Oh, Lucy!"

"Oh, I missed you!" Lucy whispered back. "What are you doing here? Why aren't you in The State?"

"Well," Lucy's grandmother said as she pulled out of the hug and took a long, earnest look at her granddaughter. "You know, that's a long story."

"No, it's not," the tall, lanky man said, looking a little perturbed.

"Mind your own business, Howe," Naunie said, shooting him a dirty look. "You don't know everything."

"Howe?" Lucy asked. "My Uncle Howe? I know who you are! You died in that combine accident when I was a little kid!"

Uncle Howe's face melted into a huge, wide, nearly proud grin. "Why, yes, I did," he said sheepishly. "Chopped me up like egg salad."

"Well, when you stick your idiot hand up into those mowers, what do you think is gonna happen?" Naunie confirmed.

"Am I related to you, too?" Lucy asked the stern-looking Victorian woman. "Are you my great-great-great-grandmother? This is so exciting! It's like being a Mormon but without ruffles and tithing!"

"No," Naunie answered quite flatly. "She is not a Fisher. Her name is Geneva Franks. I don't even know why she's here. She needs to mind her own business, too."

"That is a blatant lie, Clovis," Geneva Franks staunchly replied, boring angry eyes into Naunie. "You have endangered the status of my eternal existence. That is every bit my business."

"A little push wouldn't kill you!" Naunie shot back, not minding her manners at all. "You've been stuck in the same rut since before Abraham Lincoln died!"

"Clovie," Ruby sternly interrupted. "Is this necessary? Is it? I have a fresh batch of Surprise Demisers attending their funerals today. We need to get this thing settled up and figured out now. Time is of the essence."

"She's an interloper!" Naunie shot back. "She and Howe just want that house for themselves! Three's a crowd, I'm telling you. Three is definitely a crowd, and now because these two have eyes for each other, I'm getting kicked out of my own house!"

"It was my house *first,*" Geneva asserted firmly.

"I'm very confused," Lucy said, trying to make sense of the bickering. "I don't think I understand what's going on. What are we settling?"

"Clovie has been reassigned," Ruby tried to explain. "There was an incident at the farmhouse, and Howe and Geneva feel it is urgent that we remove her from the situation."

"It was more than one incident," Geneva commented.

"And I wouldn't call them 'incidents,'" Howe chimed in. "They were more like the final scenes from horror movies."

Naunie scoffed and rolled her eyes.

"They were destroying my house," she retorted as she threw her tiny gauzy arms up. "What did you expect me to do? They were ripping out my pink toilet! Do you know how much I paid for that?"

"My house was the first in the county to have indoor plumbing," Geneva reminded Naunie. "And I didn't go berserk when you pulled out that cast-iron claw-foot bathtub, threw it away, and replaced it with that terrible pink atrocity!"

"You had a hundred years with that rusted old hulk of metal," Naunie argued. "My toilet was beautiful, sleek, and modern!"

"Sure, it was modern," Howe agreed. "In 1956! I kind of liked the toilet they were putting in. It looked like someplace you could sit awhile, relax."

"Okay," Lucy interrupted. "Let me get this straight—the people who live in the farmhouse now—"

"The people *you* sold it to," Naunie interjected, "are very busy destroying it."

"They're remodeling," Ruby explained. "And Clovie was very upset at losing her pink toilet."

"All this fuss over a *chamber pot,*" Geneva said, giving Naunie a look of disgust. "And you say *I'm* in a rut!"

"Either way, she went a little overboard in expressing her opinion of the new bathroom," Ruby went on. "To the point where professionals have been called in."

"Professional remodelers?" Lucy questioned.

"No," Ruby said quickly. "Professional presence house cleaners. As in cleaning out the spirits that may be lingering around."

"You are all making a big deal out of nothing," Naunie objected. "So I did a little spooking, big deal. They took my pink toilet and sink out and threw them away, like they were trash! They ripped out my brand-new brown carpet and took down the gold drapes. Of course I'm upset!"

"That brown carpet wasn't new, Naunie. I learned to crawl on it," Lucy reminded her.

"And now you know how I felt when you pulled out my cast-iron claw-foot bathtub and replaced it with a nozzle that spits water out of the wall, and covered up my wood floors with that dusty carpet," Geneva added. "But did I ever hiss in your ear in the middle of the night? Did I ever open and close the door to the bathroom when the living were in there having their private time? NO, I did not, and I've existed with your decorating for half a century now. And I will not get pulled into the white light because of you, Clovis Fisher. I will not."

"Maybe if you had hissed in my ear you wouldn't have been stuck in that old farmhouse for all of eternity," Naunie shot back. "Maybe if you would have been the least bit active, you could have met your objective and been sewing a quilt or churning butter or milking a dead cow or whatever nineteenth-century farm women do in The State. I may be getting kicked out of my own house, but at least I was a real ghost!"

"You mind your own business!" Geneva said, pointing a cross finger at Naunie. "You don't know anything about that. One minute I was dead, and then the next thing I knew, it was 1918 and everyone else in the house got the flu and died, and I was out of an objective! I was stuck and lonely until Howe came, and now we're getting along just fine, thank you!"

"I've only been here for a matter of days and I'm already bored beyond belief," Lucy admitted. "I don't know how you roamed around alone for all those years. You were both in the house the whole time I was growing up. Why haven't you moved on, Uncle Howe? Why aren't you in The State by now?"

"Well, I'm just kind of used to it now, I guess," he answered. "Besides, it hasn't been that long."

"You've been dead for twenty-plus years," Lucy informed him.

He shook his head and laughed at her. "Are you sure?" her uncle questioned. "It doesn't feel that long. Nah, feels like a couple of months! Twenty years! Who're you foolin'?"

"Well," Lucy said with a shrug, "it's been long enough for me to grow up, get a job, almost get married, and then get smashed by a bus."

Uncle Howe thought for a moment, then nodded.

"Even if it has been that long, I'm good where I am," he decided. "I know where I am, and if I moved on, I wouldn't know where I was going. Clovie was in The State, but that sure didn't last long."

"Really?" Lucy exclaimed, turning back to Naunie. "You were there? What was it like? What did you do? Why didn't you stay?"

Lucy's grandmother sort of shrugged and then looked away.

"Sometimes, things don't take, not even in The State, and they need to be readjusted," Ruby began to explain. "Clovie was slotted for The State, and did stay there for a while until she was reassigned. The first time. And that's how I met Clovie, and how she came to be in my class."

"Naunie was your student?" Lucy asked excitedly. "Really? Why didn't you tell me?"

"Oh, I had no idea," Ruby answered. "I get very little history on my students. Name, cause of death, and just how freshly they have expired. I really don't need much more than that."

"Naunie, what was The State like?" Lucy asked again. "Why didn't you stay?"

"Hell if I know. They zapped me," the old lady said, slapping the top of her head. "I don't remember a thing."

"I have a feeling I'm not getting the whole story here," Lucy said to everyone. "Who can tell me what happened? Was she sent there by mistake, was her place not ready, what?"

Naunie didn't say a word, just looked around the room as if no one was talking to her.

This continued for several long, silly seconds until Ruby jumped in.

"Clovie was expunged. There are several rules of conduct in

The State—there have to be to ensure its status and quality of being. They are minor, simple issues, and typically, there is never a problem and people abide by the guidelines. However, there was an issue Clovie had difficulty with."

"She tried to slaughter one of the ark animals, didn't she?" Lucy guessed.

"No," Ruby replied.

"Did she complain that the harp music was too loud and flowery?"

"No," Ruby said again.

"Did she blow her nose on one of her Ethereal White Lady sleeves?" Lucy took another shot.

"Repeatedly, but everyone tried to ignore that," Ruby answered. "The issue was regarding a disturbance."

"A what?" Lucy asked Naunie. "What kind of disturbance? Who did you disturb?"

"Who *didn't* she disturb was more like it," Uncle Howe commented, to which Geneva simply shook her sorrowful head. "People were hiding from her."

"People were *not* hiding from me!" Naunie objected. "How can you say such a thing?"

"Frank Sinatra!" Uncle Howe yelled. "Frank Sinatra was hiding from you. You wouldn't leave the man alone! We read it in the report when you got shipped back to us! Asking that man to sing 'The Lady Is a Tramp' over and over again. The man had no choice but to hide. And poor Steve McQueen, constantly begging him to take you for a ride on his motorcycle. That is shameful, Clovie, just shameful! People have their deaths to live, you know."

"Don't act so surprised!" Naunie countered. "You saw *The Great Escape*! He just looked so . . . so damn *salty*! I just wanted to grab that boy and hold on tight!"

"I can't believe you stalked Frank Sinatra and Steve McQueen to the point that you got expelled from all eternity," Lucy said.

"Oh, no," Uncle Howe continued. "That's not what got her the boot. When she got wind that Paul Newman was coming to town, so to speak, she lost her mind and decided she was going to be the first one to greet him. The very second that poor man stepped foot into The State, what did your grandmother do?"

"I'm afraid to ask," Lucy said quietly.

"She screamed, 'Take your shirt off, lie down, and I'll feed you fifty eggs!'" Geneva finished. "I don't even know who Paul Newman is, but that is not a siren's call I think anyone's ears would welcome."

"I'm not ashamed." Naunie shrugged. "I have a thing for blue eyes."

"So," Ruby picked up, "Clovie was relegated back to ghost status and was placed back at her farmhouse, but as you can tell, things have not been going very well over there and we have reached a crisis point. To avoid a white light situation, it's been decided that she should be relocated here, with you."

"That's wonderful," Lucy cried, and embraced Naunie. "I'm so happy you'll be haunting with me."

"You two," Ruby said, wiggling her finger back and forth between them, "had better take care. And watch yourselves. Do you remember, Lucy, when you kicked the chair and I told you I had only seen one other ghost do that without extensive training?"

Lucy nodded.

"Here she is," Ruby said, pointing to Naunie, who sheepishly grinned. "Her genes must be strong. They've surpassed even death. Watch out, the both of you, and don't get into too much trouble, you hear? I don't want to have to come back here again!"

They both nodded accordingly.

"All right, then," Ruby concluded. "I'll expect you to behave. It was very good to see you again, Lucy. Get your job done quickly. Move outta here."

And with that, she turned to go.

"Wait," Lucy said, almost in a panic. "What *is* my job? I just woke up here. I have no idea what I'm supposed to be doing. I didn't get an instruction sheet or anything. What do I need to be doing to get out of here?"

"Oh," Ruby said, her eyes widening. "I have no idea, Lucy, just like I told you on the last day of school. I don't decide that. Other forces do. Sometimes, I think, the purpose might be rather obvious, but all assignments are different. It may take some time for you to figure out why you're here."

"There has to be a better answer than that!" Lucy scoffed. "Nothing happens here. She watches TV, he works. That's it. I don't want to be stuck here forever, trying to figure it out."

"Oh, dear, you won't be," Ruby reassured her. "Whatever it is that you're supposed to do will present itself. Hopefully."

"Goodbye, Clovie," Uncle Howe said as he put a hand on Naunie's shoulder. "Maybe I'll see you sometime."

"Aw, Howe," Naunie said, patting his hand. "You always did like older women. You hated it when I butchered aged livestock."

Uncle Howe turned and followed Ruby to the front door, as did Geneva, but not before she leaned in quickly and hissed, "You are a menace!"

"You're older than the wood of my coffin," Naunie spat back. "You've been dead five lifetimes over!"

That sparked something in Lucy, and without knowing it, she reached forward toward her old teacher.

"Ruby!" she called out, and the hooded figure stopped and turned back around.

"The calendar is different in the kitchen," she said, pointing behind her. "And Tulip has more gray on her face than I remember, and it's just starting to get warm again."

Ruby raised her eyebrows, but didn't say anything.

"It was just getting warm when this all started," Lucy explained. "How long has it been? Because I didn't think it had been that long, but . . ."

Ruby paused and smiled, then took the hand that had reached out for her robe.

"It's been nearly a year, Lucy," she said softly. "You've been dead almost a year."

Lucy stopped for a moment, looking shocked, and then nodded, attempting to take it all in.

Ruby patted her hand in a series of light, quick little taps.

"I know you're on your way to being a great ghost," she said, and she smiled. "And I'm betting you were a great girl. You will find what you're looking for, Lucy."

Lucy was puzzled by that last comment, even after Ruby had pulled her hand away, turned around, and walked right through the front door, followed by Uncle Howe and Geneva.

Lucy waved goodbye, and then proceeded to give Naunie a grand tour of a house that was no longer hers.

"I am so bored," Naunie whined as she sat next to Lucy at the end of the sofa with the overzealous spring. Nola sat on the other end, the television blaring, and tears getting ready to spill from her eyes. "This is so boring."

"I know," Lucy agreed, mostly to placate her grandmother. Tulip, who was also bored, was spread out between the two of them, Naunie petting her little doggie head and Lucy rubbing her belly. "But look on the bright side; somewhere, some little girl who can only see with night vision and has a clubfoot is about to get a ruffly canopy bed and a jungle gym in her backyard."

"This is the dullest haunted house in the history of haunted houses," the old lady complained. "Nothing happens here. Nobody does anything. All she does is watch TV, and all he does is work, come home, sleep, and then go back to work. It's a good thing you didn't marry that loser. Otherwise, this would have been your life instead of your death."

Lucy shook her head. "He wasn't like that when I lived here," she admitted. "He worked a lot, but not like this. We did lots of things together, took Tulip for walks, watched movies, took trips. I don't think he's done any of that since I've been here now. Maybe they're shorthanded at work. He's the manager of the produce department. It's his job to fill in for anybody that goes on vacation or calls in sick."

"At least at my house, I had places to go and conduct my own business," Naunie said, sighing heavily. "I could go to the attic, stomp around up there. I could knock things over in the basement. I could run up and down the stairs! There's no place for us to go here! What possessed you to agree to live in a ranch style cracker box with a crawl space and a carport? People need to think about these things when they buy houses. Ghosts need a decent work space; otherwise it's just futile. What a waste of time! This is a ridiculous setup for haunting, and I don't know how either one of us is going to complete our mission in a house as big as a tent."

"How am I supposed to complete a mission when I don't know what it even is?" Lucy asked, raising her voice. "I have no idea what I'm supposed to be doing. I keep waiting for Martin to say he's lost his keys, or someone's been locked out of the house, or someone wonders where all the lost socks go. Because *I know. I have them*. But nope. I just sit here, day in, day out, waiting for someone to lose something, hoping that eventually my mission will present itself, I can attend to it, complete it, and get the hell out of here."

"Tell me about it," Naunie agreed. "You know there is fifty thousand dollars stashed in the one wall of my house that the new tenants were not going to knock down? Had they been halfway decent people and retained the house the way it should be, maybe I mighta led them to it. Who knows? But I sure was going to keep that secret to myself as long as they were throwing away and ripping out everything that was mine!"

"What do you mean there was a stash of money in the wall?" Lucy gasped. "How do you know? How did it get there? Did you always know?"

"I had no idea when I was living in the house," she said. "But afterward, Geneva was always going on and saying how her father had been accused of robbing a payroll stagecoach when she was a girl, and even went on trial for it, but the only witness was a prostitute and they dropped the case."

"Didn't Geneva know the money was there?" Lucy asked.

"Nope. She never looked, I guess. As soon as I heard that story, I went through every wall in that house, and sure enough, there was a big old bundle of money bricked up in the wall between the living room and the dining room. Geneva and Howe—that was probably both of their missions all along, to let whoever was living in the house know that the money was there, but those two just didn't get it."

"How did you know it was fifty thousand dollars?" Lucy wondered.

"Well, I don't really, but that's how much Geneva said was taken from the stagecoach, and she said her father couldn't have been guilty because sometimes they were so poor they were in danger of the bank taking back the house, and that surely, if her father had had that kind of money, they would never have been in that predicament."

"Unless coughing up so much money would surely confirm his role and render him guilty," Lucy added.

"Exactly," Naunie agreed. "He couldn't touch it if he wanted to. So it just sat there. And it's still there. All of that old currency. It must be worth far more than that now."

"Just think, it was there the whole time we were growing up," Lucy pondered. "Why didn't you give us a sign that the money was there when you found it? Alice could have really used something like that, especially since the divorce."

"Oh," Naunie answered, shaking her head. "By the time I got back to the house, the new tenants had moved in. Frankly, I was surprised that one of you girls didn't keep the house. I would have liked to see another generation of Fishers grow up there."

"I'm sorry, Naunie," Lucy said earnestly. "I'm sorry that when you came back we were gone. It wasn't practical to keep the house. Neither one of us could have afforded to. Alice lives so far away, and I already had this house with Martin. If I only knew then what I know now."

Naunie sat there for a moment, thinking, it seemed, but she didn't say anything. A certain kind of sadness passed over her face, but just as quickly, the fire returned to her eyes, signaling the entrance of a terribly wicked thought.

"Let me pinch her," Naunie said, her harsh gaze concentrated on Nola. "Just one pinch. Maybe two. She won't even know it's me. She'll think it's a bug or something like that. Just let me liven things up a bit in this joint. One pinch. That's all I'm asking."

"No," Lucy said, shaking her head. It wasn't that she didn't want Naunie to pinch Nola, or even that she didn't want to pinch Nola herself, but she was afraid if she let her cranky grandmother start dabbling in nonsense, next time it wouldn't be a pinch. It would be a tug of her hair. After that, it would be a push, and after that, knowing Nola, it would be something that could turn this silly, tiny ranch house haunting into a white light situation.

"Come on," Naunie urged. "How could you not want to pinch her? She got you fired, she's living in your house, watching your TV, and now your boyfriend is her boyfriend. Lean over there and just pinch her, Lucy!"

Lucy shook her head. Eventually, at some point in her life, Nola would get hers. And if Lucy was lucky or unlucky enough to be around to see it, she was pretty sure that would be all she'd need.

chapter fourteen I Thought I Just Saw Her

Lucy was in the kitchen looking over the morning paper that Martin had left out, when she heard a high-pitched, hysterical bloodcurdling scream from down the hall.

"Oh, my God! Oh, my God! Oh, my God!" Nola shrieked uncontrollably.

"What's the matter?" Martin called out calmly from the living room, where Lucy could hear he had just picked up his keys and was ready to head out the front door to go to work.

"It's Tulip!" Nola bellowed. "She—she—she just pushed open the bathroom door, and now I'm *exposed*!"

"That's impossible, Nola. I just put her out," Martin replied a little drolly.

"I swear to you, Martin, she just pushed that door open and I am sitting here completely showing!" Nola insisted.

Lucy heard Martin take a deep breath and then exhale.

"Nola, I'm leaving for work right now, and after I'm gone, there will be no one left in the house," he assured her. "Even Tulip can't see you. Compose yourself, get a towel, and then shut the door so you can preserve your modesty."

"OW!" Nola replied shrilly. "Something just bit me! OW! Ouch! I think we have fleas, Martin! I think that dog has fleas!"

The vibration of the front door closing rattled a framed picture in the hallway.

Lucy chuckled slightly, grinning. "Naunie!" she called out. "Get in here and stop pinching her!"

"But it's so much fun," she heard her grandmother protest. "Her rump is so fleshy and pinchable! It's like bread dough!"

"Ow!" Nola cried again. "Mar-tin! Martin! We're going to need to spray this weekend!"

Naunie strolled into the kitchen with a spring in her step.

"I'm sick of hanging around this dump," she said matter-of-factly. "I have a fantastic idea."

"You've been here for a day and a half," Lucy said, not even raising her eyes from the paper. "Let Tulip back in first."

Naunie swung the door open, and Tulip slowly trotted in. Lucy had noticed she was slowing down a bit, but it made sense with the gray on her muzzle. She was getting up there, and for an old girl, it was time to relax. Tulip nestled herself tightly next to Lucy, panting happily, and looking content.

"Whaddya think," Naunie whispered tauntingly, "about going to work with her? Huh? Whaddya say? Change of scenery, change of pace, and you'd get to see your friends? Just catch a ride with Roly-Poly-Noly and we're as good as gold."

"I don't know," Lucy hedged. "I'm not so sure I should let you out in the open to roam wild and free just yet."

"Oh, come on!" Naunie pouted. "Where's my free-spirited granddaughter, huh? The one who used to make me stay up all night waiting for her to come home? The one who could not have too much fun? Where is that girl?"

Naunie playfully punched Lucy in the shoulder.

"Where is that girl?" Naunie said again, delivering another punch.

"A bus turned her into a free-spirited rug because she wasn't looking where she was going," Lucy retorted. "Apparently, when the wheels stopped, I was simply a pelt and so much so that I didn't even get a burial. I just got incinerated like a leftover pot roast."

"Whatever," Naunie scoffed. "I had a stroke on a pink toilet. Uncle Howe ended up as meat loaf in the middle of a cornfield. Big deal. Who cares. If it's a beautiful memory you're after, stay alive. How you died isn't who you were, Lucy. Because you're still that person. Your body wasn't so fortunate in the end, but I hate to tell you, it wasn't your body that I loved. It was you. And you're still here. So let's go to work with our hostess and tear some shit up."

Lucy burst out laughing. She couldn't help it.

Even if they couldn't see her, she would still love to see Jilly and Marianne, she thought, and it might be good to have a change of scenery.

"You'd better hurry up and make up your mind," Naunie warned. "Nola's already on her third coat of foundation. It won't be long before she leaves. She just has to wax and buff her face now like the front end of a Buick."

As Tulip nuzzled against her leg, Lucy petted her loyal friend, and laughed when she found a little bump on Tulip's front leg.

"Oh, Tulip," she gushed into her dog's deep cocoa-brown eyes. "I won't love you any less, because they can't bite me, but I think you really might have fleas!"

Lucy kept petting Tulip as she thought about Naunie's idea. The thought of seeing her friends again made Lucy incredibly happy. She wondered if they had changed much, if they had thought about her often. The thought, although fleeting, even crossed her mind that maybe they had a memorial—a tiny, tiny, *tiny* one with just a couple of pictures, some flowers, a burning candle—dedicated to her somewhere in the office to make up for being no-shows at her funeral. In a nook, by the coffee machine, or maybe on the counter in reception. After a moment, she laughed at herself heartily, as if Nola would ever allow that. Just the thought of seeing Jilly and Marianne lightened Lucy's mood up considerably.

"I'm ready!" she said as she turned to Naunie.

"Oh!" Naunie gushed, squeezing Lucy's shoulders. "This is going to be so much fun!"

The office looked like it had the first day Lucy had gone to work there; not a thing had changed. As Naunie and Lucy followed Nola in, Lucy noted details that had remained intact and stagnant, despite the great change there had been in her own world. The patients' chairs in the waiting room were the exact ones that had been there for years, and in the same arrangement. The silk flowers on the reception counter in front of Marianne's desk sat where they always had in shades of forest-green, red, and pink, with excelsior moss shoved haphazardly to mask the Styrofoam brick beneath the blooms.

It was the sameness of the office that alarmed her. Everything around her had been kept intact, kept the same; only she had been plucked out of the scenario.

Nola, always the early arriver and keeper of the time clock, got to the office about a half hour before everyone else, including Dr. Meadows, Lucy remembered. She made sure everything was in its place for the start of a bright, new dental day. As they moved through the technical rooms of the office and back toward the admin section, Lucy kept her eye out for any trace, any *thing* that signaled she had once been there. She didn't remember doing anything specifically to mark her spot, but you never know, she reasoned. It's the unconscious things we do that are the most telling. They passed by the individual chairs and stations where Lucy had spent so much time assisting Dr. Meadows with gauze, the suction tool, and finding the right drill bit.

Nola passed her own work area, which was set up in an alcove next to the break room, and plopped her worn fake leather purse on top of the desk. Without stopping, she continued on to Dr. Meadows's office, where she entered and, without hesitation, began opening the drawers of the dentist's desk.

"Look at that!" Lucy cried to Naunie, who pushed up against Lucy in the doorway to get a better view. "She's spying! She's going through all of his things, like a thief!"

"That woman has no shame," Naunie added. "What could she possibly be looking for? Money? Drugs? Dirty pictures? Wouldn't it be great if she was blackmailing him?"

Nola ruffled through another drawer before the question was answered.

In Nola's hands were a cloth rag, a spray can of something, and a feather duster. She used the duster first and twirled it over the pictures, clock, phone, and calendar that were precisely arranged on Dr. Meadows's desk. She immediately straightened any item she may have knocked out of alignment. Then she deployed what was in the spray can on the rag and wiped down his desk, his chair, the oak file cabinets, and the additional two chairs that faced his desk, one in which Lucy had been sitting when she was falsely accused.

Lucy couldn't believe what she was seeing; Nola, the chieftain and holy ruler of Dr. Meadows's dental office, was also his maid.

"I can't believe it," Lucy whispered. "I had no idea she did this."

Before Lucy and Naunie knew it, Nola came marching at them,

and the two separated barely a moment before she would have passed through them. From a closet in the break room, Nola pulled out a vacuum cleaner and headed right back to the office.

"I've seen enough of this show," Naunie said, pretending to yawn. "I'm going to go explore."

Lucy nodded, and wandered off to the cubbyholes where everyone in the office kept their personal stuff. It was all as she remembered it. She meandered up to Marianne's desk in reception and poked her nose around, although she was not even remotely tempted to open a drawer. Marianne had a new, single picture up by her phone, and Lucy leaned in closer for a better look. It was of Jilly and Marianne drinking enormous piña coladas on chaise longues in the warm sand of the beach. Lucy knew the picture, even though she had never seen it before.

She had taken it during their vacation in Hawaii.

It was a quarter to nine, the rest of the office were due to arrive in fifteen minutes, and the bustle of the day would begin. Lucy had looked over almost the entire office, noting the familiar things, and surprised by the new things. In the hallway was a boastful, behemoth piece of equipment, what Lucy could only figure was a brand-new panoramic X-ray machine, top of the line. This certainly had not only a bell, Lucy thought, it had whistles, spotlights, and fireworks attached to it. It would have been fun to have been able to use it, she thought as she poked around the gargantuan piece of equipment that was now stationed just outside the door of the break room. Just by messing around near it, Lucy felt the pull of it and sensed the tingling in her hands that was the first sign of gathering power. *That thing just must suck it in,* she thought. *I bet their electricity bills doubled. It's amazing what can happen in a year.*

Lucy couldn't help but feel hurt as she rummaged through the break room cabinets. She told herself she had every right to feel that way; here she was, dead a year, and although her best friends hadn't gone as far as Martin to erase all traces of her, they didn't have even one thing around to remember her by. It was a stupid idea to come here, she realized. What did she think she was going to find? Did she really expect to see some shrine of herself in the lobby or a huge Lucy portrait in the break room?

While scanning the coffee mugs to see if her favorite was still there, Lucy laughed out loud when the thought crossed her mind that, at the very least, the guilt Dr. Meadows ought to have felt for firing a girl in the last hours of her life could have been expressed with something small, yet tasteful. A plaque with an impression of Lucy's upper and lower teeth etched onto it would have been a nice remembrance, or just a bronze-dipped suction tool with Lucy's name and dates of service engraved into it would have been a nice gesture.

But no, there was nothing except Lucy's favorite coffee mug, which she pulled out of the far back of the cabinet with the energy from the unexpected charge from the X-ray machine. The mug had a very light layer of dust on the bottom, as it had been placed that side up for apparently a lengthy period of time. It had a picture of Paul Bunyan and Babe, his blue ox, from one of the only times she'd been able to talk Martin into stopping at a roadside attraction the year before last when they'd driven up to the redwoods. She smiled when she thought of him scowling as she handed over the fifteen dollars for the overpriced mug, but Lucy had been living at the moment and had thought it would be a fond memory of their trip. Now it was the only hint in the whole office that Lucy had ever been there, and it was hiding deep in the back, gathering specks of age.

Just then Lucy had an idea. She put the mug on the counter,

right side up, went back to Marianne's desk, and opened the cabinet she had seen Nola open on Lucy's last day in the office. If no one was going to have any kind of remembrance to Lucy, she decided to make one herself. She propped the picture of Marianne and Jilly in front of the mug, spelled her name on the counter using the brightly colored letters that Marianne stuck on the spine of every patient's file, and as a finishing touch, she slipped a drug test right into the mug, where it landed with a tiny *clink!*

Lucy smiled as she looked at her rather playful tongue-in-cheek hello. If some things had still remained the same, she knew that Jilly would be the first one to see her "memorial" when she went to make the coffee, as she did first thing every morning.

She heard Jilly and Marianne laughing as they entered the front door, their voices continuing to chatter as they moved through the office, Marianne stopping at her desk, then Jilly continuing on back to the break room.

Lucy could hear Jilly's soft, muffled footsteps approaching, hear her getting closer as she said, "Morning, Nola," and passed the alcove, and then suddenly, there she was. Lucy's best friend. There was Jilly, walking right past Lucy, so close that she could reach out and touch her.

If Lucy had had any breath, she would have lost it. Seeing Jilly in the flesh was so overwhelming that it shocked her. Lucy had had so much happen, had been to so many extraordinary places and done so many things that all she wanted to do was run right up to her best friend since dental school and spill it all right out in front of her. Lucy realized that if there was one thing she really missed about living, it was the living. She wanted to throw her arms around Jilly and be the friend she used to be, and then, in the next second, she wanted to pull back and demand, *What the hell, Jilly? Where were you? I was at my funeral. Why weren't you?*

Jilly stopped at her cubby, placed her purse inside, threw her lunch bag into the fridge, and then turned around, moving toward the coffeemaker. Lucy had seen her do this a thousand times, rinsing out the pot, tearing open the foil packet, tossing the coffee pouch into the machine. Jilly then went back toward the cabinet that held the mugs, with Lucy's little hello directly beneath it on the counter.

Just then, Lucy heard some rustling, and there was a woman, older than either Lucy or Jilly, her gray hair pulled tightly back into a bun, her office scrubs flashes of teal, pink, and orange, some sort of abstract design. Obviously, Lucy's replacement.

"Howdy, Jilly," the woman said with a smile.

"Hey, Marcia," Jilly replied. "Oh! I brought that book I told you about, the mystery about the Russian girl with the art gallery? It was fantastic. I read it in two days."

"Great!" Marcia replied as she opened the fridge door and set her lunch on the top shelf. "Are we still on for Saturday night? I'm making Warren's favorite—Gooey Butter Cake!"

"He'll be thrilled. He loves your cake!" Jilly laughed as she opened the cabinet and reached for a mug. "He would have joined the Manson Family if they'd baited him with a slice of—"

Lucy saw Jilly staring at the mug, her mouth dropped, her eyes unmoving.

Jilly pointed at the mug. "Who did this?" she questioned. *"Who did this?"*

Lucy at once realized what a terrible, horrible thing she had done. What she'd meant as playful and goofy was not that at all. It was a bad memory, a hurtful reminder.

"Marianne!" Jilly called. "Come back here!"

Marcia stood there, not saying anything. Marianne made it to the break room in seconds.

"Look at that," Jilly said, pointing to the shrine. "Did you do that?"

"No," Marianne said, shaking her head, looking as in shock as Jilly did.

"It's your picture," Jilly pointed out. "Is this supposed to be funny?"

"I d-don't know," Marianne stumbled. "I didn't do it, Jilly."

Jilly bit her lip and thought for a moment, then marched right past her co-workers, right past Lucy, and into Nola's alcove. Lucy followed right behind her. They found Nola on the phone, imploring, "Hello? Hello?" while Naunie sat on the corner of her desk, watching her intently.

Lucy snuck behind the panoramic X-ray machine.

"Nola," Jilly said starkly, standing before the desk rigidly.

"Yes," the office manager replied, preoccupied with dialing a number. "Oh. Thank heavens! It's ringing this time."

Naunie leaned over, her crooked finger poised and rapidly going for the disconnect button.

"Hello? Hello?" Nola pleaded, then finally slammed the receiver down. "WHAT is wrong with this phone? I can't make any calls out!"

"I think someone is playing a joke on me," Jilly explained. "Who was here last night when you left?"

"No one, just me," Nola answered. "I locked up."

"Then who was here this morning? There must have been someone here. I don't know, landlord, the cleaning people, was there a repair person here?"

"That's ridiculous. It was just me," Nola said as she picked up the receiver again. "There was no one here. The office was empty like it always is in the morning. Ow! Ow! Something is biting me! I've been bitten! They must have followed me to the office! That dog has fleas. They've been waging war on me all morning!"

"Someone has taken Lucy's mug out of the cabinet and spelled out her name in chart letters in front of it. And I want to know who did that and why," Jilly informed her, then turned around. As she began to walk back to the office, she glanced past the X-ray machine. Lucy quickly slunk back, just in time to miss being caught in Jilly's double take due to the charge Lucy was pulling from the machine.

"How would I know that?" Nola called after her. "She'*s your* friend."

"*Was* my friend," Jilly said almost beneath her breath.

Still perched behind the giant X-ray machine, Lucy watched as Nola chugged into the break room to see the display for herself. Once she caught a glimpse of the mug shrine, her brow tensed.

"I don't know what that's all about," Nola huffed. "Why on earth would you think I would have anything to do with that? I'm the *last* person who wants anything to do with *that* person. I have to deal with her enough as it is. She's still everywhere I look. This morning, I found a Lucy Fisher sticker on my lunch bag."

She snatched the drug test out of the cup, threw the mug into the trash, gathered up the letters, and shoved them into the pockets of her smock.

"Now it's gone," she announced. "Problem solved."

No one said anything as Nola stormed out of the break room and back to her alcove, tripping in the doorway on her suddenly untied and extended shoelace.

After a long silence, it was Marcia who spoke first.

"So . . . ," she started. "I take it this is the Lucy you told me about."

Jilly nodded. Lucy moved out from behind the machine into the doorway of the break room.

"We're not supposed to talk about her in the office," Marianne whispered, gesturing her head toward Nola's way.

"Do you think Nola did that?" Jilly asked, also in a whisper. "Just to get a rise out of us?"

"I don't know," Marianne answered simply. "It's kinda weird."

"Marianne, the whole thing is kinda weird," Jilly said rather firmly.

"She did look shocked when she saw it," Marianne concluded. "I don't think it was Nola."

"Then, who would do it?" Jilly questioned. "Who else would set up some creepy thing like that for me to find except for the woman who kind of took over Lucy's life here?"

"But why would she do it?" Marcia asked quietly.

Jilly shook her head. "Who knows?" she replied. "And you know what else? Who cares? Lucy was such a good friend to us that she took off, left her dog behind, and her stuff in my garage, and that's it. That's a really great friend, isn't it?"

Lucy was quite taken aback. *That was some response,* she thought, *like I'd planned on getting killed that day. What a crappy thing to say,* she wanted to yell at Jilly. *Like this is my fault! Like I knew this was going to happen and left my stuff in your garage just to piss you off? Sorry to saddle you with your dead friend's rocking chair and a box of books! What a hassle.* What was wrong with her?

Marianne looked down at the floor. "I haven't heard from her either, Jilly," she said simply.

What? Lucy screamed in her head. *How were you supposed to hear from me? None of us were able to send any kind of message back once we were in school.* What did Marianne think, that there was a special ghost phone she could call on? *She's dumber than she was the last time I saw her.*

Jilly shook her head disgustedly. "I don't know what I did aside from being a good friend to that girl," she said harshly. "I got her this job, nursed her through one heartache after another, and encouraged her to stop being such a flake and get her shit together when she met Martin. But apparently, that's not enough to give me a ring or drop me a line after she starts a new life wherever the hell she is. Nola said Martin got a letter from her, but me, no. Not a word. Not one single damn word."

"I'm sorry, Jilly," Marianne said.

"You know what the funny thing is?" Jilly said, biting her lip. "I miss her. *I miss her.* I thought I saw her in the hall, just now. How crazy is that? No matter what she's done, no matter how much she doesn't care about any of us, I still miss her. But the next time I see her, I am kicking her ass. I'm so tired of worrying about Lucy. I've spent years doing it."

Naunie, who was crouched on the opposite side of the doorjamb after attacking Nola's shoe, looked over and saw the jaw hanging open on her granddaughter's stunned and dazed face.

"Lucy," she said, not able to believe it herself, "they don't know you're dead."

Lucy couldn't stay at the office after that. She had too much to absorb. Despite her aversion to large city-run vehicles, she still remembered the bus route from all the times her truck had broken down and been in the shop. She and Naunie left the dentist's office and headed back home. They found a quiet seat in the back and scooted in. They noticed there were several other ghosts riding the bus, too, evident by the shining that surrounded them, and they exchanged small, knowing nods with two old women both dressed as White Ladies, except both of them clutched their pocketbooks, terrified that even in their invisible, spectral form, they were still vulnerable while taking city transportation to getting mugged by some ruffian wayward youth.

"I don't understand," Lucy said for the fifth time after they had been sitting for a while. "Why didn't Alice tell anyone? Wasn't it worth mentioning?"

"A fellow in my class at ghost school was dead for almost a year before anyone found him in his recliner, TV still on," Naunie mentioned. "At least they found you."

"Well, I don't think that could have been helped," Lucy replied. "I was kind of scattered all over an intersection."

"All right, then, let's think about this," Naunie said. "How many of your friends did Alice know?"

Lucy thought for a moment. "Not many, but she certainly knew Jilly. They've met before, numerous times. I can't understand why she wouldn't tell her."

"Maybe it's not that she wouldn't," Naunie suggested. "Maybe it's that she couldn't. Did you have an address book, or somewhere that had all of the phone numbers of your friends?"

"An address book?" Lucy laughed. "I haven't had an address book for years. Everything I needed was on my phone."

"Okay. Did Alice know how to access those numbers, did she know that's where everything was?" Naunie questioned. "Was the phone at Alice's house?"

Lucy slowly shook her head. "No," she finally answered. "It was with me the day I was killed. In my purse."

"Oh." Naunie understood. "Chances are it didn't fare any better than you did. Well, there must have been other ways you kept in touch with people, right? Didn't you write letters? Maybe you had some that had return addresses on them?"

"I'm sure I got a postcard here and there, but nothing that I held on to," Lucy remembered.

"There has to be another way to find your friends," Naunie insisted. "What about email?"

"Yes!" Lucy almost shouted. "I did email almost everyone I

knew, but when Martin kicked me out, I lost my primary account. Jilly set me up with a free one on my laptop before I left for Flagstaff, but I never really had a chance to use it, just gave a couple of people my new address. I never even turned the laptop on when I got to Alice's. It was in my bag in a box with some other stuff."

"Nothing else?" Naunie asked. "What about your work phone number?"

"Are you kidding?" Lucy laughed. "With Nola watching us like a hawk? No, if Alice wanted to get ahold of me, she'd call home or my cell. I don't think I ever gave her my work number. And after the threat of a malpractice suit last year, Dr. Meadows changed the practice into a corporation to protect his personal assets. It's listed under 'The Molar System' in the phone book now. I guess I didn't leave her much to go on, did I? I don't even think she knew Jilly's new married name. I never thought that once my phone got creamed, I would become obsolete and lost to the ages. I never thought about leaving an 'In the Event of My Death' list of contacts. Was I really that easy to just wipe away? And no one came looking for me, either, I notice."

"If people still wrote letters, this would never have happened, Lucy!" Naunie insisted. "Damn technology only lets you down when you need to send the most important message of all."

"Well, apparently, I wrote a letter to Martin! Why would Nola make up such a stupid lie, except to create drama and to have one up on everyone else?" Lucy almost hissed. "Now instead of wondering what happened to me, my friends hate me. All I can tell you is that someone is going to get pinched tonight."

The pair made it back to the house just in time for Lucy's favorite activity of the day: mail delivery. Naunie was hoping that it was just what her granddaughter needed to cheer her up.

"Lucy!" Naunie screeched as she saw the mail carrier, a man close to retirement age with flushed red cheeks and a receding hairline typical of Franciscan monks, starting up the driveway to the house. The fatty skin above his knees jiggled recklessly with every step, and as Lucy ran into the living room in response to Naunie's screech, she saw the mailman pass the living room picture window and looked into his eyes at the exact same moment he looked into hers.

He looked shocked, then furrowed his brow.

"You," he said as he pointed a finger at her, "did not fill out a change of address form! You have to do that, you know! You can't just keep writing 'Whereabouts Unknown' on everything with your name on it and expect me to pick it back up again! You've had me carrying *pounds* of returned mail and *you are no longer on my route*!"

Lucy couldn't say anything; she just stood there with her mouth hanging open. He, clearly, could see her. Not just catching a glimpse like Jilly out of the corner of her eye, but he was talking to her as if she was really there.

"Lucy!" said Naunie, who had collapsed to the floor, which she was now desperately hugging to stay out of sight. "Walk over here! Give me your foot and transfer your energy to me!"

Lucy produced a huge, affable smile for the mailman and gave him a friendly wave.

"Too late," she tried to say through her Cheshire cat grin. "He's already seen me. He's still looking at me . . . Still looking at me . . . Still looking at me. What if I start to fade? I'm beginning to get that not-so-fresh-feeling. . . ."

"Hang on," Naunie instructed as she commando-crawled toward Lucy. Naunie grabbed Lucy's ankle and then, with her foot, made contact with a power outlet on the closest wall.

Lucy felt the surge immediately, albeit thinly.

The mailman, who was still staring at Lucy, tucked the bundle of mail under his arm, knocked on the window with his postal knuckle, and gestured for her to come closer, or perhaps even outside.

Lucy shook her head and pointed to the mail slot in the door, and quickly thought to point to her back and grimace as if she was in sciatica pain.

Looking disgusted, the postman shook his head, reached into his mailbag, pulled a pad of pink paper from one of the pockets, and ripped the top sheet off. Then, as his fleshy knees trembled, he took several steps to the front door and aggressively shoved the mail through the slot. It landed on Lucy's side with a mad thud. On his way back, he turned to give Lucy one last expression of loathing and disdain as he marched past the window and down the driveway.

"He's gone!" Lucy whispered to Naunie, who released the death grip on Lucy's ankle.

Lucy, in turn, dropped the grimace and looked down at her grandmother, who was still sprawled out on the carpet.

"You can get up now," Lucy informed her. "I said he was gone."

"I'm halfway charged," Naunie protested. "What if he forgot something and comes back? And by the way, why were you charged when you ran in here? You have to be more careful than that!"

"I drained the batteries in Nola's home electrolysis pen, and I was changing her alarm clock to the Mexican polka station," Lucy explained.

"Good choice." Naunie smiled admiringly as she got up cautiously, checking to see if the coast was indeed clear. "They have the commercials for the stereo store with the guy who screams *'OCHO! OCHO! OCHO! CUATRO TRES UNO DOS!'* over and over and over."

"The phone number to the stereo store," Lucy confirmed wickedly.

"Nice move," Naunie approved. "That's my girl!"

Lucy walked over to the bundle of letters and flipped through it.

On top of the stack was the pink change of address form the mailman had torn off and left. Under that was a thick cushion mailer the size and width of a paperback book, and beneath that was a plain white envelope addressed in handwriting.

"Well, look at this," she said as she picked it up, a substantial portion of her charge remaining. "What a coincidence. It looks like I've been writing letters to Martin again."

"It would appear that way, wouldn't it?" Naunie said, noticing the return address with "Fisher" written above it in black ink. "Except that this is not from you. This is from Alice."

That night, Nola came home to a darkened house. When she turned the key in the lock, not even Tulip raised her head to welcome her. Nola was surprised that Martin wasn't home yet; she had run some errands after work, and had thought for sure he would have beat her home. Instead, only Naunie and Lucy were there, peering out from the shadows, watching her flip the light switch on that was closest to the door as she struggled with her shopping bags, dropping one. Its contents—tape, some fancy paper, and what looked like scrapbooking supplies—shot over the floor in a long, straight line, like a streak. She bent down to pick them up, and came upon Alice's letter instead.

When the letter had arrived, Lucy and Naunie had wanted to tear open the envelope and read the letter for themselves. Certainly, opening mail not addressed to them was not within their realm of ghostly objectives or duties, but still, they felt the letter more or less belonged to them, mainly because Alice belonged to them. If she'd taken the time to write it and mail it down here, it was something they wanted to read, and there lay the dilemma; Alice wanted to tell Martin something, and that message had every right to get to him, regardless of what either Naunie or Lucy wanted. Opening the letter would have destroyed that possibility, and so they'd had no choice. Although each of them had taken turns holding the letter up to the sunlight and trying to read the scribble, eventually they'd put the letter back where it had fallen with a thud with the other mail.

Nola stared at the return address for a moment. Obviously, she thought she knew exactly what it was. Quickly, Nola stood up and marched down the hall. Lucy and Naunie suddenly heard a grinding mechanical noise—the sound of Martin's shredder in the hobby room. "Goodbye again, Lucy," they heard Nola say just before the mechanical sound turned muffled and ragged. "Get your own life, because you're not getting this one back. You've never known when enough was enough."

She then came back into the living room, scooped the scattered items off the floor, put them back into the bag, and then tossed the bag over onto the couch. She picked up the thick paperback-size bubble mailer that had also come in the mail and tossed it onto the couch as well, narrowly missing Naunie, who ducked. Her commando-like reflexes were becoming quite honed. From the bookcase next to where Lucy was standing and watching her, Nola pulled out a photo album. Lucy recognized it, since it was filled with pictures of past vacations and camping trips. Album in hand, Nola plopped down, nearly right on top of Naunie, who finally scurried away and found a safer place to observe from on the other side of the room.

Nola ripped open the small bubble mailer and pulled out a colorful envelope from inside it. She flipped the top of the envelope open and revealed a large stack of photos. She smiled as she went through them, her face softening on some, and she giggled at others. This surprised Lucy—she had never seen Nola do anything much more than act irritated, bothered, and demanding when she wasn't sobbing during makeover reality shows. Looking at the pictures made her seem content and calm, nearly gentle. When she was done flipping through all of them, she put them aside and then reached for the photo album, opened it, and turned to the first page, which Lucy could see was the camping trip she and Martin had taken to the Mogollon Rim.

Nola looked at it for several seconds. Then she turned back the protective plastic sheeting and promptly tore every photo from the adhesive page. She did this on the next page and the page after that. She threw the old, now curled photos next to her on the couch, and Lucy watched as they grew into a pile, then eventually tipped over and scattered over the cushion.

Nola was ripping Lucy out of her own photo album, scene by scene, smile by smile. Nola didn't particularly seem to enjoy doing it, but did it methodically and mechanically without any feelings attached, kind of like shredding a personal letter that was not addressed to you.

"What the hell is she doing?" Lucy asked angrily. "Why take all of the photos out of my album when she clearly went to the scrapbooking store and could have bought her own album?"

Naunie was quiet for a moment and simply shook her head.

"It's not about creating something new for her," she finally said. "It's about elimination and inserting herself where you once were."

The sound of a truck door slamming interrupted the ripping sound as Nola stopped mid-tug on one of the photos of Lucy and Tulip sitting alongside a brook. It took only a second for Nola to slam the book shut, shove it into her bag with all of her supplies, and then grab the handfuls of photos and ram them into the small drawer of the side table. She closed it at the precise moment Martin opened the door and took a step into the house.

"I'm so glad you're home," Nola said immediately, turning around with a charming smile on her face. "I'm making a big surprise for you!"

Lucy looked at the man that she had lived with for several years, the man whose quirks she knew, the man who had torn her out of his life without explanation, the man who did not know she had been dead, cremated, and sitting in an urn almost since the last time he'd seen her.

"That's nice," he said with a small reciprocating smile, and headed off toward the kitchen. Nola dutifully followed.

What was he doing here? Lucy wondered. What was he doing in this? *This is not like you,* she wanted to scream at him. *She is not like you. What happened to you, Martin? What is wrong with you?*

It had been a day of wonder, Lucy thought as she leaned against the wall and looked at her grandmother, neither of them needing to say anything, until Naunie thought differently.

"Lucy, I don't know if you can see it," she said, crossing her arms and nodding in the direction of the kitchen. "But your mission is pretty clear to me. I know that man wrecked your life and tore it apart like a rabid dog, but it's her you've got to get rid of."

chapter fifteen The Other Woman

Nola was planning on enjoying her day off.

Lucy could tell by the way Nola carefully set up her operation on the coffee table: First, she had her stack of chronologically arranged photos placed precisely in the most strategic spot, next to the tape, her sticker embellishments, and her scrapbooking flair. Next to that grouping was the set of remote controls for both the television and her recorder, which held the viewing pleasure that was a foundation for every Saturday. And last, but not least, was a space for her lunch, which consisted of a giant hero sandwich that looked like a conglomeration of every type of processed meat and cheese known to the free world, and which had taken her more than twenty minutes to construct. For side dishes, she had a perfectly sliced pickle spear and a tub of store-bought potato salad, and for dessert, she had decided on just one maple-frosted donut.

Nola loved Saturdays. She *loved* them. They were the only day she had completely and entirely to herself, with no one to demand anything from her or spoil her solitude. Martin worked every Saturday, as it was the busiest shopping day of the week and he needed to be available should a cabbage or eggplant avalanche suddenly strike the store and trap the elderly. Saturdays were all hers to relax, indulge, and pamper herself. And she was about to do just that. She had brought her lunch in and set it on the coffee table in its designated spot, when the doorbell rang.

She sighed heavily, shook her head, and slapped her palms on the tops of her thighs to truly demonstrate her disgust at having to get up and bother herself. She shuffled to the door, hoping that in the four drags of the feet it took her, the interloper would have thought better of being such a nuisance and would have simply vanished. But he had not. When Nola opened the door, there stood the mailman, his knees quivering with every breath, his arms outstretched with a medium-size package.

"You need to sign for this," he said. A bead of perspiration ran down the left side of his face in a mad dash. Nola took the pen he had positioned in his left hand, took the delivery slip from his right, and signed by the *x*.

"Thank you," she said, and took the package from him.

"If you have the other slip filled out, I can take that back," he informed her.

Nola shook her head. "What slip?"

"The change of address form I gave to that girl the other day," he replied.

Nola shook her head again quickly. "You must be mistaken," she said immediately. "Wrong house. I'm the only woman here."

"The other woman," the mailman said emphatically. "The *other* one. She never changed her address. The girl on whose mail is written 'Whereabouts Unknown' when you consistently give it back to me."

"What?" Nola said, starting to get irritated. This nonsense was taking a serious bite out of her glorious alone time. "I'm pretty sure you have the wrong house, but fine, fine, whatever. Thank you."

Nola had nearly succeeded in closing the door all the way when the mailman suddenly blurted out, "LUCY! That's her name! I gave it to Lucy!"

The closing door came to an abrupt halt and quickly opened again.

"Did you say Lucy?" Nola asked slowly and with clarity.

The mailman nodded. "Cute girl, curly hair, cowboy boots," he said. "Younger than you."

"We're the same age," she corrected him with a glare.

"No, this girl's younger," he insisted. "You know, the one who lived here before you."

"Same age," Nola repeated through clenched teeth. "Are you sure it was her? She was here? She was at the door when you got here?"

"Oh, no," he answered. "She was inside. Right behind where you are now."

He pointed past Nola to the middle of the living room, exactly where Lucy had been standing. "Right there," he added.

Nola looked at him for several seconds without saying anything.

"You are saying she was inside this house," she clarified. "Lucy was inside my house."

"Yes," he confirmed. "She wouldn't come to the door, so I put the form through the mail slot with the other mail. It was the day you got the photographs processed by Walmart."

"Nice of you to notice," Nola said, flashing a fake smile. "Thank you for the package."

"Tell her to return it as soon as she can," the mailman said quickly.

"To return what?" Nola asked, now visibly agitated.

"The change of address form," he reminded her. "It's been a year now that I've been carrying around unnecessary mail for her. Unless she's back here now."

"No," Nola said firmly. "She's not. I can guarantee that."

With that, Nola slammed the door shut and stood there for what seemed like a year.

"Idiot needs water and to lower his body temperature or he's going to have more heatstroke-induced hallucinations," Nola mumbled to herself. "Because she is definitely not back here."

"That's what you think," Naunie said from the doorway to the hallway, where she had watched the whole thing. "What a fat blue snitch in kneesocks. I have a thing or two up my sleeve for him."

Nola returned to the couch with her package and put it aside. Then she picked up the photo album and with a new ferocity went to work tearing out the rest of the photos while Lucy and Naunie watched her, unable to do anything.

When she was done and had removed every photo, Nola took the bunch of them and marched into Martin's hobby room to deposit them in her weapon of choice—the shredder. She fed the pictures in by twos and threes, which took a considerable amount of time, since she had a whole album's worth of pictures to destroy, but that was all right. It was all the time Naunie needed to offer Nola's masterpiece of a sandwich to one very lazy, but deserving, dog, who—perhaps wisely—refused it.

Sandwich in ghost hand, Naunie panicked as she quickly panned the room for a place to hide Nola's grub.

"She shredded every picture of me in that book," Lucy complained to Naunie, not believing what she was seeing. "Well, she can destroy whatever she wants. I am still very much a presence in this house. She cannot eradicate me. I am not polio!"

"Damn right you aren't," her grandmother agreed. She finally spotted the perfect place and rushed to the front door to shove the sandwich right through the mail slot.

When Nola was satisfied that she had shredded Lucy to bits and then had taken the colored shards of smiles, eyes, and assorted backgrounds to the garbage tote to remove the evidence, she was finally ready for the candy center of her day. She turned on the television to watch the stockpile of shows she had recorded throughout the week. She settled in, clicked the remote to turn the TV on, and clicked again to get to the menu to see delightful shows she had waiting for her.

"Wait. That's not right," she said aloud.

She scrolled through everything that had been recorded, and while all of the shows she had already watched but could not bring herself to delete were still there—along with Martin's numerous newly recorded fishing shows—all of her new makeover shows were missing. She painstakingly went through all of the "Now Playing" menu, even as far back as the recording of the previous year's Academy Awards and the red carpet commentary preceding it, but with no success. Every single show she had taped that week—all four of them—was gone.

"Martin's shows recorded over mine!" she said to herself in a pissy little huff. "I can't believe it. *I can't believe it!* I've waited all week to watch a woman get ready to go to her high school reunion by having a chin implant and neck liposuction and getting her ears reduced! I've been waiting all week! What am I supposed to do now?"

Naunie observed from the other end of the couch and burst out laughing.

"I am so glad we're haunting in this day and age," she said. "I could have never accomplished that ten years ago."

Lucy shook her head and grinned right back.

"Who would have thought the act of pressing a button could be so much fun?" Lucy added. "I would have failed the 'screwing with the remote control' section of school if it hadn't been for my friend Bethanny. I was pretty busy feeling sorry for myself that day and acting like our friend Nola here."

"The tantrum is going to get better here, just wait and watch," Naunie said, barely able to contain her excitement.

Nola threw down the remote control, which bounced off the table, hit the floor, and then slid under Martin's rotting La-Z-Boy recliner, but she didn't notice. She was too busy staring at the empty spot where her lunch used to be. Ridiculously, she began searching for it, lifting up the photo album, magazines, even her napkin.

"Do you think we'll ever see them again?" Lucy asked.

"See who?" Naunie replied, her eyes glued on Nola, who was now bent over and looking under the coffee table.

"Friends . . . ," Lucy added, "from ghost school."

"Did I eat it?" Lucy heard Nola ask as she hung upside down.

"Oh, I dunno," Naunie said as she waved Lucy away. "Five bucks says she looks in the cushions. Hee, hee. Watch this."

While Nola searched under the couch, Naunie grabbed the pickle spear she was hiding behind a pillow and placed it where Nola had placed her sandwich—but on top of the donut.

"Didn't you make any friends in ghost school?" Lucy asked her grandmother. "I made a good one. I would love to see her again. At least she knew I was dead, right?"

"Oh, my God!" Nola gasped, spotting the pickle lounging on her donut. "Oh, no!"

She looked at the display as if it was a gruesome car accident that she was afraid to approach because the horror was too great.

"You should have put it in the photo album," Lucy joked.

"I would have needed more of a charge," Naunie said wistfully.

Nola shook her head angrily and looked over at the slumbering, snoring, drooling Tulip.

"You," she said simply as she got up, pickle and donut in hand, and stomped to the kitchen. "I will not forget this."

"Aw, Tulip," Lucy said as she bent down and rubbed the dog's belly. "We'll get a house to fall on that wicked witch, just you wait."

Tulip woke up and gave Lucy a wide smile as her tongue dropped out of her mouth and laid itself on the floor.

"Watch out, Tulip, I'm going to tickle you!" Lucy warned as she lifted up her dog's leg and went straight for the armpit. Tulip was panting in the way that dogs laugh, and Lucy was laughing, too. The dog loved the attention, and Lucy loved giving it to her. In the middle of the rampant ticklefest, Lucy suddenly stopped.

She felt something odd on Tulip's leg, in a spot tucked up under her body. It was a lump, hard and egg-shaped, the size of Lucy's thumb from the knuckle up. She remembered the flea bite from earlier in the week and returned to that spot with her hands. It hadn't gone away; it was still there, and it was clear to Lucy that it was not a flea bite after all. There was no scab in the middle, no fleshy swelling around it. While not as large as the other spot, this one felt hard and solid, too. It was bigger than she remembered it being.

Lucy looked at Tulip, and Tulip looked back for several seconds before she laid her head back on the floor and panted. Lucy knew, and Tulip knew, but Lucy wouldn't allow herself to think it. She stretched an arm over Tulip and the other arm through her front legs, and hugged her softly.

When Martin came home that night, Nola wasted no time notifying him of the tragedy of the day the minute he walked through the front door.

"When you recorded *your* shows, you deleted *my* shows," she complained. "It would be nice if you could try to figure out how to get them back."

"Maybe you could give me time to clean some mayonnaise and lettuce off my shoes," he volleyed. "It appears that we've been attacked by a sandwich."

"What?" Nola said as she rushed into the living room and looked at the carnage of ham, salami, and lettuce that was every bit as shredded as a photograph of Lucy. "My sandwich! Where did you find that? I've been looking for that! All I had to eat for lunch today was a tub of potato salad!"

Martin emitted a small sigh, and shook his head as Nola collected the sandwich from his meaty hands.

"How did this even happen between these two?" Naunie said, pointing her finger back and forth between Nola and Martin. "This brings up something I've wanted to ask for a while, and I just can't hold it in any longer. Did this happen after you, or was he fooling around and kicked you out to move her in? Because if that's the case, more things than sub sandwiches can get shoved through the mail slot."

Lucy shrugged and threw her hands up. "I honestly don't know," she admitted. "I try not to think about it. The Martin I knew wasn't the kind of guy to mess around, and honestly, I never would have thought that Nola was his type at all. Clearly, however, weirder things have happened."

"So you two were getting along fine, nothing seemed odd or out of the ordinary?" Naunie questioned.

"Nope," Lucy replied. "Everything was fine. I mean, we were getting married in eight weeks when I found my stuff outside."

Naunie paused. "Really? Everything was fine?" she asked again. "Because this is the first time you've mentioned that you were engaged and weeks away from a wedding. That doesn't sound fine to me."

Lucy laughed a little and nodded. "Yeah, I guess you're right," she confirmed. "It probably wasn't so fine. Things weren't exactly great. I think we might have both been having second thoughts, but the suspicion of him cheating—especially with her—never crossed my mind until after I wound up back here."

"Wanna find out for sure?" her grandmother said with her trademark wicked grin.

"I don't know." Lucy hesitated. Naunie certainly did carry tricks up her sleeve, but so far, they consisted of pinching people on the toilet and ramming food through mail slots. "How?"

Nola returned to the room with a dish towel for Martin to wipe his hands on.

"Watch and learn," Naunie said slyly, then sidled right up to Nola.

Lucy couldn't help but feel wary.

"Remember when we met?" Naunie said directly into Nola's ear.

Nola smiled pleasantly, then cocked her head slightly to one side.

"Martin, remember when we met?" she repeated, as if being fed lines for a role.

He, in turn, looked puzzled as he wiped condiments and lettuce bits from his palms.

"What?" he asked, scrunching his brow. "What do you mean?"

"I mean do you remember when we met?" Nola continued on in the delight of her memory. "Remember, I came into Safeway and you were busy picking the bad grapes off of the display?"

"Sure, sure. But I never have bad grapes on my display, although there might be some overextended ones. Why do you ask?"

"I don't know. I was remembering," Nola explained. "It was fate, don't you think?"

"You got me, Nola," he answered. "Do you think it was fate that you needed boiler onions that day?"

"This is stupid. Give me something I can use!" Naunie nearly hissed, then went back up to Nola's ear. "Where was Lucy?"

"Well, not exactly," Nola replied. "But running into you at the store was fate, I think. That was a nice surprise, wasn't it? And Lucy—"

"Lucy had been gone for a while, and it certainly was nice of you to invite me to dinner," he said, handing her back the dish towel. "I sure did need the company. But it wasn't as if that was our first meeting, since we talked on the phone when the girls were in Hawaii. Maybe that was the fate part."

"Oh, I was just doing my job," Nola reminded him. "Someone had to track down that deposit."

"Very true," Martin said, and smiled. "Your strong work ethic is something that I've always greatly admired about you."

"That's terribly sweet of you, Martin," Nola gushed.

"I'm glad you think so," he replied, then leaned over and kissed her lightly on the cheek.

She blushed.

"Now, what's this about your missing programs?" he asked her. "Let me see if I can help."

Naunie looked at Lucy. "Answer your question?" she asked.

"I can't say it's not some sort of relief," Lucy said. "But why on earth would Nola not call me directly about the deposit? Why did she call Martin looking for it? What could he have possibly done? I never heard a thing about her calling him. Not a thing."

"When was the last time you spoke to him? Do you remember?" Naunie asked. "He didn't mention her calling?"

Lucy thought for a moment. "It had to have been the night I ate the bad shellfish, but to be honest, I was so sick I couldn't talk. Jilly talked to him, though, and told him what was going on."

"And Jilly never said anything about the deposit being missing while you were in Hawaii?" Naunie questioned.

"No, no, no," Lucy said, shaking her head. "She didn't know a thing about it until we came home, and that's when she told me."

"At least you weren't dumped for that," Naunie said, then reached out and pinched Nola on a fat flap on the back of her arm.

"Ouch!" she cried, and immediately slapped the spot.

Naunie chuckled. "If you think that's something," she said, clapping her wrinkled hands together, "wait till I show you how Freudian slips are not so Freudian unless Freud is the spook whispering them in your ear."

Martin, in his noble effort to assist Nola and rescue her viewing choices, could not find the remote control. He searched the coffee table, under the couch, ran his hands along the ends of the sofa cushions, scoured the tops of each side table, rolled Tulip over side to side, and still came up empty.

"Nola," he called out to the kitchen. "Where is the remote for the digital recorder?"

"Um, it should be right there," she answered, clearly forgetting that she had thrown it across the room in a temper tantrum. The two ghosts who had witnessed the embarrassing display had found it wonderfully delightful and would not only remember it but would reenact the fit for the rest of eternity, to howls of laughter from many of the dead.

"I'm not seeing it," Martin said to no one other than himself.

Now, it's true that Naunie and Lucy had the complete capacity to help Martin out with his search, since they were both aware of where the remote had ended up while Nola had had a cow, but neither one of them was feeling generous enough to stick their hand through the chair and nudge it out.

Martin stood in the middle of the living room, hands on his hips, and almost declared himself defeated until he spied two more possible options. He went to the table nearest the side of the couch with the springing coil, and opened the drawer, only to find batteries, some coasters, and a dried-up pen. But after he closed that drawer and went to the table on other side of the couch, he opened that drawer and found something quite different.

Martin hadn't seen a picture of Lucy in nearly a year.

After he had stood in the shadows of the kitchen and watched her pack up her stuff into Warren's truck and leave, he knew that he had done what he had to do. If he looked at something and it had one single memory of her attached to it, he put it in a produce box and put it out on the lawn. He tried to wipe the house clean of her, otherwise it would have been too difficult. He knew that. After she was gone, he realized he had missed some things, and they offered themselves up to him over the course of the following months: the broken coffeepot, an old lipstick shoved into a corner of the medicine cabinet, a stray earring hiding between the nightstand and the wall. For the most part, however, he had succeeded in taking the Lucy part of his life out while trying to leave the Martin part in. There were some things he left, including the pictures, which he knew he wanted to keep but couldn't bear to look at. The pictures weren't like a pair of her shoes or her bathrobe; the pictures were a record of a time, a capsule of their life together, and abolishing them seemed more harmful than beneficial. Each one was like a book, to be remembered and read if needed. Once they were gone, they were gone. You couldn't get things like that back. Lucy had been a part of his life. And he realized that someday, a long time from now, when he was able to digest the truth of what had happened, he would have the photos there if he ever needed or wanted to see them.

But now, here they were, in his hands. Wrinkled, creased, crushed, angrily shoved into a drawer of the side table by someone a little too jealous to leave them alone.

Behind the closed door of his hobby room, he took them out of his pocket, and the sting returned, feeling fresh and new. He knew he shouldn't look at them, but he did, ignoring the part of him that insisted he put them away and just forget about her like he had been doing. Lucy cooking eggs on a gas stove outside a tent at Big Bear. Lucy pretending to hold up the underside the massive statue of Babe the Blue Ox in the redwoods, which happened to be very largely anatomically correct for all intents and purposes, even if they were balls of concrete. Lucy squinting in the sunlight, dirt streaked across her forehead as she struggled to stake the tent down, smiling broadly.

He wasn't sure if he would ever understand, and honestly, he never expected to. They'd had a good life, he thought, he and Lucy. It hadn't been perfect, it hadn't been grand, but it had been good and it had been solid, and there wasn't a whole lot more that he'd known how to give her. He felt foolish thinking he had been used. He was humiliated that he'd believed so much in her only to be proven so very wrong. He had wanted her to go to Hawaii, he had wanted her to have fun and enjoy herself, but he hadn't been prepared for what that had really meant for her. And once it happened, once he knew, there was no going back. There was only a life without her, and as soon as he'd hung up the phone, he had begun building it, by going back to the store and grabbing every box he could find.

Lucy had only given him one option.

She sent a letter afterward. Martin was sure it was full of justifications, pleas, and Lucy's explanation for everything she had done. He never opened it. He was so angry at her that he threw it away. He didn't want to hear her excuses. He didn't want to hear anything from her. She never even came back for Tulip when she said she would, and that told him everything he needed to know about her. If she wanted her dog, he thought, she was going to have to show up to get her, not send some letter full of reasons why she couldn't. Tulip deserved better than that. So after Lucy was gone, the thing Martin decided to look for in his life, the thing he thought he needed, was something that was the opposite of her, as far away from Lucy as he could get. He wanted no reminders, no familiars. He wanted none of it.

And then came Nola, looking for boiler onions—bulbous, practical, unadorned boiler onions. She was easy to satisfy, dependable. She needed so little.

She needed even less than he did.

From the corner of the hobby room, Lucy watched him as he went through the crumpled photos he had pulled from his pocket, the ones Nola had torn from the album and shoved into the side table drawer.

She watched him as he studied each picture, shook his head, pursed his lips, and rubbed his forehead, then returned to looking at them again. And she watched him, as the sun began to set, as the room slowly lost its light, as he placed the photographs on his desk and tried to smooth each of them out, one by one.

chapter sixteen A Shiver Runs Through It

"You haven't heard from Lucy, have you?" Nola asked Martin as he sat down to have his morning coffee.

"Mmm-mmm." Martin shook his head after he took his first sip. "Why do you ask?"

Nola shrugged as her Eggo waffle popped out of the toaster. "I dunno," she said simply. "Just thought she might have checked in or something."

"Not a word since the letter I got some time ago," he said, flipping the morning paper open. "Anyone from the office heard from her?"

Nola shook her head as she slathered butter on her Eggo. "I don't think so, but not that any of them would tell me," she replied. "Thick as thieves."

"Yeah, well, things get sticky when lines are drawn," he added. "I could see why they wouldn't bring it up in front of you. I don't know Marianne very well, but Jilly is good people. She was used by Lucy just like everyone else. Don't hold it against her."

Nola brought her waffle over to the table, smiled, and took a bite.

"Okay," she said.

Martin was quiet as he read the headlines.

Nola poured more syrup on her waffle. She watched him read.

"Because if you think she's been skulking around," Martin said, looking up, "you should tell me. I should know."

"No," she replied simply. "I don't. I was just curious."

Several weeks before, it wouldn't have crossed Nola's mind that Lucy would come back, ever, for anything, or at least that's what she told herself. She repeated it over and over again in her head that her former co-worker would be far too embarrassed after being caught stealing drugs and attempting to pilfer twenty thousand bucks from her employer. Nola tried not to really pay too much attention to the mug incident at work, chalking it up to Jilly and Marianne trying to pull a stupid trick on her, and the mailman was clearly suffering from dehydration. It must have been some heat-induced mirage when he thought he saw Lucy in the house. Half the time, he didn't even deliver the right mail to them and it was up to Nola to trudge up and down the block, handing over bills, magazines, and junk mail to their rightful owners. If she could find them, why couldn't the mailman? Wasn't he trained specifically in mail arts? It was ridiculous to even think that it was a possibility that Lucy had been in the house to begin with. She didn't have the key, and if she had been there, why hadn't she taken that dumb dog of hers? It was the only thing left of Lucy's in the whole place. Why break into the house just to hang out? Nothing had been touched, taken, or tampered with.

Until this morning.

Despite dialing her alarm back to the eighties radio station, she woke up once again to Mexican polka music, which she loathed, particularly when the alarm went off at 3 A.M. It reminded her of refried beans, and the mere thought of that right out of a dead sleep made her sick. She went to the bathroom to brush her teeth, and on the bathroom mirror was another Lucy Fisher return address sticker, just like the one Nola had found on her lunch bag a while ago. Lucy had lived here, she reminded herself. It would be completely within the realm of possibilities that a return address sticker had gotten caught on a sleeve and then had ended up stuck on a mirror, much like the way that seeds get caught in the fur of animals and spread to other regions. It was perfectly possible that that was how Lucy's sticker had wound up plastered flat on the mirror and why it had taken several applications of Goo Gone to remove. Perfectly possible.

Perfectly.

But then when Nola went to make the coffee, there was another Lucy Fisher sticker on the handle of the carafe, exactly like the first sticker. Nola scratched that one off, too, with another hearty squirt of Goo Gone.

After the coffee was made, Nola reached inside the refrigerator for her Coffee-mate, and there was yet another Lucy Fisher sticker, taping the lid closed. Almost as if Nola had to see it if she was going to have any creamer in her coffee at all.

And she was going to have creamer.

One sticker popping up was possible, Nola told herself, but three? Still, she thought, she hadn't seen Lucy, and what did stickers prove, aside from the fact that this used to be Lucy's house? She knew exactly what sensible, no-nonsense Martin would say, and she didn't really feel like being called "hysterical" so early in the morning, especially by a man who might just be trying to cover up seeing his ex-girlfriend on the sly. Instead, she finished her waffle, sopping up all of the excess syrup with the last bite, and decided to keep her eyes wide, wide, *wide* open.

"I have a surprise for you, Martin," she said gleefully, popping up out of her chair. "You stay right there."

Martin looked up as she disappeared from the kitchen, only to reappear seconds later with a box in her hands, gift wrapped in paper that cried HAPPY ANNIVERSARY! in scrolling silver letters. This gift was the item that the mailman had delivered the previous Saturday.

"For me?" he said, clearly surprised by not only the package, but the paper as well.

"It's the sixth-month anniversary of our domestic partnership," Nola said, and beamed.

"I didn't know," Martin confessed. "I don't have anything . . ."

"It's all right," Nola said. "The present is really for both of us."

Martin smiled, tore the paper off, and opened the box. Inside was a picture frame with no glass but what looked like a blank computer screen.

"Look!" Nola said as she excitedly reached across and flipped a switch on the back. Suddenly, two faces appeared on the screen, one Martin, one Nola, from their first camping trip. It was easily identifiable because of Nola's face, which had blistered from inadequate application of sunblock due to the fact that she'd insisted her skin was too sensitive to tolerate it. She'd said that an umbrella would shield her just fine, although in four days' time, her entire head had shed like a cobra's.

Suddenly, the image on the screen began to fade and another one materialized, this one looking like a green, furry bowling ball on a plate, with a candle in it.

"My birthday cake," Martin said. "You said it was supposed to be a cabbage, right?"

Nola nodded and smiled.

The scene continued as one image melted into another, faded in, faded out, materialized and then vanished. It really couldn't have worked out better for Nola, who, considering the events of the morning, wanted nothing more than to say to her domestic partner, *Lucy never existed. She was never here. We have cabbages and sunburn now.*

"How do you work this thing?" Naunie said, poking at the picture frame, turning it upside down, and all around, back to front.

"It's the same as uploading pictures onto a computer," Lucy said, her hands grasping the top of the flickering television. "I'm almost done, so put it down. Don't break it!"

Naunie put it back on the coffee table and rolled her eyes. "I'm going to lose my charge waiting for you," she said impatiently.

"Give me thirty more seconds!" Lucy replied. "Just because you drained every small appliance in the house and got a head start is no reason to be fussy!"

"I have something big planned for the mailman today," Naunie said, making conversation while Lucy finished. "It'll teach him to be a snitch."

"Don't go too nuts," Lucy warned. "The last thing we want is a spooked mailman poking around when we least expect it. Let's get this job done and get out of here."

"No kidding," Naunie agreed. "I'm sick of sleeping on this smelly old couch."

Lucy paused for a moment and looked at her grandmother.

"Really? Are you?" she questioned sarcastically. "Because I'll trade you that stinky old couch for an even stinkier La-Z-Boy recliner with a broken footrest. Just say the word. It shall be yours."

"Seriously, Lucy," Naunie said. "Why didn't you have better furniture? This stuff is all crap!"

"Neither of us made very much money, Naunie," Lucy explained. "I would have loved to have an old historic English cottage, covered with rose vines and filled with overstuffed wing chairs and white linen sofas, but that wasn't a reality. We barely had enough to live on."

"Oh, come on," the old woman argued. "What about the money from my house? You could have bought something nice with that!"

Lucy didn't say anything and pretended to be fascinated with the volume button on the TV.

"What did you do with it?" Naunie said, less a question than a demand. "What did you do with the money?"

"I spent it on Hawaii!" Lucy finally spit out.

Naunie looked shocked. "You spent it *all* on Hawaii?" she asked.

"It was supposed to be the vacation of a lifetime," Lucy tried to explain. "Not the last vacation time of my life."

Naunie looked genuinely offended. "I bet Alice didn't spend my life's work on a vacation," she said quietly.

"No," Lucy answered quickly. "No, she didn't. After her bum of a husband left her with a house payment, a kid to raise, and a piece of junk car, Alice didn't use it for a vacation. She used it to fix her car and pay the mortgage she'd fallen behind on."

Naunie didn't say anything, but just looked silently at the picture frame.

"Oh," Lucy said, nodding her head. "Oh, I see. I get it. Alice did the responsible thing with her money, and I should have done the responsible thing with mine. Like buy nice furniture so when I came back to this house as a goblin, you'd have a more comfortable spot to sleep!"

"Lucy, I don't think you do get it," Naunie said harshly. "Do you understand what's going on? No one knows you're dead. Nobody. And the reason for that is because, well, it seems like you were flying around by the seat of your pants so much that your fanny was hanging out and you never seemed to mind. Or notice. No one is out looking for you because no one thinks it's out of character for you to take off. That's why you're here, Lucy! That's why you're stuck half in and half out of this existence. At least I can say I scared the shit out of Frank Sinatra and Steve McQueen and this is my punishment. But, Lucy, sometimes you had a hard time following through. You always did. Maybe that was my fault, but now it's come back to haunt you."

"I died and my sister didn't tell anybody," Lucy protested. "I do not see how that chalks up to me being flaky! That's ridiculous! I would clearly say that's more Alice's fault than mine!"

"None of the people you knew were surprised you disappeared and didn't come back, except for one person," Naunie argued.

"Who?" Lucy shot back.

"Nola," Naunie said. "She's been terrified that you were going to come back all along. She still is. That's what the photo album is about. She's marking her territory like a cat."

"Well, she can surely have it," Lucy responded, finally feeling a big enough charge that she lifted her hands off the TV. "But I think we need to metaphorically spray on this little frame for now."

"Count me in!" Naunie cried, rubbing her wrinkled little grandma hands together.

"Okay, hand me the camera!" Lucy said as she walked over to the coffee table.

"You know how to work that thing?" Naunie said suspiciously.

"Of course I do. It's Martin's," she informed Naunie. "He never buys anything new. Smile!"

Naunie quickly delivered a pose, her hands delicately placed on her knees, and smiled like a schoolgirl.

"Say cheese!" Lucy said cheerily, as Naunie struck one hand

behind her head and another one on her hip à la Jane Russell, but in a flowing white haunting gown.

"The camera loves you, baby!" Lucy laughed as Naunie moved from one pose to another, blowing a kiss, hands cupped under her chin, looking seductively over her shoulder.

"Want me to get sexy?" Naunie asked with a wink. She raised her White Lady gown up to reveal her little bird legs and her Easy Spirit shoes. "I can roll my knee-high hose down!"

Lucy snapped away, and then turned the camera to Tulip, who had been sleeping soundly all morning long. "Tulip!" Lucy called loud enough to wake the dog up. Tulip lifted her head, and Lucy took a picture. "Come on, Tulip! Come on over here!"

It took several attempts for the old dog to get to her feet, but she finally succeeded and ambled over toward Lucy, who took several snaps of Tulip smiling with her tongue lolling out.

"Let me get a picture of the two of you!" Naunie insisted, snatching the camera from Lucy's hands. "This button here?"

Lucy nodded, wrapping her arms around Tulip's neck and smiling. On the next one, Tulip turned to give Lucy's face a long, juicy lick.

"These are wonderful!" Naunie said. "It's too bad we won't show up in any of them."

Lucy giggled and plopped down next to Naunie on the couch, flipping through the tiny digital display on the back of the camera.

"Well," Lucy remarked, "I can't see your rolled-down knee-highs, but you are one sexy orb, Naunie!"

"Yeah, that's a shame," her grandmother said, shaking her head and flipping to another frame. "A ball of light just doesn't do justice to an old woman's sex kitten pose. I had 'come hither' eyes in that one."

"Actually, you look less like a ball of light than a frenzied moth in this one," Lucy joked. "Let's upload these!"

In no time at all, Lucy hooked up the cable, transferred all of the photos over, and even overrode Nola's slide show as the current one. Instead of face blisters and cabbage cakes, there were multiple photos of Lucy, Naunie, and Tulip, although only Tulip had the nerve to actually be seen. In place of Naunie or Lucy, tiny balls of energy dotted the image. In some of the photos, the balls were in concentrated spots, and in others, the balls were all over the place, depending on how dramatic Naunie's pose had been.

"Wow," Naunie said, watching as the photos faded from one into another. "I look positively glowing!"

"You are a thousand points of light, Clovis," Lucy said, then burst into a giggle, as did her grandmother, who then put the frame back where it belonged on the coffee table.

With the frame back in place and the image in it transitioning from a photo of a couch with a bunch of what looked like dust specks and bugs flitting about to another photo of Martin's La-Z-Boy boasting the same dust, the afternoon of mischief eventually lost its novelty. Naunie and Lucy passed the time by playing cards in the kitchen, then moved to the living room to watch *Twentieth Century* with Carole Lombard on the classic movie channel. When that was over, Naunie read one of Nola's trashy magazines, and Lucy decided to give Tulip some spa time.

Naunie and Lucy, it seemed, were truly spirits of leisure.

As she walked back into the living room after letting Tulip back inside, Lucy heard the familiar *clomp-clomp-clomp* of the mailman's heavy step lumbering up the driveway to the front door. She quickly hung back in the hallway even though she didn't have a full enough charge to be seen. Naunie, however, had enough of a charge to not only be seen, but to run for public office. The glow around her was beaming, and she crouched behind the door, waiting. Naunie had closed the drapes to the large living room window so she could get close enough to hear the mail carrier as he came closer and closer to the front door, and then the footsteps stopped. Naunie turned around and gave Lucy the "Shhh!" sign and then covered her own mouth as she giggled silently in anticipation.

They both heard some rustling on the other side of the door, the squeak of the mail slot opening, and, boom, in shot the mail, landing straight at Naunie's little feet. She quickly picked up the bundle, raised it back up to the mail slot, and shoved it back with all of her might. It landed outside the house with a muffled, dull sound.

"What the . . . ," the postman commented.

In a second, Lucy heard the mail slot sing again, and then *THUD!* The mail landed at Naunie's feet, just as it had before.

She nimbly gathered it right back up, positioned it next to the slot, held it steady with one hand, and then shot it through with the open palm of the other hand by hitting it with all her might, popping it like a volleyball.

The mail scattering all over the front walkway made almost a hissing sound as it slid across the concrete, and Naunie did the best she could to stifle her laughter.

"Whaaaaaat?" the postman could be heard questioning as he gathered up mail like playing cards.

Lucy heard the wail of the mail slot again, and instead of the mail coming through on a repeat journey, the only thing that made an appearance in the opening was a big, fat, blinking, spying eye.

Wasting not even a moment, Naunie took a deep breath and blew as hard as she could. Her maneuver was evidently successful, given the clatter of the flap as it slapped the front of the door.

"My eye!" they heard the mailman wail. "My eye! There's something in my eye!"

And through the tiny break in the curtains, Lucy saw a flash of blue streak by, and heard the frenzied sounds of flat, wide feet in thick-soled shoes slapping the pavement all the way back down the driveway.

Neither Lucy nor Naunie could contain themselves.

"I can't believe you blew in his eye!" Lucy cackled with laughter. "How did you know he was going to do that?"

"I had no idea!" Naunie replied in between fits of hysterical laughter. "He coulda stuck a stick of dynamite through there and I would have had to blow that out, too!"

"That is the funniest thing I've seen since I've been dead!" Lucy chortled and bent down to rub Tulip, who didn't make a move despite all of the racket.

"Isn't Naunie funny, Tulip?" Lucy asked as she stroked Tulip's sweet face and her floppy ears. The dog responded by blinking her eyes, and then exhaled deeply. She seemed so tired.

Lucy rubbed the dog's head, and then her chest in a doggie massage, but she also had another reason. She was looking for what she didn't want to find. She ran her hands over every part of Tulip's little doggie body, looking. Tulip didn't mind; she melted into Lucy's lap and enjoyed the attention. Lucy rubbed along her legs, back, belly, ears, chest, everywhere she thought she might find another lump. When she was confident that she'd done a thorough job, she breathed a tiny sigh of relief. She didn't find another, just the two she had already felt.

Since she had felt the second lump under Tulip's leg, she had tried in vain to figure out a way to tell Martin to get her to the vet. Tulip was old, and was slowing down, but Lucy suspected that Tulip's lack of energy and appetite had more to do with what Lucy had found than with the issue of a dog growing older. This was a different kind of spirit work than Lucy had entertained; how do you play charades with someone who can't see you? How could she leave hints about something that someone should do, rather than something they *could* do? This was a whole different ballgame than finding a key under a microwave. This wasn't a case of leaving a missing wallet on a dining room table for someone to find, but something far more complex.

She decided to seek some advice from an older, a little wiser, but much more volatile source.

"Naunie," Lucy started. "We have a problem, and I need your help. I found a couple of lumps on Tulip recently, and they're not going away. I don't think Martin knows they're there, and I need to figure out a way to let him know she needs to go to the vet. I just don't know how to do that. Do you think that doing the whispering thing in his ear might work?"

Naunie paused for a moment. "I don't know. You could try it, but I've never seen it work like that," she said. "I've only seen it used to generate a sudden thought or a memory, never to get someone to do something. It's just a little 'bolt of thought' lightning."

Lucy nodded.

"Maybe we could record a TV show about animal doctors, kind of plant the seed in his head that she might need a checkup," her grandmother suggested. "Or maybe we can take a picture of her leg and put it on the frame like we just did."

Lucy nodded. They were worthwhile suggestions, but she didn't really think there was time for Martin to figure out a puzzle.

"I really need something more direct and not open to interpretation," Lucy said. "I don't think time is on our side here."

"It's too bad we can't write him a letter without channeling through someone else, and I don't even know how to do that,"

Naunie said. "It would be so easy to slip him a note in his morning paper, don't you think?"

"Neither one of us is strong enough to hold a pencil and apply that sort of pressure for that long, even if I drained the battery of a semi," Lucy said.

"Sure, we can smack the mail and press buttons, turn a page, but anything other than that . . . ," Naunie added.

Lucy suddenly looked at Naunie.

"Unless . . . ," Lucy said with a smile.

After dinner that night, the smile on Nola's face was unmistakable. It was the smile of victory, of pride, of unbridled delight. Martin sat at the dinner table taking his last couple of bites, and she approached him with an offering in her hand.

"I wanted to give this to you on our anniversary," she explained almost humbly. "But I wanted to make sure I got the quotes in the speech bubbles right."

She stretched both arms out and presented him with the masterpiece she had been slaving over every night, every lunch hour for the last week: the photo album.

Martin smiled immediately, and thought it was very sweet of her to decorate the front of a book that way, with both of their names applied in sparkly paint. He never had expressed a need to see his name embellished with glitter, but if that's the way she wanted to interpret her artistic side, he was willing to sparkle a little. She had made a good dinner.

"Open it," Nola urged.

Martin lifted the front cover, and the second he did, something hit him—this album was familiar, he knew it. The photos on the first page, however, were not the photos that had been there when he'd shoved the album into the darkness of the bottom shelf of the bookcase when he'd been sorting Lucy's things a year before. These were photos of him and Nola on their first camping trip taken not too long ago. Suddenly, the crumpled-up photos in the side table made sense; he knew where they had come from. He quickly flipped from one page to the next and saw him and Nola, him and Nola, him and Nola, and then nothing, empty pages all the way until the end.

"Don't go so fast!" Nola chided him. "You need to read all the captions and the stickers I put on the pictures, Martin! Look, in that one, you're a tomato at the Grand Canyon! You're a tomato riding a burro! Ha, ha, ha!"

Martin shut the book and looked at her.

"This is my album, right? These had my pictures in it. Am I right about that?" he asked.

"Well, I thought . . . it would be nice if . . ." Nola hesitated, her face completely drooping. "I wanted to make an album for us. For you and me."

"Then, why didn't you get a new one? Why use this one? Why did you use this one?" he asked, his voice rigid.

"It was full of . . . the other pictures, and I wanted to make it mine. I wanted to make it *ours.* You know, so we would have memories, too," she tried to explain.

"You should have bought a new one, Nola," he said angrily. "You had no business touching this one. I found the smashed photos in the side table. I would like to have the other ones, please."

Nola didn't know what to say. She couldn't say anything. She stood there, hoping that in any second he would change his mind and realize how much work she had put into this album and how some of the captions were really funny and how now they had something that was theirs and it was full of good times that they could laugh about and look at over and over again.

"Nola. I want my pictures," he said again. "Please."

Nola shook her head, like a child who has suddenly realized exactly just how deeply she is in trouble.

"I don't have them," she said quietly.

"Then, get them," he told her.

"I mean, I don't have them anymore," she replied. "They're gone. I got rid of them."

Martin stopped looking at her. He had to look down at the table, where he could still see the "tin" of his name spelled out in gleaming blue letters.

"You had no right," he finally said, shaking his head slowly. "Those were mine. How could you do that? How could you think that was right?"

Nola shook her head quickly, almost frantically. Didn't he see?

"She's gone! Lucy is gone, Martin! It is time to start over, because it's my turn now," she said, her voice rising. "I don't understand why you would ever want pictures of her. Why would you want pictures of someone that had done something so bad to you?"

"Because they were mine!" he said, one octave below yelling. "You had no right to touch anything of mine. They didn't belong to you."

No matter how much she should have stopped there, Nola could not control herself. She was like a train shooting downhill, warning lights flashing but no way to stop.

"You are seeing Lucy again, aren't you?" she said as she burst into a flood of angry and desperate tears. "I knew it! She's sneaking in here when I'm gone and you're seeing her behind my back!"

"That's ridiculous," Martin scoffed. "I haven't heard from her in nearly a year."

"Then why would you want those pictures?" Nola sobbed.

"Why would you want those pictures if you still didn't have feelings for her? If you still didn't love her?"

From across the table, where she had been sitting the entire night, Lucy looked at Martin. She had been whispering to him during the entire meal that Tulip needed his help, Tulip was sick, and that she needed to go to the vet, but there was no sign or acknowledgment that he'd heard her. Now she studied his face, watched his eyes, the eyes that would not look at Nola. He looked confused, furious, unsure. His hands were clenched together in front of him, gripping each other tightly. She hadn't seen Martin look this way since they'd had the fight about chicken skin.

Without even thinking, she reached out and gently touched his hands, offering a reassuring pat. She meant it to be gentle and kind. Instead, his reaction was sudden and quick, jerking his hands and body backward and away in a reactive move.

"What's the matter?" Nola asked. "Are you all right?"

"Yeah, yes," he said, unsure himself, shuddering. "I felt a chill; a shiver went through me. I don't know how to explain it."

"I hope you're not coming down with something," Nola said, putting her hand on his shoulder. "I'm sorry I upset you. I thought you would be surprised."

Martin nodded, wanting to understand why she'd done it, but not able to. "I have copies of some of the photos on my computer," he said quietly. "And I have not seen Lucy. I don't know where she is. You're just going to have to take my word for that."

Nola agreed. It didn't appear as if she really had a choice. "All right," she finally said. "I will."

The next morning, after Martin had had his coffee, read the paper, and closed the bathroom door after going in for a shower, Lucy put her plan into action. She knew that if there was one thing that Martin loved more than a hot cup of coffee in the morning and reading his paper, it was phase two of Martin's morning routine: taking a hot, and she meant HOT, shower. Oftentimes when Martin had finished his steam bath of sorts, there wouldn't be enough hot water left for the duration of Lucy's shower. And with that nugget of information in her invisible ghost hand, she marched her way through the bathroom door and waited.

Martin was in the shower, and the steam was billowing over the shower curtain. Lucy grabbed his electric razor and held it tightly on its stand, and when that was drained, she went for the twin electric toothbrushes, until she felt she had enough energy built up to send a message from beyond. She had no idea if her plan was even feasible, but she couldn't risk not trying; she didn't know if he had heard her last night or not, and she wasn't willing to bet on it. She needed a sure thing, and she thought this was the only way to get it.

She put her finger up to the mirror, thinking it was a little nuts that her most important lesson in ghost school thus far had been learned by watching a Demi Moore movie.

"MARTIN," she wrote in the steam gathering on the mirror, "Tulip is sick. Take her to vet asap. PLEASE."

Lucy waited to make sure her message wasn't going to get fogged over, then slipped out of the bathroom.

She nearly fell into Nola, who was waiting on the other side of the door with the digital frame in her hand. She had found it, and was gripping it so tightly her knuckles looked like they were glowing white.

Naunie was removing herself from the line of fire by staying safely in the living room, and she motioned to Lucy to join her. They heard the water turn off and the clatter of the shower curtain being drawn back.

Then the silence of the house was sliced with the shrill ringing of the phone, and it suddenly occurred to Lucy that during the whole time she had been there, she had not heard it before.

Nola remained in the darkened hallway, unmoving, her fingers still clutching the frame.

The phone rang again.

"Nola!" Martin called out as if she was on the other side of the house. "Get it, will you?"

She didn't budge.

Another ring choked the interim quiet.

Martin emerged from the bathroom quickly in the plaid robe Lucy had given him, his hair completely wet, not yet tousled with a towel, and his face flushed with the heat of the shower. He, too, nearly ran right into Nola, who remained as still as a garden statue. Martin got to the kitchen phone just as the fourth ring erupted, and he answered it gruffly.

"Hello. Yeah. Yeah," his muffled voice said. "No, not today, he's not scheduled till ten. That sounds like a mess. No, don't do anything until I get there. Give me ten minutes."

Nola had moved. Instead of standing in the hall, she was now standing in the bathroom doorway, frozen.

Lucy suddenly realized that she was staring at the mirror. Lucy held her theoretical breath.

Martin hung up the phone and headed down the hall toward the bedroom.

Nola turned and began to slowly walk toward him.

"Martin," she called out—not angrily, not agitated, but simply, plainly. She walked down the hall until she was out of Lucy's sight.

"I gotta go, Nola," Martin huffed, and Lucy heard him scurrying around the bedroom, trying to get dressed quickly.

"Martin," she called again. "Why did you take away my pictures?"

"I don't—" he began, and then sighed. "I can't now. I have to go. The delivery is a mess. They got everything screwed up and we have a sale starting today."

"My pictures are gone," she said quietly. "Why did you do that? Are you trying to teach me a lesson—I take your pictures, you take mine?"

"Can we talk about this later?" he said. Lucy heard pounding, and imagined him hopping on one foot to get his other shoe on. She had known Martin to do that.

"No," Nola insisted, her voice harsher. "You erased my pictures to get back at me, but I know the truth. She's been in this house. I know it. *I just saw it.* Just tell me the truth!"

"I didn't do anything to get back at you. That's ridiculous," Martin replied, his voice growing louder. "I didn't take any pictures. I told you once that I have not seen her, and I will tell you again. I have not seen Lucy. I do not know where she is. Now I have to get to work. There are big problems and they need me."

"Look," Nola demanded, and Lucy heard some scuffling. "*Look.* I will prove it. I will prove it to you."

"Nola, stop it," Martin demanded as Nola pulled him toward the bathroom. "Let me go. Nola, *let go*."

From the hallway, Lucy heard hurried footsteps, and Nola appeared first, pulling Martin by his wrist.

"I will show you," she insisted. "Because I saw it. I saw it, Martin! She was just in here, wasn't she?"

She had just reached the bathroom doorway, when Tulip, who had gotten spooked by the yelling and the footsteps, made the wrong decision and tried to run to the bathroom to hide from the commotion. Tulip collided with Nola, who'd been pulling Martin and walking backward down the hall. Tulip dashed under her feet, and Nola lost her grip on Martin. There was no way that Nola could have stopped as she toppled backward and, trying to regain her balance, fell forward, smacking her face against the bathroom doorjamb as the digital picture frame slipped from her other hand and tumbled to the floor.

Red was everywhere instantly, as if a paintball had popped. It was smudged on the doorjamb, and smeared on Nola's lip and chin. It was not a lot of blood, Lucy realized, but the appearance and color of it was vibrant and striking.

"That dog," Nola said as she grimaced, holding her lip. "Get rid of that dog, Martin. That dog is the reason she keeps coming back! It's her dog, and if she's not going to take care of it, I'm not taking care of it, either!"

"Tulip just got scared, Nola," Martin said, gathering a towel and pressing it on Nola's split lip. "It was an accident, just an accident."

"Really?" Nola quickly snarled and pointed to the bathroom mirror. "Is *that* an accident?"

The mirror was clear, steam-free. Lucy's message had evaporated with every last drop of moisture.

Martin exhaled deeply and shrugged out of frustration.

"This has got to stop," he said, shaking his head. "I don't know where this is coming from. I know you've had your issues with Lucy, but I have nothing to do with that. These accusations are getting a little nuts."

"You're telling me you didn't see that?" Nola cried. "You didn't see it? Right in front of your face and you didn't see the writing on the mirror? Come on, Martin, now who's a little nuts? It was *right there*. I saw it! *She was just here!*"

"I don't know what you saw," he replied. "But I do know I am getting tired of this. There was no one in the bathroom with me, especially not Lucy Fisher. I think I probably would have seen her."

"She has been in this house. The mailman even saw her!" Nola yelled. "Lucy stickers were everywhere. They were on my Coffee-mate!"

"I think maybe it's time you talked to somebody, you know?" Martin said, handing the bloodied towel to Nola and walking out of the bathroom. "We're going to have to talk about this later, because I have to go to work now. But I will tell you that this situation is getting out of control. You need to figure it out, Nola. Figure it out."

And with that, Martin picked his truck keys from the side table in the living room and walked out the door.

From the couch where she was sitting, trying to calm a terrified Tulip, Lucy saw Nola press the towel to her lip and walk out into the hallway, where her domestic partnership present was on the floor, the front of it shattered like a spiderwebbed windshield.

Nola picked up the frame and walked into the living room, where, through the window, she saw Martin climbing into his truck and driving away.

"I am not crazy, Martin," she said, looking at the broken frame in her hand. *"I am not crazy! Lucy Fisher is destroying my life!"*

Then Nola reared back her arm like a World Series pitcher and threw the frame across the room with all her might. It shot between the side tables and flew over the couch, where it would have completely shattered on the floor. That is, if Naunie had not been there to catch it nimbly and, without a slice of hesitation, rear her own arm back and, with every bit as much force, throw it right back at Nola.

chapter seventeen Give It to the Kid

That Saturday, when the chime of the doorbell sounded and Martin answered it, Lucy did not expect to see Jilly standing on the other side.

"Hi, Jilly," he said calmly.

"Martin," she said as she nodded once.

"Come on in," he added, stepping aside. "How've you been?" he queried as she stepped past him and stopped just inside the living room.

"No complaints," she answered simply.

"And Warren?"

"Same," she said.

Martin nodded politely. "Good to hear, good to hear," he replied.

He closed the door, and then stood there for a moment.

"You know, this whole thing," he began, not sure where he was going. "It's—You know, I just think that it's a better place for her now, until things settle down. I don't want you to think that I . . .

I'd be doing this if it wasn't for . . . Well, it's just for *right now*. Just right now, and I am appreciative that you—"

"It's all right, Martin," Jilly interrupted. "Of course I'll do it. There's no question."

"Thank you," he said humbly. "I appreciate it."

"Holy crap!" Lucy spat, almost choking. "Did you hear that? Is Nola moving in with Jilly? Martin is kicking her out? I haven't seen her pack anything, have you?"

Naunie shook her head and shrugged. "I'll be glad to get rid of her," she offered, "but I will miss pinching that doughy behind."

"Does this mean our job is done?" Lucy cried, nearly ecstatic.

"We could be in The State by tonight, kid." Naunie cackled. "Whaddya think about that?"

Jilly took a deep breath and just stood there, looking at Martin.

"Have you heard from her," she finally asked. "At all?"

"Nope," Martin said. "Just got one letter, but nothing since then."

"What did the letter say?" Jilly wanted to know. She had never asked Martin any of this before—it wasn't really her business, there had never been a good opportunity—but the truth was that she had never had the guts to bring it up. She didn't know what she might be opening up here. But now, here, just her and him, had to be the right time, and it might be the only time. "What did Lucy say?"

Martin took a deep breath and ran his hand over his short, cropped hair. "You know, Jilly, it may sound silly now, but at the time, I couldn't bring myself to open it. There wasn't anything she could say to fix what had happened, and I just didn't want to hear her try to. So I . . . didn't. Didn't read it. I threw it away, probably to get back at her. I don't know."

"I wish you had read it," Jilly said. "I'd like to know anything about what happened after she left here."

"So you haven't talked to her, either?" Martin asked.

"Not a word since the day she pulled out of my driveway," she said. "I sure would like to know what happened that day, when she found all of her stuff thrown out on the lawn, Martin."

"I wish I could tell you, Jilly," he replied.

"Then why don't you?"

Martin paused and bit his lip. "I've got enough on my mind for today, I think," he said.

"All right, then, another day," Jilly said. "But I mean it. Another day. Do you have everything together for her?"

"The State by nightfall," Lucy chimed. "The State by nightfall!"

"We are so good at haunting we should charge for this," Naunie said, and laughed. "We can crack 'em in no time flat!"

"Sure, I've got her things right here," Martin said. He walked back into the hallway and pulled out a shopping bag. "Again, I appreciate it, Jilly."

"He's not sending her off with much," Naunie said. "The least he could do is give her that glitter album back. Who spells their name in glitter except Charo?"

"Wouldn't have it any other way," Jilly replied. "Lucy was my best friend. We brought her home together."

Lucy gasped. "They're taking her," she said quietly and quickly. "Naunie, they're taking Tulip."

Lucy looked at her dog asleep at her feet, wedged in between the coffee table and the couch, almost all gray around her muzzle. Jilly had been there when Lucy had found Tulip at the pound. It was Jilly who'd driven home while Lucy had kept the puppy on her lap, the puppy who'd given long, sloppy licks with delicious puppy breath. One extended lick over not just Lucy's bottom lip or chin like most dogs, but right over the top, it had to be both lips. Two lips. Tulip.

"Naunie," Lucy barely squeezed out, her eyes immediately full, a wave of grief and panic swallowing her. "Don't let them take her! Oh, no! They can't take her!"

Naunie grabbed Lucy's hand firmly with one hand and held her around the shoulders with her other.

"Oh, no," Lucy whispered, trembling.

"Lucy," Naunie said sternly. "You need to listen to me. *Listen to me.* Jilly loves Tulip, you know she will care for her. Tulip can't stay here anymore. You don't know what Nola will do. She's safer with Jilly. You can't protect Tulip the way you are. You can love her, but you have to love her enough to let her go."

Tulip, sensing Lucy's distress, woke up and licked her hand. Then she struggled to get up, and laid her chin on the smelly couch cushion next to Lucy.

Lucy broke down and sobbed. Through everything she had been through—being dumped, fired, killed, and forgotten, Lucy had not shed one tear. Not one. She had changed physical proportions, purposes, and realms. But not once had she allowed the tears to pass; she'd always been able to keep them back. Now it was too much. It was too hard, and she wept with anger, sadness, frustration, and now, most of all, emptiness.

"I can't lose her again," she cried to her grandmother. "I just got her back."

Lucy stroked Tulip's head while the dog looked at her reassuringly.

"I'm so sorry," Lucy said.

"Tulip, come," Martin commanded, and Tulip gave Lucy a long, warm look, rubbing her nose into Lucy's palm. Then she turned and padded off toward Martin, who kneeled down in front of her and rubbed her ears.

"You are a good girl," he said, and looked at her for a long time.

Then he pulled her leash out of the bag, clipped it onto her collar, and stood up.

"Thank you," he said earnestly, and cleared his throat, handing the leash to Jilly. "I couldn't imagine her going to anyone else."

"Neither could I," Jilly agreed, then took the bag of Tulip's things from Martin.

"I'm sorry to bring this up, but she hasn't been to the vet in a while. I have a nagging feeling that she should get checked out," Martin added. "I'll gladly pay for it and anything else you need for her."

He heard me, Lucy thought. *Martin really did hear me that night.*

"Okay," Jilly agreed. "I'll make an appointment. Tulip has the same vet as my dog. Come on, Tulip. Have I got things to show you!"

And with that, she turned around as Martin opened the door for her, and both she and Tulip walked out of the house. Lucy watched them go until they were both completely out of her sight, but not before Tulip got to the end of the driveway and looked back one last time.

Alice coughed immediately after hoisting up the garage door. Dust filtered in from everywhere, drifting in the rays of the sun that were hitting all of this stuff for the first time in what seemed like a lifetime.

She hated packing, she hated moving, she hated all of it. She especially hated telling her son, Jared, that they would be living in an apartment closer to town because she had lost the house. She simply couldn't keep up with the payments and had fallen behind, and had quickly found herself in a void that ended with packing tape, boxes from Starbucks, and a notice from the sheriff. Naunie's money had helped for a while, and it had seemed to be a perfect solution when Lucy came, but that . . . brought the accident. She refused to think about that now. If she did, she'd never get through this. It was bad enough that she was going to have to start packing up her sister's possessions and move them into storage. There would barely be enough room for Alice's and Jared's things in the apartment as it was.

She looked over the pile of Lucy's belongings, a heavy layer of dust on everything, since few of Lucy's boxes had lids—they were all produce crates with peaches, grapes, or cherries printed on the side. Alice shook her head. She should have covered this stuff up a long time ago. It had never even occurred to her.

Alice ran her finger over a framed photo of her and Lucy when they were little, tiny girls, wearing the smallest bikinis in their plastic play pool. Both were laughing and beaming, Alice looking at the camera while Lucy's eyes were nearly shut, her head thrown back in laughter, her hands frozen together in a clap. On the side of the photo, a woman's thin arm held a hose, her thumb over the nozzle, creating a fountainlike spray. She wondered if it was Naunie's hand or their mother's. Either way, Alice realized somberly that she was the only one left.

Next to the photo was a nylon bag, which looked like some sort of luggage. Alice pulled and tugged on the long strap to get it free from the box, and when she did, she recognized it immediately. Lucy's laptop bag. Alice didn't even remember shoving it in the box or bringing any of this to the garage. Then again, for some time after the accident, she hadn't remembered much at all, and frankly, she was glad about that one small favor. Losing Lucy was— Well, she had never known something so profound and weighted as that before, so bottomless and vast it couldn't possibly be real. It didn't make sense; it never made sense. She felt hollow and empty, cracked. She woke up one night and instantly thought, *Lucy is gone. If I looked all over the world for her, if I spent the rest of my life, I would never find her. She's not there. She's not anywhere.*

After the accident, Alice felt that even by breathing, it was a lie. Everything was a lie. It was simply not possible for things to continue on when so much she had loved had stopped existing and vanished. She found herself furious one day at a potted plant she had placed on the mantel because it got decent sun there. It had been there for years, growing, twisting, opening, living, and Alice looked at it one day and thought, *How dare you. How dare you go on like you were the same as you were last week, how dare you stay there, the same, while such a horrible thing has happened, and everything has changed. How dare you not be affected by this.* And in her anger, she pulled the plant off the mantel and put it outside, where the sun was not so kind and giving.

Time wasn't supposed to move forward, time wasn't supposed to pass, Alice thought. A world, a life, without her sister was ridiculous, preposterous. After Lucy's death, there were moments that would seem normal again, but as soon as Alice got comfortable, the grief came roaring back, slapping her for even thinking anything could be right. When she thought of Martin, she seethed. It was damage enough that he had thrown Lucy out and caused all of this, but to never answer her letters, to never respond was unimaginable. To not even reply with condolences was unforgivable. A reaction from him was needed, and on a couple of instances, Alice sent another letter to remind him that her sister was dead. The letters never came back, and she never heard a word. What had Lucy been doing with a man like that? Alice had wondered bitterly. Lucy had had a knack for bringing home terrible boyfriends, but this one was so far beyond that. He had put on a good show in front of Alice, but his actions had changed her life forever and caused exceptional loss. There were times when, in her fury, she was convinced that she needed to drive down to Phoenix and let him know just how much of a bastard she thought he was, that he needed to know just what he had done. But she eventually realized that with his resounding, silent indifference, nothing she could possibly say would matter to him, and by the same account, he didn't deserve to understand how angry he had made her.

He wasn't good enough to know how much she hated him.

Alice patted the nylon bag, trying to release the dust and make the cover clean again. She coughed. She zipped open the side, and there was the shiny white plastic top of Lucy's computer. Alice was sure it still worked, and felt around for the power cord, which was tucked into a pocket on the inside.

She knew just what to do with it, and when Jared came home that afternoon from school, she handed him the bag and the computer, because she knew that if Lucy'd had a say, she would have wanted him to have it. Her sister had died with less than $400 to her name, but in her typical but reckless generosity, she had bought Jared an iPod with what little money she had the day before.

Alice heard Lucy's voice.

"Give it to the kid," she said.

To say that Lucy was inconsolable was an understatement. She wanted to punch Martin in the face for letting Nola get away with that. He had done some stupid things—as in pairing up with Nola—but this was unforgivable, giving away her dog. *Their dog.* Tulip was a member of the family, and to surrender her, even to a good friend, because she'd tripped an unbalanced woman was simply criminal in Lucy's eyes. For days, Lucy roamed around the house lifeless, not wanting to do anything but sit in the memory of Tulip. Lie on the cushions she'd lain on, and collect whatever hair she could find on the couch and rugs and hold it in tight furry little bundles in her hand.

Naunie did whatever she could to bring Lucy out of it, telling dirty jokes, doing little dances, singing songs, and reenacting Nola's remote control hissy fit, but after a while, even she figured that she needed to back off and let Lucy grieve. Lucy needed to work through this in her own time, in her own way. Even if that meant curling up on the living room rug like a dog, her nose buried in the fibers, for hours on end.

All of that was going to need to change, however, and rather quickly. A couple of weeks after Jilly took Tulip, Nola brought a friend home after work. It was odd enough to entertain the thought that Nola could even make a friend, but that she had brought one home puzzled Naunie. Lucy was burrowed into the couch, and Naunie had to pull her arm to get her attention.

"Who's this?" Naunie said, pointing to the strange woman now in the house, who Nola was leading back into the kitchen.

Lucy saw the back of the woman's head, with long stringy hair, go by as she walked into the hallway. "I dunno," Lucy said, sniffling.

"I don't like the looks of this," Naunie said. "She doesn't look like Nola's type. She's wearing some crazy big floor-length skirt, long feather earrings, and a ton of turquoise. Something's not right."

"How do you know?" Lucy muttered, not even looking at Naunie. "What would Nola's type be?"

"The only thing she even owns aside from her fake nurse's uniform is a pair of sweatpants and a Hello Kitty T-shirt," Naunie reminded her. "That friend woman had bracelets on. *Like, forty of them.*"

"Leave me alone," Lucy whimpered. "I'm pretending that Tulip is here."

"You wanna pretend? Okay," Naunie said agreeably. "Let's pretend there's some hippie dippy psychic sitting at the kitchen table listening to Nola's story about a picture frame boomeranging back at her. All right, then, don't pretend. You don't have to, because there is a hippie dippy psychic in there right now."

And with that, Naunie grabbed Lucy's arm, yanked her off the couch, and led her, stumbling, into the kitchen.

"Holy shit," Lucy gasped immediately.

"No kidding," Naunie agreed. "What did I tell you? She's already taken her shoes off. That is disgusting. Her feet are filthy. Only a hippie has feet like that. They've got more dirt on them than an archeological dig."

"No, not her feet," Lucy said, peering around the refrigerator. "I know that woman. She's a patient of Dr. Meadows's. It's Almighty Isis! She was always trying to give me readings and tell me my future. She did that to everyone in the office to try and drum up business."

"Wasn't much to tell there, huh? 'Beware of buses, Lucy,'" Naunie added. "What do you think she's here for?"

"Oh." Lucy laughed sarcastically. "Us. She is here for us. Nola's got the picture frame in her hand."

"How is your tea?" Nola asked Isis.

"Orgasmic," Isis replied. "It would be meta-orgasmic if you had any simple agave syrup for sweetening."

Nola shook her head and frowned dramatically. "No, I don't have that, but I do have Sweet 'N Low," she offered. "Shall I get it?"

Isis ignored her. "Now tell me, Nora, what you have been experiencing that you feel is paranormal."

"Well," Nola said, very impressed with herself that she had a story to tell that someone wanted to hear. It was clear that she was about to tell her tale of the supernatural in detail, not sparing one little iota that might be crucial in Isis's expert diagnosis. "I was standing—"

"I sense something," Isis interrupted quickly.

"Is it the spirit?" Nola said, sitting up in her chair, her eyes darting about the room. "Is it here?"

"It is you," Isis said, stretching the "oo" sound in "you" out for an unnecessarily long period of time. "You have medium tendencies, don't you?"

Nola's eyes got sad, and she shook her head. "No," she said, clearly ashamed. "I'm an XXL. It's really hard to find work pants with a good fit. They get all bunched up right here."

And then she pointed to her crotch.

"I'm referring to your antennae, your ability to pick up on things otherwise unseen," Isis explained. "Your gift to sense things perhaps not of this world, but of the next."

"I guess sometimes," Nola gave in. "I certainly did see that picture frame coming at me."

"Now," Isis said, reaching into her Guatemalan fabric purse with the very dirty bottom to pull out an enormous pad of paper and a sparkly pen. "Recount the incident for me."

"Well," Nola said sharply, then stopped to take a deep breath. "I was just standing in the living room when the frame fell out of my hand. All of a sudden, it was flying over across the room, and it turned around and then came back at me. Directly at me. I ducked, and it landed on the big blue recliner out there."

"And you didn't have a window open? There wasn't a breeze blowing?" Isis investigated.

"No," Nola said. "It was early in the morning. There was no breeze."

"And no one else was in the house?" Isis continued. "You were alone, Nora?"

"I was," Nola confirmed.

"May I see the frame, please?" the psychic requested.

"Oh, of course," Nola replied, and handed it over.

"Was it already broken like this when it flew across the room?" Isis queried.

Nola nodded with a crooked, forced smile.

"Can I turn it on? May I see what's on here?" the psychic continued.

Nola nodded again and directed her to the switch on the back of the frame, which Isis turned on.

"I didn't take those pictures, though," she explained. "And I haven't gotten a straight answer about who did."

Isis pressed the manual button at the bottom of the frame and flipped through the photos, one by one, noting each frame and studying them with interest. Suddenly, her brow furrowed mightily.

She looked up at Nola. "Have you looked through these?"

"Just enough to know that they aren't my photos," Nola offered.

Isis scooted her chair closer to Nola's until they were side by side and Nola could fully experience the aroma of Isis's patchouli, the same aroma that clings to ancient recently unearthed Egyptian mummies or is infused to the mold that grows inside cheaply built houses.

"I'd like to show you something," Isis said as Nola held her breath, not figuratively, but as a survival mechanism.

"We start out here with just basic shots, not much to them, of the couch, the chair, and in all of these, we are seeing these circular blurs—we call them orbs," Isis explained as she went from frame to frame. "They're in all of these, these light spheres. They are supernatural anomalies, and they are quite often captured on film when there is a paranormal presence at work."

Isis continued to flip through the photos, pointing out the orbs to Nola in each one.

"Oh, that's odd," Isis muttered to herself when she flipped to a photo of the pink electric toothbrush resting on the open toilet seat with a splatter of orbs glowing brightly like Christmas lights.

She continued on through the pictures, until she stopped at one.

"Well, look at that," she said, with one eyebrow raised. "What do we have here?"

"What? What?" Nola asked anxiously.

Isis paused for a moment, thinking. "In all of the other photos," she said carefully, "orbs abound. But in this one—this must be your dog—it's just a picture of the dog with no orbs. Yet, there's something behind it. Can you see that?"

"I'm not sure," Nola said, still trying to not take a breath or get too close.

"What I'm seeing is in this area right behind the dog," Isis said, circling her hand over the area on the screen. "There's an outline there. In fact, it's more than an outline. Do you see it now?"

Naunie looked at Lucy with alarm. "I think we should see this," she said, and Lucy followed right behind.

On the screen, in the area where Isis was pointing, was a somewhat hazy spot up and to the left of Tulip. It was completely transparent, and difficult to make out, but there, slightly layered on top of Martin's blue La-Z-Boy, were a pair of eyes, a nose, and a mouth.

Lucy gasped. "It's me!" she said to Naunie. "There I am! Damn it."

"Uh-oh," Naunie warned. "This is not what we needed. I should have known better. You're hugging Tulip, and transferring energy from her, whether you meant to or not. Not enough for a full manifest—just enough to suggest an image if you really want to see one."

And it was clear that Isis really, *really* wanted to see one.

"I can make out a face right here," she pointed out to Nola. "Eyes, nose, mouth, shape of the head. It's obviously a man, with that jawline, wouldn't you say?"

Nola nodded vigorously as her face turned purple.

"I think it's an older man," Isis said thoughtfully as she studied the photo. "I see a receding hairline and some jowls. Do you, Nora?"

Nola didn't answer per se. She was too busy choking and trying to catch her breath after her will to survive kicked in right before she was due to lose consciousness.

"A man, huh?" Lucy said, trying desperately to resist picking up the frame herself and throwing it at Isis. "She thinks I'm a man? She is such an idiot. You deserve your periodontal disease, and I wish I had stayed alive long enough to root plane you."

"She's an asshole," Naunie said.

"Oh, yeah, that's certainly a man," Isis said to herself, and nodded. "In his fifties, maybe sixties. Older. Frustrated. Resentful that he is no longer alive."

Lucy leaned over toward the psychic's frizzy head and bellowed, "Isis, you're a jackass!"

Somewhat recovered and now breathing through a paper towel she had plastered over her face, Nola couldn't have agreed more.

"A man! That would explain how the frame could have been thrown at me with such force," Nola concluded.

"I'm getting an *M*," Isis said as she closed her eyes and laid her palm flat on the screen. "Ma . . . Mar . . ."

"Martin?" Nola questioned, her eyes widening.

"Mar . . . cus!" Isis concluded. "Marcus . . . I'm getting a *W* . . . Waaaahhhh . . . Wahhhhh . . . Wel . . . Welp . . . Welby!"

"Marcus Welby?" Naunie questioned. "I suppose that makes me Barnaby Jones, then."

"Marcus Welby." Nola breathed with awe at Almighty Isis's unbelievable skills of pulling names from a thirty-year-old *TV Guide*.

"Is it familiar?" Isis asked. "Does it at all sound familiar to you?"

Nola bit her lip and shook her head.

"What a fraud," Naunie said, laughing. "I can't believe we were afraid of that!"

"Is he an angry spirit?" Nola asked, afraid to know the answer.

"Marcus Welby is not happy you are in his house," Isis replied. "I think he'll do anything to get rid of you. The frame was just the first level in his wrath. Things could get very dangerous for you here. I think a cleansing is in order right away. And I can help you."

"What a sales pitch!" Lucy said, amazed that she had just seen such a spectacle.

"You can?" Nola breathed, clearly quite relieved.

"Certainly," she said. "I'll have to consult my removal team and see what works with our schedule, but as soon as I have a date, I'll call you and let you know."

"That's wonderful," Nola said. "I don't know how I'm going to sleep tonight knowing that Marcus Welby is dangerous."

"Here is my own brew of ghost repellant," Isis said, pulling a spray bottle out of her purse with a label on it that had obviously been printed on her home computer. "It will keep you safe from Marcus Welby and other spirits until we can get them all where they need to be, and that's out of here!"

Nola took the bottle, sprayed a tiny amount, and then sniffed it. She wrinkled her nose immediately, smelling something familiar.

"This is what you're wearing, isn't it?" she asked.

"It is," Isis confirmed. "I need protection constantly. I am an open portal and am therefore quite vulnerable to spirit attacks and hostile takeovers. This keeps me safe."

"And it will keep me safe, too, from Marcus Welby?"

"Very safe," Isis counseled. "But be generous with it. The more you use, the more you are protected. And I can always make more!"

Then she tapped the bottle with the tip of her dirty fingernail.

"Thank you, Isis!" Nola said, relieved.

"That'll be twenty-nine ninety-nine," Isis replied, reaching into her giant Central American bag. "Cash, check, Visa, MasterCard, or American Express?"

"Um . . . Visa?" Nola said, a little confused, and then reached for her purse.

"Perfect," Isis said with a perky smile, drawing a portable credit card processor terminal from her brightly colored hobo knapsack.

"Piece of cake," Naunie said after Isis had bamboozled Nola out of a hundred bucks for a "consultation" fee and then had left the house. Nola had also left, opting to wait out the rest of Martin's shift at the local Starbucks rather than be left alone in the house with the terrifying and ominous Marcus Welby. "She's absolutely nothing to worry about. She was nothing like the last psychic I encountered. She didn't make up some 1970s television series doctor and pretend he was haunting the house, oh, no. She zeroed in right on me, knew where I was sitting, knew what I was doing, and she certainly heard every word I said to her. But this one—Isis—she's no better than a nickel fortune-teller at a school yard carnival. We have nothing to worry about."

"I agree," Lucy said cautiously. "But I think we need to be careful about this all the same. She did spot something in the picture with Tulip—and even though she identified me as a middle-aged man, I didn't see that in the picture, you didn't see it, and Nola didn't originally see it. There may be some skill there. Agreed—it's minuscule, but it might be something. I don't feel good going into this blind."

"Oh, what's she gonna do?" Naunie scoffed. "Spray some of that hippie Glade room freshener on you and toss some glitter around? Really, Lucy. You're too easily spooked for a spook. She's after the money. Let her have it. 'Nora' in there deserves to get bilked."

"Of course she does, but I don't want to end up as a space rock circling Saturn for all of eternity next to the last bozo who was certain he could outfox a fake medium," Lucy decided.

"Fine," Naunie said, sounding half-insulted. "But I'm not making the call."

"I have a feeling you never do," Lucy said, then cupped her hands around her mouth. "RUBY!" she yelled, figuring if it had worked to get her out of a funeral home, it would work in this mess, too.

Within five minutes, Lucy and Naunie's spook schoolteacher walked out of the bathroom.

"That's so odd," she said as she walked into the living room, smoothing her long black robe. "I've never had the elevator let me out in a bathtub before. You people must have a thing with restrooms."

"We may have a slight problem," Naunie began very nonchalantly.

"Good to see you, too, Clovie," Ruby said with a smile. "What did you send flying through the air this time?"

Lucy sighed and rolled her eyes. "You did the same thing before?" she said somewhat angrily.

"What can I say?" Naunie said as she shrugged. "I have an MO."

"She threw a digital picture frame at my boyfriend's girlfriend," Lucy explained.

"I did not," Naunie protested. "I merely returned it to her."

"Sure you did," Lucy agreed. "At forty-five miles per hour."

"Clovie, that temper of yours is going to throw you and your granddaughter into orbit if you don't watch it," Ruby warned.

"A 'psychic' was here today, talking about cleaning the house," Lucy began, and the news made Ruby wince.

"That's not good news," Ruby replied.

"No, that's the bad news," Lucy reiterated. "But the good news is that she ID'd me as Marcus Welby, an angry middle-aged male ghost."

"Marcus Welby, the kindhearted doctor from the seventies TV series played by Robert Young?" Ruby asked. "I saw every episode. He was never angry, and had a terrific bedside manner. You look nothing like him."

"Which is more good news," Lucy added. "She's clearly not that skilled or fine-tuned. But the bad news: She did see my outline in a photo when neither Naunie nor I had."

"So she may be remedial, but not that powerful," Ruby said, thinking.

"And don't forget the 'ghost spray,'" Naunie reminded Lucy. "It protects her from 'hostile takeovers.' And she sells it."

Ruby burst out laughing. "All right," she started after she wiped the tears from her eyes. "If she didn't sense you soon after entering the house, I don't think there's too much to be worried about. I think it's a sham, but, to be on the safe side, you should be prepared. The best way to combat a psychic is to present a powerful front. Clovie, you're the more powerful of the two of you, so you need to take charge in this. Together, if you combine your forces, you can fight it off, depending on how strong the light is, but that will depend on how strong the medium is."

"That's all?" Lucy asked. "That's all we have to do—stick together? That sounds easy, unless we get sprayed with ghost mace, of course. Are you sure?"

Ruby shrugged. "That's about it," she said. "The only other thing that can add to your power is gathering energy through thought."

"That seems simple. We need to stave off the white light by thinking about it?" Naunie asked.

"No, not exactly," Ruby cautioned. "It's not your thoughts that give you energy. It's the thoughts of other people when they're thinking about you. Can you do something to encourage something like that?"

"Great," Lucy said, not exactly folding, but sensing that this tactic was useless. "Everyone is angry with me for flaking out and disappearing. No one gives me a second thought. You can count me out on that front. Just in case Isis becomes the real thing overnight, I want to be prepared."

"What did you say? Her name is Isis?" Ruby asked, holding her side and wheezing. "Why didn't you say that in the first place. *Isis?* You have nothing to worry about. No self-respecting medium would ever call themselves that. If her name was Andrea or Dee Ann, I'd worry. But Isis? Please. She made that name up, just like her magical abilities."

"She has a credit card terminal in her purse," Naunie added.

"I would be surprised if she *didn't,*" Ruby said. "You're going to be fine. Don't worry. Hopefully, you'll get a couple of laughs from the whole thing."

"Thank you, Ruby," Lucy said, giving her teacher a hug. "I'm sorry if we bothered you."

"Naw," she said with a grin. "I was just getting ready to demo pulling sheets off a bed in the middle of the night."

"I loved that section," Naunie said with a gleam in her eye. "Maybe I'll have to try that tonight!"

"You are going to behave," Lucy demanded. "Unless you can get the whole world talking about you."

Ruby said goodbye, walked back to the bathtub, and went back to teaching new ghosts how to pull sheets off the beds of the living.

The sun had just gone down, and Lucy and Naunie were busy watching Nola's newly recorded makeover show before they erased it, when their laughter was interrupted by the shrill, still-unfamiliar sound of the telephone ringing.

The phone rang four times before the answering machine picked up.

Lucy heard a voice she knew, a voice she liked, on the other end. She motioned to Naunie to mute the TV, and when she did, she heard Jilly's voice suddenly bloom and take over the entire house.

"—like you said, and I'm afraid you were right. I don't have good news," Jilly said. "Um, I'm so sorry to say this, but Tulip has several tumors on her leg, so the vet ran some tests. It turns out it's cancer, Martin, and when they did X-rays, they saw it had spread to her chest cavity. Because of that, because it's in such a risky spot, there's little they can do except make her as comfortable as possible. I thought you should know. I'm sorry I had to leave a message like this, but I thought it was important to tell you right away. Call me if you want to. Goodbye."

Lucy looked at Naunie, and Naunie reached over to the blue recliner and took her hand.

"I'm sorry, dear," her grandmother said, tightening the grip of her paper-thin hands. "I'm so sorry."

chapter eighteen The Dog and Phony Show

"I HAVE TULIP. YOU MUST CALL ME IMMEDIATELY."

Jared read the subject line, the first in a long list of emails.

His mother had given him the laptop the day before, even though school was almost out for the summer. He had been anxious all day to come home and see what he could do on it, and the minute he and Alice had walked through the front door to their new apartment, he'd run right to the kitchen table and flipped it open. With rules firmly established by his mother and agreed upon by both parties, Jared had clicked his Internet connection and it had popped up in a second, just as it had the day before, along with the home page of the browser. And just as he'd been about to type in a different address, he'd seen something he hadn't noticed the day before. It looked like an email address next to the word "username," with a series of stars in the box underneath, next to the word "password." Out of curiosity, he'd clicked the button in the third line, which read "Sign in."

And up had popped Lucy's email, the account she and Jilly had set up the night before Lucy had left for Alice's, the email account that had gone unread and untouched for almost a year.

Lucy's in-box was overflowing, each subject line still in bold, signifying that none of her emails had ever been read. It was a solid page.

"Come back!" one subject line read, along with "Where are you?" and "We miss you."

And then, at the top, was, "I HAVE TULIP. YOU MUST CALL ME IMMEDIATELY."

Jared stopped for a moment, unsure of what to do. Should he click on it and read it, or ignore it? It wasn't his email. He knew he shouldn't read it, but it seemed kind of important.

"Mom," he finally called out from the kitchen table. "I think someone sent Aunt Lucy a ransom note."

Alice couldn't believe what she was reading.

It was truly incomprehensible.

She checked the date again. The year was this year. It was from the week before.

> *Lucy, please call me as soon as you get this. I need to talk to you. I have Tulip. She is living with me and Warren. I am taking good care of her but she needs you. Please, please call me. As soon as you can.*
>
> *Love, Jilly*

Alice's mind was jumbled. Why would Jilly send such a message, any such message, actually, to her sister a year after? No matter how many times Alice read the email, it didn't make sense to her. Was it some sort of joke, or was it something else, maybe Jilly trying to deal with Lucy's loss by emailing her, just as if she was alive?

Alice knew Jilly—not very well, but she had known her since Lucy had started dental school years ago. Alice had known her long enough to know that Jilly wasn't a fruitcake or a psycho, metaphorically propping up a dead friend in cyberspace to have regular conversations with her.

Something definitely didn't feel right.

Alice read the email again, and opened the next message from Jilly, dated a week before the ransom note. It began like any other regular email, a cordial greeting, how are you, and then the conversational things people always put in letters—what had happened in her life, what she hoped would happen, the things she laughed about. Jilly narrated her life for Lucy, telling her the things she had done, stupid things Marianne had said, annoying policies Nola had put into practice at work. That Warren had fallen asleep in the sun and awoken with sunburned neck rings once he'd lifted his head. That she had heard from Martin, and that he had asked her for a favor.

Alice read through the next email and the next one, and the one after that. Jilly, it seemed, wrote to Lucy every week, catching her up on the latest news, gossip, and developments in the world that had been their lives. Alice scrolled all the way down to the first one Jilly had sent; it was the day Lucy died.

Jilly had done this for a year, fifty or so letters in once-a-week installments, all in the hopes that when Lucy decided to come back, she wouldn't have missed a thing.

Jilly had no idea that her best friend was dead. And had been for almost a year. That she was writing to no one, and that she was never going to receive a reply, at least not from Lucy. Jilly didn't know what had happened, despite Alice's letter to Martin and the news coverage, *both* in the papers and on TV.

Jilly, it was apparent, had never given up on Lucy, and was still waiting for her to come home.

Alice nearly hit reply, and then thought better of it. She wasn't sure what to say, but she did know that she was not going to break the news to Jilly in a beyond-the-grave email from her sister.

Instead, she copied Jilly's address and composed a letter using her own account. Alice hadn't been planning on going to Phoenix anytime soon, but if there ever was a reason to head back down there, she supposed this was it.

A week had gone by without a return visit from Almighty Isis, and Naunie and Lucy were getting tired of waiting. Even though they were sure that her alleged psychic gift was of the charlatan variety, there was still a sense of anxiety that went along with the word "exorcism." Lucy could tell that Naunie was becoming restless, so she tried to placate her by letting her throw Nola's washed sweaters into the dryer, take Nola's favorite foods out of the fridge and leave them out on the counter to spoil, and hide Nola's fake nurse shoes in different parts of the house. But Naunie really wasn't satisfied. She still begged Lucy relentlessly to let her whisper "Duck! It's Marcus Welby!" into Nola's ear, or write "Marcus Welby + Nola FOREVER" when she was feeling bored and of little supernatural worth.

But all of that wanting to create mischief came to an end one night when Nola rushed into the house after work and immediately began tidying up, arranging her *National Enquirer* and *National Examiner* magazines in a fan on the coffee table as if they were academic journals or *National Geographics*. She fluffed the pillows on the couch and brushed the crumbs off of Martin's recliner.

Then she stood up, tried to smooth the pouf in her work pants, laid what looked like a bud from a pot plant and two candles next to her magazine fan, then positioned herself on the couch and waited.

Within minutes the doorbell rang, and Nola sprang into action. She ran to the door and opened it just in time for an army of Isis disciples and their leader—dressed in a rainbow outfit of gauze, heartily embellished with child labor embroidery and bells—to march through the front door and begin setting their equipment up in the living room. The rest of her crew consisted of several young men dipped in tie-dye who Isis probably bought pot from, and a girl in her twenties who looked relatively normal, dressed in shorts and a plain T-shirt.

"What's all this?" Naunie questioned, her eyes a little alarmed. "I didn't realize she was bringing her hippie hive."

"She said she had a removal team," Lucy reminded her.

"I thought she meant herself, her dream catcher, and her air freshener spray," Naunie said.

"Nora," Isis commanded, her voice booming. She motioned toward the odd collection of people standing in the living room. "I would like you to meet our investigation team. This is Spliff; he's our tech manager and will sweep the house first with our thermal camera and thermal scanner to search for cold spots and temperature fluctuations. Solstice is also a tech person, and he will handle the digital voice recorders for the EVPs. Ramses will monitor the EMF detector, and this is my protégée, Andrea Riner, who will be the mediator to communicate with the lost souls."

Naunie and Lucy just looked at each other with wide eyes.

"I thought you said there was just one. Marcus Welby," Nola said.

"Don't worry," Naunie said, tapping Lucy on the arm. "They're all shysters. This is a dog and phony show."

"There's two of them," Andrea mentioned blithely. "They're right over there." And then she pointed directly at Naunie and Lucy.

"Ah, shit," Naunie whispered, grabbing Lucy's arm. "We're toast."

Nola ran into a corner and cowered there, covering her head.

"Remember what Ruby said," Lucy whispered back. "If we stick together and combine our energy, we can beat this."

"Spirits of the dead aren't atomic bombs," Andrea said to Nola. "There's no need to cover your head."

"I'm afraid Marcus Welby is going to throw something else at me!" Nola cried. "He nearly decapitated me with a digital picture frame! He threw it right at my neck like it was a Chinese star!"

Andrea shook her head. "I get the sense that these are two women. One is young, one is older. I think they're related," she continued, and then became very aware of the filthy warning look Isis was shooting at her sideways.

"Or maybe not. It could be a man," Andrea quickly covered. "A dreadful, angry man. Spiteful, with hate in his heart. He's raging. Beware, all."

"I thought we would set up here, in the living room, and then invite our spirit friend to join our circle, and help him to the other side," Isis commanded, to which Nola simply nodded.

"Will we be done by nine o'clock?" Nola asked. "That's when Martin will be home, and I don't think he'll be too happy to see all of this set up here. Can we get the evil spirit out by then?"

"Completely doable," Isis reassured her. "You'll have a clean house by then, I guarantee it. Ramses, how are the readings?"

"Nice and clear," he said, giving Isis a knowing smile. "It all looks good, Nora. Come on out of the corner."

Nola, clearly still quite wary, released her grip on her skull, but remained staunchly where she was.

"Marcus Welby is afraid of us," Isis informed her, and held her hand out to coax Nola out of hiding. "He will not come out until we call for him."

"We're almost done setting up," Spliff volunteered. "We can start in about a minute."

"So exciting!" Isis cooed, clapping her hands. "I love a good exorcism!"

"We're all set to go," Spliff said.

"All right!" Isis said, spreading her arms wide and making motions with her hands to have the team gather, including Nola.

"Now, this is what we're going to do," she gabbled. "Spliff and Solstice will man the thermal image recorders to see if we can catch the spirits on videotape and capture any EVPs, and Ramses will keep an eye on the EMF detector."

"I don't know what any of that means," Nola admitted as she timidly moved forward. "Is the EVP anything like EVOO?"

Isis looked at Nola with a blank expression. "No," she said plainly. "'EMF' stands for 'electromagnetic field'—that's a force that's been created by electric particles, and when we see a rise on the EMF detector, that shows us that spirits are present. EVPs are electronic voice phenomena, which are voices of the disembodied that we don't hear but that are recorded with our sensitive device. The thermal image camera will let us capture anything on tape that has a heat register—including paranormal figures. Anywhere they are in the room, we can see that. They simply can't hide. And we also have a thermal scanner that helps us determine cold spots—ghosts will suck energy out of the atmosphere to manifest themselves, and we can find those spots with this."

"I already have a reading," Spliff said excitedly as he walked closer and closer to Lucy and Naunie. "I have a cold spot!"

"I'll give you a cold spot!" Naunie said as she took two steps and grabbed the thermal scanner, and from the glow that intensified around her, Lucy could tell Naunie was sucking every bit of energy out of it like a vampire.

"Hey—wait!" Spliff said. "It's flickering. What the he— It's . . . I can't believe this! It's *dead*."

"I told you to put new batteries in," Isis scolded him.

"These were brand-new," he replied. "I just put them in this afternoon. I have an extra set, though."

"Lucy, quick!" Naunie hissed. "Drain the batteries! Drain all of the batteries!"

Lucy nimbly made her way to the thermal camera, which was resting on the coffee table, and grabbed it with both hands. Naunie abandoned the already dead thermal scanner and attacked the EMF detector next, determined she wouldn't leave as much as a spark left in it.

"Take it easy!" Lucy warned, still pulling from the camera. "Your glow is getting too bright—"

But before Lucy could finish telling Naunie that she was taking on too much too quickly and beginning to manifest, Isis let out a scream and pointed.

"A ghost! It's a ghost!" she shrieked.

Now, to the seasoned spook or even a freshly dead member of the other side, Naunie's "appearance" was novice at best, if not downright amateurish. But for the living, the easily excitable and overreactive living, Naunie's fuzzy, light, quite transparent little cloud of an image was enough to render them completely unhinged. Scarier apparitions have swirled out of the tailpipes of cars.

"What did I tell you, Nora?" Isis clamored. "It's him! Didn't I tell you? Didn't I?"

"Marcus Welby!" Nola shrieked. "Please don't hurt me! Please don't hurt me! Take my purse, take my wallet!"

"Naunie!" Lucy called. "Let go! Let go! They can see you!"

"Yes, we can see you," Andrea said quite calmly, adding to the confusion.

Naunie immediately recoiled from the EMF device, and within seconds began losing her charge, and thankfully started fading.

"So you can hear me," Lucy asked softly, to which Andrea slowly nodded, her eyebrows raised.

Then the protégée held up the digital voice recorder, which had been recording all along, its tiny red light burning powerfully.

"Shit," Lucy mumbled.

After Naunie had successfully frightened everyone in the living room, including Lucy as well as herself, the group took a minute to calm themselves down while Spliff loaded a new set of batteries into the thermal scanner. Nola, close to hysterics, sat in the recliner as Isis tried to tell her everything was going to be all right, and now that the entity had presented itself, it would be that much easier to get rid of it. Particularly since Isis would not get paid if the exorcism did not take place.

"Didn't you see it?" Nola insisted dramatically, as if this was her reality show. "It had beady red eyes and flames for hair! It tried to swipe its claw at me! I heard it call my name! Didn't you hear it?"

"Of course I did!" Isis confirmed. "I heard it cry, 'Nora, Nora!' But you see, that's all the more reason for us to get rid of it! You can't live with that in your house! We must remove it! And we must do it now!"

"Did you see fangs?" Nola asked the remainder of the crew. "I am pretty sure I saw fangs! And it had a giant spider sitting on its shoulder, like a pet!"

"Don't be afraid," Isis encouraged. "Remember, we have the ghost repellant spray. It will protect you."

Lucy saw Ramses smirk to himself, and Andrea roll her eyes.

"Come," Isis demanded of everyone. "Come, let us gather into the circle of light so that Nora will be protected. I will release the spray, and all it reaches will be safe. You can't hurt us, Marcus Welby, once we are in the protective circle! You are dead! You may roam this earth, but the living control it!"

She fumbled to find her purse, and then proceeded to pollute the entire room with the unfortunate patchouli, which stunk even more pungently of a mixture of decomposing, rotting forest foliage and acrid spice when sprayed directly on the air that did not have the benefit of time to dilute it. Isis waved her arms wildly about, trying to spread the spray over everyone.

"Will you look at her? Jesus, lady, put on a bra! Those feed bags are going to slap someone in the face!" Naunie complained, and Lucy was about to shush her when Lucy saw the young protégée turn her head, cover her mouth, and giggle.

Lucy got Naunie's attention and pointed to Andrea. She mimicked the girl laughing, and then pointed back to Naunie. Naunie nodded. She needed a plan.

"How are the readings?" Isis asked.

"The EMF detector is pretty much worthless, too," Solstice said, shrugging with the dead instrument in his hand.

"Let's just use the thermal camera," Isis demanded, and pointed at it on the coffee table.

Spliff picked it up, and his face fell. "There's no charge left. We could plug it in, but it would take a couple of hours before we could use it."

"We don't have a couple of hours," Nola protested. "We have to hurry. Martin will be home soon."

"Let's join hands, then," Isis instructed. "Everyone. All we have is the digital voice recorder and the thermal scanner, and they're useless if everything else isn't working. Join the circle, Nora. I want you next to me."

They all obliged, and within a minute, Isis's circle of light had been formed, with Naunie and Lucy watching from several feet away.

Isis cleared her throat and puffed up her voice. "We are here tonight to help any souls trapped in this house to move over to where you rightfully belong; to free you from this earthly prison and release you to a plane where you can exist for all eternity," Isis bellowed as if she was delivering a sermon. "Join us, spirits, in the circle of light. Let us help you in your journey so that you can cross over to the other side."

Isis raised her hands up, signaling the rise for everyone, nearly looking like a very overgrown version of "London Bridge." Lucy had the urge to giggle, and she would have, had Naunie not nudged her in the ribs and nodded over to Isis, where behind the perfumed phony was a minuscule but growing circle of white light.

Not very far away from Isis's circle of light, two or three miles at best, a doorbell rang at a little brick house with a perfect little hedge that bordered the entire yard. The visitor could have knocked, but she'd decided instead, under the circumstances, that ringing the doorbell was much more appropriate. After a minute or so, the door opened, and Jilly let Marianne in.

Inside, the chatter was plentiful but quiet, a little subdued. There were people Marianne knew, such as Warren, of course, and Marcia from the office. And there were a couple of people she had seen at some of Jilly and Warren's barbecues that she didn't know all that well, such as the neighbors. Then there were other people she had never met but had heard about in stories told again and again by Jilly and Lucy—friends of theirs from years and years before. People they knew from dental school, from previous jobs, some from the bar, and each time she met someone she didn't know, the question was always the same: "She was great, wasn't she? Just the sweetest thing. How did you know her? I knew her from when she was this big!"

Marianne had just gotten a glass of wine when Jilly stood up in front of the room and tapped her wineglass with a spoon.

"Thank you so much for coming," she began. "As you know, I've asked you all here to help me give honor to a wonderful friend with a loving personality, and a heart that was so very brave and strong. I know we'll all miss her, and feel like we were lucky we knew her, even if we might not have seen her for a while. So please join me in celebrating the life and beauty of Tulip, who we will all truly miss, and hope that wherever she is, she's getting a good belly rub and a nice, meaty bone."

Jilly raised her glass. "To dear Tulip," she said.

"To dear Tulip," the guests repeated.

And then Jilly moved aside, and behind her on a table was a framed picture of Tulip as a puppy, sitting on Lucy's lap, her long tongue mid-kiss, right at the bottom of Lucy's lower lip. On a stand was Tulip's red collar and matching leash, well worn, with her smell still on them. Below that was her water bowl and dish, her favorite ball, and a bag of biscuits, the kind that Jilly remembered Lucy used to buy for her. Jilly had gone to the pet supply store and bought her more, throwing the generic ones away. Tulip had been too good, everyone would agree, for generic biscuits. Marianne was standing at the table looking at Tulip's things, when she heard someone ask Jilly if she had heard from Lucy recently.

Jilly shook her head and said "No."

"She'll be back," someone else said confidently. "You know Lucy. When you least expect her, she'll pop up again."

"Yeah, maybe she's living on some tropical island with no phone and no stress," a girl Marianne didn't recognize said.

"You said she loved Hawaii," the guy next to her said. "I bet she hopped the next plane back there."

"Maybe she met some rich and wealthy old count and is sailing around the world on a yacht," the man behind him said. "And being attended to by servants."

"Maybe," Jilly said with a slight smile.

"Don't you miss her?" the girl asked.

"Very much," Jilly said, same smile still intact.

"I loved her laugh," someone from the back of the group added. "No one had a laugh like Lucy. It was as contagious as the flu."

"She was hilarious," a girl with red hair said. "Do you remember that party where she hid—"

"In the bathtub to get away from that guy who had that enormous crush on her and wouldn't leave her alone?" someone else finished. "She finally fell asleep in there!"

"We didn't find her till the next morning," the girl added. "And her back was messed up for weeks!"

"Well," a guy in a plaid shirt chimed in, "you couldn't exactly count on Lucy, but you always knew you'd have fun with her. But she'd surprise you. She once loaned me rent money and was late paying her own because of it."

"She drove me all the way to Tucson when my car broke down and I had to be down there to play a show with my band," another guy with longish hair said. "But then she hooked up with the guitarist from the band we opened for and went on tour with them for five months!"

"That is classic Lucy," a girl with a blond ponytail reminded them.

"On our vacation to Hawaii, she wouldn't let me go to this guy's room alone," Marianne added. "And it was a good thing, because I'm pretty sure he was a creep."

"In the end, she'd come through. Well, sometimes!" The man in the plaid shirt laughed. "But really, Lucy was a great friend."

"Lucy was. She really was," Marianne agreed.

"To Lucy!" the guy in the plaid shirt said, and raised his beer.

"To Lucy!" everyone chimed in, and cheered to her.

"See that, Jilly," someone yelled from the back. "Lucy wouldn't leave and not come back, not without saying goodbye. She's probably touring with the Rolling Stones. She'll be back. You'll see."

Jilly nodded, and took a sip of wine. She hoped he was right, but she wasn't betting on it. She had gotten an email from Alice, who was coming down in a few days and wanted to drop in and say hi. Jilly found it odd, since she really didn't know Alice that well, but she'd said sure, she'd love to see her, it had been a long time. She'd left it at that. See you in a couple of days, she'd replied.

Everything else, she figured, was better left for then.

Behind Isis, the light—swirling, churning, and powerful—had grown to the size where it was almost blocking the entire front door, and Lucy and Naunie were beginning to feel it. The brightness that emanated from it was nearly blinding. It was not the comforting sort of light that people who have reported near-death experiences claim to have seen, but a blatant, coarse, almost violent light that was paralyzing in its ferocity. The roar of the light filled the house, although it was apparent that only Lucy and Naunie could hear it. It was loud, mechanical, and angry.

Lucy could see that the light was actually more of a tunnel, and the pulling force it possessed was daunting, spiking fear in Lucy, and no doubt in Naunie as well. As they clung to each other and fought the tugging draw of the light, Naunie yelled over the crush of the tunnel's roar.

"Hang on, Lucy!" she demanded. "Get behind me, but don't let go!"

"No," Lucy argued, shaking her head. "We need to stay together! If I'm behind you, you have to fight off more!"

"I'm stronger than you are!" she reminded her granddaughter. "I think I have a plan!"

"What is it?" Lucy yelled back. "You're going to have to tell me or I'm not moving!"

"Isis didn't open that light. It was Andrea!" Naunie replied, looking Lucy dead in the eye. "She's the only one with the power to do it. Trust me."

Lucy knew she was right; their only other option was to cling to each other until they could no longer fight the suction of the light. And, by the looks of it, with the light growing in size and showing no signs of breaking, that wouldn't take very much longer.

In careful, tiny steps, keeping her grasp on Naunie firmly in place, Lucy worked her way behind her grandmother and held on tight.

"Lucy, I need you to focus," Naunie yelled over the light's incessant whirling roar. "And I need you to move forward with me."

"No!" Lucy screamed. "Don't go toward the light! It will pull you in!"

"Keep pulling back on me," Naunie screamed. "You need to keep the resistance going!"

Naunie took a step forward, and Lucy followed, trying to keep them steady and pull back at the same time. The more they moved forward, the more pressure they felt, the more powerful the suction of the light became. By Naunie's careful third step, Lucy began to understand where they were going.

"ANDREA!" Naunie yelled when they got close enough to the protégée that the sound of the light, which was deafening on the spectral plane but not audible to Andrea on hers, would not drown her out.

"ANDREA!" Naunie called again, and this time, the girl's eyes flew open and she looked in Naunie's direction.

While Lucy didn't think that Andrea could actually see them, she could certainly sense them, and she knew they were there.

"Stop the light, Andrea! It's not what you think it is. You have to stop it or we will be lost in limbo circling Saturn forever!"

Lucy watched Andrea, and was waiting for her to say something, when instead, she faintly heard

Don't you miss her?

Lucy looked at the faces in Isis's circle of light. No one was speaking but Isis, who was chanting the same thing over and over again, "Spirits, join us in the circle of light. Cross over, children. Go into the light. There is peace and serenity in the light. . . ."

Oh, good God, Lucy thought. *Really? That movie is practically looped on at least three basic cable channels.*

No one had a laugh like . . .

Lucy looked around again, trying to place the voice, but there was no one she could attribute it to.

. . . you always knew you'd have fun with her. . . .

"ANDREA," Naunie called again. "You have to stop the light. Only you have control over it! Focus your mind and stop it. There is no peace in the light. It's a vacuum that will throw us out into eternal limbo. You must help us! It's going to destroy us!"

Lucy felt the pull of the light weakening; the snarl of the light was lessening, and the brightness was not as blinding as it had been before, even if only by a slight amount.

"It's working, Naunie!" Lucy shouted. "She's listening to you!"

Lucy kept her grip tight on Naunie for what seemed like a very long time. She could tell that the old woman was getting weaker, too.

. . . all the way to Tucson when my car broke down . . .

"Keep turning it off, Andrea," Naunie kept yelling. "Block the light from your mind. Push it away!"

"They're gone!" Andrea cried, releasing the hands of the people on either side of her and breaking the circle. "They're gone! They've gone into the light. The light is gone."

"Are you sure?" Nola barked. "Are you sure it's over?"

. . . was a great friend . . .

Andrea nodded vigorously. "Yes. Yes. I'm sure they're crossed over now. It's over."

Except it wasn't. Although the power of the light had lessened, Lucy and Naunie still fought determinedly to keep out of its grasp. Lucy clung to her grandmother, and pulled back as hard as she could, but she was struggling. She didn't think she was strong enough to pull them both back despite the weakened light. She wasn't sure how long she could hang on, because if Andrea couldn't close the light she had opened, this tug of war could only end up one way: with Naunie and Lucy sucked into the middle of it and spit out on the other side, shriveled, compressed, and circling a gas giant until the end of time.

"I won't let go," Lucy told Naunie.

"Why are you looking over there, then?" Nola demanded of Andrea, who was still tuned in and could hear all of what Naunie and Lucy were saying. "I think you're lying. Isis, I think your worker is lying to me. I don't think Marcus Welby is gone at all. In fact, I think he is right there!"

Nola grabbed the thermal scanner off of the coffee table, where Spliff had put it after he'd replaced the dead batteries with the extra set. She marched full force right at Lucy and Naunie. She charged at them, swinging the scanner and pressing every button, as if she was trying to Taser them like a cop at a peace rally.

Lucy's reflexes, still very present, made her automatically duck and try to avoid Nola's swinging bearlike paw and raise her hand to shield herself from the blow. Nola's arm came swinging down, slicing through Lucy and continuing to swing, as if Nola was batting at flies.

All Lucy heard was the scream as Naunie shot away from her and toward the light, despite the fact that it was still decreasing in size. It still had enough pull to yank a startled, weightless ghost and drag her across the floor to its open, gaping glow.

"Naunie!" Lucy screamed, as Naunie managed to grab on to Isis's leg, stopping the light from devouring her as she held on for dear death.

"Hang on!" Lucy called to her as she tried to regain her own balance. "I'm coming!"

"Don't, Lucy, don't!" Naunie replied. "It's too dangerous!"

Lucy frantically looked around for something to grab on to as she made her way toward the front door, where Naunie was a foot from getting sucked away into the monstrous hole. All Lucy could do was watch as her grandmother's grip loosened finger by finger, and she got closer and closer to the light.

. . . Lucy . . .

. . . To Lu . . .

. . . To . . .

. . . cy . . .

. . . To Lu . . .

. . . Lucy . . .

. . . cy . . .

To Lucy!

Lucy watched as the light dimmed, more, more, more, and pulled away, getting smaller, retracting, smaller, farther away, smaller, until in a moment, it was gone.

The pull was gone. Lucy had felt the pull slipping away as the light had melted into nothing and left her wobbly. Naunie was still clinging to Isis's leg, covered by layers of fiesta-colored gauze.

"This is ridiculous," Naunie said, trying to hunt her way out from under Isis's skirt. With one reach, well-placed or an ill-timed mistake, Naunie grabbed the skirt and yanked it down, maybe in an attempt to pull herself up. Instead, the elastic waistband skirt from the clearance rack at JCPenney came shooting down, revealing that a bra was not the only undergarment Isis felt she didn't require.

Lucy grabbed Naunie, yelled "RUN!" and scrambled out of the room as Andrea blocked the path for Solstice after he yanked the thermal scanner out of Nola's hand and, panicking, began to try to get a reading on the only true paranormal activity he and most of the people in the room had ever seen.

Lucy and Naunie punched through the back wall, just as Lucy had through the double doors at her funeral, and collapsed on the grass in the backyard, relieved and still more than a little unsettled, trying to process and figure out what had just happened.

"I was so scared," Lucy admitted. "I really thought I had lost you."

"Lucy, you stopped it. How did you stop it?" Naunie asked.

"I didn't," she replied. "I didn't do anything. It just started shrinking, and then it vanished."

"I don't understand," Naunie said, still very startled. "If Andrea didn't close it off, what did?"

Lucy shrugged. "I did hear some voices," she mentioned. "It sounded like chatter at a party. Did you hear that?"

Naunie shook her head. "I couldn't hear anything over that racket. I was really scared, Lucy."

"Me, too," her granddaughter agreed.

"Excuse me," a voice whispered, coming from the shadows on the side of the house. "I don't mean to bother you, but . . . It's Andrea."

The girl crept forward and stepped into the light from the house.

"If I just helped two mean ghosts escape, I'm going to be mad," she said.

"We're not mean," Naunie replied. "We're just misunderstood."

Lucy burst out laughing. "We're not mean, or misunderstood,

we're just on assignment," she said. "Thank you for helping us in there. We both know you didn't have to."

"Explain to me what you mean about the light," Andrea probed. "It doesn't help people cross over? Then, what is it?"

"It's a psychic vacuum cleaner, sort of," Naunie tried to explain.

"But whatever it sucks out—bad energy, bad intent, bad spirits—gets compressed and is forever in limbo," Lucy finished.

Andrea quickly covered her mouth. "I always assumed they were screams of joy!" she gasped.

"Good ghosts shouldn't get sucked up like bad pennies," Lucy said plainly. "It's a terrible fate."

"ANDREA! ANDREA!" they heard Isis yell. "We're about to start the smudging! Quickly!"

"I have to go," the girl said quickly. "Even though I can't see you, it was nice to meet you. And you might want to steer clear of the house for about a half hour. Smudging stinks. And I don't think it works."

"It doesn't," Lucy and Naunie said in unison.

Then Andrea took off in a sprint back around the corner of the house, and disappeared into the shadows.

"Ditch the braless broad," Naunie called after her. "She's only the name; you're the talent!"

And then Lucy and Naunie collapsed into laughter.

At Jilly's, almost everyone had left Tulip's wake, when the doorbell rang one last time that day. Marianne, who had volunteered to stay and help her friend clean up, answered it.

She had not expected to see Martin.

He was holding a small bouquet of flowers, little pink carnations wrapped in green cellophane.

"I don't know if this is appropriate," he said, and nodded at the flowers. "But I saw them, so I got them."

"Jilly," Marianne called. "It's Martin."

They walked into the living room, where Jilly had set up Tulip's little memorial, and Martin took a minute to look at the photos and toys Jilly had set out.

"She was a good girl," he said as he tapped his fingers on the table.

Jilly came into the living room, drying her hands with a dish towel.

"I'm sorry to be so late. We had a late delivery and things took longer than I thought," he explained.

"That's all right," Jilly said, with a little smile. "I'm just glad you came."

"I'm—I'm not sure what to say, you know, except that I'm sorry about all of this and that this is all just such a mess," he said, clearly flustered. "I didn't expect this would happen. I didn't know. I had no idea she was that sick."

"Well, you had good intuition, Martin," Jilly said. "We didn't get to her illness in time, but at least we were able to help her a little bit at the end."

"What did—" he started. "Where is she?"

"We'll have her ashes back soon," Jilly explained. "If you like, I can bring them by."

"That would be good," Martin agreed. "I think that would be good. Has anyone told Lucy?"

Jilly and Marianne looked at each other and then looked at him.

"Martin," Jilly began, "when I told you that I hadn't heard from her since the day she left here, I told you the truth. I wasn't lying to you. You were the only one who heard from her. You got that letter. We never got anything."

Martin pressed his lips tight and nodded. "I thought you might have heard something," he said quietly. "I thought she actually might have been back around."

He laughed abruptly. "At least Nola's convinced that Lucy is back," he finished. "And if she was back, you know, I know she'd drop by to see you. I figured at least. You sure she hasn't come back around?"

"I wouldn't lie to you, Martin," Jilly said calmly. "But don't you think it's time you told us what happened between the two of you?"

"Aw, Jilly, you have to know!" he said, getting slightly louder. "You were there. You knew. You knew what she had done! Why do you wanna make me say it?"

"Martin, I have no idea what you're talking about," she replied. "Even Lucy had no idea. We are all completely in the dark. It's time somebody knew what this was all about."

"She cheated on me!" Martin exclaimed, throwing one arm up into the air. "She cheated on me when you were in Hawaii. What else was I supposed to do, let her come back and get married?"

Jilly's face dropped. "That's not true—that's not true," she stammered. "I know it's not. She would never do that to you, Martin, never. Besides, we were with each other the whole time, every minute of every day. There was no time for anything like that to happen. You're wrong, I'm telling you."

"I caught her!" he cried, shaking his head. "Red-handed, I caught her. And it wasn't like she hadn't done it before. I *caught* her. I heard it with my own ears."

"What do you mean," Jilly asked. "I don't understand what you mean by that."

"Nola called looking for the deposit, the one Lucy lost, right?" Martin explained, his face getting red. "So I called Lucy right after I hung up with Nola, to ask her if she knew anything about it, and a guy answers the phone. *Her phone.* I asked who the hell he was, and he tells me that he's a friend of Lucy's, and when I told him to put her on the phone, he said she was too busy in the bathroom, getting ready for the party the two of them were going to have and that they did not want to be disturbed and that maybe she might call me later if she wasn't too tired. So how's that, Jilly? What do you say to that now?"

Jilly was quiet, and shook her head. "I don't know anything about that, Martin," she replied. "I'm sorry."

Martin didn't know what to say, either. There was a still quiet between them.

"I do," Marianne finally said.

Martin and Jilly looked at her.

"I know about that," she said. "But it's not what you thought. I met that guy at the bar downstairs, and Lucy wouldn't let me go to his room to play poker by myself, so she went with me. When we got to his room, I remembered I'd left my key card at the bar, and went down to get it. I was only gone for a few minutes, and when I came back, Lucy had just thrown up in the bathroom. She was still sick from the luau. We left, and she said he was a creep. Nothing happened, Martin. We went back to our room and watched a movie on cable. Nothing happened, she didn't cheat on you. I was there. She had to have been in the bathroom when you called, and he just answered it. It was all a mistake."

Martin looked at her and didn't say anything, couldn't say anything. He swallowed hard. Then he handed the flowers to Jilly and without another word walked back across the living room and out the door.

chapter nineteen Boo

The next morning, Martin was already showered, coffee-ed up, and looking for his keys when Nola shuffled into the kitchen.

"You were out late last night," she said, looking puffy with her short, dark mannish hair askew. "You didn't tell me you would be out so late."

"I didn't know I would be," he replied curtly, clicking the closure of his watch into place.

"Did you have coffee already?" Nola asked, looking at the empty pot.

"I did," he said, looking at her.

"What time did you get home?" she asked. "I didn't hear you come in."

Martin shrugged. "I don't know," he said simply. "It was late."

"It was well past midnight," Nola informed him with an edge in her voice. It was this edge that tipped Lucy and Naunie off that this was most likely a conversation they should indeed be eavesdropping on.

"I suppose it could have been," Martin replied.

"It *was,*" Nola confirmed. "You told me you'd be home at nine."

Naunie and Lucy slid into the hallway, where they were in earshot of the conversation.

Martin shrugged again and tried to move past her.

"Where were you?" Nola said, grabbing his arm.

"I was driving around," he answered quickly, and ended it with a sigh.

"All night long? Are you sure?" she demanded.

Martin laughed.

"Why, Nola? Do you want to correct me again? Were you in the backseat?"

She opened her mouth, but nothing came out. It remained hanging open, waiting for Nola to fill it with something, but she didn't. She finally closed it and looked away.

"I was at Jilly's," Martin said matter-of-factly. "There was a wake, and I went. Tulip died."

Lucy was immediately absorbed by numbness. Naunie grabbed her by the shoulder and drew her close in.

"Oh, sweetheart, oh, sweetheart," Naunie said softly as Lucy broke into waves of sobs.

"You just can't break free of her, can you?" Nola accused as Martin abruptly walked by her into the hallway and went for the front door. "She's not coming back, Martin. She's not. No matter how many pictures you hide of her in the top drawer of your desk, Lucy is not coming back for you."

"Nola," Martin said as he stopped dead in his tracks and turned around. "What is in my desk drawer is none of your business, but what you tried to get rid of in the side table drawer is my business. I don't have to listen to this. I don't have to listen to you. And I won't."

With that, he picked up his keys on the console next to the door and walked out.

If Nola had had another digital picture frame within reach, it would have gone flying. Instead, she stood there for a moment, pouting and breathing angrily, her fists clenched on either side of her.

"I never liked that stupid mutt," she forced out between her teeth, then marched into the bathroom and slammed the door.

The sound of the shower turning on followed within seconds.

Nola's heartless comment was enough to make Lucy break from Naunie's embrace. She put her face in her hands and took several deep breaths, neatly gathering her sorrow and her anger.

"I'm okay," she reassured her grandmother. "I'm okay."

She stood there for several moments, breathing in and out and collecting every bit of herself. She hadn't been this angry since the day of her funeral. Then, after one final deep breath, she took three steps to the refrigerator and grabbed either side of it with both hands, standing in front of it as if she was pushing it up a hill.

"Lucy, what are you doing?" Naunie cried, watching Lucy's glow getting more and more luminous and bright. "Lucy, stop and think for a minute!"

"I *am* thinking, Naunie," Lucy replied staunchly. "I should have done this a long time ago."

The refrigerator made a strange clicking sound, then the motor faintly ground to a halt.

Lucy moved on to the television, the answering machine, every lamp she could find, the microwave, even her very own broken coffeemaker. She mercilessly drained everything in the house until she heard the shower stop and her shine was almost as fiery as the sun.

When Nola emerged from the shower wearing a bathrobe with a towel around her head, it was hardly how she'd expected to look the next time she ran into Lucy Fisher.

Who was now sitting on the couch in the living room. Waiting for her.

"Boo," Lucy said simply.

"How did you get in here?" Nola immediately demanded.

"I was already here," Lucy said, getting up and walking toward her.

"You need to leave," Nola barked. "I think you should leave, Lucy. You aren't wanted here. You don't belong here."

Lucy smiled. "You see, Nola," she said with a grin, "that's where I think you're wrong."

Nola shook her head. "I was right, wasn't I?" she declared, pointing her finger at Lucy. "I was right about you hanging around here, putting stickers on things, writing on the mirror. Even the mailman caught you. I *knew* it. I knew I wasn't making things up! So, what, now you want it all back? What is it that you want, Lucy?"

"I want you to leave," she said simply. "I want you to pack up your things and go. Because I promise you, I'm not going anywhere until you do."

"You think I'm going to leave Martin just because you said so? You think that you're the only one for him?"

"No," Lucy replied. "I'm not the one for him, but neither are you. And you know that."

"What makes you so sure? What makes you think that you can come in here and take this away from me, huh? What makes you think that I'd let you? I will never let you take anything from me again! You think you can decide to come back and just waltz through the door like nothing happened?"

"You can't even imagine what's happened, Nola," Lucy said. "So much that it isn't even a possibility. Everything I had is gone."

"Everything *you* had is gone? Really? You think you know about losing everything? Well, let me tell you about that, Lucy, because I once had everything. I had a fiancé, too. Did you know that? I was planning on getting married, starting a family. Everything was all set. But then my fiancé, Ricky, went home with another girl one night. He was at the Round About when he met this girl. They started dancing, drinking, and the next morning, he woke up with her in his bed. He told me about it, said she was a friend of Jilly's and her name was Lucy. He decided after his night of fun that he wasn't ready to get married after all and broke it off. A few months later, a friend of Jilly's came to interview with Dr. Meadows for a job. He told me to get all of the paperwork ready; he had hired her. Her name was Lucy."

"Icky Ricky was your boyfriend?" Lucy gasped, amazed, disgusted, unbelieving, horrified, and wanting to take a shower even though she theoretically no longer had a body. "No, no, no, wait. Wait, wait, wait a minute, Nola. You mean that you think I ruined that all for you?"

"No, Lucy," Nola barked back. "I don't *think*. I know it was you. You ruined the rest of my life, and I swore I'd make you pay for at least some of it. I waited, and waited, and waited, and finally, the time was right. You made the wrong move, just like I predicted you would."

"The deposit," Lucy said, shaking her head. "I gave you too much credit, Nola. Even I didn't really think you would stoop that low. You put that money in there on purpose, so that I would be responsible for it, and you counted on me being distracted."

"Well, it *had* to be that night." Nola chuckled. "A typical day's draw would be maybe a hundred dollars in cash, the rest in checks and credit cards. No big deal if it went missing. Most of it could be replaced. But if twenty thousand dollars of the doctor's money turned up missing, that was a different story altogether. I took a chance and waited a couple of days before putting it in the deposit the day before you were leaving for Hawaii. It was just a matter of perfect timing."

"Perfect for you," Lucy replied. "How on earth did you manage to sneak the drug test in there? And how did you know it would be positive? Did you rig that, too?"

"Oh, that was luck in its purest form," Nola said, and smiled. "I had nothing to do with that. There were pharmaceuticals missing. I had no idea whether you had anything to do with that or not. Turns out, you did."

"I *didn't,*" Lucy protested. "I had nothing to do with that, Nola. I didn't *take* the drugs, I didn't *do* the drugs, I knew *nothing* about the drugs. Just like I had nothing to do with your boyfriend. If he broke up with you, it had nothing to do with me. I did have too much to drink that night and I should have left with Warren and Jilly, but my biggest crime was passing out before I could tell Icky Ricky where I lived. That's how I ended up at his apartment, and believe me, when I woke up the next morning, fully clothed, I should have been quarantined. *Had* something happened between us, I would have turned myself in to the Centers for Disease Control. At this point, I would love nothing more than to tell you I ruined your life, but the truth is, I had nothing to do with it. Nothing. Your jealousy, your rage, your hate, it's for nothing. You wasted all that time and energy when you could have been doing something good with yourself. And, if I may impart some advice, I'd start working on your good deeds list now if I were you. You can make your first contribution by moving out of this house."

"I will not," Nola said adamantly. "You have no control over me, Lucy. I have a nice life here. A life that is owed to me."

"Think about it, Nola," Lucy said carefully. "Because the decision you make could very well haunt you for the rest of your life."

"He won't take you back," Nola insisted. "Not after what you did. You can try to get rid of me, but Martin will never take you back after you cheated on him."

"I already told you, Nola," Lucy sternly replied. "Nothing happened between me and Icky Ricky. I'm sorry you formed a life of revenge around a lie, but you did. I've told you the truth, and you're going to have to drop it."

"I'm not talking about Ricky!" Nola said, her voice rising. "Martin knows nothing about Ricky. I'm talking about Hawaii. I'm talking about when Martin caught you with another man. He called you, and that man answered your phone and told him everything!"

"Nola, your lies are getting ridiculous," Lucy answered. "I was rooming with Jilly and Marianne. Don't you think they'd have noticed a strange man in their bed talking on the phone?"

"Not your room phone! *Your* phone! He called you on *your* cellphone and a man answered. He said that you were in the bathroom getting ready to 'party' with him and then told Martin not to call back!"

"That never happened," Lucy insisted. "It's impossible. Martin would never tell you something that never happened. You're making this up."

"It was the night before you came home, Lucy," Nola added. "A man answered your phone and basically told Martin he was going to have sex with you. He said you were in his room, in his bathroom. You were there; you know it."

Lucy felt as if she had dropped seventy feet in an elevator with no cables. *That's what this is all about?* she thought, trying to keep the room from spinning. *That's what changed my life into death? The fact that I was throwing up in the bathroom and the most disgusting, vile man on the face of the earth answered my phone because he thought he was going to get lucky?*

That is why I'm here?

It's all been for that?

"Lucy!" Naunie whispered from her vantage point in the hallway. "Wrap it up. You're losing the charge!"

Lucy snapped back, her anger even more intensified. Everything that had seemed unfair had just been brought into a much sharper, closer view. And Nola was certainly a part of it.

"Whether Martin takes me back or not is not the issue; what matters is that you leave him alone and let him have something real," Lucy said as she started to walk toward the front door and try to get out of the house before she became nothing but the tailpipe exhaust figure Nola had seen of Naunie the night before. "This isn't real. It's not genuine or true, and you know it. You're here because you wanted to take from me what you thought I stole from you. And you've been terrified ever since you stepped foot in this house that I would always return and come back for what was mine."

"I—" Nola started as Lucy opened the front door.

"I'm back," Lucy concluded as she walked over the threshold and shut the door behind her.

Nola said nothing to Martin about Lucy breaking into the house and confronting her. She didn't want to start another fight with him, and she didn't want to give Lucy the satisfaction of knowing that she had gotten to her. She weighed her options and planned out her strategy, staying quiet and keeping her eyes open. She listened carefully. She knew she could wait this out, even though she was positive that every time she came around a corner, Lucy would be there, waiting for her, telling her what she already knew.

Because she was right. Lucy *was* back.

It was confirmed a couple of days later when Nola saw Lucy's truck pull into the driveway. There was no hiding this time, no skulking around, no behind-the-scenes mischief, Nola thought as she peeked out the living room window. The truck sat in the driveway for a long time, simply idling. Martin's truck was in the driveway too, as plain as day, right in front of it.

Today, Nola thought, *is the day that Lucy is going to stake her claim.*

She'd brought reinforcements, too, Nola realized when she saw Jilly get out of the passenger side of Lucy's truck and walk around the front of the vehicle. *What are they going to do,* Nola asked herself, *beat me up? Why would Jilly even remotely need to be here? That was a bad move on Jilly's part,* she said to herself. She, too, could be easily replaced at the office. It had taken Nola years, but she had found a way for Lucy to go, and she could be patient and find a way for her little friend, too.

Martin saw Lucy's truck pull into the driveway, after he heard the familiar sound of its engine and peered out the bedroom window to investigate. While Jilly had called and said she'd be over with Tulip's ashes, he'd never expected this. A part of him felt ambushed, while another, truer part of him felt relieved, as if the whole last year was finally over, everything had been fixed and was now working the way it should have been. That feeling, however, only lasted for a moment. The driver's side door opened.

Instead of Lucy sliding out of the driver's side, it was someone Nola didn't know, didn't recognize. After the doorbell rang and Martin walked past her and answered it, Nola realized that only two people had arrived in Lucy's truck, and Lucy wasn't one of them.

Jilly looked terrible. Her face was drawn and tired, her eyes puffy and red. It was apparent that she had been crying. But once Nola saw what she had in her hand, she understood. A small brass urn, no bigger than a mayonnaise jar. Nola wanted to scoff, but couldn't. She understood what it was to love something and lose it, even if it was just a dog.

"Alice?" Martin said as the next woman walked into the house. He looked very surprised. His mouth opened to form another word, but he couldn't finish it, and he stood there, as if frozen.

Naunie gasped from the couch, where she had been reclining. "Lucy, it's Alice!" she nearly screamed. "It's Alice! It's Alice!"

Lucy ran in from the kitchen, where she had been reading the flap of the newspaper Martin had left open on the table. Naunie was already next to Alice, getting as close as she could.

"How are you, Martin?" Lucy's sister said, and she gave him a faint smile.

Martin nodded, but still didn't say anything.

"Lucy, look!" Naunie said, pointing. "It's Alice! She's here!"

Lucy stood in the doorway and looked at her sister. She was relieved, grateful, overjoyed to see her. Just as when she'd seen Alice at her funeral, she wanted to embrace her and hug her tightly. Now Alice looked far better than she had at the funeral home, and Lucy was glad. She couldn't stand the thought of her sister being in any kind of distress, and to see her looking better was a huge relief to Lucy.

Naunie was simply giddy. The look on her face said it all; a wide, bright smile, her eyes sparkling like the sun off water. She could not get enough of Alice, and danced around her almost like an elf, trying to take all of her in.

"I wish I was here under better circumstances," Alice said to Martin. Nola lurked silently behind him.

Martin agreed, although he was curious why Alice had come with Jilly to deliver Tulip's ashes, and thought for a moment that this might indicate a tug of war over them. In that instant, he decided, if Alice really wanted them, he wouldn't fight her for them; he had his memories of Tulip and didn't feel entirely entitled to them, since he'd given the dog to Jilly.

"May we sit down?" Alice asked politely.

"Of course," Martin replied, and motioned toward the couch. "It's hot out there. Can we get you something to drink?"

"Water. Just water would be wonderful," Alice said as she took a seat on the couch. Jilly sat next to her, Martin took the recliner, and Nola stood there for a moment until she understood that she was in charge of refreshments.

"Water would be great, thanks," Jilly said, and Nola scooted off to the kitchen, looking quite unsettled as she passed Lucy.

"Martin," Alice started right away as Naunie squirmed in delight, sitting behind her on the top of the couch, "I need to say something that is not easy to say, and I'm sorry. I thought I had already said it, but after talking to Jilly I realized that I hadn't, so here I am."

Martin decided to jump in. "I have no problem with you taking Tulip's ashes, Alice; I know Lucy would like to have them. I completely understand, or we can share them," he said. "Either way, whatever you decide is fine with me. You won't get an argument."

Alice clasped her hands together tightly. "That's not it, Martin," she said, shaking her head softly. "About a year ago, I tried to contact you. Your phone number had changed and I didn't have your email address. Because of that, I thought the best way to reach you would be by letter. It wasn't an easy letter to write, but I hoped you would understand my reasons for writing it and not coming down to Phoenix to see you. At the time."

Martin looked confused, but hung on Alice's every word, thinking that the next thing she said would piece it all together.

"I never got a response from you, Martin. I gave you my phone number and all of my other contact information, but I never heard from you," she explained. "So after several months—more than several months—I wrote you again, and again, and again. You never answered any of my letters."

"Alice, I don't know what to say," Martin said, knowing the situation to be a misunderstanding. "I'm sorry you've been upset about this, but I never received anything from you, a year ago or since. I certainly would have replied to a letter from you had I gotten it. I'm terribly sorry."

"Martin, you did get the letter," Jilly interrupted. "But you thought it was from Lucy. That was the letter you threw away, the one you got right after she left."

Martin looked puzzled. "What?" he asked. "What do you mean? That wasn't from Lucy? Of course it was from her. It had her name on the return address."

"It was *my* name on the return address," Alice said. "I changed it back after the divorce."

"I thought it was from her," he said, not looking at anyone. "I always thought it was from her. Well, you see the confusion now, Alice. I apologize. I don't know what else to say. But whatever was in the letter, I'd be happy to discuss it with you now."

"It's about Lucy," Alice said, hesitating a bit.

"I assumed so," Martin said, and nodded. "What is it? Do I have something of hers, did she need money, was it an issue with the wedding? Because I canceled all the arrangements, and all the deposits were forfeited. There was nothing left to split. I lost everything."

"I really don't think any of that ever crossed her mind," Alice said. "It isn't about any of that."

Then Alice went on and told Martin about that last day, how Alice's car wouldn't start and how Lucy gave her the truck, saying she'd take a bus to the unemployment office, and then what happened after that. Then about the accident.

What she didn't mention, Lucy thought when Alice had finished, *is that it was a beautiful day. The sun was shining brightly and the breeze was perfect. My hair looked great for a change. I was wearing my favorite boots, the ones I'm wearing now. I never saw the bus. I never saw it. I just saw the bus driver's eyes and then heard it on me. She was nice, the bus driver. Everything was perfect that day. I feel terrible that she hit me.*

No one would ever know that, Lucy thought. No one would ever know that part of the story.

Martin didn't respond to Alice. He said nothing and looked far, far past her.

Lucy watched Martin, who was confounded by what he couldn't grasp, not yet. He sat there in a moment of shock, the last moment he would be able to push it away for a long, long time.

Jilly reached out and took his hand.

"I'm so sorry, Martin," she said so lightly that it was barely audible. "I didn't know, either. Lucy's phone was destroyed in the accident, and without it, Alice didn't know how to find me under my married name. She counted on your reading that letter and then telling the rest of us what happened."

"See, Lucy?" Naunie said, with comforting eyes. "Alice didn't just let you vanish. She did try to tell them. It's just that no one heard her."

"They're lying," came a bold declaration, and everyone in the room looked up to see Nola standing in the doorway. "Lucy Fisher is not dead. She was standing in this living room, two feet from me, a few days ago. I saw her. The mailman saw her. She's broken into the house numerous times, and whatever you've said, it's not true. I saw her."

"That's impossible," Jilly said. "Why would you say such a thing?"

"Because it's true!" Nola asserted. "She told me I needed to leave and that she was back. That was the last thing she said before she walked out the door, 'I'm back.'"

"I don't know you," Alice interjected. "But I can guess who you are. My sister was killed in a terrible accident almost a year ago, and I happen to think that your little joke is in poor taste. For you to call me a liar is unthinkable. What would I possibly have to gain by saying and pretending my sister is dead?"

"Get her, Alice!" Naunie cheered from the sidelines.

Nola scoffed. "Well, her life insurance policy, for one," she huffed.

"Again, that's ridiculous," Alice protested. "Lucy didn't have a life insurance policy."

"Yes, she did!" Jilly said quickly.

"I did?" Lucy said.

"We all have one at the office," Jilly added. "It's included in our benefits."

"But she had gotten fired. She was no longer employed," Alice reasoned.

"Her benefits were good until the end of the month," Nola said with a wry smile. "So if you're claiming she died when she did, she just made it under the deadline. What a coincidence. Another coincidence is that there is an accidental death benefit rider to the life insurance policy we have, double the amount of the benefit. And another coincidence is that you have a year to make a claim. And your time is almost up."

Alice tossed up her hands. "I don't know about a life insurance policy, and I don't care about a life insurance policy," she said angrily. "I lost my sister. Just when she lost everything, I lost her."

"It all adds up very nicely to a case of insurance fraud," Nola barked. "But I won't let you get away with it. Lucy Fisher is alive and well, and I can prove it!"

Jilly gave Nola a dirty look. "How?" she questioned her coworker. "How are you going to prove that, Nola? I'm sure Alice has a death certificate and a coroner's report. I've seen the clipping from the story in the newspaper, and it seems no one has seen her, not one single person, not a loved one, best friend, or ex-fiancé in almost a year. No one has seen her but you. Only you, Nola. And she never liked you. Why would she stop in and chat with you?"

"And she stole drugs from Dr. Meadows," Nola added. "She's lucky he never pressed charges against her! Now I will see that he does!"

"That's not true," Jilly said, shaking her head. "Lucy didn't touch those drugs. Marianne did. She finally told me the truth at Tulip's wake, feeling bad because Lucy had been such a good friend to her. She took them before we went to Hawaii, but was too scared to do them, and actually put them back the day Lucy got fired. You noticed when they were gone, but you never noticed when they were returned."

"That's why she never came back for Tulip," Martin said quietly. "I should have known something was wrong when she didn't come back for her."

"Don't listen to them, Martin," Nola demanded. "Don't fall for it. It's all a scheme. I swear I saw her a couple days ago. I don't know how they're pulling this off, but—"

"Enough, Nola," Martin said harshly, finally breaking out of his daze to look her. "That's so much more than enough. Not one more word. I mean it. I can't bear *one more word*."

Nola spun on her heel, charged down the hall, and slammed the bedroom door.

Martin stood up and raised his hand to Jilly and Alice. "I'm so sorry. You'll—You'll . . . please excuse me . . . ," he said, and went into the hallway, disappearing into the shadows.

Oh, he is not *chasing after her,* Lucy thought. *He can't be. Martin, where are you? What* happened *to you? Is this what you are now? How can I help you if there's nothing left to save?*

Lucy left the living room, determined to do whatever she could to stop him from making another concession, another mistake. She walked almost to the bedroom door and stopped. He wasn't in there. He couldn't be in there, she could feel it. She took two steps backward and peered through the open doorway of the hobby room.

She saw the back of him, just a silhouette, sitting in his chair in front of his desk. She walked in and stood just inside the threshold, listening to him breathe.

The room was quiet, static, like it had been flash frozen. As if this moment in time, this very moment, would always remain, never disintegrate, fall away, or erode.

Martin didn't move, as if he could keep the truth farther from him if he didn't react, respond, or feel.

Lucy walked toward him and put her hand on his shoulder. Unlike the time in the kitchen, he didn't flinch or pull away. She went around behind the chair and put her other hand on his other shoulder, and then slowly wrapped her arms around him. With her face next to his, she stood for a moment, then whispered, "I'm all right. I am here. I am fine where I am."

He breathed in one sudden, impatient breath, and then choked slightly as he let it back out.

"Oh, no," he said, his eyes narrowing, his breath quickening. "Oh, no."

chapter twenty Over the Hills and Far Away

A week later, the last spirit Lucy expected to see walking out of the bathroom was Ruby Spicer.

Her teacher greeted her with a warm hug.

"Naunie!" Lucy called. "Look who's here! You won't believe it!"

Naunie came into the living room almost bursting. Her smile, though, quickly faded when she realized why Ruby had probably come.

"I'm getting transferred again, aren't I?" she asked. It had been a couple of weeks since the boomerang frame incident and the exorcism that had resulted, and truth be told, Naunie had been waiting for Ruby to pop up.

Ruby just smiled slyly and put her arms around her two students. "WE," she said with a bold, wide smile, "are going to a party."

"You're kidding!" Naunie said, clapping her hands. "Really? I had no idea there were ghost parties! Is it a mixer? Do you think I might meet someone? It really is too bad that alcohol has no effect on me anymore. . . . I was such a lively drunk!"

"Speaking of lively," Ruby said, looking around, "this place is dead! This is the quietest haunted house I've ever seen! Where is everybody?"

Lucy nodded, then shrugged.

That morning, Martin had called in sick to work as he had done every day for the entire week. By 6 A.M., he'd had his coffee thermos by his side and had pulled out of the driveway in his truck. Lucy could only guess that he had gone to one of his favorite fishing spots, though he'd neglected to take a pole.

Nola, too, had been going in early, and coming home late. Several nights before, she hadn't walked through the front door until 9 P.M. Her shows had been entirely neglected, even to the point where they were getting deleted on their own because so much time had passed.

"That's too bad," Naunie had said, shaking her head as she'd checked the menu for the recorder and had seen that Nola's programs were already gone. "She would have bawled her eyes out on the one where the lady got her feet narrowed and her toenails permanently dyed red. Even I teared up a little."

The day before, a small van had pulled up in the driveway, and Nola had hauled out a dozen boxes and loaded them into the van herself. There had been no words, not even a note; she'd simply left her key on the console by the front door and locked the door on the way out. She hadn't looked back, and neither Naunie nor Lucy had waved goodbye.

It had been very quiet around the house since Jilly's and Alice's visit, to the point where Lucy and Naunie were even getting bored with their own company. There was only so much TV watching and card playing they could do. A party was going to be a very welcome change of pace for them both.

"Where are we going?" Lucy asked as the three of them walked through the front door and out into the yard.

"Oh." Ruby laughed. "You'll see."

"I'm excited," Naunie exclaimed. "I hope I'm the only White Lady there! I don't want to blend in."

"It's just a short ride on the bus," Ruby said, fishing something out of her cloak pocket as they walked to the corner. Once they got there, she lifted her hand, which held a cigarette between her forefinger and third finger, all the way up to her shine, which instantly lit the end of the cigarette a fiery orange.

"I didn't know you still smoked!" Lucy gasped.

"Chica, I'm off the clock," she replied, exhaling a tremendous haze of smoke. "Don't be surprised if you see me tie one on. Just don't let me go home with anybody, no matter how haunting their good looks may be."

When the bus pulled up, the three specters slid on board and made their way to the back, where, to Naunie's great dismay, another White Lady and a mining prospector were already sitting and glowing.

"Are you going to tell us what this is about?" Lucy asked as they jostled and swayed with the bus's movement. "I really prefer not to take city transportation if I can at all help it."

"Relax. We're almost there. Next stop," Ruby reassured Lucy. A minute later, Ruby reached up and pulled the line, which immediately rang out a pleasant, tinkly chime.

The bus came to a stop soon after, the three of them climbed off, and Ruby started off in one direction.

"Hold on. Hold on. Stop, please!" Lucy called. "Lucy Rule: Cross behind the bus, please. Never in front unless you want to wear the same thing for the rest of your death."

They walked a couple blocks farther, until Ruby stopped in front of another ranch style brick house similar to Martin's, with a perfect short hedge all the way around the yard. Music could be heard loudly playing from the inside, and through the windows, Lucy could see the place was packed with people laughing, dancing, talking, and having the time of their lives.

"This is Jilly's house," Lucy remarked, a little startled. "They're playing 'You Can't Always Get What You Want.' That's my favorite song!"

"Lucy," Ruby said, standing behind her and grabbing her by the shoulders, "welcome to your funeral!"

"Oh, Lucy!" Naunie said, and clapped her hands in delight. "You've earned it, kid!"

Passing through the front door, Lucy saw what seemed like everyone she had known in life; her best friend, Jilly, and Marianne, people she had gone to dental school with, high school with, hung out with at the Round About, and even people whose teeth she had cleaned. As she worked her way through the crowd with Naunie and Ruby by her side, Lucy beamed at the dining room table overflowing with photos of her from her teenage years on, beads that she and Jilly had acquired at Mardi Gras one year, ticket stubs from concerts they had seen together, and even Lucy's fake nurse's dental smock.

They eavesdropped on all of the conversations, Lucy stories being recalled again and again, most getting a little grander with each pass.

"Led Zeppelin—'Over the Hills and Far Away!'" Lucy shouted as another song started. "This is my favorite song!"

Lucy sidled up to Marianne, who was busy talking to Scott, one of the cutest bartenders at the Round About, not that there was an assortment to choose from, but still. Marianne was doing well; she didn't seem too nervous, hadn't spit food out on him yet, and was apparently telling a great story by the looks of it.

"Oh, it's definitely true. I work in the office. I was there when the agents came in and talked to my boss," Marianne relayed. "Lucy was still covered by the insurance policy. It had three days left on it. Can you believe that? *Three days!* Can you believe that luck? Well, I guess that depends on how you look at it, but . . . And, yep, there was a double death thingy attached to it because it was an accident. I forget what you call it. So, yeah, in the end, it came to a pretty, pretty penny. Everything goes to her sister and her nephew. Isn't that nice? I'm thinking about leaving everything to my sister and my nephew, but I really don't want to get hit by a bus, you know?"

"Lucy, look at this!" Naunie shouted over the laughter and noise of the crowd, and pointed to a photograph in the assortment of everything on the Lucy shrine. It was of her, in the redwoods, standing underneath Babe the Blue Ox, pretending to hold up the legendary figure's Volkswagen-size blue balls of concrete.

Lucy burst out laughing. "I cannot tell you how much Martin *did not* want to take that picture!" she cried, pointing at it. "Oh, I thought he was going to shrivel up just looking at it! He could simply not be talked into touching them, let alone letting me take a picture, so I had to do it. That's funny. That's Martin's picture. That's one of the ones I saw Nola crumple and shove into the drawer."

Lucy felt someone touch her arm and heard Naunie call her name softly.

"Look," her grandmother said, and nodded her head in the direction across the room.

Lucy followed with her eyes and saw her sister talking to someone that she couldn't make out. Alice was smiling a little, and that made Lucy want to smile. She moved through the crowd to get closer to Alice, saying hi to all of the people who had come to say goodbye to her, some she hadn't seen for a very long time. When she got to Alice, she stopped in her tracks when she saw who Alice was talking to.

It was Martin.

"No, I had no idea," her sister said. "I decided to drive by the old place on my way back up to Flagstaff after Jilly and I left your house, and that's when I saw the sign. The house was empty, completely empty, like the owners had fled in the middle of the night. I knew they were renovating it, but to up and leave like that? Anyway, the inside is pretty torn up. It doesn't look like they finished anything they started, and they're listing it for a song. I made an offer, so I'll see what happens. It would be good to be back at the old place, start over anew in someplace old, you know? Jared would like it down there, all of that room . . . The only thing is that the place really is a wreck. There's about one wall left standing in the whole place. I'll have enough from Lucy's settlement to cover the house, but the rest would be pretty costly. I'd have to really fix it back up."

"I'd be happy to help," Lucy heard Martin say. "I do okay with a hammer and nails."

"That would be great, Martin," Alice said with a smile. "Thank you."

And Lucy smiled, too, big and wide and honest. She smiled as she watched them talk, as she watched other people laugh, as she listened to other people tell stories about her that might have been only slightly exaggerated.

"I never toured with the Rolling Stones," she corrected one guest as she passed by. "I only got backstage."

She snuck up to Jilly, who was watching all of the goings-on next to Warren, his arm around her tight. Lucy moved in and gave her a big hug, melding into her best friend like Silly Putty.

"Thank you, Jilly," she whispered into her ear. "For taking care of me and for being so good to Tulip. I know it sounds creepy, but I can't wait to see you again. I have a feeling you're going straight to The State."

Then, as one song ended and another began, Lucy pulled away from Jilly and gasped with glee.

"'Once in a Lifetime,' Talking Heads!" she yelled. "This is my favorite song!"

Jilly laughed. "Lucy really loved this song," she said to Warren, who smiled a big, bearded smile, kissed her on the forehead, and brought her into him even closer.

When Lucy's "funeral" was wrapping up, Ruby gathered her charges and told Lucy to say her goodbyes to the guests who were left.

"We need to go," she said simply. "There's something I have to talk to you both about."

Lucy took one last look around the living room, blew kisses to Jilly and Warren, who were beginning to clean up, and gave a Silly Putty hug to her sister.

"I think you're going to be fine," she whispered. "I hope you have a happy life, Alice."

With Martin, she just smiled and touched his arm. "I'm all right, Martin," she told him. "I am here. And I want good things for you."

She could have sworn she saw him smile.

"Lucy," Ruby called, "are you ready?"

She nodded, and together the three of them walked back through the front door.

When they got to the sidewalk, Ruby stopped.

"I have good news for you, Lucy." Ruby beamed as she put her arm around her student. "You're not going back to Martin's. You've been elevated. You've made it to The State."

"You're kidding!" Lucy breathed, barely able to contain her excitement. "Oh, that's wonderful! That's so wonderful! Oh, I can't believe it! Can you believe it, Naunie? We're going to The State! *We're going to The State!*"

She grabbed Naunie's hands and began jumping up and down in unadulterated happiness.

"Wait," Ruby said cautiously, reaching out for Lucy's arm. "Wait."

Lucy stopped jumping and looked at Ruby suspiciously. "You can't be serious," she said, her joyous face fallen.

"Clovie is being transferred back to the farmhouse," Ruby told them. "I'm so sorry. I don't make the rules, the decisions, any of that, Lucy. I am just the messenger."

"I don't want to go without her," Lucy said, her face flushing red. "I can't go."

"You have to," Ruby replied. "I can't change that. You completed your mission. Clovie hasn't."

Lucy shook her head in opposition.

"When is this supposed to take place?" Lucy asked. "When does this happen?"

"Now," Ruby answered. "We're taking Clovie to the farmhouse, and then you and I take the elevator back up, and after that, you'll move to The State."

"All right," Lucy said, definitively as an idea clicked in her head. "Let's go, then."

Once they got to the farmhouse, Lucy saw that Alice was right. It was a wreck. It wasn't that the house needed to be repaired so much as *rebuilt*. Lucy had hardly expected the home of her childhood to look like it had been bombed, but that's the impression she was left with.

"This is terrible," Lucy said, walking with Naunie and Ruby

though the darkened skeleton that had once housed holidays, birthday parties, and weddings.

"Well, hello, Lucy," a voice said from the shadows, and Lucy nearly jumped out of her ethereal skin. "Clovie," the voice added.

It was Uncle Howe and Geneva, coming out of hiding.

"It is terrible what they've done, isn't it?" Geneva said, sadly shaking her head. "I thought Clovis was a tornado with her pink toilet, but this . . ."

"Some kids tried to break in last night," Uncle Howe said rather sadly. "We were just trying to stay unnoticed."

"You were doing a fine job," Lucy said, and chuckled. "You scared the crap out of me. What appliances are left here that I can drain?"

Uncle Howe sighed. "Nothing. Absolutely nothing," he replied sorrowfully. "It's all gone. I'm not even sure how much wiring is left."

Lucy took a deep breath and thought. *I can do this,* she told herself. *I can. I moved a chair without even knowing what I was doing, so this should be a piece of cake.*

She looked around for something, anything to use. She saw a claw hammer just poking out of the shadows by Howe and Geneva, and she motioned to them.

"I need your help," she said simply, and waved over Naunie, who had been standing in what used to be the foyer, with Ruby. "We need to pick this up."

"That's impossible," Geneva balked. "I'm going to need access to an oil lamp if I'm going to do anything."

"No, it's not impossible," Lucy asserted to them. "We can do this. Ruby said Naunie has strong ghost genes, so that means I have them and so do you, Uncle Howe. I'm just including you, Geneva, to be polite. You can help or not help, but you simply must stop talking because you're sort of a downer and I need to build a sense of enthusiasm right now. We all need to focus and tap into our ghost potential, and if we can do that, we can pick this up."

Uncle Howe bent down and grabbed the handle, while Lucy tried to pick up the neck. It slid through their hands on the first several attempts, although on the last one, with a bit of focus, Lucy was able to lift her end off the ground. Uncle Howe, however, couldn't get a grip and gave up in frustration.

"It's impossible," he asserted. "Unless I can get a charge, I'll never be able to pick that up."

"Work together," Ruby urged. "Pool your forces."

"Naunie," Lucy called, seeing her grandmother at the opposite side of the living room. "Give us a hand. We need all the strength we can get."

Naunie didn't answer, and when Lucy looked back over after several moments of silence, she saw why. Naunie, standing in a corner, was seething. Her house, the house that she'd put everything into and had kept meticulously maintained, had effectively been destroyed. She stared fiercely at the damage all around her, her anger growing like a fire. Every hole in the plaster, every exposed beam, and every molding that had been removed fueled her like a splash of gasoline.

She couldn't control it, and her rage grew as she thought of all the time and effort she had spent making this old, antique farmhouse into a home. She had grown up here, she had raised her children here, and it been a perfect place for Lucy and Alice when they'd come to live with her. To see it ravaged, and carelessly so, made her want to erupt.

She shook her head repeatedly in disgust. How dare they! She just couldn't believe that someone would move into an old place with history, memories, a life, and strip that all away and try to build something different on top of it.

Her fists clenched like tiny balls of rage, she charged over to where Howe was crouched, pathetically trying to pick up the hammer, and in one swoop she bent down and grabbed it, leaned back, and hurled it at the wall that separated the living room and the dining room. Lucy and Ruby gasped. The claw hammer chewed into the plaster and stayed there, now firmly planted into the wall as if it was a light fixture. Naunie stared at it for a while, her eyes not moving, simply concentrating.

Then she marched to the spot where the hammer protruded, grabbed the handle, and yanked it out. Chunks of plaster and fine white dust spewed from the hole as if the wall had exhaled. Naunie examined the hole she had made in the wall, and then, without a second of hesitation, she leaned back and smacked the wall again with the hammer, in almost the same spot. Naunie gnawed at the gash in the wall until she was satisfied, then took a good long look at it up close.

"It's good," she finally said, and turning to Lucy added, "I can see it. It's right there. Anyone who is going to have to fix this hole can't help but get in there and see it."

"Clovis, do you have to be so dramatic?" Geneva said, her voice full of disdain. "See what? What could there possibly be in there to see?"

"The money your father robbed from the stagecoach," Lucy said. "It's been there all along."

"That's ridiculous," Geneva shot back. "How do you know that's what it is?"

"Any of us can slip through this wall and see it," Naunie replied. "It's still in canvas payroll bags."

"That's got to be worth a fortune, all of that old currency," Uncle Howe added. "That's all highly valuable now, worth way more than what's printed on it."

Geneva didn't say anything in response, and simply looked away.

"Lucy," Ruby said from behind Naunie. "I'm sorry, but we have to go."

Lucy looked at Naunie. She couldn't believe this was it, that she'd be going on without her.

"It's not fair," Lucy said. "Naunie helped get Nola out of the house, too."

Ruby nodded. "I know," she replied, "but that wasn't her objective."

Lucy moved toward Naunie and they met in a hard, clinging embrace.

"You'll be there soon," Lucy told her. "She's going to see it."

"I love you, Lucy," her grandmother said. "I'm so happy for you."

Naunie let go and pushed Lucy gently toward Ruby, who reached out her hand. Lucy took it, and together they walked into the dining room, where the elevator was waiting.

"Lucy?" a voice called out, followed by several loud knocks at the front door. "Lucy? Are you in there?"

"I'm in here," Lucy called from the kitchen, where she was making a bowl of brownie batter and was planning to eat every last bit of it herself with her finger. She took off her apron, tossed it onto the enormous butcher-block island, and hurried down the sunlit hallway and into the living room, where a homey fire was burning.

"Bethanny!" Lucy cried, throwing her arms around her friend, hugging her tight. "Oh, it is so good to see you!"

"Lucy, this is the cutest house!" Bethanny cried. "I love the brick and stone, and the roses that climb all the way up to the chimney. The fragrance is beautiful!"

"Are you far from here?" Lucy asked, holding her friend's hand and inviting her to sit on the marshmallowy down-filled cushions of the white linen couch.

"No, no, I'm a five-minute walk," she explained. "I'm in the tall mirrored high-rise with the steel beams right on the beach."

"Oh, that's a great building!" Lucy exclaimed. "Have you been here long?"

"I guess so," Bethanny said, after thinking a moment. "As soon as I got to my assignment, I found some kids on a sinking boat and a shark that was ready for lunch."

"You're kidding!" Lucy replied. "What did you do?"

"I flashed the shark, then punched him in the eye," Bethanny said with a nonchalant wave of her hand. "That shark had it coming. He looked a little too familiar."

"I'm so happy to see you," Lucy reiterated. "I was about to eat a bowl of brownie batter. Can I make you one?"

"Oh, no." Her friend laughed. "I'm good. I have a carrot cake in my purse. Isn't this great? Welcome to The State!"

"The State of Elated Bliss," Lucy emphasized. "Boy, they aren't kidding, huh?"

Bethanny shook her head happily and laughed. "Elliot lives right down the road from me, and he still hasn't taken off his Socrates outfit yet. I saw Kirk and the Countess when they drove through last; they have a massive RV and they just drive around The State, on a permanent vacation like a retired couple!"

Frantic, loud banging suddenly interrupted their visit, and the creak of the screen door followed.

"I don't believe it! I don't believe it!" a voice cried excitedly. "Lucy, Lucy, Lucy! Guess what!"

"We're in here," Lucy called, laughing, and Naunie appeared in the doorway in a flash of a second later.

"Bethanny, this is my grandmother Naunie," Lucy told her. "She was a White Lady, too! She lives next door."

"Ooooh," Bethanny cooed. "In the big old white farmhouse? It's so pretty!"

"Thank you," Naunie said, catching her breath and smiling. "My other granddaughter lives in the earthly version, and they did a fantastic job fixing it back up, but now it's a little too fancy for my taste. *She has a garbage disposal.* In my house, though— Lucy, you're not going to believe this, but my toilet and bathtub are pink! I got them back! I've got a pink toilet!"

"Naunie is just moving in," Lucy said to Bethanny. "She is newly arrived and is discovering all about The State, as long as she promises to leave Frank Sinatra and Steve McQueen alone."

"Congratulations." Bethanny beamed. "It will be great to have you here, I just know it."

A sudden, snorty snore rose up from behind the couch, followed by a high-pitched yawn.

Bethanny looked at Lucy oddly. "What was that?"

Lucy smiled as a fuzzy head with a long tongue peeked around the corner.

"That," she said, feeling happier than she ever had in any moment of her life or her death, "is my dog, Tulip."

PHOTO: © LAURIE NOTARO

LAURIE NOTARO has seen ghosts twice in her life: once on her tenth birthday and again when she mistakenly assumed her husband had come home at 2 A.M. dressed as Dashiell Hammett. Notaro hasn't made her bed in thirty-two years, was said by *The New Yorker* to have "positively cackled" (a gross exaggeration), and once saw Billie Jean King while eating lunch. She (Notaro, not Billie Jean King) still lives in Eugene, Oregon, with her opaque husband and absurdly charming dog, Maeby. This is her eighth book (note to the newspaper editor who fired her [Notaro, not the dog]).

www.laurienotaro.com